GAME OF SCONES

A BEAUFORT SCALES MYSTERY - BOOK 4

KIM M. WATT

BEAUFORT SCALES

Seriously, don't steal books. Share them. Talk about them. Review them. Tell your friends about them. Writers *love* that. But book thieves will be fed to dragons.

For further information contact: www.kmwatt.com

Cover design: Monika McFarland, www.ampersandbookcovers.com

Editor: Lynda Dietz, www.easyreaderediting.com

Logo design by www.imaginarybeast.com

ISBN: 978-1-9160780-3-1

First Edition: November 2019

10 9 8 7 6 5 4 3 2 1

To the lovely people of Skipton.
I'm sorry I took such liberties with your
street layout. And the morals of your town council.
I do love you. I promise.

A BEAUFORT SCALES MYSTERY

CONTENTS

1
ALICE

Councillor Thomas Wright, a light sheen of sweat on his forehead due to either the surprisingly warm Yorkshire sun or the close proximity of the ten ladies of the Toot Hansell Women's Institute, leaned over the table and peered at the contents of a large glass bowl.

"Um," he said. "Is this … are these potatoes meant to be blue?"

"I used Blue Danube potatoes," Jasmine said, her face pink with the heat. "I bought them especially."

Alice leaned in next to Thomas and examined the salad as he poked it with the serving spoon. The thing with Blue Danubes was that they weren't actually blue. The skin was a lovely purple colour, and they made for very nice roasties, but not only had she never used them in a salad, she'd never seen *any* salad this colour. The potatoes were the colour of the bluebells down by the river, and the mayonnaise dressing had the delightful azure tones of a beach holiday brochure.

"Should I eat it?" Thomas whispered to her. "I don't want to be rude."

"Just put some on the side of your plate," Alice said. "And make sure you don't get any on your shirt."

"It actually tastes rather nice," Rose said. She was sitting in a round-bottomed chair in the flower-crowded confines of Rosemary's garden, her feet swinging.

"Your lips are blue," Alice observed.

Rose shrugged and turned her attention to a feta and spinach pastry.

"I think the last time I had anything that blue was when we used to get blue ice lollies," Teresa said, then patted Jasmine's arm. "They were very nice, too."

"I just thought it'd be a bit summery," Jasmine said. "You know, something different."

"It's perfectly lovely," Rose said. "I think it's just the colour putting people off." Her teeth had taken on an interesting turquoise tinge.

Jasmine frowned. "The colour? It's a *blue potato* salad. It says so right in the recipe."

"The potatoes turned it this colour?" Gert asked. She had her face lifted to the sun, heavy arms flushed with heat. "Where did you get them from, Smurf's Produce?"

Alice managed not to laugh as Jasmine put her hands on her hips. "They're Blue Danubes. Blue potatoes!"

"Well, it's very interesting," Thomas said, seating himself in a slightly unsteady folding chair. "It's good to be adventurous with one's cooking."

"Interesting is one word," Teresa said.

"Don't listen to them, love," Rose said, lifting another forkful of salad. "All the more for me."

"I have to admit I've never seen potatoes *quite* this blue," Alice said, spooning some bulgar wheat salad onto her plate. It was full of herbs and seeds and fat cherry tomatoes, and looked rather like a Miriam creation. "Blue Danubes, you said?"

"Well." Jasmine twisted a napkin in her hands. "That's what the man at the market said they were, but they didn't stay that colour at all, so I don't know if I believe him. It was most disappointing."

The women looked at the blue salad for a long moment without speaking. Thomas moved his serving carefully to the side of the plate, where it couldn't touch anything else.

"They didn't stay blue?" Alice said finally.

"No, they just went sort of dull and boring-looking. So I put some colouring in."

Gert burst out laughing, and Alice covered her mouth.

"What?" Jasmine demanded. "He said they were blue! I was counting on it!"

"Very adventurous," Thomas repeated.

The Toot Hansell Women's Institute were taking advantage of a particularly warm and windless day, and were holding their meeting in Rosemary's fragrant, sunny garden rather than in the confines of the village hall. An old green table had been covered with a Provençal-style tablecloth and loaded with Tupperware containers and trays and bowls, all overfull with salads and quiches and little cheese-stuffed pastries, and, oddly, pigs in blankets. Alice had a suspicion that was Rose, who seemed to be using her recent eighty-eighth birthday as a reason to become distinctly eccentric. Alice had mixed feelings about eccentricity. On the one hand, she didn't see any reason to act as society expected, other than in the instance of laws (and even those could be open to interpretation). On the other hand, it seemed a little … careless. Although making pigs in blankets for summer lunches and turning up with different coloured hair each week were hardly things she could disapprove of.

She sat back in her folding chair, crossing her feet neatly at the ankles, and said to Thomas, "It was very good of you to take the time to come and talk to us."

"Oh, well." Thomas had exchanged his plate (still bearing a

scoop of blue potato salad) for a large glass of elderflower cordial and a slice of lemon drizzle cake. "You ladies were wonderful supporters when I decided to run for council. And it's always a pleasure to spend time with you."

Alice thought that was laying it on a bit thick, but that was politicians for you. Never knew when to stop.

"Go on, then," Gert said. "Give us your spiel."

"My spiel?" Thomas wiped his face with a napkin.

"You know the one. We should donate money, or re-elect you, or whatever, because …?"

"I, well, yes." He took a large swig of cordial, then spluttered. "Is this *alcoholic?*"

"Oh, sorry," Teresa leaned over and took his glass, replacing it with a new one. "That's Gert's cordial. Adults only."

"It's only slightly alcoholic," Gert protested, and Rose raised her glass.

"Tasty, too."

"I'll stick with plain, thanks," Thomas said, taking a cautious sip from the new glass, then relaxing. "I still have some driving to do."

"Nothing wrong with a little tipple in the afternoon," Carlotta said. "In the old country—"

"You were all having pints down the pub at 10 a.m.?" Rosemary suggested.

Carlotta glared at her. "*No.*"

"Funny, whenever I've been to Manchester—"

"Ladies," Alice said, before Carlotta could throw her Victoria Sponge at Rosemary. "Thomas, you were going to talk to us about the proposed communal garden project."

"Yes." He looked nervously at Rosemary and Carlotta, but they were both watching him with interest. "So, naturally, we are aware that you ladies do a fantastic job with flowers and so on, but there have been some wonderful programmes popping up about the country where public areas are being transformed into food gardens."

"I like that idea," Priya said. "Everyone should have the opportunity to grow their own food."

"Until some silly sod steals it, or digs it all up for fun," Teresa pointed out.

"No one would do that around here!" Pearl said.

"I think it'd be okay," Miriam said. "I put all my extra veg in a box by the gate, and no one's ever stolen anything."

There was a pause, then Gert said, "You don't charge for it, Miriam."

"I know! But I mean, no one clears it out or anything."

"Well," Thomas started, and Rose interrupted him.

"We should have wildflowers. For the bees."

"Well—"

"My Ben's allergic to bees," Jasmine said.

"He's a *police officer*," Priya said.

"So? They can be allergic to stuff!"

"Bees are probably allergic to *him*," Rose said. "They still need homes!"

"We were going to have insect houses," Thomas offered, wiping his forehead.

"Are you too hot?" Pearl asked. "We need more shade. Do you want to move under the trees?"

"I've got an umbrella," Rosemary said, pushing herself out of her chair.

"No, no, I'm fine." Thomas folded his napkin and smiled at them all. "As I was saying—"

"Bees don't live in insect houses," Priya said.

"Honeybees don't," Rose said. "Others do."

"Honey would be nice," Rosemary said.

Rose shook her head. "Oh, that's a whole other thing. Hives and stuff."

"Maybe we could mix wildflowers with the veggies?" Pearl offered. "You know, best of both worlds."

"We should companion plant," Miriam said. "It's good for everyone then, and you don't need to use pesticides."

"Well, sometimes you need some," Teresa said. "I mean, we're not feeding the slugs of the world here."

"Chickens," Carlotta said. "In the old country we used chickens."

"That does seem to be the right level of technology for Mancunians," Rosemary said.

"I like chickens," Priya put in, before Carlotta could respond. "Can we get chickens anyway?"

"Then we'll have chickens wandering all over the village," Jasmine said. "That's not hygienic, surely?"

"At least we'll know why they crossed the road," Rose said, and cackled in delight.

Alice uncrossed her ankles and got up to refill her water glass as the W.I. argued about chickens and whether that would be any more problematic than the terrifying geese that lived in the duck pond, and took the jug of Gert's cordial over to Thomas. "Are you sure you wouldn't like some?"

He held his half-empty glass up. "I don't suppose a little would hurt."

"Sometimes it can even help."

He snorted, and took a sip of the drink. "Do I take this as the W.I. being behind the idea, though?"

"I think it's safe to say that, yes. We'll be happy to help."

"Thank you. That would be wonderful. I think this project could be really good, and if it works it may even get pushed to other villages."

Alice nodded. "Toot Hansell isn't exactly like other villages, though."

"I think that's a pretty safe statement." There was the clang of a mobile phone, and Thomas fished in the pockets of his jacket where it hung over the back of the chair. Alice sat back down, not wanting to intrude, but she couldn't miss the way Thomas' shoulders tightened, the way he leaned forward in his chair with the phone clasped between his knees as he opened the message. She couldn't see his face for a moment, just the way his forehead grew lines and the reddened skin showed through his hair. Then he straightened up, sliding the phone back into his pocket.

"Is everything alright?" Alice asked.

"Yes." He gave her a singularly unconvincing smile. "Someone wanted me to go and meet them, but it can wait. We have gardens to discuss!"

And he waved at Rose, declaring that she was entirely right and they must do all they could for the bees, then told Miriam that companion planting was a wonderful idea, but he was concerned about the chickens.

Alice was also concerned about the chickens, not least because she knew of a certain dragon who had a habit of stealing poultry with the intention of releasing the helpless things into the wild. But that wasn't exactly something she could bring up in front of a town councillor. So she listened and nodded, and wondered if she could detect an odd, unhappy note in the man's voice despite his cheerfulness.

IT WAS late afternoon by the time Alice and Miriam walked home across the village green, the shadows lazy on the ground, the heat of the day still heavy on their shoulders. Miriam looked pink and flushed from the sun, and Alice was pleased she'd worn a hat. Her bare arms were a shade too warm, despite a generous application of sunscreen. It was one of those summer days that seemed to belong to childhood memories and Enid Blyton books, all high blue skies and empty streets and birds calling to each other in the trees.

The village green was spotted with people sprawled in the long grass, caught up in books or one another, and little groups flung balls and Frisbees and, in one case, a dragon scale glider through the still air, catching the lowering sun.

"Look at that!" Miriam said. "Mortimer would be so pleased!"

"It's behaving very well," Alice said. Mortimer made dragon scale baubles and gliders in the hills beyond the village, and Miriam sold them for him on Etsy. The baubles did exceptionally well at Christmas, but the gliders and boats that bloomed when they touched the water had been slower to take off. It was nice to see one being used, catching the sun as it looped and glittered above the soft grass of the green. "Miriam, did you notice Thomas was acting a little oddly after lunch?"

"I thought it might have been the potato salad that unnerved him."

"A reasonable assumption, but no. He received a phone message, and after that he seemed quite … off."

Miriam looked at the ground as if it had offended her. "I didn't notice."

"Something about the message definitely upset him. I wonder if it had anything to do with Angela Pearson retiring?"

"Why would it? She just retired. And he wouldn't have his seat if she hadn't."

"Yes, but she was rather committed and passionate about everything. Don't you remember when she came to talk to us? That was only a few months ago, and she just gave everything up all of a sudden."

"Maybe she's not well," Miriam said, still frowning at the ground.

"Thomas said she went on a cruise."

"Well, there we go. Going on a cruise with all those people! She obviously wasn't well at all."

Alice shared a very similar opinion of cruises and organised tours, but not everyone did. "It does seem odd, though. To be so dedicated, then just to throw in the towel and go off around the world."

Miriam sighed and looked at Alice finally. "Maybe she just re-evaluated her life and decided going travelling was more important than dealing with village flower beds and parking areas. You're not looking for something to investigate, are you, Alice?"

"Of course I'm not. I was just saying it seemed strange."

"Well, I don't think it does. And I've had enough investigating to last me a lifetime."

"No one said there was anything to investigate, dear." Alice rather thought that investigating added a certain spice to retirement. Quite accidentally – well, mostly accidentally – they'd become caught up in two murder investigations and a kidnapping over the last year. Miriam hadn't grown used to it at all, and still seemed to find the whole thing very stressful. Alice assumed it was because she was a civilian. They were rarely quite as prepared for criminal activity.

Miriam was still regarding Alice somewhat suspiciously and not looking where she was going. She tripped over something and managed to tangle her feet in the hem of her floating skirt, stumbling forward to the accompaniment of tearing stitches. "Oh no!"

"Oh dear." Alice relieved the younger woman of her hessian shopping bag so that she could investigate the rip. "It's just the seam, isn't it?"

"Yes. But I love this skirt!" She gathered the soft material – deep blue-green and shot through with glittery threads – in her hands. "You see? This is all because you mentioned investigating!"

Alice *hmph*-ed. "I believe you brought it up. And if you didn't take on so about it, it wouldn't be a problem."

Miriam looked as if she was about to make an uncharacteristically rude retort, but at that moment there was the sound of a revving engine. The women frowned at each other. Toot Hansell was not the sort of place people sped through. The streets were narrow and shaded by leaning trees and stone walls, and there was far too much risk of encountering a wandering duck or sheep. Potentially chickens before long, too. They turned toward the noise, looking across the green to where the duck pond sheltered under the willows, with a low fence protecting it from the street beyond. The engine was running much too loud and fast, and tyres screeched on a corner.

"Who on earth is that?" Miriam asked.

Alice glanced around. People were looking toward the noise with lazy interest, and the engine screamed as the driver changed gear. It must be coming up the lane right beyond the duck pond. The geese were honking nervously, and they followed the ducks as the smaller birds took flight, squawking their panic. A man who had been floating a model boat in the pond grabbed it and backed away as the engine grew louder. She couldn't hear brakes, couldn't hear another car, and she had a moment to wonder what the driver was running from before there was a hungry crunch of breaking wood and the man by the pond sprinted across the green. A bright red Toyota exploded through the low fence from the road like a charging hippopotamus, sending shards of wood flying. The car shot between two willow trees, sliding on reeds and lilies, its momentum carrying it across the soft ground, and plunged nose first into the duck pond with the engine still screaming. Its back end caught up with it and tilted to the sky as if the little car was trying to do a headstand before dropping slowly back to the bank, and a pale, watery woman with dark hair surfaced next to it.

"*Really*," she said, and put webbed hands on her hips. "*Humans*."

Alice dropped her bags and broke into a run, her hip twinging. She recognised that car.

She had a feeling Thomas was no longer on the council.

2
MIRIAM

Miriam froze for only a moment after the car planted itself in the pond, which made her feel that she was maybe improving when it came to crisis situations. Of course, she rather thought that Alice might not have frozen at all, but that was Alice. It would take more than an unexpected red Toyota in a duck pond to make her hesitate. However, Miriam, unlike Alice, didn't have a bad hip brought on by the goblin attack last Christmas, so she kicked off her flip-flops, broke into a run, and overtook the older woman just as she reached the chipped wood border at the edge of the pond.

"Miriam!" Alice shouted, but Miriam ignored her, charging into the pond with a squeak at the chill. She splashed determinedly through the lilies, mud squidging between her bare toes and blooming in the clear dark water, hoping the geese didn't come back. Something jabbed her instep and she wondered briefly if she should have left her flip-flops on. They'd only have got tangled up in things and slowed her down, though. "Miriam, wait!" Alice called.

"I'm almost there!" The water was rising over her knees, and she gathered her skirt up in one hand, holding the other out for balance.

"Be careful." Alice sounded as if she wasn't far behind, but Miriam didn't turn around to check. She was concentrating on staying upright. The plant-tangled bottom was uneven and treacherous, and she wasn't entirely sure what she was stepping on. A lily stem slid between her toes like something alive and she yelped, tried to kick herself free, and almost fell face-first into the water. She dropped her skirt, flailing for balance, and the fabric floated around her, sinking toward her legs as it soaked and darkened. Well, it was already torn. What was a bit of mud?

"*Miriam*. Slow down." Alice was using her RAF voice, which was normally impossible to ignore, but Miriam could see a man slumped behind the wheel of the car, head resting on his arms as if in exhaustion or despair as the water rose around him. He was wearing a familiar pale blue polo shirt and his hair was thin and fair, and he wasn't moving. Miriam tried to go faster. She was over halfway across the pond, the water still only just above her knees, but the car seemed to be *sinking*. Its nose was well under the green-brown surface, and as she watched, the water began to investigate the open window. She gave up on trying to be careful and galumphed across the pond, arms pumping as waves of her own making surged around her legs.

People were shouting on the green behind them, and a roundish man was struggling through the ferns at the edge of the pond, still cradling his model boat in both arms.

"Call an ambulance," Alice shouted at him. "Quick as you can, man!"

Miriam glanced at the man as he gave an alarmed yelp and stopped where he was, trying to keep hold of the boat while he dug a phone out of his pocket. She looked back at where she was going just in time to see a face appear in the water in front of her. She gave a screech of alarm, tried to stop her forward momentum, tangled her feet in some roots or her skirt or just each other, and pitched face-first into the pond with her arms windmilling.

The water washed up around her, the brown turned to amber by the glow of sunlight, and she tasted mulch and silence. She put her arms out and tried to push herself off the bottom, but she couldn't reach it. She bubbled alarm, bringing her feet underneath her – only, oh, was it underneath? She couldn't tell, couldn't find anything solid to push against, and she knew there was something about watching your bubbles to know which was up, but there were bubbles *everywhere*, and all was confused green waters and the sneaky grip of lily stems around her feet. She thrashed in fright, trying not to scream, clinging to her breath, then cold strong hands gripped her arms and she was pulled firmly to the surface.

She spluttered mud and pond water, hair plastered to her head, finding herself sitting on a very solid and present bottom with the water washing under her armpits and lilies tangled around her hands.

"Soz," her rescuer said. "Didn't mean to give you a fright."

Miriam drew a whooping breath, then managed, "What happened?"

"You fell in the hole," the creature in front of her said, brushing mud off her scales. She had exceptionally sharp teeth, and clear third eyelids slid across her eyes as she blinked.

"The hole?"

"Yeah. It's bottomless. You shouldn't go stumbling about in it."

"The hole's bottomless?"

"The pond. Although, I guess, yeah."

Miriam pushed hair out of her face and looked at the car. Alice had obviously decided Miriam was in no danger and had carried on to reach it, which Miriam felt was a little unfair.

"I'm fine, thanks," she said to no one in particular, then looked at the water sprite, with her lank weed-green hair and clammy skin. "Are you Nellie?" They hadn't exactly met before, but thanks to the dragons she knew *of* the sprite.

"Yeah," Nellie said. "What's with the car in my pond?"

"I don't know," Miriam admitted. "Is it in the hole?" The hole thing seemed a little dangerous, really, with Alice next to the car directing efforts to get the man out, her voice clear and crisp over the splashing of people arriving off the green and the road.

The sprite frowned. "It kind of moves. Takes what it wants, you know."

"Oh dear." Now it was a sentient bottomless hole.

"Well, it's not going to take the car, if that's what you're worried about. Too many witnesses."

"It tried to take me." She sounded aggrieved. She *felt* aggrieved.

The sprite snorted, and caught a water beetle, popping it in her mouth and crunching noisily. "You pretty much dived head first into it. What was it going to do, spit you out?"

Miriam thought that was exactly what the mysterious hole should have done, but as she was still likely sitting within easy reach of it, she decided not to say so.

"I'm off," the sprite said. "Too many humans. Worse than a Sunday afternoon."

"Where are you going?" Miriam asked.

"Around," the sprite said, waving vaguely. The village of Toot Hansell nestled within a network of streams like a jewel in a complicated setting, and they cut and bisected the streets and yards in unexpected places. Miriam supposed it was quite handy for a water sprite. "Anyhow, you best stop talking to me. People'll start wondering about you, sitting in a pond talking to yourself." The sprite chuckled and vanished beneath the surface, and, with some difficulty, Miriam clambered to her feet and busied herself with getting disentangled from the overfamiliar embrace of the water lilies.

The sprite was right, of course. Miriam was Sensitive, and,

more than that, she and the ladies of the Women's Institute, being accustomed to dragons, had become rather used to seeing the magical Folk of the world. But Folk are *faint,* not invisible but unnoticeable, and as most people don't expect to see them, most people don't. Which was to the advantage of the Folk, but also did make it look to the uninformed observer as if one were talking to nothing.

There was a sudden commotion over by the car as it started moving and the nose slipped deeper into the pond, the back wheels lifting off the bank again. Miriam struggled to her feet and waded over to join Alice just as two young men dragged the driver out from behind the wheel and hauled him to the shore. The car groaned and wobbled, and with a noisy gurgle the front end dropped as if a chasm had opened beneath it. Miriam grabbed Alice's arm and they staggered back, watching as the boot lifted to the sky like a whale raising its tail to dive. Then it stopped, shuddering, vertical in the pond with the water lapping over the back of the front seats.

"Well done," Alice called to the two rather pale young men. "Just in time."

"It really shouldn't be able to do that," Miriam said, staring at the car.

Alice smiled. "One would think you'd just arrived in Toot Hansell, with that sort of talk."

THEY WADED to the bank and scrambled ashore, Miriam slipping on the slick sides of the pond. She was trying not to look at the … the person lying on the crushed ferns and chipped wood, unmoving as an older woman with short grey hair checked his airway.

"Nothing," the woman said, and positioned herself at the man's side, elbows locked and her back straight as she started chest compressions. "Anyone with first aid training? It's been a while since I had to do these."

Miriam made an unhappy gesture. "I think I remember." She didn't want to touch him. Maybe if she didn't touch him it wouldn't be real. It'd just be some emergency drill, a mannequin made up to look like Thomas, who'd sat smiling and sweating in the garden with them only a few hours ago.

"I can do it," Alice said, shooing a couple of bystanders out of the way and getting carefully onto her knees. "Do you think there's much chance?"

"I don't have any of my kit with me," the woman said. "But it's always worth a try, isn't it?"

Miriam tried not to think of Thomas laughing at one of Gert's off-colour jokes, and to remember what else to do in an emergency. "Has someone called an ambulance?"

"Yes," the man with the boat said. His face was so pale Miriam wanted to tell him to sit down and put his head between his knees. "They're on the way."

Alice pinched Thomas' nose and breathed for him, then looked up. "They'll be a while if they're coming from Skipton."

Miriam nodded, then suddenly thought of something. "There's a defibrillator in the village hall." She pointed at the two young men who had pulled Thomas from the car. "One of you lads run over there and get it. Hurry!"

They glanced at each other, then took off for the road at a sprint, wet trainers squelching. Miriam thought they probably wanted to get well away from the body, and she didn't blame them.

"Well remembered, Miriam," Alice said, and took over the chest compressions, the other woman correcting her hand placement before going back to breathing for poor Thomas. Miriam thought her own effort was a sorry contribution, and wondered what else she could do. She wanted to do *something*, but it had been so long since she'd done her last first aid course, she wasn't at all sure she'd be able to do any of it right. The ambulance had been called. The defibrillator was on its way. There was nothing she could do but be here, a witness to a man's passing. She swallowed, her throat clicking, and watched the two older women working in unspeaking rhythm, trying to catch a life that was already gone. She could feel its absence in the way the sun had lost its heat and the day had grown shadows longer than they had any right to be. She could smell the fuel from the car, and she didn't try and stop the tears that stung the corners of her eyes.

After the ambulance had arrived with lights flashing and sirens screaming, it left in short order and at a rather more sedate pace. The police, who had arrived at much the same time, stayed a little longer, unrolling crime scene tape and taking names and phone numbers of the witnesses. The sun had crept behind some clouds, as if unable to watch, and Miriam rather wished she could do the same. She still couldn't quite believe what she'd seen, although the car stood resolutely upright in the pond, reminding her.

"We just had lunch with him!" she said to Alice. "How could this happen?"

"I don't know," Alice said. "Poor Bryan."

"Poor Bryan," Miriam echoed, the words distant to her own ears. Thomas and Bryan would come – *used* to come – and sit on the green on Mondays, when their pub was closed. It was the nicest pub of the three in the village, not far from the green and the church, restored respectfully and lovingly, with garden tables for the summer and open fires for the winter. They'd bring a picnic down to the green, with rosé wine if it was warm and a thermos of something if it was cold, and sit back in deckchairs reading books and talking to anyone who happened by. Once she'd stopped to have a drink with them and had watched Bryan present Thomas with a daisy chain. Thomas had still been wearing it on his head when she'd left them, the petals shining in his sensible hair like gems. She swallowed hard.

"Do you want a drink?" the woman who had started CPR asked. Her name was Nora, Miriam had eventually remembered, and she had five cats and a nice husband who had rushed over, seen Thomas, and promptly fainted. "I've got some whisky in the cupboard, and I could rather do with something after all that." She nodded at her husband, sitting on the bank looking pale. "And I think he needs one, too."

Alice shook her head. "I think we'll just head home. Our bags are still over on the green somewhere."

"Alright," Nora said. "Come on, Lionel." She helped her husband up and they headed across the road to their house, and Alice patted Miriam's arm.

"Shall we get home?"

"Yes, please," Miriam said. "I need a cup of tea."

"That seems like an excellent plan," Alice said, and they started to pick their way around the pond arm in arm, Miriam hoping her muddy skirt wasn't making too much of a mess of Alice's white capris. Not that they were looking any too clean anymore, either.

"Ms Martin?" someone called behind them. "Ms Ellis?"

They stopped, turning back to see Ben, Jasmine's husband, padding toward them. He looked worried, and there was a smear of blue on the corner of his mouth. "Hello, Ben," Alice said.

"Hello." He hesitated, then said, "You were first on the scene?"

"We were." Alice agreed, and Miriam made a small noise. It was hard to be nervous of Ben, who was tall and young-looking and red-faced, but he was still the police. And talking to the police always made her feel she'd done something wrong.

"Um, so, I know I took your statements and everything, but I think the inspector will still want to see you."

"Colin?" Alice said. "That'll be quite alright."

"I'll make some carrot cake," Miriam said. "Colin always likes carrot cake." Detective Inspector Colin Collins was her nephew, which made him about as unfrightening as any police officer could be.

"He'll probably be by tomorrow," Ben said, checking his watch. "So, you know, if you can be around . . .?"

"Don't leave town," Miriam said, and a little bubble of laughter popped up from somewhere. She covered her mouth with one hand, her ears getting hot as Alice and Ben looked at her curiously.

"Not really," Ben said. "I mean, he's got your phone number and everything."

"He knows where we live," Miriam agreed, and tried to swallow a giggle.

"I think we'd best go home," Alice said. "We've had a long day."

"Yes," Ben said, scratching the back of his neck. "I can imagine."

"You've got something just there," Alice said, touching the corner of her mouth, and they left Ben scrubbing at the blue dye as they padded off across the green in search of their abandoned bags. Miriam wasn't terribly surprised to find she was crying again.

3
DI ADAMS

"It can't do that," DI Adams said. She stood on the bank of the duck pond in a pair of sodden wellies, arms crossed, glaring at the car as if it was standing on its nose just to spite her. Late afternoon light turned the windscreen into a blinding beacon.

"And yet it is," DI Collins said.

"Yes, but *how?* That's got to be against the laws of physics or something."

"Maybe it's just really well balanced," he offered, and she gave him a withering look that was entirely wasted, as he was inspecting a skinny greyish creature with slick green hair that had just surfaced among the lilies. "Hello."

"Hello," the sprite said, favouring him with a sweet, sharp-toothed smile before grabbing a frog that was pretending to be invisible among the reeds.

"Who're you, then?" Collins asked. He'd been using a torch to inspect the inside of the car, and now he played it over the creature. She hissed, shielding her eyes with the frog. "Sorry. Are you photosensitive?"

"Collins, you're shining it in her eyes. I'd hiss, too." DI Adams checked for the uniformed officers, but they'd retreated to beyond the crime scene tape, letting the techs and inspectors get on with things. No one was close enough to overhear.

"Right." Collins switched the torch off. "Sorry about that."

"I'm Nellie," the sprite said. "I don't know you two."

"We're ... friends of Beaufort," DI Adams said, feeling that it was maybe more useful (and less incriminating) to say they were friends of the High Lord of the Cloverly dragons than friends of the W.I.

"Huh," the sprite said, and examined the frog, apparently losing interest in them.

"So ... Did you see anything unusual today?" DI Collins asked.

The sprite looked up. "You mean, apart from the bloody great car in my pond?"

"Well. I mean, anything that could have led to that."

"I was minding my own business," Nellie said. "I *always* mind my own business. Then there's this horrible great crash, and there's a car and a bunch of noisy humans thrashing about, scaring the fish." She put the frog back in the reeds and it paddled away. "And so far I still have the same problem." She gave them a pointed glare.

"We're very sorry about that," DI Adams said. "We're going to try and get this cleared up as soon as possible." She hesitated. "Only – well, how *is* the car stuck?"

The sprite sighed. "The pond's bottomless sometimes. But it gets shy. So when all the people started running in and shouting, it stopped being bottomless."

"It gets shy," DI Adams said.

"It's not very social."

"The pond's not very social."

Nellie looked at Collins. "Is there something wrong with her?"

"She's from down south," Collins said, and Nellie said "Ah," as if that explained anything.

DI Adams shook her head and watched the sprite lunge forward and grab a small brown fish, which flopped about in panic until she started stroking its belly. DI Adams decided not to wonder how a pond could be a) bottomless; and b) only bottomless sometimes. She also decided it was definitely best not to think about it being shy. That seemed like a slippery slope. What would be next? Passive-aggressive wells? Anxious becks?

She opened her mouth to thank Nellie for her time just as the sprite stopped petting the fish and bit its head off. Both inspectors gave voice to an involuntary *Ew!*

Nellie looked at them. "What?" she demanded, her mouth full of half-chewed fish. "What do you think I eat?"

DI Adams made some half-articulated sound, thinking that it least it hadn't been the frog, and the sprite tossed her lank hair dismissively then melted into the surface of the water, taking the twitching body of the fish with her.

"Well," DI Collins said. "That explains a lot."

"The car?"

"That too. But there always were rumours that the duck pond was bottomless. I thought it was to keep us out of it when we were kids."

DI Adams nodded. "I suppose it depends how shy the pond was feeling."

"Evidently." Collins turned away to watch the crime scene techs shaking the car cautiously, and DI Adams wondered how they were going to write that particular report up.

Rather them than her.

DI ADAMS ROLLED out of bed, threw the window open, and bellowed into the early light, "*Shut up, you horrible bird!*"

There was absolute silence for a moment, then the rooster

crowed again, and someone tutted rather loudly. DI Adams looked down into the next-door yard and sighed.

"Not you," she said to the woman in the pink dressing gown. "The rooster."

The woman just tutted again and went back to hanging up her washing. DI Adams closed the window. There was no point trying to reason with anyone who was doing laundry at 5:30 a.m. on a Saturday.

She considering trying to get more sleep, but the rooster was still doing his best impression of an air raid siren, and at some point in the night Dandy had crept onto the little double bed and expanded to take up pretty much all of it. She poked him in the side and said, "Dogs don't belong on beds."

He rolled onto his back, exposing his dreadlocked grey belly, and panted at her happily. She still wasn't sure what to make of him. She didn't consider herself a dog person, but she hadn't exactly had a choice in the matter when he adopted her in the spring. And, to be fair, he wasn't exactly a dog. He was a dandy, and no one seemed entirely clear on what that was. What she did know was that he liked tummy rubs, disdained dogfood, and wasn't exactly visible to most humans. Well, to any other than her.

She pulled a hoody on over her pyjamas and padded downstairs into the unfamiliar little kitchen of the terraced house, wondering again how she'd ended up in Skipton. Transferring from London to Leeds was one thing, but *Skipton?* Her youngest brother had asked her if she was having a midlife crisis and planning to buy Hunter wellies and a Labrador. She'd suggested he come up here and tell her that, then he could see what country jails were like. He'd responded by calling her Jeanette, which was actually her name, but didn't mean he got to use it. She'd hung up while he was still snorting with laughter and offering to send her a Barbour jacket for Christmas.

It was all because of Toot Hansell, of course. Well, it was

because of dragons, but the dragons lived in the general region of Toot Hansell, and somehow the Toot Hansell Women's Institute had become ground zero for dealing with anything dragon-related. And as she and Collins were the only two people outside the W.I. who seemed to know about dragons, it made sense that they dealt with any police business involving Toot Hansell, the W.I., dragons, or any sort of magical carryings-on rather than risk someone else stumbling across the secret. And it was surprising just how many carryings-on seemed to come up. The village hardly looked like a hotbed of criminal activity, but she'd spent so much time out there since transferring up from London that her DCI hadn't even been surprised when Skipton requested that she assist them. In fact, he'd been almost unseemingly happy, which DI Adams felt was a bit rude. But then, no one had ever accused DCI Temple – known unaffectionately as The Temper – of being particularly diplomatic. He'd just walked up to her desk and said, "Adams. Pack a bag. Skipton needs you on a case."

She'd started to point out that she *had* a case, which was exactly what she'd said to Collins when he'd called her an hour earlier, but the DCI had cut her off.

"Hamilton can handle it. I'll supervise him. DCI Taylor's an old friend, so if she says they need you, you'd best go."

She'd considered protesting, but The Temper had evidently made up his mind, and Collins was texting her every five minutes with an update and pictures of cake, so it wasn't as if she was getting any peace over it. She had a sneaking suspicion that her DCI was pleased to see the back of her. In addition to suffering from a lack of diplomacy, he was also a product of the school of stiff upper lips. Dealing with a new DI who had transferred from London following a work-induced mental health break was sufficiently out of his comfort zone that she was half-surprised he hadn't packed her bag himself.

So she'd left Leeds an hour later with a gym bag and her coffee machine on the back seat of the car and driven straight to Toot Hansell, to be confronted with physics-defying cars. And now she'd been woken by roosters after spending the night in someone's aunt's holiday let, the place all done up with pink floral towels, knitted doll toilet paper covers, framed photos of kittens, and an extravagance of doilies and souvenir plates.

I'm only on loan, she reminded herself, plugging her coffee machine in and topping it up with coffee. This was for one case, and one case only. As soon as it was done, she was going back somewhere that didn't have roosters in the backyard.

THEY RAN BEFORE WORK, DI Adams listening to the fall of her feet and the harsh rhythm of her breathing, Dandy loping alongside her. His size was oddly variable, and today his head was almost level with her waist as he kept easy pace, grey dreadlocks flopping in the wake of his movement. The sun was already warm on her back, and the woods smelt of night-damp and rotting leaves and new growth. They ran the loop of the castle woods, the trees green and whispering, the river gold and the dirt track forgiving under her feet. Other walkers and runners nodded to DI Adams but gave her a wide berth without seeming to know why, and their dogs strained away in fright. Dandy ignored them, although apparently he wasn't above chasing squirrels. The first time he'd raced off after one DI Adams had spent half an hour hissing at him to come down out of the tree, trying to look casual every time someone went past. Apparently, dandies were good climbers.

Back at the house, she took a moment to stretch at the gate, her eyes drawn to the fell that lifted itself above town. She seemed to be able to see it from almost anywhere, immovable grey stone and green grass like a monument to something unspoken. It was a constant reminder that the town was anchored to wild country, that the luminous green fields led to higher and less tamed places. She tried not to like it. She didn't want to start liking things around here.

She was almost ready to go in when a car pulled into the spot in front of hers.

"Morning, Adams," Collins said, as Dandy went to investigate the bag he was holding. "Good run?"

"Morning," she said, then added, "Dandy, no."

"Dandy what?" Collins asked, looking around in alarm, but it was too late – the bag was jerked from his hand. "Hey!"

"Put it— oh. Too late. Sorry." Dandy gulped the bag down without bothering to even separate the contents, then stood on the pavement with his tail wagging softly, looking at Collins as if he might produce another.

"Does he have to be invisible?" Collins asked. "I wasn't prepared for that."

"I have no idea," DI Adams said. "I know nothing about him." Which was true. Dandy had adopted her during a rather bizarre case involving pheasants, elderly thieves, a suspicious death, and the W.I. Of course. And not even the dragons knew very much about him. The cat had opinions, of course, but the cat always had opinions. She was just glad that, unlike the cat, Dandy had so far shown no inclination to talk. "Do you want some coffee?" she offered.

"Don't you have any toast?"

"I haven't exactly had a chance to go shopping. Besides, I don't want to have to cart loads of stuff back to Leeds with me."

"You could be here a while."

"You don't know that." She went through the gate to the front door, ignoring his snort.

Collins poked at her coffee machine and complained about the breakfast sandwiches the dog had stolen while DI Adams showered and changed into a suit and shirt. She tightened her hair more firmly into a bun, half-listening to him shouting up the stairs that buying a vegetarian sausage sandwich for her had seriously damaged his standing in the community. She poked at a stray curl and thought she should probably try straightening her hair again, but it took too long, and never worked anyway. She shoved a couple of extra bobby pins in for luck, then padded down the stairs.

"Is Dandy in here?" Collins asked.

"Under the table."

"Well, *bad dog*," the big inspector said, leaning over and shouting in the general direction of Dandy's hindquarters. The dog looked at DI Adams – well, pointed his head in her general direction, his red eyes invisible behind the flopping hair, and thumped his tail.

"He looks very contrite," she said, putting her to-go mug under the coffee machine spout. "Want one?"

"Sure. Why not."

"Any news from the techs?" she asked, retrieving another mug from the cupboard.

"Other than the fact the car's apparently concreted into the bottom of the pond?"

"Wow."

"Yep. They haven't been able to inspect it properly yet. It's going to have to be cut out. But initial forensics on the deceased suggest a heart attack."

"So maybe an accident?" she asked.

"Could be. Awfully sudden, though, not to pull over. And no brake marks, not even on the bank. He went in full-tilt."

"And that was fast, especially for someone who knows the way the village works and would have wanted to stay in everyone's good books."

"Yep. And the last people to see him alive that we know of were the W.I."

DI Adams sighed, and switched the coffee machine off. "Of course they were."

DI Collins looked at the mug she handed him. "You have no food but you have two to-go mugs?"

"I have four. I only brought two."

"That seems excessive."

"I'm not going to lose one and then be stuck with no to-go mug."

DI Collins got up and looked in the fridge, which was empty except for an elderly apple she'd transferred from the car. "Milk?"

"Sorry." She pocketed her phone. "Toot Hansell, then?"

"Let's see what the ladies can tell us. And if they can feed us."

DI Adams led the way out into the crisp summer morning.

❧

THEY TOOK DI ADAMS' car, and Dandy sat on the back seat with his head out the window. He seemed very put out that Collins was in the front, and kept breathing on his ear, making him yelp in surprise. DI Adams ignored his complaints, watching the world become greener and wider as the roads narrowed and the houses scattered to odd buildings and the occasional hamlet, watched over by red kites and sleepy-looking cattle.

"Just push him away," she said, as Collins tried to wrestle his coffee back from the dog.

"How can I? I can't even see him!" He gave up and let Dandy take the mug. "I don't want it anyway. You'll have slobbered on it."

"But if you can't see the slobber, is it really there?" DI Adams asked, slowing to pass a group of walkers in heavy socks, maps in clear pouches hung on string around their necks.

"Definitely," Collins said, glaring in the general direction of the dog. "Although I'm starting to see why you have so many coffee mugs now."

"No. I had that many before." She went back to ignoring him poking Dandy as the dog sat there with the to-go mug in his mouth, wearing an air of long-suffering patience.

They went to Rose's first, parking outside her little bungalow and letting themselves in the gate. An enormous volley of barking greeted their knock on the door, which Dandy entirely ignored. He was busy investigating the meadow of wildflowers that had once been a lawn.

Rose opened the door with her Great Dane, Angelus, bounding around behind her. The dog was almost as tall as she was. "Inspectors!" she shouted over the barking. "I heard you might be by!"

"Of course you did," DI Adams said. Angelus forced himself past Rose without much difficulty, rushed into the garden, and stopped so suddenly his long back legs didn't quite get the message. He pitched nose first onto the path, recovered himself, and bolted back into the house with a whimper. Dandy watched him go, flowers festooning his dreadlocks.

"I made scones," Rose said, ignoring Angelus.

"Oh, thank heavens," Collins said, and hurried after her as she led the way inside. DI Adams left Dandy romping in the flowers. He seemed happy.

COLLINS ATE at least three scones with jam and cream at Rose's, by DI Adams' count, and by the time they'd visited Pearl and Teresa, Priya, Gert, Rosemary, and Jasmine both of them were awash with tea and DI Adams was fairly sure she'd broken her previous W.I.

record for the amount of baked goods consumed in one morning. Dandy had been the willing recipient of some very stodgy banana cake that made DI Adams' teeth go funny at Jasmine's, and he had scared Jasmine's little Pomeranian so much she'd gone under the sofa and refused to come out. Which DI Adams felt was an improvement, as it was a very nippy little thing. Jasmine had been terrified she'd poisoned the councillor with blue potato salad, and DI Collins had spent twenty minutes explaining that they already had the tub she'd made Ben take to the police lab, and it was absolutely fine, and she shouldn't fuss herself. DI Adams made encouraging noises and tried not to check her watch.

What they hadn't gained was any useful information. Everyone said the same thing: Thomas had seemed fine at lunch, he hadn't rushed off, and he hadn't talked about anything except communal gardens and chickens. Or possibly bees and wildflowers, depending on who you were talking to. Certainly nothing suspicious.

DI Adams pulled the car up outside Carlotta's house and said, "I can't take another cup of tea."

"Just have some water," Collins said. "You don't have to drink it, anyway."

"But then it's a waste."

He shrugged. "They have to offer it, you have to accept. These are the things you're going to have to get used to around here."

"On loan," she reminded him.

"Keep telling yourself that," he said, and DI Adams made a face, then stretched before she followed him, as if that'd somehow make more room for tea and cake.

Carlotta opened the door before they reached it. "Hello, inspectors," she called.

"Hello, Carlotta," they chorused, DI Adams still having to remind herself not to use last names.

"Come in, come in. I've just put the kettle on."

DI Adams wondered if Thomas Wright could have died of tea overdose. She felt it was possible.

❧

TWENTY MINUTES later they were back in the car, DI Adams resting her forehead on the wheel. "I'm done," she moaned, and pushed Dandy away as he shoved his nose into her side in a sympathetic sort of way. "Why are we interviewing them all separately again?"

"You do remember what it's like when they're all together?"

"I know, but …" she rubbed her belly. "I may never recover."

"You didn't have to have three ginger cookies."

"They were good!"

"Pace yourself, Adams. It's a marathon, not a sprint."

She lifted her head and glared at him. "Oh, is that what you were doing with all Gert's custard tarts and Priya's cookies?"

"Nankhatai."

"What?"

"Nankhatai. The cookies."

She waved him off. "Either way, I hardly call it pacing yourself."

"I've been in training." He grinned at her. "Anyway, let's go see Auntie Miriam and Alice. Just two more stops, Adams."

DI Adams wondered if her stomach could take two more stops.

4
MORTIMER

Mortimer was arguing with Gilbert.

Well, he was actually trying not to argue with Gilbert, but the young dragon wasn't making it easy.

"I'm telling you," Gilbert was saying, his orange nose turning a little red with emotion, "these gliders will be *amazing*."

"I just don't think that having fire-breathing gliders is a good idea, Gilbert," Mortimer tried.

Gilbert shook the glider at him. "You old dragons! You have no sense for innovation!"

"*Hey*," Amelia said, before Mortimer could object. "That old dragon is the reason we have a trade in dragon scale toys *at all*, Gil. Never mind innovation – he created the whole damn industry!" She was wearing magnifying goggles and using specially made tongs to shape thin, light dragon scales into a mobile, creating birds that lifted and swam in the slightest breeze, running with colours that defied categorising. It was tricky, working with dragon scales. Only dragon fire was hot enough to make it malleable, which meant they went through an awful lot of tongs and hammers. Even dwarf-made tools could only take so much.

Now she was distracted and the bird she was shaping was taking on a dangerously lopsided look.

"All that aside," Mortimer said, trying not feel aggrieved by being described as *old*. He was hardly *old*. He was only a hundred and fourteen! Just because these two hadn't even reached their century yet.

Gilbert frowned at Amelia. "I know that. I'm just saying—"

"*Fire*, Gilbert," Mortimer said. "These are toys for human children."

"Yes, but—"

"Their coordination isn't always quite what it could be. If they don't set themselves on fire, they'll put half the town alight."

Gilbert opened his mouth to protest, then closed it again. "Okay. Yes. I see what you're saying." He thought for a moment. "How about if we made them for grown-ups only?"

Mortimer resisted the urge to shout that this workshop should be for grown-ups only, and Gilbert clearly wasn't there yet, and Amelia threw the lopsided bird at her brother, her eyes rather alarmingly huge behind the goggles.

"Gil! That'll only make the kids want it more! And you've seen enough humans – you really think the adults will be that much better?"

Gilbert ducked the bird easily and stared at the glider in his paws. His talons were painted in alternating shades of lime green and gold, which was rather fetching against his orange scales, although Mortimer still didn't quite understand it. But then, he didn't understand Gilbert's tail piercings, either, which made him wonder if one hundred and twenty-one did actually count as old.

"Alright," the young dragon said. "I get it. No fire."

"No fire," Mortimer and Amelia agreed.

"But it was so cool. Want to see?"

He looked at them so hopefully that even Amelia couldn't protest, and they followed him dutifully out of the workshop, with its baskets of unworked scales waiting near the entrance, chimineas in the corners and great prisms collecting light from outside and reflecting it onto the low stone workbenches. The three dragons padded single file down the passageway to the rocky face outside, and sat on the ledge in the early morning sun. The lake below the mount was gently ruffled with the fingerprints of the wind, shattering light on every ripple, and the trees in the woods beyond were heavy with summer growth in every shade of green. Distantly, they could see the roofs of Toot Hansell, and beyond that the bright fields of farms rolling toward distant fells.

"Watch," Gilbert said, and flung the glider into the wind. It spiralled away from them, sleek as a flying fish, its wings broadening and unfurling, angling to catch an updraft. It executed a flawless loop-de-loop, barrel-rolled to its left, then came sweeping back again, wings trembling.

"Where's the fire?" Amelia asked, sounding unimpressed. "You said it breathed fire."

"Any minute now," Gilbert said, as the little glider continued with its acrobatics, glimmering with pink and rose. "Aaaany minute."

Mortimer took a moment to appreciate the fact that Gilbert really was an extraordinary craftsdragon. The glider was perfectly balanced, following every small shift in the breeze with its own minute adjustments, rolling through a recital of moves with effortless accuracy. He wasn't so sure about the skulls painted on the fuselage, though.

Just then, the glider gave a shudder and stalled. "What? No!" Gilbert shouted. "Pull up, pull up!" The glider plummeted toward the rocks below, rolling over and over, turning from pink to purple as it went.

"Oh dear," Mortimer said.

"It's stopping! Just a glitch!"

The glider *was* stopping. It had darkened to a deep royal purple and seemed to be expanding, tail lengthening as it began to rise again. Soon it was roaring up the cliff face, and Mortimer could see the hammered scale stretched taut and translucent against a raging fire within.

"Take cover!" he bellowed, and they piled back into the passageway as the glider screamed toward them. It hit the ledge just above theirs, eliciting an enraged shriek from Lydia, an older dragon who'd been sunning herself at the mouth of her cavern. Billows of purple flame spilled across the cliff face, falling over the workshop entrance like a particularly brilliant waterfall. The three dragons stayed where they were for a moment longer, waiting, then there was a scraping noise and a sad thud as the wreckage slid back down and landed on the ledge outside.

"I can see where this wasn't really ready for market," Gilbert said after a moment.

Amelia snorted. "Go apologise to Lydia."

"Aw. She'll tweak my tail!"

"Serves you right." Amelia went back into the workshop, and Mortimer patted Gilbert awkwardly on the shoulder.

"Never mind," he said. "It was a good effort. Great aeronautics."

"Really?" Gilbert had started to fade to an unhappy grey colour, but now he perked up. "You thought it was good?"

Mortimer wrinkled his snout. "Just so we're clear, not the fire bit."

"But the rest?"

"The rest was wonderful."

"Awesome! I'll keep working on it."

"Not the fire bit!" Mortimer shouted after him as the young dragon hurried out onto the ledge to collect the wreckage, yelling apologies to Lydia, who shouted something back about carelessness and tweaked tails. Mortimer hoped none of her blankets had caught fire. Since he'd set up the dragon scale trade with Miriam as his human partner, the Cloverly dragons had rather quickly moved on from buying gas barbecues for sleeping on (much more comfortable and reliable than fires), to requesting blankets, coloured sheepskins, hats, and, in the case of the younger dragons, talon paint and piercings. He was slightly bewildered by what he'd started, but mostly just happy that no one had to worry about finding enough fuel to stay warm through the winter anymore, or choosing between being warm and finding enough to eat. But dragons did tend to forget that not everything was fireproof.

He started to turn back into the workshop when the semicircle of blue sky at the entrance was blocked out by a rather bulkier body than Gilbert's.

"Morning, lad," Beaufort said cheerfully. "That was quite the display! New range?"

Mortimer winced. Beaufort's voice was very loud in the confines of the passageway. "Not exactly," he said.

"Did you like it?" Gilbert called from outside, and the High Lord shuffled in the entrance so he could see both younger dragons.

"It was most impressive," Beaufort said.

"*No*," Mortimer said, before Gilbert could say anything else. "It was dangerous. Not for use by humans."

"Oh," Beaufort said. "It wasn't a firework or some such, then?"

"It was a fire-breathing glider," Gilbert said.

"Which is not practical." Mortimer tried to make himself sound authoritative. "And we will not be continuing work on them."

Gilbert sighed, rather theatrically, and Beaufort looked at Mortimer with the corners of his old gold eyes crinkled in amusement.

"Quite right," he said. "One must know what to pursue and what to leave alone, especially when in business."

"Yes," Mortimer said, a little uncertainly, then nodded. "Yes, exactly. Did you need something, sir?" He still found the habit of calling the High Lord "sir" hard to get rid of. After all, it was only in the last couple of years, ever since Mortimer had instigated the idea of redefining treasure to include such things as barbecues, that he and Beaufort had become ... well, whatever they were. *Friends* still didn't seem right. Beaufort was the High Lord of the Cloverly dragons, and Mortimer was, well, just Mortimer. He wasn't even a lord, and no matter what Gilbert thought about his age, Beaufort was much, much older. He was so old he'd lost count of the centuries, and still bore Saint George a grudge for killing off his predecessor, High Lord Catherine, while she was sleeping peacefully in a bramble patch. And Mortimer could understand that grudge, considering that even in the glory days of the Cloverlies they'd never grown bigger than a small pony. It cast a rather different light on Saint George's heroism.

"Fancy going for a little jaunt?" Beaufort said.

Mortimer frowned. *Jaunt* sounded a little suspicious. He wasn't sure about *jaunts* where the High Lord was concerned. Beaufort tended to get very interested in things. A *jaunt* sounded like it could lead to those sorts of things. He looked down at his tail reflexively. The scales were just beginning to grow back from the manor house thing in spring. He wondered if a *jaunt* could induce stress-shedding. It sounded like it could. "Well, we do have quite a lot on," he said aloud.

"Of course you do," Beaufort said. "Summer fete this month, isn't it?"

Mortimer nodded. Miriam sold the dragon scale trinkets on the Etsy, but much of their sales came from Toot Hansell's fetes and markets. They could barely keep up with demand.

"Well, I can always go on my own. Just thought you might like to get out," Beaufort said. "Don't work too hard, lad." He turned and padded back out onto the ledge, and Mortimer dithered for a moment. On the one paw, they did have a lot to do. On the other – Beaufort, out unsupervised. On a *jaunt*. He could almost feel his scales threatening to let go at the thought.

"Wait!" he shouted. "I'm coming!"

THEY KEPT low as they flew toward Toot Hansell, their shadows painted on the trees below them. With the clear skies, it was always possible that someone Sensitive might actually see them if they flew too high, but just above the trees they were safe enough. No one could see them through the leafy cover. Birds watched them go suspiciously and squirrels dived for cover, chattering angrily. Dragons – or certainly Cloverly dragons – preferred rabbits, but it was always best for small creatures to be careful.

"Are we going to see Miriam?" Mortimer asked. She'd been the first human to not only see a dragon, but to befriend one, in centuries, and she made him much less nervous than Alice did. Plus she made very nice banana cake, and always had extra bread on hand to make cheese toasties for hungry dragons. Mortimer considered these fine attributes in a friend.

"I rather think so, yes," Beaufort said.

"Has something happened?"

Beaufort gave a thoughtful rumble that Mortimer didn't much like. "Perhaps, lad," he said. "Although perhaps it's just human business."

Human business should have sounded more encouraging, but Mortimer was quite aware that the High Lord wasn't very good at staying out of human business. He always managed to find some angle that meant he could get involved.

As they drew closer to town and the trees thinned out, they dropped to the ground, folding their wings against their backs and ambling through the underbrush with the earth cool and dew-damp beneath their paws. Miriam's garden backed up onto the stream that looped around the village, encircling it like a natural moat, and they paused before they stepped onto the little path that ran on the woods side of the waterway, checking for dog-walkers. No one seemed to be about, so they hurried across the path and over the little stone ford that served Miriam as a bridge, then let themselves through the gate and into her cheerfully overgrown garden. Flowering plants and vegetables fought for supremacy among overflowing herb pots and clambering vines, and an apple tree drooped heavy under an abundance of green fruit. Bees massed around the wildflowers that grew on the borders among the long grass, and birds squabbled over the seeds in the feeder. There was an almost embarrassing excess of life going on.

There was no one in the garden, so Beaufort led the way to the kitchen door and knocked briskly before Mortimer could even protest. The younger dragon ducked behind a broken pot overflowing with tomatoes and said, "Beaufort! Anyone could be in there!"

"I don't think so," the High Lord replied, peering in the kitchen window. "I don't see anyone at all."

"Maybe she's out."

"Quite." Beaufort considered for a moment, then said, "Let's see if Alice is home."

Mortimer supposed that was safe enough. Alice's house backed onto the woods on the eastern side of the village, and they could go all the way there under the cover of the trees without crossing a road or doing anything else dangerous or silly. And Alice might not be one for cheese toasties, but she did make an excellent egg salad sandwich. He started to say exactly that when there was the sound of footsteps coming around the side of the house. He flung himself into the shadow of the tomatoes, trying desperately to convince his anxiously grey scales to take on the mottled green of the garden before some horribly perceptive person walked around the corner and found themselves face to face with a dragon, and then they were exposed in national newspapers – or international – and dissected or tased or put in zoos or—

"Detective Inspector Adams!" Beaufort boomed cheerily. He'd merely sunk in among the plant pots under Miriam's window, taking on the stone-grey of the flags beneath him, and now he stood up, regarding the inspector with a toothy smile as his scales flushed back to green. "And Detective Inspector Collins. How lovely to see you both!"

"Beaufort," DI Adams said, not sounding quite as enthusiastic. She looked around until she spotted Mortimer, who was trying to look casual under the tomatoes. "Mortimer."

"Hello," Mortimer said weakly, and sat up. There was a tomato squashed under his belly, and he wiped it off distastefully. He still hadn't decided which of the inspectors made him more nervous. DI Adams was terribly serious, but DI Collins was *friendly*. That was almost worse.

"Hello, lads," DI Collins said. "Have you seen my Auntie Miriam?"

"We were looking for her ourselves," Beaufort said. "In fact, we were about to go around and see if she was at Alice's."

DI Adams gave a rather weighty sigh. "We were too."

"Oh, we'll come with you, then," Beaufort said. "You can give us a lift."

DI Adams looked alarmed, and Mortimer began to stammer out a protest, but DI Collins clapped his hands together and grinned at the dragons. "Makes sense," he said. "Everyone in!" He turned and led the way back around the house, Beaufort trotting after him with his nose high, and DI Adams and Mortimer exchanged horrified looks.

"Is that wise?" she said. "I mean, someone might see you."

"I know," Mortimer said, plucking at his tail. "But you try telling him. He likes cars," he added, to underline the difficulty of the situation.

DI Adams looked at him for a moment, then gave him a clumsy

pat on the shoulder and said, "Well, no helping it then. Come on. We'll miss our ride."

"Well, we don't want *that,* do we," Mortimer said, then immediately said, "Sorry. That was rude."

"No, you're fine. I'm glad to see not everyone around here thinks this sort of thing is normal." She put her hands in her pockets and headed for the front of the house, and after a moment Mortimer followed. It could be worse, he reminded himself. Beaufort could be buying mulled wine in a dog costume at the Christmas market. Again.

5
MIRIAM

Miriam was standing at Alice's gate, trying to disentangle her fingers from the handles of her shopping bags without poking herself in the face with the rhubarb or squashing the cherries when a car pulled up next to her. She peered around, and promptly dropped the bag with the strawberries in it on her foot. "Oh no!"

"Are you alright there, Auntie Miriam?" Colin asked, climbing out of the car and rescuing the bag.

"You surprised me," she said, trying not to sound accusing. "Are my strawberries alright?"

He peered into the bag. "I think so."

An urgent tapping on the car window made them both look around, and Miriam spotted a very grey Mortimer squashed against the glass as if trying to stay well away from something in the middle of the car. Beaufort was already climbing out the other door while DI Adams held it open, looking like a particularly impatient chauffeur. "Out," she said, leaning down to peer in, then checked the lane for observers. Miriam could hear a mower running somewhere, but she couldn't see anyone out in their front garden or dog-walking down the lane.

"Hello," Miriam said, putting as much cheerfulness in her voice as she could manage. It wasn't a lot. There were going to be Interviews, she could feel it.

DI Adams nodded at her, then slapped her leg and said, "Come on! Out!"

Mortimer scrabbled at his door desperately, not moving toward DI Adams, and Colin stepped forward to open it. Mortimer spilled out of the car in a tumble of wings and tail and legs, whimpering as he bumped his nose on the kerb, found his feet, and took cover behind Miriam.

"Hello, dear," she said, looking down at him. He was trying to take on the cheerful green of the grass, but it wasn't getting past his knees. Did dragons have knees? She supposed they must. "Are you alright?"

"We had to ride with the dandy," he said. "He kept *breathing* on me. And staring at me."

Miriam thought of pointing out that at least he could *see* the detective inspector's invisible dog, but didn't think it'd be much comfort, so she just said, "Oh dear."

"Hello Miriam," Beaufort said, trotting happily around the car. "Lovely day, isn't it?"

DI Adams muttered something about lovely days being overrated, and Alice called from the house, "Are you going to come in, or just stand at my gate all day? I've popped the kettle on."

"Right you are," Colin said, relieving Miriam of her other shopping bag, and DI Adams made a despairing noise that Miriam thought was a most unusual response to the offer of tea.

ALICE SHOOED everyone straight out the back door again, with instructions to get the cushions for the chairs out of the little summerhouse at the bottom of the garden. Miriam stayed in the kitchen to help with the plates and mugs, and also to avoid having to make small talk with DI Adams. She had a feeling the detective inspector might be even worse at it than she was, and she wasn't sure she was quite prepared for that.

"Were you expecting them?" she whispered to Alice as the older woman took a golden cake studded with the pink stems of rhubarb from a tin and set it on a plate, then handed it to her.

Alice smiled. "Of course. We were most likely some of the last people to see him alive, after all."

Miriam squeaked and almost dropped the cake, then followed Alice out into the neatly trimmed garden, catching the scents of fresh-cut grass and lavender.

DI Adams was arguing with a smoky tabby cat who was standing on the table with his tail bushed out to impressive proportions.

"He's not doing anything," the detective inspector insisted. "He's just sitting there!"

"Being all devilish and dandy," the cat said. "And stinking."

"Does he still smell? I seem to have got used to it."

"He's a *dog*. All dogs smell. And he's a dandy devil dog, so he stinks like the devil."

"How do you know what the devil smells like?" Collins asked. "Have you met him?"

The cat bared his teeth. "Humans. Always so literal."

"Lovely to see everyone getting on as well as always," Alice said, setting the teapots on the table.

"She needs to stop dragging that dandy around," the cat said.

"I'm not dragging him anywhere. He's just sort of *there*." DI Adams shrugged. "Besides, maybe I like having an invisible dog."

"I wouldn't mind an invisible dog," Collins said. "Seems like the sort of thing that'd come in handy." He picked up a piece of cake with a sigh and took a huge bite, scattering crumbs on his shirt. Alice handed him a plate and a napkin, and he looked guilty.

"I don't know," DI Adams said. "He hasn't really done anything yet."

"He's a *dandy*," the cat said. "How many times do I have to tell you?" He shook his head and stuck his nose in the milk jug. Alice grabbed him and lifted him away. "Hey!"

"You'll get hair in it," she said.

"What's a little hair between friends?" The cat sat down on a chair to groom himself, radiating a put-upon air. "It's all, 'Hey, Thompson, help us find the goblins', or 'Oi, Thompson, find us a lost inspector'. But gods forbid I tell you to stop hanging out with nasty dogs. Oh no. Just a bloody effective marketing campaign, that one. Man's best friend. Huh." He apparently had a lot more to say on the subject, but found a particularly matted patch of fur and started to lick it frantically, muttering unintelligibly the whole time.

"Well," Beaufort said. "At least we know his thoughts on the matter." He gave Miriam a toothy grin as she handed him a soup mug of tea. "Now, how can we help you, inspectors?"

"We actually came to see Alice and Miriam," DI Adams said, and Miriam tried to take a calm sip of tea but slurped it instead, her cheeks growing hot at the sound.

"Ooh, an Investigation, is it?" Beaufort took a piece of cake while Mortimer retreated under a large clump of geraniums. "Maybe we can help. Is it about the crash?"

"I was asking Alice and Miriam," DI Adams began, just as Colin said, "How do you know about the crash?"

They exchanged equally obstinate looks, and Alice set her mug down. "Shall I start?" she suggested.

"Yes," DI Adams said. Colin shrugged and brushed crumbs off his belly.

"There's nothing much to add to what we told the officers last night. But it was very out of character for him to be speeding."

"And he wasn't upset at the meeting yesterday?"

Alice considered it. "Not really, no. He did get a phone message that seemed to bother him, but it didn't send him rushing off or anything."

DI Adams made a note on a pad she'd put on the table, and looked at Miriam. "Did you see him get the message, Miriam?"

"Me? What? No!" She swallowed hard, and Colin patted her shoulder.

"You're not in any trouble, Auntie Miriam. Just tell us anything you remember."

"I don't remember anything. He was worried about Jasmine's potato salad, and I think he didn't agree with me very much about the companion planting."

"Companion planting?" DI Adams started, then shook her head. "Never mind. Had he been drinking?"

"He had a very small amount of Gert's cordial," Alice said. "He certainly wasn't drunk."

"He was very against it," Miriam said. "Not drinking, I mean, he owned a pub. But being drunk. Bryan used to joke that the last time Thomas had been tipsy was on his mum's sherry trifle when he was nine."

"I see." DI Adams tapped her pen on the notepad. "And he was well-liked enough?"

"Yes," Alice said. "He was a nice man. And very good on the council, too. Did what he said he was going to, and never fussed around talking like a politician."

"How does one of those talk?" Beaufort asked. Next to him, Mortimer was beginning to get his colour back as he ate his way steadily through the rhubarb cake.

"With lots of words but very little meaning," Alice said.

"Oh. I wonder if that's where I went wrong with our election."

"You have elections?" Colin asked.

"We tried them. It didn't go quite as planned."

"That's one way of putting it," Mortimer muttered, apparently addressing the cake.

Colin looked as if he'd quite like to pursue this line of inquiry, but DI Adams said, "Well. I guess that's it, then."

"There's not much more we can tell you," Alice agreed. "So, have you transferred to Skipton, DI Adams?"

"*No!* No," the younger woman continued, as if aware that she might have been a little too overenthusiastic. "Just on loan."

"She'll come round," Collins said cheerfully, setting his mug on the table. They were Alice's outside mugs, squat and green and solid. Miriam, to her shame, was the only person who'd ever managed to break one.

"There's no coming around to do," DI Adams snapped.

"I'm just saying, Toot Hansell keeps having cases. I can't request you every time or the DCI will start thinking I can't do my job at all."

DI Adams made a non-committal sound that suggested that wasn't her problem, and that the DCI might not be entirely wrong, which Miriam felt was a little unfair.

"More tea?" she offered, and DI Adams made an alarmed pushing away gesture.

"No, no. We better go. We need to head up to the pub and interview the husband."

"Now?" Miriam said. Nervous as she was, she felt vaguely safer with the inspectors here, which was a new experience. Rather than worrying that they might arrest her for some undefined crime, she rather felt that their presence might stop Alice and Beaufort wanting to Get Involved, which she was sure was actually going to lead to her arrest one day.

"Can we help at all?" Beaufort asked the inspectors.

"Absolutely not. You can just carry on as usual," DI Adams said, and Thompson snorted so loudly it turned into a hacking cough.

DI Collins patted the cat on the back and said, "I told you to stop smoking."

The cat made a noise that suggested he was being strangled and hurked a hairball onto the cushion.

"*Ew,*" Miriam said.

"*Ew,* yourself." The cat sat up and licked his lips. "Have you not figured out that their usual *is* sticking their noses into things?" he asked DI Adams.

She scowled at him. "I'm hoping common sense will prevail."

"Yeah, good luck on that one."

The inspectors exchanged glances, and DI Adams looking from Alice to Beaufort as she said, "You understand this is not an invitation to investigate. This is a police interview."

Alice raised her eyebrows and took a sip of tea. "Are you suggesting we can't be trusted?"

"No, just that the W.I. and … friends have a tendency to get involved."

"Not deliberately. You really can't blame us when we're targeted by murderers or kidnappers, or shut up in a country house with a killer."

"That would be victim blaming," Colin said agreeably, taking another piece of cake. DI Adams glared at him.

"*I mean,*" she said, "you can't start poking around in this. You either," she added, frowning at Beaufort, who had crumbs on his nose.

"Especially not that last one," Colin said, then frowned. "I don't think. Which would be worse, Adams? Dragons crashing the investigation, or the W.I.?"

"I think both options are equally bad," she snapped. "We don't want *anyone* involved, scaled or otherwise. Understood?"

"Understood," Mortimer and Miriam said together.

"I understand exactly what you mean," Alice said, and Beaufort grinned.

DI Adams looked as if she wanted to start shouting, and she put her pen down very carefully. "Alice?"

"Yes?"

"Is there any point in telling you again to stay out of this?"

"Oh, there's always a point," Alice said. "We all know where we stand, then."

"Well, that's *such* a relief," Mortimer mumbled, and everyone looked at him. He was a rather blotchy mix of anxious grey and his own purple-blue, and now his nose went bright pink. "I'm sorry! I keep coming out with these things. I think I'm spending too much time with Gilbert."

"The vegetarian dragon?" Colin asked.

Mortimer covered his nose with both paws, trying to hide his flush. "Yes. He gets like this when Amelia tells him his baubles are no good."

"I can see how that would upset him," the big inspector said gravely, and got up. "Adams is right, though. You do need to stay out of this. None of you are involved in any way, so you really have no excuse."

Miriam squinted up at her nephew, looming over them with his big hands clasped in front of him, his round face serious. He seemed to block out the sun, and she hoped desperately Alice was listening. But when she looked at her friend, Alice just smiled and said, "I'll wrap you up some cake to take with you."

Miriam held onto her own smile until the inspectors had followed Alice into the house, then she slumped back into her chair and clutched the loose cloth of her dress in both hands. "Noooo," she said to the dragons. "Not *again!*"

Mortimer nodded miserably, but Beaufort just gave her a toothy grin.

"Cheer up, Miriam," he said. "I'm sure it'll have nothing to do with us at all."

Miriam thought, rather darkly, that the odds of that were pretty low when certain people went around making sure things had to do with them.

MIRIAM WONDERED, if she'd been a different person – or Alice had been – if she'd have dared get up and say, "I would like to not be involved in this, please." Or maybe even just rise wordlessly from her chair and walk out of the garden, leaving her half-finished tea behind her. *Sweep* out of the garden, in a suitably dramatic manner, if she was going to really daydream about this.

But she wasn't. This was just like the many W.I. events she kept finding herself involved in, such as creating fliers for church fundraisers when she was a very firm non-believer in any sort of organised religion. Or being the person who made up the numbers when not enough people wanted to go to the macramé museum, or the bug exhibit that had come to York. Only this was even worse. Although the bugs had been rather nasty. She shuddered, and Alice said, "Are you alright, Miriam?"

"Oh yes. A cat walked over my grave."

"Hey! Don't blame us. We spend far less time strolling about graveyards than people seem to think."

"Sorry." Miriam tried to sit up straight.

"You should be. All these negative stereotypes attached to cats …"

"Do shut up, Thompson. You're only causing trouble," Alice said.

"It's true."

"That's entirely beside the point." She wiped a few crumbs off the table. "That was most instructive, wouldn't you say?"

"Instructive?" Miriam said.

"Yes. They obviously have no leads."

"They don't?" She reached for another piece of cake, then decided against it. She was going to have to break into her emergency stress-eating cheesy puffs this afternoon, it was obvious, so she'd best save some room.

"We shall have to find them some, then," Beaufort said.

Mortimer said something under his breath and scowled rather ferociously at a rosebush.

"You mustn't become too involved," Alice said. "This is local politics. There will be times when the situation won't be suitable for dragons."

Miriam rather thought that there were many times when the situation wasn't very suitable for her, either. Such as now. The whole conversation was feeling most unsuitable.

"Really?" Beaufort said, as if such an idea had never occurred to him.

"Alice, what on earth are you talking about?" Miriam asked. "We can't just start investigating when we've been told not to!"

"Of course not," Alice said, lifting her face to the sun.

"So, what do you mean to do?"

"Well, I believe Toot Hansell is currently missing a council representative."

"Oho," the cat said, and gave his curious, huffing laugh. "Alice for prime minister."

"Don't be so silly, Thompson."

"Hey, I can arrange it. I know cats in high places."

"Alice, is this wise?" Miriam twisted her fingers in her skirt. "If someone really did ... if Thomas' death wasn't an accident ..."

"Then things are very serious indeed. And rather someone who understands that than someone who doesn't."

"But you've never had the slightest interest in politics," Miriam said. "And don't you have to run for elections and things?"

"This shall be a most fascinating look at modern democracy, don't you think lad?" Beaufort said, nudging Mortimer.

"*Fascinating*," Mortimer said, and groaned.

"I do believe that, with the right signatures, I can step in as an emergency replacement, so to speak," Alice said. "It's not as if I want to hold on to the position." She tapped her fingers on the table. "Doesn't Gert's second cousin twice removed, or sister-in-law's cousin's niece, or something to that effect, work in the council offices?"

"Probably," Miriam said weakly. Gert had such a convoluted and extensive family that the odds were good someone worked pretty much everywhere. "But what will you do? We've been told to stay out of it!"

"Out of investigating, dear. Not out of ensuring Toot Hansell is individually represented in the council, which has been in the town charter ever since we accepted we couldn't be our own county."

"In 1901," Beaufort supplied helpfully. "Only sixty-three years after you stopped fighting to be declared an independent nation."

Miriam raised her hands as if she could trap the ideas floating around the garden and lock them away somewhere safe. "Alice! We don't even know anything! No more than the police do. And it's really nothing to do with us, anyway."

"I understand that you're worried, dear," Alice said. "But it is to do with us. It's our village that lost its councillor. One of our own who's been killed. One can't stand by and pretend to be disconnected. The world doesn't work like that. Or it shouldn't."

There was silence for a moment. Mortimer had curled his tail tightly around him, and was worrying at it with his forepaws. Beaufort was looking on with enormous interest, and even Thompson was, for once, silent, his green eyes narrow. Miriam squeezed her hands together. The cake felt heavy and suddenly unpleasant in her belly, and the sunny day had dark edges.

"I don't like it," she said finally. "And what are you going to do, anyway?"

"I shall poke around a little. Ask a few questions. Nothing risky."

"But why you? You hate politicians."

"I have never been a politician," Alice said. "I may change my mind about the matter."

"You'll make a great politician," the cat said. "You've got the right mindset for it."

Alice frowned at him. "I'm not sure that's a compliment."

"I'm pretty certain it's not," Mortimer muttered.

"Marvellous!" Beaufort exclaimed, ignoring the younger dragon. "And we will, of course, be security."

"We will?" Mortimer said, and Thompson snorted.

"Well, of course! In the event that there are criminal elements involved, we must be around to protect Alice."

"Criminal elements?" Mortimer said faintly, and grabbed a slice of cake, stuffing it into his mouth whole. "Criminal elements?" he repeated, somewhat indistinctly.

Miriam only just managed not to join Mortimer on the ground. Beaufort had flushed an even deeper green, vying with the grass for brightness.

"That's very kind of you," Alice said, "but I'm sure it won't be necessary. I have no intention of getting into trouble."

Thompson snorted so loudly it turned into another coughing fit, and Miriam thought protection might actually be very necessary once DI Adams heard that Alice was entirely disregarding the police's directions. "How are you going to explain this?" she asked. "You know the inspectors will find out about it."

"I'm quite sure they will. But you know the old adage about it being easier to beg forgiveness than ask permission. Thrown around far too often by reckless individuals as an excuse for not thinking things through, but the exception proves the rule. It applies in this scenario."

"Of course," Beaufort said, grinning. "Once you're in the council, the inspectors will have no choice but to let you help. They can't force you to resign, and they can't turn down that sort of information."

"Quite," Alice said. "And I can think of no finer support in getting started than you three. Four," she added, as Thompson opened his mouth.

Miriam's cheeks heated up, even though she was trying to remain upset. "It still sounds terribly dangerous to me."

"Miriam," Alice said gravely, "we have faced much more dangerous things together than local council meetings. And we shall have the full support of the police."

"Once they find out," Mortimer pointed out.

"Yes."

"And assuming DI Adams doesn't arrest you."

"Yes."

"Or tase you." Mortimer was almost entirely grey, just his wings retaining a little purple and blue. "Or tase all of us!"

"I really think this tasing thing is a much smaller problem than you make out," Beaufort said. "I've never once seen her even threaten to tase anyone."

"It only takes once," Mortimer muttered, and checked his plate for more cake.

"Are you sure about this?" Miriam asked Alice. "If Thomas really was murdered, this is serious."

"I'm serious, too," Alice said, and smiled.

Miriam sighed. She never liked that smile. It wasn't a nasty smile, not at all, but it was the sort of smile that said Alice was going to do exactly what she intended to do, no matter what anyone else said. It was the sort of smile that suggested the smiler could take over a small country, if she so desired, never mind a local council.

“Alright,” Miriam said. “What do you need me to do?”

6
DI ADAMS

The Skipton police station was more modern than one might expect, and freshly painted, but that didn't change the fact that her desk was small, wooden, and appeared to have one leg shorter than the others. But she'd arrived prepared this morning, and was underneath the desk with an assortment of cardboard scraps when an amused voice said, "You alright there, Adams? I don't think there's an earthquake drill scheduled today."

She peered around the offending desk leg to glare at DI Collins until he offered her a takeaway cup of coffee, then extricated herself from the computer cables and dust bunnies and sat back in her chair with a sigh. She prodded the desk. It still wobbled, just not as violently. She'd half thought her to-go mug was going to slide straight off this morning when she'd set it down. The lean really did seem to be getting worse, and she was starting to suspect Dandy of chewing on the legs.

"Coffee?" she asked him, taking the cup. "Is it any good?"

"I told them to add three extra shots, since you're a Londoner and all." Collins sipped his own coffee and gave a pleased sigh.

"I don't need extra shots." DI Adams took the lid off and scrutinised the coffee. It *smelled* good, and there was still a slick of crema on the top. "I just need something that doesn't come out of a bloody packet. Or some ancient filter that's never been cleaned."

"We're not entirely backward, you know."

"There's a queue outside the pork pie shop every morning. Not lunch, *morning*."

"They're bloody good pork pies. You don't know what you're missing out on."

DI Adams rather doubted a cold, sausage-stuffed pastry would be the thing that would break almost two decades of vegetarianism, but instead of saying anything she sipped the coffee, then spluttered. "You actually told them three *extra* shots?"

"No, just one. It comes with two already." Collins sat down at his own desk, leaning back in a dangerously creaking chair. "Have some of mine if you want. Mocha."

"That's sacrilege."

"Delicious, delicious sacrilege." He grinned at her, took another gulp of coffee, then leaned forward to turn the computer on.

DI Adams took another sip and discovered that, once her taste buds had got over the shock, it was actually rather good.

She put her cup on the table just as Dandy pulled her carefully stacked pieces of cardboard out from under the leg and swallowed them. Her coffee lurched, along with everything else, and she barely saved the keyboard from the small tidal wave it unleashed. "*Bad dog!*"

Dandy *whuff*-ed at her, and Collins scratched his chin. "That's unfortunate."

"It's bloody impractical, is what it is."

"Dandy?"

"No! This bloody wobbly table. Can't you get some new furniture? Doesn't IKEA exist up here?"

"Sure. In Leeds. Or Manchester."

"That's a lot of bloody use," she mumbled, and went to find some kitchen roll to clean up the mess.

"Alright," DI Adams said, the spill mopped up and a packet of chocolate digestives liberated from her bag. Ever since encountering Toot Hansell she seemed to find it impossible to have a cup of coffee without accompanying it with biscuits. The Women's Institute were an insidious influence, it seemed. "Where are we with everything?"

"In regards to this case, or in general?" Collins asked. "Because in general seems a rather big question. Bigger than it did a year ago, what with dragons and so on."

"Yes, in relation to the Thomas Wright case." DI Adams suspected he was being facetious, but it was hard to tell with Collins. He might have thought she was asking a serious question about life in general. She took another sip of coffee, upgrading her opinion from rather good to excellent. Although it wasn't a very big cup, and the third shot was making her eye twitch. She pushed Dandy away as he snuffled the mug. One of the things she was learning about him was that, along with an ability to run up trees after squirrels, he had an insatiable appetite for coffee. He really was her sort of creature. Especially with the not talking. There were far too many things around here that talked, and the fact that Dandy didn't made her feel really rather fond of him.

"Well, the lab says Wright had a cardiac event, whatever that is when it's at home, despite having no history of heart problems. No word on possible toxins yet. No sign of Wright's phone, and we're waiting on phone records still. We've interviewed the W.I., discovered the deceased did not appreciate blue potato salad, liked communal gardens, and may have had mixed views on chickens. His widower says that while maybe not everyone loved him, no one had a grudge against him. Said widower was tending bar, which a surprisingly large proportion of the village seems able to testify to." Collins leaned over to take a biscuit and thought for a moment. "The widower does say that upon leaving the W.I. meeting the deceased called him to, quote, 'make sure he was okay'. Should have been the other way around, really."

"But apparently that wasn't an unusual thing for Thomas Wright to do, to check in."

"Apparently not."

DI Adams sipped her coffee, looking at the notes on her screen. "But then there was a second phone call. About half an hour before the crash, so presumably when the victim was either driving back to Toot Hansell, or just about to – and that was unusual."

"Yes. Once a day was normal. A second time was, apparently, not. And the widower says that although Wright didn't say anything out of the ordinary, he sounded anxious."

DI Adams took another biscuit and tried to remember if she'd already had two or just one. "But we still don't know where he was coming from, or what might have made him anxious, as the only event in his diary was the meeting with the W.I."

"Which is enough to make anyone anxious, but was apparently not related. Unless it was a delayed reaction."

DI Adams wondered if it was possible to have a delayed reaction to the W.I. Her reaction was always pretty immediate. She moved the biscuits as Dandy ventured a little too close to them, and found a dog chew in her bag. He might disdain canned food, but he loved chews. "We need to find out where he went after the meeting. I can't believe there are *no* traffic cameras around there."

"Well, the tech may turn up something on the mobile phone location," Collins said. "Otherwise we shall have to rely on good old-fashioned police work. And Alice Martin poking around, of course."

DI Adams discovered she'd finished her biscuits, and took two more, as the situation seemed to call for it. "Alice Martin is not a part of this investigation."

DI Collins made a non-committal sound.

"She's not!"

"Not of our investigation, no, but this is Alice we're talking about. She's hardly going to sit by quietly if she thinks someone's causing trouble in her village."

"Yes, but—" DI Adams stopped as there was a tentative knock on the open door. "Yes?" she said to the tall PC lingering in the doorway, his brow furrowed with worry. "PC Shaw, isn't it?" Jasmine's husband, the one who survived blue potato salad, among other delicacies.

"Yes. Hi," he said, and rubbed his lips. "Um, ma'am." He raised a hand to Collins, who nodded and offered him a biscuit.

"DI Adams or Detective Inspector's fine."

"Okay." He took a biscuit and sat down in one of the spare chairs. It was almost as wobbly as the table.

"What's happening, Ben?" Collins asked.

"Right. Yes." He took a deep breath. "You asked me to let you know if the W.I. seemed to be up to anything. Well, Jas was really excited yesterday, because they had a sort of emergency meeting in the afternoon."

"Oh bloody hell," DI Adams said, and Collins sighed.

Ben went pink. He was that type of round-cheeked, permanently young-looking sort that was halfway there most of the time anyway. "They all went around to Alice's – Ms Martin's – house for it. It was about the council candidate for Toot Hansell."

DI Adams put her cup down before she could crush it and waste the coffee. "What do you mean? Toot Hansell has no candidate at the moment."

"Um, yes." He'd gone past pink into red territory. "The thing is, there's a clause in the town charter that states there has to be a representative for Toot Hansell at all times. If we lose the sitting one, a stand-in has to be brought in pretty much immediately."

"No elections?"

"Not for a stand-in. They just need a couple of signatures, then they take over until there's time for a proper election to be held."

DI Adams thought that was both ridiculous and completely expected. "Who's the candidate, PC Shaw?"

The constable looked distinctly unhappy, and DI Adams could see sweat on his hairline. "Alice Martin, ma'am. Detective Inspector, sorry."

She managed not to either hit her head on the desk or bury her face in her hands, and gave a stiff nod instead. "I see. And did Jasmine say anything else about the meeting?"

"It sounded like the rest was fairly normal. Alice – Ms Martin – was just letting them all know and making sure they agreed she should do it, I think."

DI Adams wished Alice had extended the same courtesy to them. "And this didn't seem like an odd move to Jasmine?"

"Not really. I mean, it is Alice." He thought for a moment. "I can't imagine anyone else doing it, to be honest."

"That does sound about right," Collins said. "Did Jasmine say anything else?"

"Just that she was surprised Alice was doing it, because she doesn't like politicians. Alice, I mean, not Jasmine. I'm not sure Jasmine has an opinion on politicians." He considered it. "No more than the rest of us, anyway."

DI Adams clasped her hands on the desk, then winced and tried to ease her grip as her fingers ground together. "Thank you, PC Shaw," she said. "I appreciate you coming to us with this."

He nodded. "Jasmine would only be doing what she's told, ma— Detective Inspector. She wouldn't be meddling." He lifted his chin and looked at the inspector directly for the first time, his eyes wide and startlingly blue. "She won't mean anything by it."

DI Adams smiled. "I know. She won't be in any trouble, um, Ben."

He blinked at her as if more alarmed by the fact she'd used his first name than by the possibility of Jasmine facing arrest for interfering with a police investigation.

"Nice one, Ben," DI Collins said. "Let us know if you hear anything else, although I imagine Alice is controlling information better than the damn MI5." He looked at DI Adams. "In fact, are you sure she was RAF and not a bloody spook?"

"I'm sure of nothing when it comes to Alice Martin," DI Adams said, wondering if another biscuit would help.

Ben got up and put the chair back in place carefully, as if afraid he might break something. "I'll be off, then."

Collins raised a lazy hand and watched the other man cross the room and head out of the office, then looked at DI Adams. "Thoughts?"

"I have no idea. Do you think we can stop her? Call her off before she gets registered or whatever? It could be dangerous."

Collins snorted. "Good luck with that. And knowing her, she's probably already on the council."

DI Adams groaned and gave up, folding her arms on the desk and resting her forehead on them. "This is impossible. *She's* impossible!"

"Hey, you're the big city cop. You can't tell me you didn't deal with worse in London."

"Criminals. I dealt with *criminals*. Not the Toot bloody Hansell W.I."

"I'm pretty sure there are plenty of W.I.s in London."

"Not like this one. *Nothing* like this one."

DI Collins nodded. "You've got a point there. But what can we do? Got to work with what we've got."

DI Adams made a small growling sound that made the dandy jump to his feet in alarm. "What does that mean?"

Collins grinned. "We've got someone on the council now. Alice is not the worst person to have in place."

DI Adams stared at her biscuits, thinking that eating another was possibly a good tactic. She felt like shouting. She didn't *want* to shout, but something about Toot Hansell kept bringing the urge up. In the calmest voice she could manage she said, "This is a police investigation. Ex-RAF or not, Alice is a civilian these days."

"Do you want to tell her that?" DI Collins asked. He'd taken the lid off his coffee so he could dunk his biscuits in it.

DI Adams opened her mouth, shut it again, then took a weary bite of biscuit. "We shouldn't need to tell her," she pointed out.

"Well, I'm certainly not telling her."

"I just said we shouldn't have to tell her."

"So we're not going to tell her."

DI Adams sighed. Collins was right. Alice was smart, adaptable, and alarmingly observant. She was, in fact, just the sort of person DI Adams would have chosen to have working for them, if she hadn't been Alice, and therefore just as likely to try and deal with the whole thing on her own as she was to actually pass them any information. "Surely your DCI won't approve that."

"Maud knows all about the W.I. She grew up in Toot Hansell."

"You're not serious."

"Sure. Before Alice moved there, but she knows her. She's Pearl Davies' niece."

DI Adams looked at him for a moment, then said, "Are you actually all related out in the country, then?"

"Oi. We can't all be suave southerners like you."

"Evidently not." She didn't feel very suave. "We need to tell her about Wright's cardiac event. The fact that maybe it was induced. And about that Gavin Peabody."

"We're not sure that was connected. It was ruled a natural death at the time."

"True, but two councillors dropping dead in not much more than six months seems odd. And that was a heart attack too."

"He was out on the town in Leeds at 3 a.m. with not one but three lovely young ladies, all indulging in some illicit substances. And he did have a heart condition."

DI Adams frowned at him. "It's still odd."

"I know. But maybe we're best not to tell her. Maybe it's safer, if there is something going on, that she doesn't have all the information. She might get even more enthusiastic about poking around."

She sighed. "Knowing her, she probably already knows."

"You could be right." Collins popped the last of his biscuit in his mouth.

"There's probably some underground Women's Institute information network," DI Adams continued, not entirely joking. "Morse code in the knitting and secret messages in the jam."

Collins shook his head. "I'm not sure the country agrees with you, you know."

"Neither am I."

THE YOUNG CONSTABLE on the front desk, PC McLeod, called DI Adams and told her there was someone to see her. "He says he knows you from the manor house case?"

"What's his name?"

"He says it's a surprise."

DI Adams put the desk phone down with a sigh.

"What's up?" Collins asked.

"Press, I think." She walked out of the office and down the little corridor, letting herself into the waiting room with its photo prints of Dales landscapes and information posters and grey plastic chairs. A couple in walking gear sat in one corner, looking distressed and talking quietly in a language she didn't recognise, and a shrivelled woman was loudly berating a distressed PC McLeod for the fact that he wasn't doing enough to stop whoever was stealing her daffodils. DI Adams was no gardener, but she was quite certain daffodil season was long over.

"DI Adams!" a young man exclaimed, bouncing to his feet and advancing on her with one long-fingered hand outstretched, his dimples on full display. "We must stop meeting like this."

DI Adams ignored his hand. "Quite right. At some stage all this following me around becomes stalking." She glanced at Dandy, who was sniffing the journalist's legs, and wondered what happened if an invisible dog bit you. Unfortunately, Dandy didn't seem to share her dislike of the young man, and he lost interest and wandered out the front door into the sun. "What do you want, Mr Giles?"

"Maybe just to catch up, for old time's sake."

She just looked at him, hands in her pockets, waiting. Ervin Giles had been writing a profile on how old country houses were surviving in the modern day when they'd last met, at the manor house owned by Miriam's sister. He'd been a nuisance during that investigation, and she didn't expect him to be any different now.

"Alright, alright. The Thomas Wright death. Can you tell me how the investigation is going?"

"No."

"Oh, come on. Not even one statement?"

"I thought you wrote articles on country house hotels."

"I did, but my coverage of the manor house death in spring was so good that the paper put me on crime."

"Such a promotion for you. In Skipton." Trying to ignore the fact that she was in the same place, and *she'd* started in London.

"In Leeds, actually, but when I saw you were on the case I thought I'd pop over."

"Lucky, lucky me."

He pushed his hands through his dark hair and smiled at her.

"Look, I know you hate the press. Police always do. But you have to admit I did a good story last time. I'm not going for tabloid fodder."

"The investigation is still in its very early stages, Mr Giles. I have nothing to say to you."

"What about what you're doing in Skipton, then? You do like keeping the Toot Hansell Women's Institute close, don't you? Word is Mr Wright's last stop was one of their meetings."

DI Adams nodded, then turned to the woman at the desk and said, "Ma'am? This journalist here is a crime reporter. I think you should tell him all about your daffodils."

The woman wheeled around in a swirl of pink tartan coat and matching skirt. "Finally! This constable is doing *nothing* to help me!"

"Hang on," Ervin said, eyeing the door, and DI Adams patted his shoulder.

"Balanced reporting, Mr Giles." She followed Dandy out into the sunlight as the woman backed Ervin into a corner, already describing which of her neighbours she thought was the culprit. PC McLeod mouthed *thank you* at her, and she grinned at him.

With any luck he might actually stop looking terrified every time she came in the door now.

7
ALICE

Alice climbed the old stone steps to the town hall, a quiet breeze lifting grey hair off the back of her neck. It was warm today, the air smelling of hot streets and baking ground, and the lobby when she stepped inside was wonderfully cool. She clipped across the floor in her low heels, spoke briefly to the receptionist, and was directed to the next floor.

It hadn't been difficult to get the signatures she needed to be put forward as the temporary representative for Toot Hansell. And with Gert's brother's niece's second cousin – or whatever dreadfully complicated relation it was – putting the application letter in front of the right people, she'd found herself entering politics rather rapidly. Miriam was still exceptionally nervous about the whole thing, and it had been very hard to convince Beaufort he couldn't accompany her to the meeting, but otherwise everything was under control. The inspectors had found out rather more quickly than she would have liked, which she thought might be due to Jasmine feeling the need to share everything with Ben. She never quite understood people who did that, but then, her own husband had been most unsatisfactory, so she'd never really felt the need to share that much with him.

And be that as it may, the inspectors had at least known not to bother trying to tell her she couldn't do it. DI Adams had made a lot of warning noises about not poking around in things and just getting on with council business, which had had Thompson choking with laughter, and DI Collins had muttered about the importance of Alice staying in constant contact, but after that they'd left her alone. Which was a little suspicious, and she had found herself checking for police cars behind her on the drive in, but she supposed it didn't really matter. What did matter was that she was now on the council. She smiled as she walked down the upstairs hall, stopping in front of a dark wood door with a plaque labelled *Conference Room 3*. Now it was time to investigate.

She let herself into a rather stuffy conference room that smelled of wood polish and too much cologne and talcum powder, and nodded at the six people scattered around a long table. "Good morning," she said. "Alice Martin, temporary representative for Toot Hansell. Anywhere in particular I should sit?"

"Oh, come sit next to me, dear," a pretty woman with dark hair said, waving her over. "We're not very formal. It being summer and all, half of us are missing anyway."

"Dropping like flies," a lanky man with a weather-darkened face said. "Off to Bermuda and what have you."

"That seems very irresponsible," Alice said, taking a seat one chair away from the woman. If there were going to be spare spaces she didn't fancy being crowded.

"All the serious work gets done in winter," a red-faced man with a shirt straining across his belly said. "We're just keeping things ticking over, really."

"I see." Alice set a notebook and a pen on the table and tucked her bag beneath her chair. "Well, that gives you plenty of time to catch me up on everything I've missed, doesn't it?"

The lanky man snorted, stretched, folded his arms over his chest and appeared to go to sleep immediately. Alice looked at the woman next to her, eyebrows raised.

"Oh, that's Len. Don't mind him. He says council meetings are where he does his best sleeping."

"I see," she said again, trying not to sound too disapproving. Not on her first day.

"Lily Dean," the woman said, extending a hand.

"Pleased to meet you." Lily's dark hair curled about her face rather fetchingly, and she had the sort of clear-skinned look that made her age hard to place. Alice thought she might be around Miriam's age, early fifties or thereabouts. "Do you live in Skipton, Lily?"

"Yes, recent transplant." She pointed around the table. "Rob," she said, pointing at the red-faced man. "Charles," this a man who was eating a custard tart with every evidence of enjoyment and waved at them cheerily around a mouthful of pastry, "Ed, and Lee." The remaining two men were comparing something on their phones, and they looked up, nodded, then went back to what they were doing.

Alice poured herself a glass of water from the jug on the table, condensation spreading around it in a pool on the stained wood. The windows were cracked open, but despite that, the room was choked with a heat that managed to be both dusty and sticky at once. "Is it just us?"

"Probably. Honestly, everything runs much better when it's not school holidays and so on."

Alice didn't share the somewhat uncharitable thought that it could hardly run worse. "Can't we get some fans in here? No wonder everyone's half asleep."

"Oh, we ask after every meeting." Lily took a little battery-powered fan out of her purse and switched it on, planting it on the desk in front of them. "Nothing ever happens."

"I see." Alice opened her notebook. "Well, then, if everyone's here, we may as well get started, hadn't we?"

ALICE DID NOT CONSIDER it to be a particularly successful meeting. Len snored so loudly at one point that she couldn't hear what Rob was saying, and Ed and Lee never looked up from their phones. Charles had a seemingly limitless supply of pastries that he offered around the table, and he paid more attention to them than he did to what was happening in the meeting. He was rather a skinny sort, too. Lily leaned over and whispered in Alice's ear that his wife had him on a no-sugar diet, and this was the only chance he got to indulge. Alice thought both the diet and the meeting was a lot of foolishness, and the W.I. was a rather more efficiently run organisation. Or the Toot Hansell branch was, at least. She couldn't speak for any others.

Lily kept the minutes in a laborious scrawl, and Alice was sure she missed at least half of what was said. Rob led the meeting, in a manner of speaking, flipping through some printed sheets and calling out now and then, "Who was getting quotes for the new tourist maps? Ones *without* fairy houses and river monsters on them?" or "Who was responsible for getting rid of that damn silly typo on the dog park signs?" Inevitably, the answer seemed to be someone who wasn't there.

Alice folded her arms and leaned back in her chair, reminding herself that she was there to gather information, not to restructure the council. "Is it normal for everyone to go away at once?" she asked Lily, while Rob paged through his sheets, muttering to himself.

"Oh, well. I've actually only been on the council since the end of last summer, but it seems so. Lots of people off on nice holidays, it seems. I wish *I* could go to Barbados."

Alice personally thought it sounded a bit overrated, sitting on a beach drinking things with umbrellas in them, but she just said, "I imagine."

"Flowers for Thomas?" Rob demanded. "Tell me someone did that!"

"I did!" Lily exclaimed, almost bouncing out of her seat.

"Great. So we can actually get something done around here." He went back to his notes.

LILY WALKED out with Alice as the meeting ended, nodding goodbye to the other councillors and leaving Len snoring in the stuffy room. The two women stood on the steps, Lily fanning herself with her notepad as Alice lifted her hair off her neck to let the wind cool her.

"That wasn't a great first impression of the council," Lily admitted. "It really isn't always so slipshod."

"Well, it explains an awful lot about the state of politics in this country," Alice said, then smiled. "I'm sorry. That was rude."

"No, you're right. And I think I came in feeling quite idealistic about it all too, as though maybe I could make changes and really help around here, but you just sort of get worn down by the indifference."

"Did you say you've been here since last summer?"

"Yes, about nine months or so. There was a vacancy not long after I arrived in Skipton, so I went right out and got myself selected." She smiled at Alice, her teeth bright white and not quite straight. "Early retirement. I couldn't stand the idea of sitting around doing nothing."

"Quite." Alice nodded toward the centre of town. "I really fancy a decent cup of tea after all that. And probably a bite to eat. Will you join me? You can fill me in."

"Oh yes! That would be lovely."

The two women headed down the main street, and Alice wondered if it was odd or not that no one had mentioned Thomas except to ask about flowers. It felt odd to her.

THEY ORDERED salads and a large pot of tea in one of the cafes on the main street, sitting in the bay window upstairs where they could watch people pass below. Alice spotted Ben sitting in a patrol car in one of the parking bays, and wondered if he was trailing her. Then he got out of the car and, with a guilty look around, emptied a tub of something into the bin and went into a baker's, emerging a moment later with a fat sandwich and a bag of crisps. Which answered her question about whether he actually liked Jasmine's food, although not the lingering doubts she had about how neither he nor Jasmine had come down with food poisoning yet.

Lily had been chattering on about her husband, who she was very enthusiastic about, and her previous career building up a chain of clothing shops, which she was even more enthusiastic about. Alice was wondering why Lily had given it up when she suddenly said, "Are you married, Alice?"

"Oh, no," Alice said. "Not at all."

"Oh." Lily looked at her plate, then said, "Well, there's no knowing when it'll happen. I met my husband only last year."

"Really."

"Yes! Do you know, he literally tripped over me at a cafe. Knocked my coffee all over my tablet and asked to buy me another one."

"Another coffee?"

"No, silly. Another tablet!" Lily laughed delightedly. "Although he did buy me a coffee, too. And then dinner. And, you know ..." She winked, rather alarmingly, and Alice smiled back.

"So, he works here, does he?"

"Well, he's a bit of an international businessman. He's out of the country all this month, more's the pity. But he's marvellous. He gave me wonderful advice on selling my shops. I'd probably still be slaving away in them otherwise."

Alice thought the whole thing sounded highly dubious, but she wasn't about to say as much. Instead she just said, "Did you know Thomas well?"

"Thomas?"

"My predecessor."

"Oh, Thomas. Of course. Sorry, I was still thinking about husbands. Yes, he was such a lovely man." Lily took a mouthful of salad and ate. Alice waited. After a moment Lily put her fork down and said, "I mean, I knew him from the council. I wouldn't say I knew him well."

"It was quite tragic, his death."

"Oh, awful. Just awful." Lily busied herself with her food again. "I hear it was a heart attack. So sad. He was so young!"

"Indeed." Alice chased a cherry tomato around her plate. "Did he get on with everyone at the council?"

"Oh yes. Usual thing – everyone clashes with everyone else at some point, but everyone liked him. It really is so sad."

Alice wondered if Lily could fit sad into every sentence for the rest of lunch. "He wasn't working on anything in particular, was he?"

"I don't think so. Why?" Lily tipped her head to the side, suddenly birdlike, her eyes bright. "You think something happened to him?"

Of course something happened to him, Alice thought. *He died.* Honestly, people were so obtuse sometimes. Aloud, she said, "No, of course not. Just if he was dealing with anything specific to Toot Hansell I should probably take a look at it."

"Oh! Of course. Well, I put all the minutes of the meetings in emails, and send them to everyone. I'll email all of the last month or so to you when I get home."

"That would be lovely," Alice said, and checked the tea pot. "I think we need a refill."

"Yes! And now tell me about you – you're not married, but is there anyone special? Come on, girl talk!"

Alice tried not to let the horror show on her face, and wished she hadn't mentioned the refill. "No," she said, when Lily poked her arm, still grinning. "I tried marriage. It didn't agree with me."

"Oh, how terrible! Do you want to talk about it?"

Alice leaned forward and said, "He vanished. I retired from the RAF, and about a week after I got home, I went out to get some milk. I came home, and he had vanished."

"Vanished!" Lily whispered, her eyes round. "Was he … was he *murdered?*"

Alice leaned back in her seat. "The police thought *I* might have murdered him."

Lily was rather gratifyingly quiet for a moment, then said, "But you didn't, of course?"

"And have him be even more trouble than he already was? No." She smiled at the young waiter as he delivered a fresh pot of tea to the table. "Thank you, dear."

"And you never found him?" Lily asked, when the waiter had retreated.

"I never looked."

BY THE TIME Alice made it back to her car, her ears hurt. All she wanted was to go home and not talk to anyone – or rather not be talked at – for at least the rest of the day. She leaned on her car for a moment, savouring the sun and the silence and wondering if it was really necessary to stop at Morrisons. She didn't think her ears could take it.

Movement across the car park caught her eye, and she looked around to see Len slouching his way along from the direction of the hall. He looked rumpled and mostly asleep still, which she imagined he would if he'd slept all through lunch. She hesitated, then tucked her hands into her pockets and let her shoulders relax as she strolled across the tarmac to intercept him.

"Len, isn't it?" she said, smiling up at him.

He looked at her, then grunted and nodded, continuing toward his car. "Alice Martin, temporary representative for Toot Hansell."

"That's the one." She fell into step with him. "Hardly thrilling, these meetings."

"Nup."

"You know, except for Thomas dying."

He glanced at her, fishing his keys out of his pocket. "I wouldn't call that thrilling. More unfortunate."

"Quite." She nodded, as if thinking about it, and looked up at the sky. "You know him well?"

"Not outside the council."

"You think he was working on anything dodgy?"

He leaned against his car, following her gaze up into the high blue of the sky. "Lot of questions."

"First day. One wants to know what one's getting into."

He smiled at that. "Read the minutes."

"Is everything in the minutes?"

There was a pause, then Len said, "Everything you need to know."

"So not actually everything."

"Alice," he said, the word almost a sigh, "you're not here for long. Just make things easy on yourself. Come to the meetings, have a brew and a bit of cake, then go home. It's all you need to do."

"What if I decide to stay?"

"The council can be a very easy place to be if you just get along. Very rewarding, even. Or you can make it very hard for yourself."

"Is that what I'm doing now?"

"You're heading that way." He beeped the car open.

"Nice Range Rover." It was. Brand new, a glossy British racing green with gleaming alloys. It looked like it had the sort of engine that made her hands itch.

"Thanks." He opened the door and got in. "Just get along, Alice. It's easier on everyone." He closed the door firmly, and Alice stepped back as he started the engine, giving him a friendly little wave as he backed out of the parking space and headed off. It really was a very nice car. She thought about Angela Pearson, who had been very committed and passionate about protecting Toot Hansell, and who also spent an inordinate amount of time clipping coupons from fliers and driving across half of Yorkshire spending more money on fuel than she was saving on the deals she hunted down. Angela, who had up and headed off on a world cruise which she was unlikely to have got on coupons. Alice wondered if any of the other councillors had nice new cars. She'd have to remember to check next week. Or, even better ... She pulled out her phone as she wandered back to her car and pulled the detective inspector's number up. Her thumb hovered over the call icon as she considered it. She didn't exactly have anything concrete. So one person had a new car, and some indeterminate number of others were off on fancy holidays. And who knew if they were even fancy? You could go anywhere on a package holiday these days.

She hit the lock button instead and put the phone back in her bag. The last thing she needed was DI Adams accusing her of getting involved in an investigation when she hadn't even got started. No, she'd wait until she had something a little more concrete before she went to the inspectors. And she knew where she wanted to start next.

AS MUCH AS she wanted to drive straight home, she went to Thomas and Bryan's pub first, parking in the empty car park and crunching across the gravel to ring the bell by the kitchen entrance. The grass was neatly cut in the garden, and the hanging baskets tumbled flowers from every corner of the building, but the big chairs and benches were devoid of cushions and life, and there were crates of bottled beer and wine stacked by the door with an invoice stuck to them. She pulled it off as she waited, noting that none of the delivery seemed to be missing as yet. Even in Toot Hansell, it was a bit of a temptation leaving it all outside like this.

She rang the bell again, and this time she heard reluctant footsteps shuffling to the door. Locks rolled, and Bryan peered out at her, his face red and blotchy.

"Hello, dear," she said. "I'm so sorry to disturb you. You must have had just everyone coming by this week."

He nodded, but stepped back from the door. "Would you like a cup of tea?"

"Oh no. I don't want to bother you."

"It's no bother. It's all I seem to be doing. Drinking tea and crying."

"Ah." She patted his shoulder, not quite sure how to respond, and barely held back a squeak of alarm as he hugged her, his face heavy and hot on her shoulder.

"I can't believe he's gone!" Bryan wailed. "It's not possible!"

Alice rubbed his back gingerly. From the smell of him, he'd been drinking more than tea. Not that she blamed him, but still. "I can see how you must feel that way."

“I keep thinking he’ll come in the door from one of his stupid council meetings any minute!”

“Ah, yes.” His tears were wetting her shoulder, and it was all rather distasteful. She should have brought Miriam. Miriam was much better at this sort of thing. “Come on. Let’s sit down and I’ll make you a nice cup of tea.”

“But I was going to make you one.” Bryan straightened up and wiped his nose, snuffling noisily. Alice decided her blouse was going straight in the wash when she got home.

“Let me do it. You just sit down. Come along.” She ushered him ahead of her into the shuttered pub, and decided that, despite his state, whisky would probably be better. For both of them.

8
MIRIAM

Miriam hurried around the pub and let herself in the back door, hoping nothing awful had happened. The text from Alice had been even terser than usual – it just said, *At pub come quick*. Oh, what could have happened? She hoped Bryan hadn't done anything foolish, like getting drunk and falling down the stairs. Not that the getting drunk part was necessarily foolish, not with what he was going through, but he'd be better to remain downstairs if he was going to do that sort of thing. Oh, but what if someone had been after both Bryan *and* Thomas? What if it was some sort of pub warfare? She paused at the door between the kitchen and the pub, preparing herself for the worst, and pushed through into the dim-lit room beyond.

For a moment she couldn't see anyone at all, then her eyes adjusted to the shadows after the bright afternoon outside, and the sound of muffled sobbing drew her to one of the big sofas in front of the unlit fireplace. Alice was sitting in it with her back stiff and a glass resting on the table in front of her. The sobs were coming from somewhere in the region of her lap, and Miriam crept closer, unsure whether to say something or not.

She stepped on a creaky floorboard as she passed the bar, and Alice craned around to see her.

"Miriam," she said, the relief unmistakable in her voice.

"Is … is everything alright?"

"Not really." Alice looked down at her lap as a fresh gust of sobbing broke out, and Miriam inched her way around the chair to see Bryan with his head buried in a cushion that Alice had balanced on her knees.

"Um. What should I do?" Miriam asked.

Alice patted Bryan's head awkwardly, the way someone scared of dogs pats a very persistent Labrador. "If I knew that I wouldn't have had to call you. More whisky, perhaps?"

Miriam looked at the bottle on the table and leaned over to sniff Bryan. "No, rather the opposite, I should say."

"Well, please do something, Miriam. My leg's going to sleep."

Alice's voice had a strained note to it, and Miriam tried not to feel a very teeny bit smug. Alice was always so good at everything. But then, she realised, as she hurried around the sofa to crouch in front of Bryan, calming crying men didn't really rank that highly on valuable life skills. Or maybe it did. Maybe not enough people were good at it, just as not enough men were good at crying. She placed a hand on Bryan's neck and said softly, "Bryan? Sit up for me a moment, dear."

Bryan turned his face out of the pillow and snuffled at her. "He's gone."

"I know." She wasn't surprised to find her own tears sneaking up on her. "And it's okay to be sad, and it's okay to cry – it's more than okay – but Alice's leg's starting to cramp."

"Oh." Bryan wiped his face and sat up. "I'm sorry. I'm a mess."

Alice stood up and gave a little stretch, a look of enormous relief on her face. "I'll put the kettle on," she said, and almost jogged out of the room. Miriam didn't think her leg looked very asleep at all.

Miriam took Alice's place next to Bryan and folded her hand over his. "When did you last eat?"

He shrugged, reaching for the whisky bottle. Miriam moved it away.

"We'll get you some food," she said. "Then I think a good sleep is in order."

He looked at her, then down at his crumpled shirt. "I suppose."

"Do you have any family coming to stay?"

"My sister. Not until tomorrow, though. She couldn't get away."

"Well, then. That means you've got tonight to get organised." Miriam got up, still holding his hand, and pulled him up with her. "Now how about you have a quick shower while I get you a bite to eat?"

He sniffled. "A shower does sound good."

"There we are, then. Deciding to do it is the hardest part." She turned him around and guided him to the door marked *Private*. "Do you want me to come start it for you?"

He wiped his eyes, and gave her a reluctant smile. "I'm grieving, not helpless."

"Sometimes it can feel like the same thing." She watched him wander unsteadily through the door, then went to find Alice.

ALICE WAS SORTING through a mountain of Tupperware in the pub kitchen, the colours glaring lime greens and yellows against the stark stainless of the worktops and polished cabinets.

"Should they be in the fridge?" Miriam asked.

"No, they all seem to be cakes and things," Alice said, opening yet another and setting it aside. "There's more in there already, anyway."

"Really?" Miriam opened the double doors on the big commercial fridge and found multicoloured containers shoved in higgledy-piggledy around crates of vegetables and jars of conserves, and balancing on massive tubs of cream and spread. "Ooh. There's even more than when the vicar died."

"Well, I think rather more people came to the pub than the church," Alice pointed out, just as the kettle clicked off. "Tea?"

"Yes, please. Bryan's gone to have a shower."

"Well done, Miriam."

"That's alright." Miriam watched Alice topping three mugs off with boiling water. "What were you doing here, anyway?"

Alice sighed. "I wanted to find out if Thomas had mentioned anything about the council. Anything that wouldn't have been on the minutes."

"It's barely been a week, Alice."

"Yes, well. I realise now that I might have been a bit premature." She fished the teabags out. "But one does have to return to real life at some point."

"But everyone has a different point." Miriam started hunting through the Tupperware. "Do you think any of these are any good?"

"The ones that were on top are to the left. I think the others might be a bit old."

"Ugh. Yes." Miriam had opened a box of carrot cake that was forming its own ecosystem in the bottom of the tub. "I think we might need to do some clearing out."

Alice handed her a tea. "That's a very good idea."

By the time Bryan came downstairs the Tupperware mountain had, for the most part, made its way from the counter to the sink, and Miriam had lugged a bag full of dubious (as well as beyond dubious) food out to the bins. Alice had put a cottage pie in the oven, and the kitchen smelt of gravy and potato and comfort.

"Oh no," he said, hesitating in the door. "You didn't have to clean up!"

"It's quite alright," Alice said. "You sit down and I'll bring a cup of tea through in a minute."

"I can't." He picked up a tea towel and started drying the Tupperware. "Let me get these done, at least."

"If you want." Alice went back to clearing sprouting vegetables out of the fridge, and Miriam smiled at Bryan, her arms soapy up to the elbows. Commercial sinks were terribly deep, and she thought she might have got less wet if she'd just climbed in.

"Are you feeling a little better?"

"A little. I'm terribly embarrassed, though. I'm sorry, Alice. I didn't think anyone would come by today. The whole village seems to have been by over the last few days, and the staff don't start again until tomorrow, so I just thought … you know. Kind of indulgent, I guess."

"Not at all," Miriam said firmly. "Very sensible of you to take some time for yourself."

"And don't be embarrassed on my account," Alice said, handing Miriam a crate with the remnants of squished tomatoes still clinging to the bottom. "We all have our lows."

Miriam wondered if Alice did indeed have any such thing, but she kept that thought to herself and concentrated on getting the tomato seeds out of the ribs in the crate.

"Please don't worry about those," Bryan said, dropping the tea towel to take a bag of rubbish from Alice. "Really! The staff'll be back tomorrow, and we'll tackle it all together."

"Nonsense," Alice said. "We're almost done."

"Well," he waved his hands vaguely. "What can I do to repay you?"

"There's no need," Miriam said. "It's just what you do, isn't it?"

"Is it?" Bryan asked. "I mean, bringing food, yes. But this?"

"Of course it is." Alice gave him another one of those awkward arm pats. "Now take that outside and I'll plate you up some cottage pie. It looks excellent."

Bryan pottered obediently out the door, and Miriam frowned at Alice. "You're not still going to ask him?"

"Of course I am. It'll do him good to be doing something toward catching his husband's killer."

Which rather confirmed for Miriam that Alice was not as familiar with lows as she made out, but she just set the crate to drain and put the kettle on again. She felt it was too early for cottage pie, but she'd spotted some shortbread biscuits that looked very like Rose's, and it was always the right time for them.

THEY SAT at one of the old wooden tables in the pub, and the cottage pie smelt so good Miriam almost revised her opinion that 4 p.m. was too early for dinner. Bryan took the first bite tentatively, but by the time he'd eaten a quarter of the plate he seemed to have rediscovered his appetite. His cheeks had lost their hectic colour, and he was smiling as Miriam recounted a problem she'd been having with an Etsy client.

"So she wanted to buy fifty boats, but claimed they were all for gifts! And she wanted a sixty percent discount, so it was obvious she wanted to resell them."

"A victim of your own success, Miriam," Alice said.

"Well, it's hardly me," she began, then spluttered on her tea.

"Do you have a business partner?" Bryan asked. "You said you didn't make the baubles yourself when we bought ours." There were eight of them drifting sedately around the pub, fine-petalled flowers lit from within by a flame that burned cold and never went out unless you closed the flower up again. Miriam had sold Bryan and Thomas twelve last Christmas, but after four had been liberated during the busier Christmas services they'd tethered the rest permanently to the heavy wooden beams that ran through the building.

"Um, yes. Business partner. That's it," Miriam managed.

"Not in the village then?"

"No, he's, um—"

"From abroad," Alice said. "That's where he gets the unusual material from."

"Oh." Bryan took another forkful of mash, doused liberally in brown sauce, and Miriam slumped into her chair. She had to remember not to talk too easily about the bauble business. Dragons seemed such an everyday occurrence these days that she sometimes forgot not everyone knew about them. Never mind talking cats and invisible dogs and bottomless ponds. She gulped tea and helped herself to another shortbread biscuit. But really, such things were easier to deal with than Investigations. Even the goblins were better than that.

"Bryan," Alice said, folding her hands on the table (Miriam took a moment to wonder how her friend's nails stayed so neat and clean with all the gardening she did. Her own had a permanent rim of earth under the nail, no matter how hard she scrubbed). "I've stepped into Thomas' place on the council, just to keep an eye on things."

"Oh. Yes. That's … well, that's quite right, of course. You'll be very good at it." Bryan looked at his plate as if it had suddenly snapped at him.

"Well, it won't be permanent, but we do have to make sure all his hard work to support the village is continued."

"Yes. Yes, you're right." Bryan looked up at her and gave a very small smile, more willpower than feeling. "He cared very much about this place."

Alice reached across the table and put her hand on Bryan's with much more confidence than she had earlier. "We all do, dear. So I need to ask – did Thomas mention anything about the council that maybe wouldn't be in the minutes? Gossip about the members? Any problems? Anything that might help me do his job better?"

Bryan put his fork down and pushed his plate away with his free hand. "The police already asked me about any clashes on the council."

"Of course they did. But now you've had time to think about it, and maybe there were things that weren't concrete enough to tell the police."

The room was silent for a moment, and Miriam could hear the hum of the drinks fridges behind the bar, and a car passing on the road outside. Bryan started to lean back, as if to pull his hand away from Alice, then stopped and looked at both women carefully.

"You didn't come here just to check on me," he said.

Miriam started to mumble a denial, but Alice said, "No."

"You're always getting tangled up in stuff," he said. "Police matters and things."

"It has happened," Alice said.

"None of this is … I mean, it's just talk, you know."

"We understand," Alice said. "It's nothing you could really tell the police."

"But are you going to look for who did this? Because I know it wasn't an accident. His heart was *fine*. He had it checked just last year, after his aunt got sick. He fussed about that sort of thing." Bryan smiled for a moment, then it faded. "And then the police were asking about drugs. He would *never*. That is— was— just not him. Someone did something. I know they did. Someone killed him and made it look like an accident."

"That's what we were afraid of," Alice said. "And why I need all the information I can get, Bryan."

"What if they come after you?"

"It's always a possibility," Alice said, and Miriam swallowed hard against an unexpected obstruction in her throat. How could she be so calm? How could anyone say that and be calm about it?

Her cheeks had been hot with shame a moment before, but now the temperature in the room seemed to have plunged to midwinter. She glanced around, half-expecting to see a door swinging open to let in a draught.

Bryan took a deep breath. "Okay. He didn't really know a lot, or he didn't tell me a lot, but someone was approaching the councillors individually."

"What for?"

"That was the thing, it was all very cagey. They were just approached and told that it wasn't going to be anything illegal, they didn't even need to vote on anything, they just had to be 'helpful'. But if it was legal, why all the secrecy?"

"And Thomas didn't agree."

"Of course not! He didn't know what they were going to be asked to do. And he couldn't exactly go to the police and say, someone wants to give me money to be *helpful*. It sounds silly."

"I guess it does, in a way," Alice said. "But dangerous, too."

Bryan nodded. "I think that's what Tommy – Thomas – thought. And then the odd person started turning up with a new car, or fancy clothes, so he figured some of them had agreed."

"But he still didn't know what they'd agreed to."

"Not really, no. He thought it was to do with a new development going up on the other side of Skipton, all posh homes and so on, but he couldn't see why. He pulled all the plans and everything was in order for them, so I think it was just the timing of it that made him think that." Bryan sighed. "Maybe it was the digging around that got him in trouble, you know?"

Miriam wanted to protest, to say, *no, that can't be right,* but she seemed to have forgotten how. And she thought she might have been lying, anyway.

"How many councillors did Thomas think were involved?" Alice asked.

Bryan shook his head. "He does— didn't know. Gavin asked

him if he'd had any letters, apparently. They were talking, I think Thomas trusted him, but that was when, um, you know." Bryan suddenly flushed a rather appealing shade of pink. "Gavin, um, he seemed to be enjoying himself when he died. And there were a few others – Angela retiring, for instance, vanishing off on that cruise thing. But he couldn't be sure."

"Do you know where he went after he met with us last week?"

Bryan touched his mouth, the fingers trembling. "I'm not sure. It wasn't planned. He called when he left you and said he was dropping by a farm, but he wouldn't say who or why. The whole thing had really got to him, you know? He got a bit funny and paranoid about everything, and wouldn't tell me very much. I'm sorry. I wish I knew more."

Alice squeezed Bryan's hand. "That's very helpful, Bryan."

Bryan clamped his free hand down on hers in a panicky grip. "You'll be careful, won't you? If they did this …."

Alice smiled at him, and it was that terrifying, may-take-over-a-small-country smile again. "Then they will be found out."

After a moment, Bryan smiled back at her, a tight and angry sort of smile, and Miriam pushed her chair back. "There was jam roly-poly in the fridge," she said, her voice sounding squeaky and unfamiliar to her own ears. "I'll just use a little of your cream, Bryan."

She hurried through to the kitchen before anyone could stop her, and stood leaning over the sink with some inner wind rushing in her ears, wondering why she'd expected anything else.

There was always an Investigation, and Alice was always in the middle of it, and what sort of friend would she be if she just left her there?

Miriam growled at the bottom of the sink, and helped herself to a large chunk of brownie from a tub she'd discovered earlier. If a day like this didn't call for generous servings of brownies, she wasn't sure what did.

9
MORTIMER

Mortimer stacked three new scales into the baskets in the corner of his workshop, and sighed so deeply he set the flowers floating under the low ceiling bobbing about in alarm. He'd been losing scales steadily ever since the impromptu meeting in Alice's garden a week ago, and the fact that Beaufort kept muttering about needing to keep a closer eye on things wasn't helping. He fancied some scones, with an inadvisable amount of whipped cream and raspberry jam, but when he'd crept into Miriam's garden this afternoon she hadn't been home, and he wasn't at all sure about going to Alice's. So he'd retreated to his workshop, his belly rumbling as he wondered if he could face eating a rabbit. He was starting to get as squeamish as Gilbert.

There was scuffling at the entrance, and he busied himself sorting through the scales, trying to find one that would give just the right sheen for a bracelet. He had some vague idea about making multi-purpose jewellery, but he really was going to have to concentrate. The last one he'd tried had transformed from bracelet to umbrella perfectly, but on turning back had started pouring water everywhere. The whole workshop had been awash by the time they'd got it off Amelia's paw and back onto the bench, and even then it had leaked so much they'd barely been able to melt the charms out of it.

"Mortimer?" Gilbert said, padding down the tunnel. "Are you about?"

"In here," Mortimer called, wondering if he should ask Gilbert about rabbit alternatives. The young dragon was very fond of pumpkins, but Mortimer was unconvinced by them. It was something to do with the squidgy texture when they were roasted, and that they couldn't seem to decide if they were sweet or savoury. He couldn't be doing with indecisive vegetables.

"I had an idea," Gilbert said, and Mortimer braced himself for flaming stars and model ships armed with actual firing cannons.

"Oh?"

"We need more help, right?"

"Well, we're managing—"

"Only just. And look at how you're shedding!"

Mortimer curled his tail protectively under the workbench. "That's not really from work."

"Well, yeah, I know, but it's not like things are going to stop with Beaufort or the W.I., is it?"

Mortimer glared at the young dragon, wanting very much to throw a handy pair of tongs at him and tell him to keep his opinions to himself. Because he'd been trying quite hard to avoid the fact that, rather than there being *less* Investigation and meddling in police business as time went on, there seemed to be more. And now there were jaunts, which he was coming to heartily dislike.

"Well, what do you want me to do about it?" he asked, a little more harshly than he intended. It was the lack of scones, he decided.

"I just mean that you could do to be doing less work here, so you only have to worry about Beaufort."

"I don't *want* to worry about Beaufort," Mortimer mumbled.

Gilbert snorted. "Yeah, I don't think you have any choice in that one, M."

"I ... well, your point, please?"

"Why don't we have bauble auditions?"

"Bauble auditions?"

"Yeah, like those talent shows Miriam likes. You know, people come on and show what they can do, and if they're really good – or really weird – they get through to the next round, and eventually one person gets to be the best baker, or the newest pop star, or whatever." Mortimer opened his mouth to argue, and Gilbert added hurriedly, "We wouldn't go with the weird ones, obviously. I mean, you've already got me." He gave such a huge, toothy grin that Mortimer couldn't help grinning back.

"Well, okay, I see what you mean, but would anyone even be interested? I mean, Amelia's already handling the scale trade, so no one really has to contribute anything more."

Gilbert shrugged. "Sure, not everyone'll be interested, but I think a lot will. I mean, old Lord Walter might mutter on about hating humans, but even he loves the barbecues and the blankets and everything. They know what you're doing's important."

Mortimer could just see his snout going a flattered orange. "Us."

"Everyone knows it's all you, really." Gilbert picked up a scale and examined the edge. "So, what do you think? Can't hurt, right?"

Mortimer scratched his neck. Technically it couldn't, but ... "Okay," he said. "But not some silly competition thing. Just give everyone some guidelines, and then we can take a look. No scores or anything."

"Awesome. This is going to be *awesome*." Gilbert dropped to all fours and scampered for the tunnel entrance, and Mortimer shouted after him, "*No flames!*"

Mortimer played around with the bracelet for a little longer, before his rumbling tummy forced him to pad out into the sunshine. That, and the fact that while this bracelet wasn't pouring water everywhere, it was refusing to let go of the pipe he was using as a make-shift wrist. Plus it kept getting tighter, and the metal was starting to groan with the strain. He shook his wings out on the ledge, and decided that he'd catch himself a fish. He hadn't had fish for a while, and the thought of it didn't seem to make him as queasy as rabbits did at the moment.

He launched himself off the ledge with the easy grace of long practise, his wings curving to catch the updraft, and took two long sweeps around the lake before he touched down in the shallows, the cold water making him squeak and shiver as it splashed against his belly. He could see Lord Pamela sunning herself on the rocks across the water, and a couple of hatchlings playing in the shallows while a large dragon called Alex watched them with his legs flopped to either side of a fallen tree. The lake – or tarn, really, as it was hardly big enough to qualify as a lake – was sheltered from the worst of the wind by the mount on one side and the forest that stalked up the hill to the others, but ripples and patterns played across the surface like the footsteps of invisible things. No one came here. There were ways of making places unseen, even in the days of humans and GPS and trail bikes. There were ways of making paths vanish and trees huddle too close to penetrate, and even more there were ways of making places *faint,* just the way Folk are. Faint in a way that means the eye passes over it and the feet turn away. It took time, and skill, but dragons had plenty of both.

Mortimer took a deep breath and let it out in a sigh that sent ripples running away from him across the water, thinking of how close they had come to having to leave last Christmas. Not all of them, just Beaufort, but he would have gone too. There had never been any question in his mind about that. Imagine having to find a new place, though. Imagine having to rebuild this? He shook his head, and stared down into the water instead. Fish. That was the thing. There.

He lunged forward.

HE WAS STILL SNAPPING at the water twenty minutes later, when Amelia and Gilbert paddled out from the shore to watch. He was drenched, wings slapping at the water wildly, and so far had a mouthful of weed and a bruised snout for his efforts.

"You alright there, M?" Amelia asked.

"*No*. Since when have fish been so hard to catch?"

"Since they don't want to get eaten," Gilbert said, and Amelia rolled her eyes.

"You're just out of practise."

"I'm a *dragon*. We don't get *out of practise* at hunting."

"Of course we do," Gilbert said. "It's not an automatic thing, like breathing. You have to practise. I couldn't catch a rabbit to save my life."

"You can't even fly," Mortimer pointed out, then immediately went an uncomfortable mustard yellow. "Sorry." He really did need to eat something.

Gilbert shrugged. "I don't care. You want a pumpkin?"

"He can't live on pumpkin," Amelia said.

"I do," Gilbert replied.

"You're a freak of nature."

"I'm a vegetarian."

"What I said."

Mortimer held up his paws to stop the arguing, but before he could say anything a shadow swept over them, and they looked up to see the High Lord of the Cloverly dragons, his scales brilliant green and running with gold, banking toward them, his wings broad and powerful against the summer sky. He came in low over the water, legs outstretched, landed heavily enough to splash them all, then tucked in his wings and grinned.

Mortimer recognised that grin, and he had the sudden feeling that he wasn't going to be getting any lunch.

"Hello, hello. What are you all up to, then? Work day out?" Beaufort asked.

"Mortimer's fishing," Amelia said.

"Oh, wonderful. Much luck, lad?"

Mortimer looked at the churned-up water washing around four sets of dragon legs, and sighed. "Not much."

"Well, that's a shame." Beaufort peered around, his old gold eyes glittering with the light reflected off the surface, then shot a paw forward and came up with a wriggling carp. He offered it to Mortimer, who just stared. "Got to sneak up on them."

Mortimer took the fish, mumbling "Thank you," and tried to ignore Amelia, who was doing a bad job of not laughing.

"That fish," Gilbert started, and his sister swatted his ear.

"Is Mortimer's lunch. He doesn't need you ascribing a personality to it."

Mortimer tried to avoid the fish's eyes. "Ah – did you need something, sir?"

"I was thinking of heading out for a while. A bit of a jaunt."

What appetite Mortimer had drained away, and he sighed. "Now?"

"Can we come?" Gilbert asked.

"We're not going to be walking," Amelia pointed out.

"No harm, actually," Beaufort said. "I wanted to take a look at something from the ridge just beyond the mount. We could walk that."

Gilbert grinned at his sister, and she huffed, then looked at Mortimer. "Are you going to eat that, or play with it?"

The fish flopped a couple of times and gave a rather despairing gasp, and Mortimer put it back in the water. It rolled over once, sinking toward the bottom, then righted itself and shot away. "I'll eat later. After our *jaunt*."

"Right you are, then. Off we go." Beaufort waded ashore, shook himself off, and trotted away through the boulders that surrounded the lake, Amelia and Gilbert ambling after him. Mortimer wished again for a scone, and padded on behind them.

THE DRAGONS LEFT the mount behind, slipping deeper into the forest, the mulch soft and fragrant underfoot, the shrubs among the trees whispering against their scales. They took on the colours of the woods, dappled browns and greens, even with no one to see them, and the birds sang on unconcerned as they passed.

It was a lot longer by foot than by wing, and by the time they slipped out of the trees and climbed to the heather-clad stone ridge that separated the forested valley from the farmland beyond Mortimer was regretting letting the fish go. His stomach was growling insistently, and it seemed far too hot, with the sun baking on his scales. He started looking for rabbit trails.

Beaufort led the way to the ridge with his head high and his wings sleek against his back, and stopped next to one of the cairns that pinned the dragons' faintness to the land. He lifted his snout, as if scenting the wind, then looked at the three young dragons as they lined up next to him. "Tell me what you see," he said.

There was a grave edge to the High Lord's voice, and Mortimer looked out across the variegated green of the fields, crosshatched with dry stone walls and garnished with pockets of woods and forest. A couple of skinny roads meandered here and there, and a thread of trees marked a waterway. Houses clustered together for company, and in the distance more fells hulked up, cutting off their view of the land beyond. The wind was stronger here, but still only enough to rumple through the heather and set the long grass leaning. He could smell sun on hot stone and grass unfurling, and the pale pink scent of small creatures hunkering down in fright lest they become lunch. But there was something missing. He couldn't quite taste what it was, but it was there, the way you know something is lost before you even see it's gone.

"It's so still," Amelia said, and Mortimer nodded in sudden comprehension.

"No tractors," he said. "No quad bikes."

"There's a car," Amelia added. "So people are still around."

They watched the little red car slip down a lane, disappearing and reappearing with the roll of the land. Beaufort didn't say anything.

Then Gilbert said, "I can't hear anyone."

Mortimer and Amelia looked at each other, then at Beaufort, who nodded. "No dogs. No shouting."

"Maybe they're at lunch?" Mortimer suggested, and his stomach reminded him that it would quite like to be at lunch, too.

Beaufort nodded at the farm below them, grey stone buildings bleached in the sun. "Keep looking."

They did, Mortimer straining to see movement in the barn, to hear cows grumbling or sheep complaining to each other. There was nothing. No cars moving on the farm tracks, no shouts from the house, no dogs in the yard or tractors rumbling across fields. The house was as motionless as a painting, and the fields surrounding it were empty.

"There's no one," Amelia said softly.

"You don't think— you don't think someone *did* something?" Mortimer was thinking of Rockford and his ridiculous fixation on dragons being dragons and eating sheep and all that nonsense. He wouldn't have even put it past the silly throwback to fancy stealing a maiden, although who knew what you were meant to do with them once you had one. It all sounded like an awful lot of trouble.

"Not one of us, no. But a whole farm doesn't just pack up and leave."

They stared out at the empty fields for a long, still moment, then Gilbert said, "If they'd been farming pumpkins, the pumpkins would still be there."

Amelia hit him.

THEY STAYED where they were for a little longer, then Beaufort said, "Shall we take a closer look?"

"No," Mortimer said immediately, then gave the High Lord a half-hearted grin. "I mean, it's still light. It's too risky!"

"I don't mean going up to the house, lad. Just down to the edge of the forest, so we can take a look at the fields."

"Yes," Amelia said. "We should do that. Find out who did this."

"Wouldn't tonight be better?" Mortimer pleaded. "It's not like we can do anything right now."

"We can gather information," Amelia said.

"They better not be turning it into an experimental site," Gilbert said, and the others looked at him.

"A what?" Beaufort asked, with enormous interest.

The younger dragon wrinkled his snout. "An experimental site. For, like, new stuff."

"New stuff," Amelia said.

"Yeah. Like new pesticides, or specially bred ducks."

Mortimer was fairly certain he'd never heard of experimental sites, let alone farms for specially bred ducks, but Gilbert did seem to learn about the strangest things. Like piercings and vegetarianism. "I don't see any ducks," he said.

"That was just an example."

"It all changes," Beaufort said, watching the land below. "I remember when this was more trees than farmland, and there was only one track leading to Toot Hansell. You couldn't even get a cart down it." He shrugged, lifting his snout to watch a plane pass. "Everything progresses."

Mortimer tried to imagine a world awash with trees and beasts and Folk, where they only considered living, not hiding, because the humans were the minority. He couldn't. And he wasn't at all sure he agreed with progress, although he realised he was the one who had brought progress to the Cloverly dragons. Maybe there were different kinds of progress. Maybe some made the world more beautiful, while others broke it. Or maybe they all broke it in different ways, and you never knew which until it was too late.

"It's bollocks, is what it is," a new voice said, and they looked down the slope to see a dryad sitting on the sparse grass with her back against a tree. "Killing trees and murdering rivers."

"You're quite right, of course," Beaufort said. "But they need to live, too."

"I'd rather they didn't do it in my woods," the dryad said, screwing her face up. "I don't mind them collecting a bit of firewood, but we can't stand much more clearing."

"I know," Beaufort said, and they were quiet for a few moments, watching the dryad tease a sapling out of the ground. "Any changes around here recently?"

The dryad shrugged. "Not really. We've had a new species of mushroom come in. It only grows on the west side of ash trees, for some reason. Want to see it?"

"No, that's alright," Beaufort said. "I was thinking more any changes with the humans."

"Oh, them. I try to keep away from them," the dryad said.

"So nothing much changed at the farm?"

"Oh yeah. Plenty." She unfolded some new leaves on the sapling.

The dragons exchanged glances. "Such as?" Beaufort prompted.

"They left."

"Left?"

"Yeah. Left. Gone."

Mortimer squinted at the house, crouching alone amid the cluster of outbuildings. One of them looked slumped and blackened, and he wondered if he could smell old smoke.

"Did anything strange happen before they left?" Beaufort asked.

The dryad stroked the leaves, and they trembled, unfurling under her touch. "Humans are strange, generally."

"True."

"There was this new one who came around. Every day, in his shiny car. All clean it was." She frowned. "He threw a sandwich wrapper out of his car window once. I threw rocks at his windscreen."

"Did you get him?" Gilbert asked.

"Of course."

"Well done," Beaufort said. "But he kept coming back?"

"Every day. On his own at first, then with a couple of other humans. Big ones."

"And then the house humans moved out?"

"Yeah. Well, first the shed burned down, then they left."

Mortimer looked back at the blackened outbuilding, and thought it wasn't smoke he was smelling. It was the scent of small animals in tight places, burrowing to escape.

"Well. That *is* interesting," Beaufort said, which Mortimer thought was rather alarming. *Interesting* sounded worse than a jaunt. *Interesting* sounded like trouble. "And what's happened since then?"

"Not much. They haven't touched my woods."

"Well, that's good," the High Lord said.

The dryad gave the sapling an approving pat and leaned back against the tree. "Sure you don't want to see the mushrooms?"

"No, thanks," Beaufort said. "But we appreciate the offer."

"Your loss," the dryad said. "See ya." Then she was gone, melted into the tree or the woods or the whispering, fiddling leaves, and the dragons looked at each other.

"I think we should take a sniff," Beaufort said, and Mortimer sighed.

"Now?"

"Lad, there's no cloud cover, a main road, a farm, no trees once we're on the fields, and dozens of walking tracks around here. Now would be a bit silly, wouldn't it?"

Mortimer thought it wouldn't be the silliest thing he'd known to happen, but he kept that thought to himself and just said, "I might go back to my lunch in that case."

"Shall we see if we can find those mushrooms?" Gilbert offered. "Mushrooms are lovely roasted."

Beaufort finally looked away from the farm and turned back toward the mount. "I knew a dragon once who was very fond of mushrooms. She used to build fairy houses with them."

Mortimer thought he might stick with fishing.

10
DI ADAMS

Ervin jumped to his feet as DI Adams walked in the door of the police station, to-go coffee mug in hand. She'd been trying to reach Alice, who should have attended her first council meeting today, but the phone just kept going to voicemail, which was doing nothing to improve her disposition toward persistent journalists. "No."

"I haven't asked you anything!" Ervin protested.

"Still no."

"Aw, c'mon." He fell into step with her, causing Dandy to give him what probably would have been a disapproving look if his eyes had been visible behind the flopping dreadlocks. "Any news on the publican with the dodgy heart?"

"Did I already say no?"

"What about the rumour that his heart was absolutely fine, and he may have run afoul of some unsavoury sorts?"

DI Adams swiped her card at the door to the offices, but didn't go in. "Do you always talk like back-cover copy for a pulp magazine?"

"I thought you might appreciate it more than, 'Oi, copper, d'you reckon someone offed 'im, then?'"

He gave her that dimpled grin, and she scowled at him. "I'm not appreciating the whole conversation, really."

"Oh, come on, Inspector. Give me something."

"I have nothing to give you, Mr Giles."

"Won't you call me Ervin?"

"No. Why would I?" She pushed through the door, and it was swinging closed when he shouted behind her.

"How about the possible connection to BelleVue Developments?"

She let the door bang shut, squeezing her eyes closed, then looked down at Dandy. Today he seemed to have settled on Labrador-size as being ideal, and he looked back at her blandly. "I'm probably going to regret this," she mumbled, then glanced around to make sure no one had seen her talking to the invisible dog. They already seemed to harbour doubts about her because she turned up in a suit every day. She opened the door, revealing Ervin hovering on the other side. He gave her an enormous smile. "Who are BelleVue Developments?"

"Well, I could explain, but in a doorway's probably not the best spot."

She considered sitting him back in the plastic chairs of the waiting area, but PC McLeod had already dropped a stack of files when she came in, and when she reopened the door he spilled tea down his front. And that was even after she'd saved him from Daffodil Woman. Maybe she should try jeans one day. She pulled her attention back to Ervin, who was still grinning at her like a kid who'd just wriggled out of detention.

"Come in," she said.

COLLINS WAS LEANING BACK in his chair and poking gravely at his phone when she led the journalist in. She installed Ervin in a chair between their two desks and sat down.

"What, no tea?" Ervin asked.

"You're not going to be here that long," DI Adams said.

"The standards of civility are very low here."

The inspectors looked at each other, and Collins got up. "I could do with one anyway. Adams?"

She waved her to-go mug at him, and he ambled out of the room.

"Now that's proper Yorkshire hospitality for you," Ervin said.

"You're not a guest, Mr Giles. You're doing your civic duty."

"Call me Ervin."

"Why?"

"Mr Giles makes me feel old."

"Diddums," she said, and leaned back in her chair to wait for Collins. She was also watching Dandy, who was cruising around Ervin, snuffling at his shoes and the canvas satchel he'd placed on the floor. He didn't seem to find anything more interesting than he had on the first encounter, and wandered back to flop at her feet. She was quite fond of Dandy, but she couldn't quite figure out the use of him. He hadn't shown any inclination to track down criminals or rescue children stuck in wells. She wondered if she should be trying to train him.

"You got milk and two sugars," Collins announced, coming back into the office and handing Ervin a pink mug with a pig's snout painted on it.

"Close enough," Ervin said, taking a sip and immediately making a face.

DI Collins dropped back into his chair and took a slurp of his own tea. "Speak up, then, lad. You've got our attention for as long as this tea lasts."

Ervin took another sip of tea, wrinkling his nose slightly. "Fine.

Right to it, then. BelleVue Developments. Have you heard of them?"

DI Adams underlined the name on her notepad and said, "Give us the basics. We can look into it further later on if we feel there's any merit to it."

"Would I waste the police's time?"

"Probably."

Collins chuckled, and pulled a packet of biscuits from his desk drawer. DI Adams took one automatically, then stared at it. "*Rice cakes?*"

"I'm trying to be a bit healthier." He offered one to Ervin, who waved it away.

DI Adams put hers on the edge of the desk and said, "Your aunt will disown you." She turned back to the journalist. "What do we need to know about BelleVue Developments?"

"On paper, perfectly respectable. However, I ran across them with one of the country houses I was profiling. It was after I stayed there – the owners contacted me. They wanted me to write a story on it, but I couldn't have, because libel is kind of a big deal. But apparently the company had been leaning on them pretty heavily to sell. As in, *heavily*."

DI Adams knocked the rice cake to the floor so Dandy could have it. "More specifically?"

"Huge incentives. Offering to pay way over the asking, and suggesting that selling was a really *good idea*." He put the last two words in air quotes, and DI Adams gave him a distasteful look. She couldn't stand air quotes. Or people who used air quotes. "But they didn't want to sell," the journalist added.

"So then what happened?"

"They started getting loads of anonymous reviews online, all saying that it was about the worst place in the world. You know, that it was filthy and run-down, and the staff were rude and so on. They reported it, but there was no way to trace who did it, and it hit their business pretty hard. BelleVue came back with more offers, still high. They still refused. Then one night one of their outbuildings burned down. Looked electrical, so the insurance agency should have paid out, but their investigator suddenly changed his tune and said it was due to poor maintenance on the wiring, or even deliberate tampering."

"So they got nothing," DI Adams said.

"Not a cent. And the police looked at them pretty hard for it, but couldn't prove anything."

"What happened then?"

"BelleVue came back. Still offering a decent price, though not as good, obviously."

"And then?" Collins said. He was nibbling on a rice cake, looking distressed. DI Adams thought that was more due to the rice cake than the conversation.

"Then their car got run off the road one night. They were both pretty shaken up, but not seriously hurt."

DI Adams looked up from her notepad. "And then another offer?"

"Yes. They took that one."

"And there was no way to say for sure it was BelleVue behind any of it."

"No. They took it to the police, but there was no evidence, and they'd already sold. BelleVue gave them an okay price, well below market but okay, so that side was pretty legitimate. Plus the police were already suspicious of them after the fire, so they weren't too helpful. You lot do get a bit fixated."

Collins made a rude noise. "What made you believe them, then?"

"Because it all added up. They loved that house. It had been in her family forever. They were going to pass it down to their children. And they were doing alright with it as a posh country house retreat. They didn't need to sell before all that."

DI Adams leaned back in her chair, rolling her pen in her fingers. "Maybe they just had bad luck and sold hastily, and are now regretting they didn't ask for more."

"It's possible," Ervin said. "But what would it gain them to blame it on BelleVue? They're not going to get any more out of them. And it'd have to be the world's biggest run of bad luck and coincidences."

"You said BelleVue looks good on paper. You done some digging?" Collins asked. He'd given up on the rice cake.

Ervin wrapped both hands around his mug and tried his dimples on them. The inspectors stared back, unimpressed. "What do I get for bringing you such invaluable information?"

The DIs exchanged glances.

"Another cuppa?" Collins offered.

"An actual biscuit?" DI Adams suggested.

"Aw, come on. We're all grown-ups here. We know the press and the police can work really well together."

DI Adams rubbed her chin. "*Can* being the operative word."

"It requires trust," Collins agreed. "Do we have a circle of trust here, Adams?"

"I'm not sure, you know. I feel this is more a triangle, rather than a circle."

"Oh, you two are just bloody hilarious."

"We are," Collins agreed. "Now stop messing us about and tell us what you know. We can always find it online anyway."

Ervin scowled, then said, "Fine. But can I at least get a decent brew? This one tastes like it was two *tablespoons* of sugar."

"I'll make you one myself if you just get on with it," DI Adams said.

"Don't do it," Collins said. "She's a coffee-drinker, and southern to boot. She makes a terrible cup of tea."

Ervin put his mug down on DI Adams' desk and leaned back again, folding his arms. "D'you know what, enough. I can't take the comedy act anymore. Do people confess just to get you two to shut up?"

DI Adams fought the smile twitching in the corner of her mouth and took a sip of coffee. "Sorry we're not to your taste. You telling us anything more or not? Because we do have actual work to do."

"Ugh, *okay*. But remember me when you've got news, right?"

"How could we forget you?" Collins asked, but Ervin ignored him and talked to DI Adams instead.

"Usual thing, the corporation's based overseas. The paper trail's a bit thin, but I'm pretty sure they were involved under other names in some of those Spanish developments that sold like mad but never got built, as well as a couple in Turkey that were built but basically started falling down again straight away."

"Who's behind it?"

"In theory, the UK face is a woman named Greta Moore. But she seems to have pretty much just popped up here, so my thinking is there's probably been a Greta Moore for Spain and one for Turkey, as well."

DI Adams was scribbling notes as the journalist talked. "So why do you think BelleVue has any involvement in the Wright death? There's been nothing flagged in his correspondence as threatening, certainly not that we've come across. And I'm not confirming there was foul play," she added, just to be sure.

"About nine months ago, BelleVue put on a bit of a do for investors and local councillors. Swanky cocktail party type thing. I noticed it, because it wasn't that long after I'd heard about the whole deal with the country house. I managed to get in, and they were basically selling off-plan plots for a development on the far side of town."

DI Adams picked her phone up, and he shook his head.

"Don't bother. It's there. Or the site's there. In nine months all that's happened is a few holes have been dug."

"So it's a scam."

"Or a cover for something else. A way to legitimately make contact with all the councillors. Maybe get them to influence planning. You know how these things go."

DI Collins snorted. "It sounds pretty far-fetched to me. There's not exactly a culture of corruption emanating from the town hall."

"Stranger things have happened, Detective Inspector," Ervin said. "Sometimes it's just a bit of wining and dining to get applications to move quicker, or discounts and gift baskets to make sure certain contractors are used. But it happens everywhere."

"Once you start talking about murder, though, it's a bit more extreme than that," Collins said.

DI Adams tapped her pen off her notepad and got up. "Thank you very much for your cooperation, Mr Giles."

"That's it? After all this exclusive and potentially vital information, just run along?"

"We don't have anything to give you right now."

"You said you'd make me a cup of tea, at least."

"Collins is right, I'm terrible at tea." She shepherded him toward the door as he got up.

"You could buy me one." He turned the full force of his dimples on her, and she heard Collins snort with laughter behind them.

"I could. Doesn't mean I'm going to." She manoeuvred him out into the station and closed the door in his face before he could protest, then hurried back to her desk. Collins was frowning at his computer, and Dandy was snoring faintly. He hadn't touched the rice cake she'd dropped on the floor. "Fat lot of good you are," she told the dog, then said to Collins, "Do you think there's anything in it?"

"I'd like to say no, but it puts an interesting slant on things."

"Thoughts?"

"Wright had a cardiac event, probably brought on by the truly spectacular amount of cocaine in his system, despite his husband saying he never touched anything harder than ibuprofen. Gavin Peabody also came up positive for cocaine, although not as much. He did have a history of heart problems, though, and he was spending the evening with three rather younger ladies at the time. It did look very much like an accident."

"And could still be." But it didn't feel like an accident. She rubbed her fingertips together, feeling the tingle of the case making connections.

"It could. But his lady friends said that he was more or less a regular, and, unlike some clients, he might have a couple of drinks, but he never touched anything more than that."

They considered it for a moment, then DI Adams said, "We're going to need to look at the council more closely, see if anyone's suddenly splashing cash."

"What about BelleVue?" he asked, nodding at his screen. "They've got offices in Manchester. We could go talk to them."

"We've got nothing to point us at them, other than that cocktail party. We don't want to scare them off."

"Fair point. I'll get the tech to check on the emails and so on again, see if the name pops up, but I imagine they're more careful than that."

DI Adams tapped her password into the computer. "Nothing on the phone records?"

Collins shook his head. "Wright got texts and phone calls from two different pay-as-you-go numbers on the day he died. He'd been in contact with one of them previously, but they're both inactive. We haven't been able to recover the messages."

They sat in silence for a moment, then DI Adams said, "We don't want to question the other councillors too pointedly."

"No. We're going to have to tread carefully. We don't know who's involved."

DI Adams sighed. "Dammit," she said. "We're going to have to use her, aren't we?"

"She's kind of put herself in the perfect place."

"I don't like it."

"Me either." DI Collins rubbed his hands over his head and sighed, then added, "Did you say you had proper biscuits? I need proper biscuits if I'm about to ask a senior citizen to gather info on potentially homicidal property developers."

DI Adams opened her desk drawer, threw a chew to Dandy, and handed a packet of Hobnobs to Collins.

"Not chocolate ones?"

"They're better than rice cakes."

"Well, there's that."

She picked up her phone and dialled Alice. It went to voicemail again, and she flung the phone down on the desk with such frustration that both Collins and Dandy looked at her in alarm. "Fancy a drive?" she asked them, and Dandy leaped to his feet and bolted for the door, sending bits of paper flying off the desk in his wake.

"Weird," DI Collins announced.

11
MIRIAM

By the time they left Bryan tucked up in bed with the TV on and a large cup of tea, it was getting on for dinner time, and Miriam was strongly regretting not having some of the cottage pie. As she climbed into Alice's SUV she said, "Come to mine and I'll make a salad. I have some nice quinoa left from last night that'll go very nice mixed in with it."

Alice wrinkled her nose in a way that suggested she wasn't so keen on quinoa, but said, "That sounds lovely, Miriam."

Miriam tried to think about whether she had any feta left, and not to fixate too much on the fact that they were wrapped up in an Investigation. Alice hadn't said anything more since Bryan had told them about Thomas' suspicions, but it was obvious she was planning *something*. It was in her thoughtful silence and the way her fingers tapped on the wheel as she drove. All Bryan's talk of bribes and accidents had just served to get her more interested, not less. As they rumbled through the village Miriam gave up on thinking about feta and burst out, "Alice, what are you doing?"

"I'm sorry?"

"Why don't you step down? Just tell the inspectors what you know and leave it to them."

"But I don't really know anything, dear."

"You know what Bryan told you!"

"Which is just second-hand guesses and hearsay. It's no help to anyone."

Miriam pressed a hand to her mouth. "People are getting killed."

"We don't know that. They could still be accidents."

"But it doesn't sound like it."

"No," Alice said, skirting the village green with the police tape still strung between the trees. "Which is why I need to find out more."

Miriam took a deep breath. "But what if … you could …"

"I won't." Alice patted her hand. "And you don't have to have anything to do with it. In fact, I want to keep the whole W.I. well away from it all. It's far too delicate a situation."

Miriam snatched her hand away. "Of course I'm going to have anything to do with it! Something. Everything." She waved vaguely. "You know what I mean. I'm your friend! I'm not just going to sit back here and let you wander off into … into political intrigue and assassinations and suchlike!"

Alice touched her mouth, and Miriam suspected she was trying not to laugh, which was simply rude. "Miriam, dear—"

"No! I shall be your secretary. I'm going to all the meetings with you."

"I don't think that's actually allowed."

"In which case, I'll go to the hall with you and wait outside."

"That might look a little suspicious. And you do have to give whoever it is a chance to actually contact me, otherwise the whole exercise will be rather pointless."

"Oh." Miriam frowned out the window. "Yes, I see what you mean. But you can't just expect me to stay out of it."

"I guess I can't, at that," Alice said, and gave Miriam a long, appraising look that made her ears go hot. "You're remarkable, you know that?"

"And you'll be the death of me." Miriam sniffed.

"Well." Alice pulled into Miriam's lane. "Miriam?"

"Yes?"

"Do stop watching those American political thrillers. I think you've got quite the wrong idea about how exciting politics are."

Miriam straightened her sleeves. "Says the woman trying to catch a murderer."

❧

ALICE PARKED outside the gate and Miriam led the way around the house to the kitchen door, wondering if she'd spoken rather hastily. Not that she had any intention of letting Alice go into this horrible mess on her own, of course, but she was a little worried that she might have given the impression she was feeling very brave about the whole thing.

And she was not.

She was actually feeling rather the opposite, and when she rounded the corner of the cottage and saw the kitchen door standing ajar she stopped so suddenly Alice walked into her.

"Miriam?" Alice asked, startled.

"*Someone's here,*" Miriam whispered, and grabbed the first thing to hand, which happened to be a glass sculpture of a bumblebee. She put it back and picked up a couple of skinny bamboo stakes she used for supporting her tomato plants.

"I don't think they'll be much good," Alice said.

"*Shh!* What if they hear us?"

"Why on earth would anyone be in your kitchen, Miriam?"

"It could be the you-know-who."

Alice looked at her for a moment, then said, "You really do need to stop watching those TV shows." She marched forward and pushed the kitchen door open, calling, "Hello?"

Miriam ran after her, still holding on to the bamboo, and reached the door just as Beaufort appeared on the doorstep and boomed, "There you are! We thought we'd lost you."

Miriam lowered the stakes. "Is that smoke?"

Beaufort shifted slightly. "There may be a little."

"What on earth have you been up to?" Alice asked, peering around the High Lord into the kitchen. Miriam craned to look over her shoulder and saw Mortimer holding a frying pan with a melted handle and what appeared to be a small scorched sponge in it. He gave them a tiny wave, his tail tucked close to his hindquarters.

"I'm terribly sorry," he said. "I don't think I was watching quite closely enough when you made those cheese toasties, Miriam."

Miriam looked at her ruined pan for a moment, then shrugged. "They can be tricky to get right," she said, and went to dig some more bread out of the freezer.

❧

THE QUINOA WAS EXCELLENT, if Miriam did say so herself. Mixed up with mint and basil from the garden, pocked with cherry tomatoes and yellow peppers and peas, then topped with a little feta and a light dousing of lemon juice and olive oil. Of course, she'd have enjoyed it a lot more if there hadn't been two dragons sticking their claws in it and saying things like, "Keen-wha? It's very fiddly. You can't even chew it. What's meant to eat keen-wha? Is it for birds, really?"

To be fair, it was really only Beaufort doing the quinoa poking, although both he and Mortimer had eaten a decent portion of it. Miriam had plenty of bread but not much cheese left after Mortimer's attempt at cooking, so she'd only been able to make the dragons three toasties each, which was a rather paltry amount by dragon standards. Mortimer had apologised so many times Alice had been quite sharp with him, and he'd apologised for apologising then gone a rather sickly yellow and retreated to the rug in front of the old green Aga stove. He seemed to have recovered somewhat, though, and was sitting with a toastie in one paw and the quinoa packet in the other, declaring that it couldn't possibly be pronounced keen-wha. Miriam was feeling a bit exasperated with them both.

Of course, a large part of the exasperation was the fact that Beaufort was adamant that they needed to go for a jaunt, which just sounded like another word for Investigating to her.

"It's hardly the time for a jaunt," Alice said. "Miriam and I have had a lot on today."

"I don't know what it is about jaunts," Mortimer whispered to Miriam. "I think he read about it somewhere."

Miriam nodded and pulled away as politely as she could. Dragon whispers are hot, and she checked surreptitiously to make sure none of her hair had melted.

"This is important," Beaufort said.

Alice looked like she wanted to argue, but eventually she nodded. "Alright. Where are we going?"

"We need to visit a farm."

"I see." Alice nodded, her face expressionless, and Miriam remembered Bryan saying, *He was dropping by a farm*. "What for, exactly?"

"We need to know if there's anyone on it."

"At this time of year?" Miriam asked. "Always. It's terribly busy."

"Only it's not," Beaufort said. "No tractors. No people. Not even any livestock."

There was a pause, and Miriam tried to remember the last time she'd really seen a sheep. They were so much a part of the landscape that you stopped noticing them after a while, like the grey stone walls that cut the fields. They were just there. "But that's not possible," she said. "They can't just be gone."

"That's what we want to check," Beaufort said. "Mortimer and I can't exactly go and knock on the door."

"No," Mortimer said, and spilled some quinoa on the floor.

Alice nodded. "That really is most unusual. You're quite right, Beaufort. We shall go and take a look."

"Is that a good idea at this time of day?" Miriam asked. "You know, with dragons?"

"If we wait until it gets dark it'll be too late for knocking on people's doors," Alice said. "I think we'd best go see what we can find." She stood up and took her plate to the sink (Miriam noted with some satisfaction that it was empty), and added, "Cake will have to wait until we get back."

Mortimer visibly deflated, and Miriam patted his shoulder as she got up. "I'm sure we won't be long."

ALICE PUT the back seats down in the SUV and spread out a blanket to let the dragons recline comfortably, peering out the tinted windows at the countryside. It was suspiciously perfect, and as they headed out of the village Miriam said, "Did you buy this car for the dragons?"

"Don't be ridiculous," Alice said. "What an odd thing that would be to base a purchase on!"

"It works very well, though."

Alice sniffed. "My poor old Prius was utterly devastated by following Thompson all over the place last Christmas. I just wanted something a bit more robust."

Which wasn't far from saying dragon-friendly, really. Miriam settled back into the seat and concentrated on counting sheep.

At first, as they left Toot Hansell, things were just as could be expected. There were sheep in the fields, and with the windows down (Alice scolding Beaufort for putting his head out where anyone could see him), they could hear a tractor working late, somewhere out of sight behind a rise. But as they looped around the village, heading northwest, things got quieter. Desperately so. The fields stood green and empty, the grass already growing long and pocked with wildflowers, and it seemed to Miriam that even the sky had become still, devoid of birds and abandoned. Alice followed Beaufort's directions off a skinny road and onto the track to the farm, rumbling over cattle grids and splashing through puddles left from the last rain. The sky felt lower and gloomier than it had that morning, and Miriam couldn't tell if it was real or just real to her.

There was a final gate into the farmyard itself, and Miriam got out to open it, looking automatically for dogs. There weren't any. There was nothing. Flowers still bloomed in hanging baskets by the farmhouse door, although they looked a little parched, and someone had left a couple of tea towels on the washing line in the yard, but there was no movement in the sheds, no lights on in the windows against the fading day. Miriam rubbed her hands together nervously. One disadvantage of being Sensitive was that one tended to be sensitive about everything. Maybe all she was feeling was the changing weather, or the disappointment of a bad lambing season. Although that still didn't explain the sheer emptiness of everything.

She pulled the gate wide and let the SUV through into the farmyard, securing the gate behind them even though there didn't seem to be anything about to either escape or break in. Alice pulled up by the farmhouse and opened the back door of the car.

"Stay here until we know it's clear," she told the dragons, and sat on the back to swap her shoes for wellies.

"I don't see anyone," Beaufort said.

"It doesn't mean they're not here," Alice said.

Miriam examined her flip-flops and deemed them practical for all conditions. "There's no cars."

"Or any livestock," Alice said, getting up. "I'll knock on the door if you check the sheds."

"On my own?"

"The dragons need to stay out of sight until we're sure no one's around."

That wasn't what Miriam had meant, and she also noticed Alice was carrying her black cane with the silver dragon's head on it. She felt somewhat at a disadvantage, and picked up a rake that was leaning against the fence. "Alright," she said, slightly reassured by the worn wooden handle. Alice smiled, and let herself in the little gate that led to the back garden.

With the rake hefted up and leaning on her shoulder, Miriam sidled up to the first shed. The door was ajar, and she peeked inside cautiously. "Hello?" she called. "Anyone about?"

There was no answer, and she slipped inside, standing peering into the dark until her eyes adjusted. It was empty except for a couple of pallets against the back wall, shrink-wrapped so thoroughly she couldn't tell what was inside them. She let herself out again, skirted an outbuilding that was nothing more than scorched stone and blackened shards of rafters, and moved on to the barn. Both the side door and the big main doors were locked with shiny padlocks on rusty hasps. She frowned at them, then crossed to the last shed, convinced for a moment she'd find something perfectly dreadful inside, that maybe it would be like a scene in a Western after the cattle rustlers have gone through— she stopped before she could scare herself out of going in entirely, and pulled the door open. Hurrying in, she tripped over a coil of fat hose, crashed to her knees in fragrant dirt, cracked herself on the head with the rake, and scrambled to her feet again, brushing off her skirt.

"I'm okay," she said to no one in particular, and blinked at the big metal drums stacked from one side of the shed to another, two and three high in some places. The whole place was ripe with fumes, and she nudged the hose that had tripped her with one foot. It was heavy and insulated, and there were rolls of plastic stacked against the wall. It didn't look very farm-y to her, but she wasn't a farmer. The closest she'd come was raising an orphaned lamb when she was little. It had run away before it was properly weaned, and she still harboured doubts about the sudden increase in lamb her family had eaten over the next few weeks.

She hurried out of the shed, and found Alice waiting expectantly by the car. "Have you seen anyone, Miriam?"

"No, no one, but the barn's locked. And there's drums of stuff in this one."

"I've not been in, but it looks like the house is empty," Alice said, opening the back of the car for the dragons. "Everything seems to have just been dropped. A pair of socks on the stairs, a half-drunk tea in the sink."

Beaufort examined the yard from the vantage point of the car, his eyes bright and interested, and Mortimer slunk reluctantly to the ground then padded toward the house. "Hang about, lad," the High Lord said. "I'm coming too." He jumped down, his wings wide enough that Miriam had to duck, and Alice opened the gate to let them in.

They trailed around the house to the back, where Alice fished a key out from under an old pot and opened the door to the kitchen. A mat still collected mud next to a rack for coats and a shelf for boots, but the hooks and spaces were empty.

"I say," Beaufort said. "How did you know that'd be there?"

"Around here, there's always a spare key hidden about the place. If it's even locked." She stood back to let the dragons lead the way, and they ambled into the empty kitchen to sit back on their hindquarters and look over the counters.

Dragons catch the traces of emotions the way a dog can catch scent, but they fade in strange ways, strong emotions lingering disproportionately. "There are little bits of happiness everywhere," Mortimer said, examining a series of lines drawn on a door frame, names and dates written next to them. "Or contentment, maybe. It smells like small flowers in quiet places."

"But why would they leave if they were content?" Miriam asked. "Something must have happened."

"Something did," Beaufort said. "But it's hard to tell. There were a lot of worries. A lot of stress. Sadness. It's everywhere, like moths. It's sort of overwhelming whatever might have forced them out, this constant background of it."

"So you can't smell violence, or fear?" Alice asked.

Beaufort looked at Mortimer, who shook his head. "No. It doesn't mean it wasn't here, just that everything else is swamping it. I don't think they were hurt. That would be much stronger."

Mortimer wandered into the hall and to the front door, his nose lifted high, and he stopped there, tipping his head from side to side like a dog hearing a noise. "It's here," he said.

"What?" Miriam asked, clutching the rake a little tighter. "Oh no, something awful did happen, didn't it?"

"Despair," Mortimer said. "Defeat."

Miriam hoped the dragons wouldn't tell them what it smelled like. She almost thought she could feel it, pressing in on her from all sides.

"Can you tell what happened?" Alice asked.

"No," Beaufort said. "But something did. They weren't hurt, but they were forced off somehow. Made to think that to stay was hopeless. It's the smell of giving up. Like—"

"I'm going outside," Miriam said.

She retreated out the back door and sat in the garden, looking at the cheery flowerbeds without seeing them, still holding the rake. It made her feel slightly better, as if she could ward off whatever hopelessness had touched the house and the people in it. She was suddenly, inexplicably tired, and she wished they'd had a cup of tea before leaving.

She glimpsed Alice at an upstairs window, just a swirl of grey hair and teal cardigan, but otherwise it was still. A bird came to investigate the feeder, chattered warningly at Miriam, then moved on to splash in the bird bath. She watched it scattering life around its tiny form, and she almost cried out when the back door opened and it fled.

"Are you alright, Miriam?" Alice asked.

"Yes. It was just a bit much. Did you find anything else?" she asked, although she wasn't sure she wanted the answer.

"No," Beaufort said, "but let's see if we can sniff out anything in the sheds." He headed around the house, Alice striding after him.

Mortimer looked up at Miriam and said, "Are you alright?"

"I just feel … icky. Like we're trespassing on memories or something."

Mortimer nodded. "We might be helping, though."

Miriam sighed. "I hope so."

They followed the others, Miriam stooping slightly to rest one hand on Mortimer's back. His warmth seemed to seep to somewhere deeper than her bones.

12

ALICE

"Sheep," Beaufort announced.

"So many sheep," Mortimer agreed, making a face.

The two dragons had their noses lifted to the air as they left the gate and ambled into the yard.

"But were they scared, maybe? Or traumatised?" Miriam asked. She was still holding onto a rake as if just waiting for the chance to hit someone with it. Alice approved.

"Have you met a sheep?" Beaufort asked. "They're always scared. People scare them. Birds scare them. Dragons scare them."

Alice thought the last was probably rather wise historically, even if they were fairly safe around modern dragons.

Mortimer had trotted ahead to the burned-out shed, and now he stopped a healthy distance away. "It doesn't make any sense," he said.

"What doesn't?" Alice asked.

"It's just all ... I don't know. Not upset."

Alice frowned at him. That seemed a terribly wishy-washy way to put things.

"Business," Beaufort announced. "Business as usual. That's what it smells like. Rubber stamps and leaky pens."

"So it wasn't an accident?" Alice asked. "Someone did that deliberately?"

"I think it's a fair guess."

Miriam shivered almost theatrically and looked around. "What an awful thing to do."

"It might have been an insurance claim," Alice said, but she doubted it. Not given what the dragons had told them of the dryad's story. She wondered if dryads were fairly reliable. It wasn't a question she'd ever had to ask herself before.

"Anything's possible," Beaufort said, and followed Mortimer over to the next shed.

"That's got the drums in it," Miriam said, and Mortimer stuck his head in the door then spluttered, backing away from it hurriedly.

"Ugh, that's awful," he said. "It's made my eyes go funny."

Beaufort squinted at him. "They look fine to me, lad. But I can smell it from out here, and it's too strong. We won't catch any proper scents through it. Let's try the barn instead."

"It's locked," Miriam said.

"Oh, well," Mortimer said. "That's a shame."

"Not like you to give up so easy, lad," Beaufort said, and led the way around to the side door.

"I did say," Miriam said, as the High Lord examined the padlock.

"Ah, bad luck," Mortimer said.

Beaufort gave the lock an experimental rattle, then *shoved*. The door bounced open with the sound of screws tearing and boards splintering, and he gave them a toothy grin. "Wood's a bit rotten."

"Really, Beaufort," Alice said. "Hardly subtle."

"They're going to know we've been here!" Mortimer said. He'd been doing quite well at maintaining the muddy brown of the farmyard, but now he flushed anxious grey so quickly Alice thought he might faint.

"What, dragons? No one's going to expect dragons."

"Quite true," Alice said, although the broken lock would indicate *someone* had been there. But it was a bit late to worry about it now. Beaufort vanished inside, the door swinging in his wake, and she followed him into the near-dark of the interior, clicking on the light on her phone and raising it to reveal a horde of beasts lying in wait. "Oh," she said, hearing Miriam give a little squeak next to her and Mortimer say something unrepeatable.

The barn still had the damp woolly smell of sheep, but inside machines were lined up shoulder to shoulder, dead headlights reflecting her light blindly back at her. There were diggers and forklifts and bulldozers, all looking terribly glossy and shiny and very much unused. She counted them, coming up with fifteen machines, which seemed excessive. She didn't know a single farmer that could afford all these new machines, let alone use them all.

"What are they doing here?" Mortimer whispered, as if afraid to wake sleeping monsters.

"Waiting," Beaufort said.

"What for?"

"I rather think that's what we need to find out," Alice said.

"This makes no sense," Miriam said. "Why force the family out? Why sneak the machines in?"

"Do you remember what I said about it being better to beg for forgiveness than ask for permission?"

"Oh no."

Alice nodded. "I think this is connected to the council. I think the bribes were to get councillors to turn a blind eye while they "accidentally" start preparing the land, and there'll be a little mix-up, and it'll be in quite the wrong place to what they applied for, but by then it'll be too late for anyone to do anything except maybe fine them."

"They can't do that," Mortimer said.

Beaufort gave an enormous, toothy smile. "Well then," he said. "We better do something about it, hadn't we?"

Miriam and Mortimer sighed in unison.

THEY FILED out into the early evening light, and Beaufort headed for the final shed. Alice started to follow, then paused. She'd heard a car go past on the road beyond the farm track earlier, but this sound was steadier, and growing. "Wait."

"Oh no – is someone coming?" Miriam asked.

Alice walked across the farmyard, peering down the track. Yes, it was unmistakable now. A car engine, rumbling powerfully, approaching fast. Alice wondered if it was just bad timing, or if there were cameras in the sheds. Either way, it was too late now. "Back into the car," she said to the dragons, and they fled to the SUV, not even Beaufort arguing. Miriam hurried after them, closing the back door and hiding them from even perceptive eyes behind the tinted window. Alice crossed to the gate, and by the time the car pulled up she was opening it, smiling at the occupant. "Hello there," she called. "Are you looking for the Elliots, too?"

The man didn't return the smile, just pulled into the yard and stopped in the middle. He got out, big and bearded, inspecting the women with a frown on his face. "I'm not looking for anyone. I'm the new owner."

"Oh, how lovely." Alice advanced with her hand held out. "Alice Martin. Chair of the Toot Hansell W.I."

The man studied her for a moment, then said, "You're trespassing."

She put both hands on the head of her cane, the tip resting in the dirt between her feet. "We're fundraising for the church. We just wanted to stop by and see if the Elliots had anything they'd like to donate to the charity sale next month. But as they're gone, I don't suppose you have anything to hand, Mr ...?" She trailed off expectantly and he scowled at her, then at Miriam, who had her teeth bared in something that was supposed to be a smile. He stared at her for a moment, then looked back at Alice.

"No. Not interested. Don't come back here."

"Understood. Terribly sorry to inconvenience you. Perhaps you'd like to pop by the fete—"

"Get out." He didn't raise his voice. He seemed like the sort of person who rarely needed to.

She smiled up at him. "Of course. Please accept our apologies." She walked back to the SUV, feeling the man's glare on her back and seeing Miriam scrambling in the passenger side. She lost one flip-flop in the process and had to go back for it. Alice paused, turning slowly on her heel.

"Just a question, though. Purely out of interest."

"*Alice,*" Miriam hissed from the car.

"I told you to get out." His voice rumbled in his chest, low and menacing, and answering rumbles came from the back of the SUV. Alice held one hand out behind her in a very small gesture of *stop.*

"Where have all the sheep gone? What on earth will you do with an empty farm?"

The man looked at the ground and shook his head. "Bloody small towns. Chair of the gossip council, did you say? None of your business, Alice Martin. Now get off my property before I call the police on you."

Alice smiled. "Well, we wouldn't want that."

"You certainly wouldn't." The man folded his arms and rocked back on his heels. "Off you go now."

Alice climbed into the SUV and backed around, leaning out the window to say, "You'll close the gate for us, won't you?"

The man waved them off, watching as they drove away. In the rear-view mirror, Alice saw him take his phone from his pocket and make a call.

"Ooh, Alice!" Miriam dropped back in her seat, pressing one hand to her chest. "What on earth were you doing?"

Alice gave her an amused look. "The worst thing one can do is look guilty."

"But you gave him your real name and everything!"

"Of course I did. Nothing to be gained from hiding. Besides, he thinks I'm just some local busybody now."

No one answered for a moment, then Miriam looked at the dragons. "What did you think?"

"I couldn't catch much from in the car," Beaufort said. "He just seemed as he was. A big angry man. Nothing unusual about that at all."

"So you couldn't tell if he was involved in forcing them off the land or anything?"

Beaufort raised his eyebrow ridges at her. "It's scents, Miriam. Not magic."

Miriam sighed and said, "Can we go home now?"

"I think that sounds like an excellent idea," Alice said.

❧

AS THEY TURNED down the lane to Miriam's house Alice spotted a very familiar dark blue VW Golf sitting outside the little gate, both front doors open. A leg protruded from each, and as they drew closer the legs were joined by the bodies of the two detective inspectors.

"Oh no," Miriam wailed. "Oh, he *did* call the police!"

"Of course he didn't, Miriam," Alice said. "A person like that never calls the police."

"Well, they're *here*," Miriam said, then sighed. "I'm sorry."

"You need some tea," Mortimer said. "Cake, too, most likely."

Alice parked just behind the Golf, and DI Adams folded her arms as they got out. "I've been calling you all afternoon."

Alice frowned, and retrieved her bag from the car. "Oh dear. It's still on silent." She had noticed the missed calls when she'd texted Miriam from the pub, but she'd had rather a lot to think about at the time.

"Oh dear," DI Adams agreed.

"How about you, Auntie Miriam?" Colin demanded. "You didn't answer either."

"I think my phone's still in the kitchen." She seemed to have gone a little grey.

Alice let the dragons out of the car and said, "Shall we have that cup of tea, then?"

"Oh yes, please," Mortimer said, and scooted for the gate, then yelped and jumped sideways. "Sorry, sorry," he said to something Alice couldn't see.

DI Adams shook her phone at Alice. "Phone on."

"As you say."

THEY SAT around Miriam's little, well-scrubbed kitchen table with mismatched mugs of tea and two banana cakes carved into generous slices. Mortimer was back on the rug in front of the Aga, hugging his plate to his chest and staring mistrustfully at a spot on the floor. The spot had inhaled three slices of cake as they were handed to the dragons, so Alice felt he was probably right to be wary.

DI Adams leaned her forearms on the table and said, "I didn't really want to meet here, but as we couldn't get hold of either of you, we had no choice."

"Why didn't you want to meet here?" Miriam asked, carving another slice of cake.

"Because there have been developments. And it's best if you're not associated with the police, Alice."

"I see," Alice said, taking the knife from Miriam, who appeared to have seized up.

"You need to know that you can stand down at any time," Colin said. His shoulders looked higher and tighter than usual.

"Well, that's all very well, but I have no intention of doing so."

"You might, after you hear what we've found out," he said.

"We've found out a few things ourselves."

DI Adams had picked up her mug, and now she all but slammed it down, tea slopping onto the table. "Tell me you haven't been poking around. That was not the agreement."

Alice gave the younger woman a cool look, but DI Adams returned it unflinchingly.

"Alice."

"We just talked to Bryan. You'd already talked to him, after all."

"No poking around. That's what we said. No poking around!"

Alice sipped her tea and said, "I merely suggested to him that maybe there were some things he couldn't tell the police, but he could tell me."

"And?"

"And someone was offering the councillors money, although he wasn't quite sure what for. It was all most unclear."

Colin said around a mouthful of cake, "Confirms what we found out."

DI Adams leaned across the table, fixing Alice with a quite impressively fierce gaze. "The people offering this money may be dangerous, Alice. We have reason to believe that they are. You do not want to draw attention to yourself, do you understand?"

Alice was a veteran of fierce gazes, so she just nodded and said, "Of course."

DI Adams scowled at her, and for a moment the table was silent. Then there was a squeak, a splash, and a sudden upheaval under the table.

"What was that?" Miriam yelped. She'd dropped a slice of cake in her cup and cracked her knees so hard on the underside of the table that everyone's tea had made a break for freedom. "I kicked something! It moved!"

"It's just Dandy. Sorry." DI Adams got up to fetch a cloth from the sink as Alice peeked under the table.

"He's still very invisible."

"Yeah, that doesn't seem to change."

"You don't really want to see him," Mortimer put in. "He's alarming."

Alice harboured a suspicion that Mortimer was more alarmed by the vanishing cake.

"So, Alice," Colin said, once the table was clean again. "You're determined to carry on."

"Of course."

The inspectors exchanged glances, and he sighed. "Please be careful. We can't have someone on you all the time, because we don't want to tip these people off. It might make things even more risky."

"I'm sure I can handle myself quite well, Colin. Forewarned is forearmed, after all."

Miriam put her cup down with a clatter and said, "Armed?"

"Figure of speech, dear," Alice said, handing her the cloth.

"We'll be around to keep an eye on you, anyway," Beaufort said. "Won't we, lad?"

"Yes," Mortimer said with great emphasis, then sighed and slumped against the stove.

"Thank you, dears," she said, and turned back to the inspectors. "Can you give me details?"

"As much as we have." DI Adams leaned forward again, talking in quick, clipped sentences with her dark eyes fixed on Alice. Alice listened carefully, asking a question here and there, feeling a pleasurable little shivering running up her spine.

Yes, sometimes retirement really was a little too easy for her.

ALICE FELT a little bad for Miriam, who had become paler and paler while DI Adams told them about the potentially crooked property developers, and who had also managed to put her feet on Dandy again and almost fall out of her chair. She was now perched on the seat with her feet tucked under her, clutching her crumb-festooned tea in both hands while Colin, steering the conversation away from suspicious deaths, drugs, and bribes, told them about a case he'd had the previous week. A garden centre had been complaining about someone stealing their rhododendrons. It had been happening every night for a week, and as they had no CCTV he'd decided to spend the night sitting behind a stack of potting mix bags waiting for the thieves to turn up. Just before dawn, a rustling at the fence had alerted him that the culprits had arrived, and he'd jumped out to confront half a dozen startled cows, who had discovered a loose fencepost and were letting themselves in every night for a snack.

DI Adams pushed her plate away and said, "See? This is what I mean. I catch criminals, you catch cows."

"You say that like it's a bad thing," Colin said, and she shook her head.

Alice smiled, and said, "I guess I see both your points."

"I prefer the cows," Miriam said. She was still curled up on her chair, but her face was a little closer to her normal colour.

"Now, then," Beaufort said. "Do you want to hear what we found out today?"

"You mean other than the husband's suspicions?" DI Adams asked.

"Oh yes. There's more," Alice said. "Go on, Beaufort. You discovered it."

He settled himself more comfortably and said, "Well—"

DI Adams' phone beeped a text message, and as she was fishing it out of her pocket, Colin's rang. She checked the screen of her phone as he answered his.

"Ah," she said, and looked at Colin.

"Yeah," he was saying. "Send a pin drop." He put the phone down, and looked at DI Adams. They both looked at Alice.

Miriam stared at them all, her eyes wide.

"It's another councillor," Colin said. "Charles Morgan."

Miriam gave a strangled little gasp, and Alice nodded. "Well," she said. "You two best be going, then."

DI Adams drummed her fingers on the table. "Alice, I really think you should stand down. This is looking more and more serious."

"Then you need inside information more than ever."

"Not when it's going to put you this much at risk."

"I agree," Colin said. "If they're removing anyone who suspects them, and they realise you're connected to the police, you're in danger just being there."

"I could take the bribe. Go along with it."

"It won't work," DI Adams said. "They'll look at your background and know you won't take bribes."

"You make it sound as if just being ex-RAF puts me beyond reproach. I assure you, inspectors, no one is."

"They may not be willing to take that risk. Especially when you've been in the papers as instrumental in three police investigations."

"And how else do you propose to move forward? You have very little to work with."

DI Adams spread her fingers wide on the table. "Alice. We're not messing around here."

"Neither am I. I am the only person you have in a position to actually gather evidence. I will be careful. Now go see what's happened to poor Charles."

There was a moment's silence, and Colin clasped both hands over his head, looking at the ceiling. "I do not like this."

"Neither do I." DI Adams got up, the legs of her chair loud on the stone floor as she pushed it back. "But you're right in that we don't have much choice. Alice, please answer your phone. Don't ask too many questions. Eyes and ears only. Please."

"I shall do my best," Alice said, and DI Adams gave her a look that said very clearly that she knew Alice wasn't agreeing with her. But she put her mug in the sink and headed for the door, Colin trailing after her with one hand rubbing the back of his neck, and for a moment there was silence in the kitchen.

Then Beaufort said in an aggrieved tone. "First they weren't interested in how I knew about the crash, now they're not interested in what I found today. One could feel very dismissed."

"I'm sure they don't mean anything by it," Alice said. "They have got another murder, by the sound of things."

"They'd probably rather you weren't finding things out," Mortimer mumbled. He'd taken on the deep green of the stove, and seemed to be trying to become one with it.

"I'm finding out very useful things," Beaufort said.

"You are," Alice agreed. "How did you know about the crash?"

"Nellie told me. She was complaining about some of the tributaries having unusual run-off in them, and then the car in the pond. That's why I was curious about the farm. That's where she said the run-off came from."

"How intriguing," Alice said.

"Yes. I mean sprites can be … what's that phrase, Miriam? For when one overreacts a lot? They use it on your television sometimes." He pronounced television with the care of a foreign word, which Alice supposed it was, for him.

Miriam frowned. "Drama queen?"

"Yes, that's it. Sprites can be drama queens, but she was very insistent that something was wrong."

Mortimer sighed. "Nellie's always insistent that everything's wrong. All the time."

"Drama queen," Beaufort said, and grinned broadly.

"Can I put my feet down?" Miriam asked. "Is the dandy gone?"

"Oh yes," Mortimer said. "He ate all the cake, then left."

Alice thought Mortimer had done quite a good job on the cake himself, but she just said, "Shall we have some more tea? Maybe some toast? I don't feel like going home yet."

"That's a wonderful idea," Miriam said, and Alice squeezed her arm as she got up to find the bread. Some days just called for second dinners.

13
DI ADAMS

The house smelled of cooking, garlic and herbs and warmth, and DI Collins' belly rumbled as DI Adams led the way to the kitchen, pulling on gloves as she went.

"Crime scenes always make you hungry?" she asked.

"There was less food involved at that meeting than I expected."

"There was banana cake."

"We were meeting W.I. members. That's normally two kinds of cake, minimum. Plus I think your Dandy ate more than his fair share."

DI Adams snorted, and stopped in the doorway to the kitchen as the crime scene photographer took a shot of the body face down on the floor, dressing gown open to either side like green plaid wings. The yellow-tiled kitchen floor ran on into a conservatory, and warm light rose from lamps on side tables, making the pink and green curtains glow. A cake box sat open on the kitchen island, and the body sprawled on a lime green rug, feet still caught in the legs of a bar stool. A pink cushion had been pulled loose and lay on the floor like a puff of cotton candy. DI Adams touched her fingers to the corner of her eye, feeling a slight twitch. It was like a decorator had been briefed to recreate a sweet shop.

"Ay-up, Colin," the photographer said.

"Alright, Lucas?"

"Better than this one."

DI Adams gestured at the room in general. "Can we?"

"Sure. Done on the photos. DI Adams, isn't it?"

"Yes." She crouched next to the body, examining the face where it was turned to the side. She knew Charles Morgan was in his sixties, but his cheeks were swollen and red, lines smoothed away. It made him look young. "Cause of death?"

"Asphyxiation due to closure of airways from swelling, from first impressions." Lucas took a step back to give her more room. "So what do I call you?"

"Adams." She didn't have to look up from her examination of the body to know the men were exchanging glances over her head.

"She claims she's not posh, but she goes by her last name," Collins said. "My DI sense says she might not be being entirely truthful." He crouched down on the other side of the body. "Allergic reaction?" he asked.

"Anaphylactic shock, yeah," Lucas said.

"Any idea what to?" DI Adams was checking the pockets of the dressing gown, but so far all she'd found were some mints and a Far Side cartoon clipped from a newspaper. She hadn't thought they still ran those.

"We'll know more after the post-mortem. Really, just Adams?"

"Yes. Is he married?"

"Yeah. The wife found him when she got home from Zumba."

"She here?" Collins asked.

"In the dining room. A PC's in with her."

DI Adams looked at Collins, trying not to show just how much she'd rather keep going through a dead man's pockets than speak to a widow. Grief was so … messy.

"We best go talk to her," he said.

"Um. Yes." She got up slowly, taking an evidence bag from the counter to pop the mints and comic in. "I suppose we should." Movement caught the corner of her eye, and she spotted Dandy nosing around the conservatory. She sighed. She'd told him to stay in the car, but closed doors didn't seem to be very effective on him. Or walls, for that matter. Still, at least no one could actually see if he left dog hair all over the crime scene.

Collins peered into the cake box. "These look nice." There were three cupcakes still nestled inside, crowned with swirls of white and pink icing and dotted with little blue sugar flowers.

"Probably the culprits," Lucas said. "Peanut allergy, if I had to guess."

"They still look nice." Collins led the way out of the room, and DI Adams trailed after him, notebook in hand. It could have been accidental. It *looked* accidental, but the way things were going, she rather doubted it.

THE WOMAN SEATED at the head of the dining room table was dressed in some very high-end gym gear, her hair bundled up into a bun on top of her head and a headband holding any stray wisps back. She was clutching a well-used tissue in one hand and the box in the other, and when she saw the inspectors she wiped her face hurriedly and straightened up.

"What's going on?" she whispered.

"Mrs Morgan?" DI Adams asked, sitting down on one side of the table as Collins pulled out a chair on the other.

"Please, call me Shirley. Mrs Morgan always sounds so old." She wiped her nose with the tissue and gave them a very small smile. Her face didn't move quite right when she did, and DI Adams thought Shirley might have serious objections to the ageing process.

"Shirley, the techs are almost done in the kitchen, then the body can be removed—" She stopped as Shirley gave a choked wail and covered her face with the tissue as well as she could, given its wadded state. DI Adams wrinkled her nose.

Collins shook his head and leaned forward, placing his big hands within reach of the sobbing woman. "Shirley, I know this is such a terrible time. Is someone coming over to stay with you?"

She snuffled and wiped her nose again. DI Adams suppressed a shudder and took a clean tissue from the box, holding it out hopefully. Shirley grabbed it, but just mushed it in with the dirty one. "Yes. My friend's on her way."

"That's good," Collins said. "Well done. You need a little company right now."

She nodded jerkily, and clutched one of his hands in both hers. "I just went out to my class! That was all! I always go to my class! Charles knows!" She froze. "*Knew*. He *knew*." She started to cry again.

Collins patted her hands with his free one. "You poor thing."

Shirley wiped her face, and DI Adams passed her another tissue. "What do I *do?* I mean, I have to tell his mum, and his sister, and, and I—" She dropped her face onto her forearms, and Collins made reassuring noises while DI Adams looked at the ceiling. She wanted to get on with the bit where they actually found out useful information, but she rather felt she'd best just let Collins do this at his own pace, painfully slow though it was.

Eventually Shirley's sobs eased, and Collins said, "Can you tell us if your husband was allergic to anything?"

She nodded, taking a new tissue without any urging. She had at least half a dozen of them wadded up into one awful mess now. "Shellfish."

"Shellfish?" DI Adams said carefully, unable to wait any longer. "Not peanuts or anything like that?"

"No." Shirley scowled at her. "Just shellfish. He was terribly sensitive to even the smallest amount. He always had an EpiPen on him."

Not this time, he hadn't. Not in his pyjamas and dressing gown, and evidently not handy in the kitchen. DI Adams wondered just how often you might find shellfish in cupcakes. Probably not often, she imagined. Even in the realm of "interesting" new flavours, that seemed a bit off.

"And what did Charles have to eat today?" Collins asked gently. "Anything unusual?"

"Just the damn cakes." She sniffled. "He was just … I *told* him he had to stop eating cake, but he just wouldn't listen! And now look what's happened!"

"Why did he have to stop eating cake?" DI Adams asked. "Did he have health problems?"

"He would have. Sugar's poison."

"Oh," the inspectors said together, and for a moment there was silence except for Shirley's small, regular sniffs. Then DI Adams said, "Do you know where the cakes came from?"

She shrugged. "I don't know. He was always sneaking them. I knew. Icing sugar on his shirts and jam on his sleeves. I used to get so angry." Her voice had grown very small, and DI Adams asked the next question carefully, hoping she wasn't about to set the woman crying again.

"Did Charles mention any troubles at work? Or at the council?"

Shirley looked up, her eyes red and raw-looking. "No. Why? It was an allergic reaction, wasn't it?"

"Of course. Just trying to get a … ah, picture of the general situation."

Shirley blinked at that, then said, "Because that might tell you where he got the shellfish from?"

"Um, yes." Something nudged her leg and she ignored it.

"But it's almost instant. It's not like he might have gone to lunch somewhere new yesterday and there was fish sauce on the veggies or something."

"Right." DI Adams drummed her fingers on the table, and this time when her leg was bumped she glanced down to see Dandy with something in his mouth. She pushed him away as unobtrusively as she could manage. "But was he especially stressed recently? Worried about anything in particular?"

"Why are you asking this? Are you suggesting someone *poisoned* him?"

"Just routine questions," Collins said, going back to his arm-patting. "We need to ask these things."

"Routine." She still looked doubtful, but said, "He was a little stressed, maybe. I think it was to do with the council. He was under pressure to agree to some business thing or something like that. I don't know. He didn't talk about that stuff much."

DI Adams rubbed the back of her neck, thinking of Alice. Dragons weren't going to be much help when apparent non-drug users in perfect health were having cocaine-induced heart attacks at the wheel and shellfish was turning up in the cupcakes of allergy sufferers. Dandy rested his head on her knee, and she petted him absently.

A uniformed officer knocked on the door and peered in when DI Adams called out, "Come in!"

"There's a Josie Fyfe here?"

"Josie!" Shirley said, rubbing her painfully red nose again. "Can she come in?"

Collins looked at DI Adams, and she shrugged. There didn't seem to be much more to ask. "Yes, I think we're done here," he said, and disentangled himself gently from Shirley's grip. "You look after yourself, okay? And call us if you need anything." He fished a card out of his phone case and handed it to her. "Especially if you remember anything that you think might be important. Anything at all."

Shirley nodded, her eyes already brimming over, and DI Adams thanked her then headed for the door at the quickest pace she could manage and not seem too rude. Hopefully. Another woman in workout gear was waiting impatiently at the door, her handbag clutched in both hands, and she gave them a look that suggested this whole thing was their fault before pushing into the dining room.

Outside, DI Adams breathed in the cooler, clearer air as she walked down the little path to the front gate, Dandy trotting next to her. He seemed to have taken a liking to a magazine and was carrying it with him, but as Collins hadn't said anything about being able to see a floating glossy mag, she didn't bother taking it off him. That would look weirder. She checked the street instead. There weren't any gawkers gathered around the police cars, but she could see people standing on front steps and peering around curtains, and there was a man walking his dog astonishingly slowly on the other side of the street. She rubbed her eyes and checked the time.

"'The body?'" DI Collins said. "I thought all you big city cops got sensitivity training and that sort of thing."

DI Adams didn't fancy admitting that she'd had to take the course three times, and then the instructor had only really passed her because he'd given it up as a bad job. "Well, what was with all the patting and stroking? I half-expected you to scratch her behind the ears and offer her a treat."

Collins snorted. "In policing around here, we're sometimes required to have these things called people skills."

"Yet another reason to dislike the country."

"Well, look. You can practise yours." Collins nodded at Ervin, who was waving enthusiastically beyond the cordon of cars.

"Not a chance." DI Adams beeped her car open and tried to ignore the journalist as he hurried over.

"Another death on the council! This is looking like a pattern, wouldn't you say?"

"No comment," DI Adams said, getting in the car.

"Oh, come on! I helped you out!"

"You did," Collins agreed, leaning on the car as DI Adams slammed her door. "But that was just you doing your civic duty, right?"

Ervin snorted. "Obviously the answer's no, but I can't say that without looking like scum, can I?"

DI Adams slid her window down. "You already look like a journalist."

"Harsh. But I feel we've got a nice back and forth going here. A repartee? A bond?"

Collins wedged himself into the passenger side. "He's right, of course. There is a bond."

"Like a bail bond?" DI Adams asked, starting the car.

"Something like that."

"Come on." Ervin leaned on the window, all dimples and dark curls. "At least give me an official statement."

"I can officially state that you're an annoying little prat," Adams said, and pulled away, leaving the journalist standing in the middle of the street scowling after them.

"You see," Collins said, "your people skills are excellent in these sorts of situations."

"I think so."

"However, for the good of our partnership, I think I should talk to victims and grieving widows."

"I'm in complete agreement." She glanced at her watch. "Dinner? Cake in Toot Hansell didn't quite cut it for me."

"Dinner," Collins agreed, leaning back in his seat. "Then we need to revisit the Alice Martin problem."

"And figure out how we're going to pin two – maybe three – deaths on a development company that we have no evidence has actually done anything wrong."

"I think this sort of mental effort calls for pizza."

DI Adams started to point out that she wasn't sure pizza was really considered brain food, but was interrupted by her phone shrilling through the car's speakers. The display flashed up *Alice, W.I.* "Got a plan yet?" she asked Collins.

"Not a one."

"Me either." She hit answer. "Hello, Alice."

"Detective Inspector. I hope I'm not interrupting."

"No, you're fine. I'm in the car with Collins."

"Hello, Alice," Collins added.

"Hello, Colin, dear. I just thought I should update you, as you did have to leave in rather a rush."

"We did," DI Adams said, heading out of the mess of quiet cul-de-sacs and back toward town. "Are you alright?"

"Yes, quite alright, thank you. However, we have discovered something rather interesting."

The inspectors looked at each other, and DI Adams said, "What's that?"

"At least one empty farm, DI Adams. Stockpiles of drums, possibly diesel. Earthmoving equipment."

"Alice," Collins said. "Have you been trespassing?"

"Merely checking on neighbours."

DI Adams thought that, even for Alice, she might be stretching the definition of neighbourly by romping around farms. "Maybe they're on holiday?" she offered.

"The houses were empty."

"You went *inside?*" DI Adams demanded.

"There might have been someone in trouble."

DI Adams pinched the bridge of her nose and decided that

pizza sounded like an excellent idea. With extra cheese, and jalapeños. "In what world is that not poking around, Alice?"

"It may be completely unrelated. But if you should like to look into it, I can text you the address."

"We can't go poking into buildings without reason," Collins said.

"Of course not. But if someone were worried about their neighbours vanishing …?"

DI Adams shook her head at the phone. "No, Alice. No making complaints. You don't want to draw any attention to yourself."

"Oh no, not me. Miriam's already taken her concerns to the police, and asked for Colin specifically."

In the absence of a handy stop sign, DI Adams considered pulling over just so she could hit her head on the wheel a couple of times. Instead she tightened her grip until her knuckles hurt and said, "This is not keeping a low profile."

"Maybe not, but, as you say, you can't go poking around without a reason. Now you have a reason." Alice's tone was dismissive. "Do let me know if you want that address."

There was a moment's silence, then the phone went dead. DI Adams concentrated on making her hands loosen on the wheel, but it wasn't easy.

"I really think pizza is the only way to handle this," Collins said after a moment. "Possibly with beer."

DI Adams looked at the car clock and nodded. "Nothing else can happen tonight, right?"

As she spoke, Dandy pushed his head between the seats, offering DI Adams his slightly soggy prize. She made a *gurk* sound, but took it, handing it to Collins.

"*Ew*. Where did that come from?"

"Dandy wants me to have it, for some reason. He got it from the house, I guess."

"Did he, now." Collins unfolded the magazine, leaning forward to catch the light as the streetlights started to come on. "It's not a magazine, Adams."

"It's not?"

"No. It's a brochure. Want to guess what for?"

DI Adams hit the heel of one hand lightly on the wheel. "Not really."

"A new way of living," Collins read aloud. *"Sympathetic to the glory of the Dales* – the glory of the Dales? Really? – *yet offering all the amenities of modern city dwelling. Exclusive, luxurious, secure. Country life, but better."* He snorted. "Offered by, of course—"

"BelleVue Developments?"

"Indeed. And"—he poked inside—"a little slobbered on, but there appear to be a couple of letters in here."

"What do they say?"

"No return address, not signed." He flicked the overhead light on. *"We understand living requires a certain standard. We can help you achieve your ideal."*

DI Adams pulled over so she could squint at the letter. "That's all?"

"That's it. Sounds like some sort of get rich quick scheme."

"What's the next one?" She scratched Dandy under the chin and scrubbed at the top of his head as his tail beat a happy rhythm against the back seats. "Good boy!"

DI Collins looked up from the brochure, his eyebrows raised.

"*Of course* not you. Dandy."

"Right." He went back to the papers. *"Your reticence concerns us."*

"And?"

"And nothing." He turned the sheet over to check the back, then flipped through the brochure. "Nothing else in here."

"Well, that proves sod all."

"Wait – one more." It was tucked into a pocket in the back page, and he unfolded it, holding it so DI Adams could see the stark black print. *"Choices have consequences."*

They stared at it for a moment, then DI Adams said, "That is no use at all."

"World's worst fortune cookies," Collins agreed. "But they were inside a BelleVue Developments brochure."

"Tenuous, but enough to ask some questions."

"Do we deserve pizza now?"

She gave Dandy a one-armed hug and said, "We should have it either way."

Collins shook his head. "I don't think I'll ever get used to the invisible dog thing."

"You and me both." She reached up to turn the overhead light out and he caught her arm.

"What's on your sleeve?"

She peered at it uncertainly. "It looks like …"

"Cake crumbs?"

DI Adams lifted Dandy's chin to the light, spotting icing on his nose and more crumbs caught in his dreadlocks. "Oh no …"

"You don't think—" Collins phone rang, cutting him off, and they both looked at it apprehensively. He tapped answer. "Lucas? Really? Gone? No, we didn't pick them up. No, didn't see anyone else around. Sure, hang on." He looked up at Adams and said, "You didn't take the cupcakes, did you?"

"No," she said, and glared at Dandy, who sat back into the seat and thumped his tail. "Not me."

"Yeah, sorry, Lucas. I'm sure they'll, um, turn up." DI Collins hung up, looked at DI Adams and said, "Well."

"Yeah." She started the car again. "Pizza?"

14
MORTIMER

"No," Thompson said. The cat had appeared at the kitchen window, peering in at them with narrowed green eyes and demanding to know why no one had considered that he might be waiting for his dinner. Miriam had found a tin of salmon in the pantry, and now he was sitting on the table with salmon juice on his chin and his tail flicking from side to side, threatening to end up in the butter. "No, we will not be asking around the farm cats to see if anyone saw anything dodgy going on."

Mortimer wondered if that was the royal we, or if Thompson really did think he could stop Beaufort and Alice from asking questions.

"See here, Thompson," the High Lord said, "we don't know what happened to the people from the farm. We don't even know if it might be more than one farm. We just want to be sure everyone's alright, and not draw too much unwanted attention by going there ourselves."

"No, you see here, Beaufort," the cat started, and Alice clicked her tongue.

"Thompson. There's no need to be rude."

"*I* am not being rude. *You* are all behaving like particularly inbred poodles."

There was a moment's silence while everyone tried to decipher just how much of an insult that was. Mortimer felt it was probably deeply offensive, given cats' low opinions of the intelligence of dogs. He personally thought dogs, terrifyingly toothy though they were, were probably quite intelligent. After all, one never saw them caught up in Investigations.

"I will withhold all fresh fish and kick you off my bed unless you stop acting like a lout," Alice said.

"You still let him sleep on your bed?" Miriam asked. "Isn't that — I mean, doesn't it feel a bit weird?"

"He's still just a cat," Alice said.

"*Just— just—*" Thompson spluttered. "Why am I even here? What have I done to be lumbered with the responsibility of Watching a village full of meddling senior citizens and misguided dragons? What god have I displeased?"

"Thompson, you are being a drama queen," Beaufort said, with some satisfaction.

The cat glared at him so furiously Mortimer would have laughed if he hadn't been just as worried about the meddling and misguidedness of certain people. "You tell me if I'm being a drama queen when word gets back to the Watch that you've been asking questions. Questions that indicate you're taking too much of an interest in the affairs of humans."

"Dragons and the Watch have always respected each other's boundaries."

"We have. But the main duty of the Watch is to keep humans and Folk apart. And that includes dragons getting funny ideas."

There was silence in the kitchen for a moment, and Mortimer could hear the low rumble of the fire in the belly of Miriam's Aga, not unlike a dragon itself.

"So, you won't help us," Beaufort said.

"Beaufort, I'm asking you to drop this. I don't know what happened on the farm. I can sniff around, but I can only ask so many questions. If it was Watch business, I'd know about it. So it's human stuff, which means I can't be too interested, and is all the more reason for you to drop it."

"I don't understand," Miriam said. She was clutching her mug in both hands as if terrified she might drop it. "If your job is keeping humans and Folk apart, surely human business is your business."

"Only as much as it impacts Folk. We don't go sticking our noses where they don't belong, unlike some people."

Alice steepled her fingers on the table. "What if it did impact Folk? Or you were worried it might?"

Thompson narrowed his eyes. "I'm not as much of a patsy as your dear police are."

"Beaufort, you did say Nelly was rather agitated about the car in her pond, and someone maybe putting something nasty in the water supply. That sounds like Folk business to me, protecting a sprite."

Beaufort grinned. "Nelly was *very* upset. And you know the dryads are going to be restless if they think someone might start chopping their trees down. Anything could happen."

"And I don't see how humans could have moved all those sheep without people knowing about it," Miriam said, then looked like she wished she hadn't. Mortimer stroked his tail, as if that might keep his scales attached. He'd lost two at some point this afternoon, and he just hoped they were in the car and not lying in a farmyard somewhere, waiting to be picked up by a nosy human.

Thompson gave a very theatrical sigh and said, "Great. So there's a possibility that the Watch may *need* to become involved, and you want me to draw their attention to it?"

"Of course not," Beaufort said, and there was silence for a moment.

Thompson muttered something under his breath that might have been *curses on dragons and the Women's Institute,* then he said, "Scallops. I haven't had scallops since, ooh, my second life, I think. I should like scallops."

"Scallops can be arranged," Alice said.

"And cream. Plus I want to try caviar."

"Don't push it."

MORTIMER KNEW he wasn't going to sleep. He never slept very much while there was an Investigation afoot, and he was starting to wonder what the consequences were of being a permanently sleep-deprived dragon. But at least he could get some more work done.

He lit the chimineas in the workshop, and angled the prisms in the roof so that they caught the light from the solar-powered lanterns and reflected it onto his bench. Amelia and Gilbert had been busy, by the look of things. Baskets full of baubles and gliders were lined up along one bench, and there was a crate with a label on it which read *Competition Entries* in wobbly dragon script. There were only five or six … things … in it, and Mortimer pulled one out, examining it dubiously. It looked like a teddy bear as designed by a mole who had read about them once, ten years ago. There were spines on its arms and concertinaed glider wings stuck between its six legs, and it had very large, very intimidating teeth. Mortimer ticked a claw off them, then put the thing back gingerly and picked up a creation that looked like a delicately folded paper flower. He lifted it to the light, admiring the thinness of the scales, and tapped it gently to test the strength. Oh yes. This was excellent. He held it a little closer, and it flung its petals wide in a sudden, violent unfurling, then launched itself off his paw. He jerked away with a yelp as it snapped at his snout, barely missing him. It bounced off the floor, still snapping, and as he tried to trap it with an empty basket it latched firmly onto his tail.

"*Ow!*" he wailed, throwing the basket at it and only succeeding in knocking the crate of competition entries flying. He looked around wildly for the misshapen teddy bear, just in case it was some sort of joint attack, and a shout came from the tunnel entrance.

"Don't touch them, don't-– Oh." Amelia skidded into the cavern, tripping on a bauble and all but falling into him. "Oh, *sorry!*"

"What *is* this thing?"

"I don't know. Harriet made it. You know she's been doing all the dragonlet care while Violet's on hunting detail. I think she's channelling some frustration."

"Well, can we get it off, please?" He was glad the six-limbed teddy hadn't started marching about, but the flower did have a very firm hold of his tail, and the tip was starting to go green.

"Yes, there's a trick—" Amelia grabbed the thing and pulled.

"*Ow!* That is *not* a trick. That's just you pulling it."

"It worked before." She tugged again, and one of his scales flaked sadly away. "Oops."

"*Amelia!*"

"Sorry, sorry!" She examined the hungry flower, and gave it an experimental shake. "You didn't see Gilbert on the way back, did you?"

"No – why?"

"He's …" she hesitated, then stuck a claw into the middle of the flower. It released Mortimer and she hurled it across the cavern before it could snap at her. It hit the wall, scattering tools off their hooks, and bounced about the bench, snapping furiously. Mortimer had the uneasy feeling that it was *growling,* and he mentally crossed Harriet off the list of potential craftsdragons, unless they decided to diversify into unusual forms of home security.

"Thank you. He's what?"

"He couldn't stop fussing about the empty farm, and when you and Beaufort didn't come back, he said he was going out to talk to the dryads."

"How long ago?"

"A while." Amelia fidgeted. "I'm worried, Mortimer. I mean, I know he doesn't fly, so everything takes longer, but what's he doing out there?"

Mortimer thought of the still, empty fields and Gilbert's theories about experimental sites, as well as the young dragon's propensity for stealing Christmas turkeys to stop them being eaten, and filling the grand cavern with chickens he'd "rescued" from what he thought was a terrible prison, but was actually a chicken rescue centre itself.

"Oh no," he said.

❧

THE LIGHT WAS ALMOST GONE, but dragon eyes catch and refract the smallest amount of illumination, and as Mortimer and Amelia launched themselves off the ledge outside the cavern they could see the lake like a shivering mirror below them, reflecting the boulders as slices of darkness and catching the stars that were emerging from the thinning cloud. There were no other dragons out. They'd be sharing rabbits in the warmth of the grand cavern or curled into the security of their own, barbecues pumping heat across their scales and setting them into dream-filled sleep. Mortimer and Amelia flew in silence, their broad wings creaking in the still air, their scales taking on the colour of the night.

If they hadn't been so quiet they would have missed it. An

explosion of shouting from the grand cavern, filtering out through the entrance in such a way that one couldn't be sure if it was cheering or fury, dimly heard and distorted. Mortimer looked away from his scrutiny of the ground, frowning.

"Did you hear that?" he called to Amelia, his voice low.

She was already banking toward the mount. "He wouldn't. He *wouldn't.*"

Mortimer had a funny feeling he would. Gilbert was terribly unshakeable in his beliefs. Mortimer wasn't at all sure the young dragon would stop to think that diving into a cavern full of dragons like Lord Walter (who was rumoured to be the last living dragon to have actually eaten a human) and Rockford (who felt they should never have stopped eating them), and announcing that humans were up to dodgy things on a nearby farm, might not be a good idea. And there were far too many dragons who were less extreme in their views, but still didn't approve of their closeness to the ladies of the W.I. Not that they ever complained about the fact that closeness gave them barbecues and blankets and wool beanies, he added to himself a little sniffily.

But Gilbert wouldn't be thinking that wars could be brought on by the smallest nudge in the right place at the right time – or the wrong place, wrong time, depending on how one looked at it. He'd probably listened to Nellie complain about bottles in her wells and cigarettes in her rivers for too long, or been convinced by the dryads that the end was nigh because there were yellow mushrooms where there used to be red ones. But whatever he was thinking, if he went rushing into the grand cavern shrieking *the humans are coming,* Mortimer wasn't at all sure what the reaction would be. Or rather, he didn't want to think what it might be. Not at all.

They crashed onto the ledge outside the entrance of the grand cavern with their wingtips a breath apart.

"I'm going to kill him," Amelia said, and Mortimer had the sense that he was just catching up with a conversation she'd been having with herself for some time. "I can handle the vegetarianism, I can even handle that he can't fly. But if he tries to get some sort of raiding party going ..." she was already stomping down the passage, her words drifting back to Mortimer in a low, furious growl, and he found himself feeling a twinge of sympathy for Gilbert.

He hurried after Amelia, and the sound of raised dragon voices grew to a roar as they turned the corner in the passage and ran to where it let onto the broad stone floor of the cavern, the vaulted arches of the ceiling smudged with smoke from the fire that burned constantly below the stone seat of the High Lord. Once, the smooth stone that formed the raised seat had been crowned with a throne of broken armour and rusting swords, but Beaufort had done away with it as soon as Mortimer introduced him to barbecues. Instead, a gleaming stainless Weber, one of the big ones with two levels for different foods and an attachment for a spit, stood proudly atop the seat, draped with fireproof blankets that almost obscured the gas bottle beneath. Beaufort sat next to the barbecue with his tail curled around his paws, regarding the cavern with the puzzled look of any older person who just can't comprehend Kids Today, and below him Gilbert was surrounded by jostling young dragons, and Lord Walter was bawling at the top of his not-inconsiderable old lungs for everyone to just *be quiet, old ones take you,* and Lord Margery had the young (but very large) Rockford by the ear, and Lord Pamela was threatening tail tweaks to the lot of them, backed up by furiously puce Lydia.

"Oh no," Amelia said, stopping so abruptly Mortimer almost fell over her. "We're too late."

Mortimer opened his mouth to say that maybe it wasn't as bad as it looked, when Gilbert shouted, "And as well as poisoning the sheep, the dryads say some were *slaughtered!* They're going to clear that land, and then what? What comes next? The forest? The lake? *Our home?"*

"Oh, wow," Mortimer said, and gave Amelia an anxious look. She was rapidly going to the same shade as Lydia.

"We have to stop them!" A young dragon with multicoloured spines shouted. "Humans are a scourge on the earth!"

"*Scourge!*" half a dozen dragons cheered, not sounding very upset about it.

"I told you humans are the *worst!*" Rockford bellowed, his voice bouncing off the walls, then let out a rather unimpressive yelp as Lord Margery twisted his ear in her claws.

"*The worst!*" the chorus agreed.

Amelia covered her snout with one paw. "Where does he find these dragons?"

"He's ... he seems to attract dragons with funny ideas," Mortimer offered.

"This one could get very unfunny, very quickly," Amelia replied.

"Down with humans!" the multicoloured dragon shouted – Isobel, if Mortimer remembered right. "Protect our land!"

"*Down with humans!*" the dragon chorus shrieked.

Gilbert gave them a startled look. "I don't mean *down* with them. They're very nice, mostly. We just need to stop these ones."

"*Scourge!*"

"I was *sleeping!*" Lord Walter bellowed. "Shut up, you ridiculous little hatchlings!"

"*Down with humans!*"

"Um, hang on," Gilbert said.

"We need to *rise up,*" Rockford roared. "Become true dragons ag — *Ow!*"

"Shut up you horrible monster," Lord Margery snarled at him. "Beaufort! What do we do about this?"

"Scourge!"

"If I don't get my sleep in the next ten minutes, I'll eat all of you!" Lord Walter thundered, baring some very worn and unimpressive teeth.

"Rise up!"

"Let Rockford go, you bully!" Isobel shouted at Lord Margery, then ducked behind a handy boulder as the bigger dragon glared at her. "Human-lover!" she squeaked from safety.

Beaufort just stayed where he was, regarding the uproar with the same interest he showed in Miriam's TV when they showed documentaries of far-off countries.

"It's past your bedtime!" Lord Walter bellowed.

"Down with the humans!"

"If we don't stop the humans now, they'll destroy *everything!*" Isobel shrieked.

"Yes, but we can't hurt them!" Gilbert shouted back. "They're our friends!"

"They are no one's friends! They're *monsters!*"

"Monsters!"

"A virus!"

"A virus!"

"No," Gilbert protested, but he was drowned out by Rockford shouting for action, Lord Margery threatening to descale him, Isobel demanding a revolution, and Walter giving up on diplomacy and hitting the nearest young dragon with one very old but very large paw.

"Oh, wow," Mortimer said again, and hoped Beaufort was going to do something, but the High Lord was nodding slightly, as if enjoying a very frank exchange of views on the subject, rather than what looked likely to dissolve into a dragon brawl.

Then a voice cut through the cavern, rising above the clamour with a note of pure fury.

"Gilbert of Cloverly, what did you do?" Amelia roared, and

everyone turned to look at her, her four paws planted firmly on the hard floor, talons drawing white lines across the stone, her wings wide and trembling. Gilbert flushed an alarmed pink.

"Well, look—"

"Don't you 'look' me! What've you been up to?"

"Er—"

"I rather think you should answer your sister," Beaufort said mildly, still looking more interested than alarmed.

"Scourge?" a very small dragon, probably only in his forties, offered, and Lord Walter lifted a paw. The little dragon dived behind a barbecue and fell silent.

"I … well, I was worried! So I went to have a look, and talk to the dryads, and they're all so upset!"

Beaufort nodded. "I see. Well, lad, dryads are …" He stopped, considered for a moment, then finished, "Yes. They're well-known drama queens." He smiled in satisfaction. "I really am getting to use this phrase a lot. Humans have such wonderful expressions."

"Okay," Gilbert said, "but that doesn't change the fact that sheep have been killed, others are missing, and the humans from *three* farms are gone. Three of them! That can't be just a coincidence."

"You may be right, lad. It doesn't mean anything terrible is necessarily going to happen—"

"But I spoke to a dryad who saw earthmoving equipment! They're going to destroy the land! Maybe the woods! Maybe our *home!*"

All eyes went to Beaufort. He nodded, apparently not at all bothered by being interrupted midsentence. "Maybe. But none of that suggests we should risk our secrecy. And *none* of it warrants you coming in here, upsetting everyone."

"And ruining my kip," Lord Walter grumbled, scratching his saggy belly. "Damn kids."

"But sir," Gilbert started, and the High Lord raised a paw.

"No. This was most educational, but when it comes to actual

decisions I think older and calmer heads than yours are called for, Gilbert."

Gilbert looked down at his toes, and Mortimer could see the unhappy lines drawn deep between his eyes.

"Everyone as you were," Beaufort said. "Nothing Gilbert is saying is news to me, and none of it is any cause for alarm. I'm monitoring the situation."

"Damn humans," Lord Walter declared. "Wouldn't put this rubbish past them, though. Bet they'd love to smoke us out."

"They don't even know we exist, Walter," Lord Margery said.

"Bah! When I were a lad—"

"A dragon could still get some respect, and a nice sheep here and there," the other dragon said. "Yes, we know. That was then, this is now."

Lord Walter grumbled, but he limped back to his barbecue, snapping at a young dragon who was standing too close and making her squawk in alarm.

Lord Margery looked at Beaufort. "As always, we trust to your judgement." Her voice was level, and Beaufort nodded.

"And I shall endeavour to be worthy of that trust." He waved at the cluster of younger dragons below the seat. "Off you go, then. That's quite enough fuss for one night."

The dragons dispersed slowly, padding out into the night to their own caverns, and Gilbert tried to sneak away with Isobel between him and Amelia.

"Don't even think about it," she hissed at him, and pointed at the ground in front of her. "Get over here."

He shuffled over, looking at Mortimer instead of Amelia. "I had to check," he pleaded.

"So why didn't you come to us?" his sister demanded. "Or even go to Beaufort directly?"

"Well, um—"

"Beaufort's cool and all, but he's like, the authority, you know?"

Isobel said. She'd stopped a couple of paces away, waiting for Gilbert. "And you two are like, puppets, you know?"

Amelia and Mortimer looked at each other, then Amelia said, "And you're like, talking rubbish. Gilbert, this is ridiculous! I can't believe you've got all caught up in this!"

"Hey," Isobel said. "Gilbert's a revolutionary. He's the new generation, you know?"

Gilbert looked rather pleased with himself, and Amelia swung her head toward Isobel, threateningly low. "What I *know*, is that if you don't get out of here and stop interrupting, I'll smack your silly head in."

Isobel looked as if she wanted to argue, but when Amelia took a step toward her she shrugged and said, "Whatever. Laters," and ambled away down the passage.

Amelia looked back at her brother. "Come with me," she said, and marched up to Beaufort. "Here he is," she said. "What do you want to do with him?"

Beaufort regarded Gilbert with his old gold eyes and said, "I doubt I'm as frightening to him as you are, Amelia."

Amelia went deep orange with pleasure, and rounded on her brother again. "Do you have anything else to tell us? And think long and hard about it, Gilbert. I'll know if you're lying."

Mortimer revised his sense of feeling a little sorry for Gilbert, and felt truly bad for the young dragon as he wilted under his sister's glare.

"I ... might have slashed a few tyres," he said.

"On what?" Mortimer demanded, as Beaufort raised his eyebrow ridges. "Did you go to the farm?"

"No. That would've been a really long way to walk. But there were all these cars parked up at the edge of the wood, and I'm sure they were like enemy scouts or something."

"You ... you just slashed some random tyres?" Amelia asked. Her colour was fading rather rapidly.

"Well, they weren't *random!* I mean, they must've been up to something, right?"

"Or they may not," Beaufort said. "They were just parked by the woods?"

"Yes, sir."

"And it was still light?"

"Yes." Gilbert's voice was getting quieter and quieter.

Beaufort folded one paw over the other and said, "Might there have been a walking path nearby?"

Gilbert looked up with round eyes. "Um. Maybe?"

"I see." The old dragon's voice was solemn, and he looked up at the ceiling. For one moment Mortimer thought Beaufort was trying to control his temper, but when the High Lord looked down again the corners of his mouth were twitching. "And how many tyres did you slash?" he asked, his voice still grave.

"Well – all of them?"

"Ah." Beaufort licked his lips, nodded, then said, "Well. Not much to be done now."

"What?" Amelia demanded. "That's it?"

"Yes," Beaufort said. "I'm more interested in the fact you said *farms,* Gilbert."

"The dryad said there were two other farms the man in the car had gone to, and they were both empty too."

"How interesting." The High Lord nodded. "How very interesting." He looked at Mortimer. "You can punish him."

"Me?"

"Him?" Amelia and Gilbert said.

"Yes, have him clean the workshop or something." Beaufort yawned. "Now let old dragons get their sleep."

"For the gods' sakes, *yes!* Go away, the lot of you!" Walter bellowed from his own barbecue, pulled up to the fire. He refused to sleep anywhere else, because he said Things needed to be kept an eye on.

"Alright," Mortimer said, and led the way out of the cavern, Gilbert trying to avoid Amelia, who was suggesting more and more extreme punishments as they went.

Mortimer wasn't listening. He was thinking, *three. Three empty farms.*

15
ALICE

"Aren't you going to get that?" Thompson asked, as Alice's phone continued to shrill on the counter.

"No."

The cat squinted at the screen. "It's DI Adams."

"That's why I don't want to get it."

"Trouble in the ranks?"

Alice finished rinsing her cereal bowl and set it to drain. "She'll merely attempt to dissuade me from returning to the council."

"She could have good reason. You don't know what she found out from the latest dead body."

"I never thought a feline would be one to advocate following instructions."

Thompson snorted, stretched, and jumped to the floor. "If you get offed, I'll have to find someone else to feed me. Scallops, remember?"

"How could I forget?"

"And caviar."

"That was not agreed."

"Yeah, yeah." The cat stepped sideways into nothing in that

disturbing way he had, leaving behind only the soft whisper of air rushing to fill the gap where he'd been, and a few stray hairs drifting onto the phone. Alice clicked her tongue and brushed them off.

In the quiet left behind, there was a rattly sort of knock at the kitchen door, and Alice peered out the window over the sink to see Miriam fidgeting on the step, trying to untangle her long skirt from a variety of foliage that seemed to have made a claim on it.

She unlocked the door and smiled at the younger woman. "Good morning, Miriam. You just caught me."

"Oh, I'm so glad I'm in time." Miriam kicked her flip-flops off and padded into the room. "I had this whole disguise figured out, but then I couldn't find my sunglasses, so I gave it up as a bad job."

"I see." Alice tried to imagine what would count as a disguise for Miriam. Probably clothes more like the ones she wore herself.

"Was that a bad choice? I just thought, if we're going to the council, everyone knows who you are, so there's no point my dressing up. Plus, I feel strange in trousers and cardigans." She smoothed the front of her top, which had a dragon embroidered on it.

Alice picked up her bag from the table. "I think you're quite right. I take it you're coming with me?"

"Of course! I wasn't joking about all that stuff yesterday. I'm not letting you wander around unprotected."

Alice took her cane from where it leaned next to the chair and wondered what exactly Miriam thought she was going to do. To be fair, the younger woman had been rather handy with a cricket bat when there were goblins to deal with, but she had a feeling that the enemy might be a little more subtle this time. Aloud, she just said, "Thank you, Miriam. It'll be good to have the company."

THE DRIVE to Skipton never failed to please Alice. The greens were always just slightly different, the shadows always drew new shapes across the fields, and even though it was summer the roads were mostly empty. She drove more slowly than usual, in deference to the fact that Miriam could be a bit of a nervous passenger, and only overtook a handful of pottering tourist cars. Miriam still looked a little pale by the time they joined the A65 and turned toward Skipton.

"Are you alright, dear?" Alice asked.

Miriam nodded vigorously, and slowly released her grip on the door handle. "I must have eaten my breakfast too quickly."

Alice was of the opinion that Miriam looked as if she might lose said breakfast, despite what she considered to be very sedate driving, but kept that to herself. "What will you do while I'm in the meeting?"

"I'll wait," Miriam said, in the tone of someone who doesn't intend to be argued with.

"You're very welcome to, of course, but I may be some time. You could always take the car and do a spot of shopping or have a cup of tea somewhere. I can call you when I finish."

"I suppose I could do with some more potting mix," Miriam said. "But I really shouldn't leave you alone."

"I'll be perfectly safe in there," Alice said, although she wasn't entirely sure if that was true or not. She didn't think anyone would come after her wielding the office stapler, but there were quieter forms of attack.

At the car park not far from the town hall, she left Miriam parked in the shade of the trees with the radio on and her knitting – a rather luminous purple and blue concoction that was, apparently, going to be a dragon beanie – out, and headed inside and up to the meeting room. She was early, and when she pushed the door open Lily and Len were talking in low voices at the far end of the room. Lily was propped against the table, Len leaning back in his chair, and the silence that fell as Alice walked in was one of unfinished business.

"Good morning," she said as they stared at her. "I was so sorry to hear about Charles. I do hope you're both alright."

Len nodded. "Yeah. Shame that." He sounded as if he was talking about graffiti on a bus stop, or a flowerbed dug up by a dog.

"It was *awful*," Lily said. "The poor, poor man!"

"Have the police said what happened?" Alice asked, sitting down and organising her notebook. She had meant to ask DI Adams last night, but had deemed it advisable to hang up before the inspector tried to order her off the council. The conversation had been going that way.

"Choked," Len said. "Probably scoffing his cakes. Some people just ask for what they get."

"Oh?" Alice said. "Asked for it how?"

Len met her gaze with an unpleasant little smile on the corners of his lips. "Gluttony. It's a sin, isn't it?"

"So was sloth, last time I checked." She set her bag down on the table. "And what sin would you like to ascribe to our poor Thomas?"

Lily clapped her hands. "He's just being rude, aren't you, Len?"

"That's me. Rude all over."

Lily gave Len a playful little swat on the shoulder. "You are that. And, I mean, there but for the grace of God and all that, right?"

"We're not all shovelling pastries in our face," Len said, then leaned back and closed his eyes.

Lily rolled her eyes rather dramatically and hurried over to Alice, putting her hand on the older woman's arm. "And you? Are you alright?"

"I only met him the once," Alice said, trying to resist the urge to shake Lily off. Why did people have to get so *touchy* over things?

"Still, to have just seen him on Monday, and then for this to happen. It's awful. Just awful."

"Not for everyone, evidently." Alice didn't bother lowering her voice, and Len opened his eyes to grin at her.

"I don't do crocodile tears. He got what was coming to him."

"Is cake such a crime in your life?"

"He made things hard on himself. Made bad choices. And yeah, there's such a thing as too much cake."

"You poor, misguided man," Alice said, but she was thinking, *he made things hard on himself. You can make it very hard for yourself.* That was what he'd said on the first day, when he'd accused her of asking too many questions. She wondered what questions Charles had been asking.

"That's enough," Lily said, her voice serious for once. "It's not a joking matter, Len." She turned back to Alice. "Thank you for coming to this meeting. I know it was short notice."

"Of course. And how are you, Lily? Are you coping?"

"Well, yes." Lily tipped her head to the ceiling and sniffed, tears glittering in the corners of her eyes. "One must carry on, mustn't one?"

"One must." Alice looked back at her notebook and tapped the pen off it gently. "Most odd, two deaths like that, just one after the other."

"I know. I do hope it isn't a case of things happening in threes."

Alice looked at Lily sharply, but the younger woman had her hands clasped gently in her lap and was looking at Alice with huge dark eyes, her mouth an uneven line of sorrow.

"Well," Alice said. "That's just superstition, isn't it?"

"I do hope so," Lily said. "One wouldn't want this sort of thing to continue."

THE MEETING WASN'T TERRIBLY LONG, which Alice was happy about. She didn't like the idea of Miriam waiting out in the car like an abandoned dog. But things moved along swiftly – it was mostly a chance to discuss what flowers to send to Charles' widow, and who would step into his place as needed.

"We're operating on a much-reduced ship, here," Rob said, his face even redder in the heat that had come sneaking back with the day's sun. "It's going to have to be all hands on deck."

Alice glanced around the table. Len was snoring, whether genuinely asleep or not, and Ed and Lee had their heads together, peering at something under the table. Alice presumed their phones – she hadn't seen the pair put them down yet. Only Lily was paying attention, her elbows on the table and her eyes wide.

"You can count on us," she said, nodding with her chin in her hands. "Anything you need, Rob."

"Well done, Lily," Rob said, leaning back in his chair with his belly pushed against the table. "It's good to have *someone* to rely on." He threw a pointed glance along the table, and Len gave a particularly loud snore.

Alice folded her hands and said, "I take it that's all for today, then?"

"*Hmm?* Oh, yes, yes. We'll reconvene on the first of next month, as per usual, by which time everyone should be back. Summer, huh?"

"Indeed." Alice packed away her notebook, and Lily waited next to her.

"Do you want to go for lunch, Alice?"

"I can't today, I'm afraid. I have a friend waiting for me."

"Oh." Lily looked almost comically disappointed, her shoulders drooping and her chin dropping toward her rather impressive chest. "Okay."

"I'm sorry," Alice said. "Next time?"

Lily sighed. "Alright. That's weeks away, though."

"Well, I suppose it is." Alice headed for the door with Lily trailing after her. "I'm sure you must know plenty of people to lunch with in Skipton, though."

"Well, I know some, but people get really funny about outsiders, you know?"

"Ah. Well, I'm sure that'll fade in time," Alice said, trying to sound reassuring. She didn't really want to put Lily and Miriam at a table together. At best, Miriam would get all awkward when she heard Lily had owned clothing stores, and would start talking about the dangerous beauty standards encouraged by the fashion industry. Or would start recommending homemade skincare. At worst – well, at worst she'd blurt out something accusatory, and the whole reason Alice was there would be revealed. No, it was best to keep Miriam out of anything even remotely resembling a delicate situation.

Lily stopped at the front desk and said, "Alice, have you checked for mail?"

"Mail?"

"Yes, memos and minutes get printed and left in your pigeonhole, as well as anything addressed to you by constituents."

Constituents. Alice wasn't sure she liked the idea of having constituents. She very much hoped she'd be able to stand down to make way for an actual candidate before it got to the stage of having constituents.

"You do have a couple of things," the woman at the desk said, handing Lily a few notes before ducking through the office door behind her. She returned with a handful of white envelopes, and gave them to Alice. "There you go."

"Thank you." Alice shuffled through them - none of them were postmarked. Two had *Alice Martin* handwritten on the front, a couple just said, *Representative for Toot Hansell,* and the other had her name typed out. She frowned at that one. The envelope was of a different sort, the paper heavier and coarser under her fingertips, and something about the feel of it made her want to drop it, as if it were poisonous or filthy. She suppressed a shiver and flipped it over, but there was nothing written on the back. Just that *Alice Martin* on the front, in some heavy typeface.

"What is it?" Lily asked, peering at the envelope. "I didn't get one of those!"

"I do need to get going," Alice said, tucking the envelopes into her bag and starting for the door. "I'll have to take a look later."

"Oh. Right." Lily hurried to keep up with her, and as they stepped through the doors the younger woman hesitated at the top of the stairs, as if hoping Alice might relent. Alice said nothing, although she knew if Miriam had been there she would have insisted Lily come to lunch with them, awkward or not. She just continued down the stairs, and after a moment Lily called, "See you next month," somewhat plaintively.

"See you then, Lily," Alice said, giving her a quick little wave and not pausing. She hurried around the corner and into the car park, and was halfway to where she'd left the car when she stopped. The car was gone. Miriam must have taken it to get potting mix after all. She checked her watch. Well, they had been rather quick in the end. She'd just call Miriam and see where she was.

As she reached into her bag for her phone, her fingers touched the envelopes. She hesitated, and drew the odd one out, the one that made her skin crawl. She may as well see what it said.

She stood there in the strengthening sun and read the two sheets inside, her hands still and her eyes dry, but when she folded them up again she had to swallow hard.

"Oh dear," she said, and heard the shake in her own voice.

MIRIAM'S PHONE RANG, rang, rang. Then there was a click, and Miriam said brightly, "Hello!"

"Miriam!" Alice said, her hand so tight on the phone she could feel pain blooming across the knuckles. "Miriam—"

"You've reached Miriam Ellis," Miriam's voice continued, still sounding as if she'd drunk three cups of coffee with a generous serving of sugar before recording the message. "I'm sorry I missed you! Please leave a message, and I'll call as soon as I can. Happy travels!"

The phone beeped, and Alice said quietly, "Miriam, please call me immediately. *Immediately*." She hung up and looked around the car park, as if Miriam might have just moved the car to a more shaded spot and left her phone on silent. It wasn't impossible. But nowhere she looked was the familiar silver roof of the little SUV, and after a moment Alice turned and walked back to the building. The receptionist smiled at her.

"Did you forget something?"

"Not quite." Alice showed her the heavy paper envelope, having to resist the urge to pinch it between her fingertips like a rag she'd found in the gutter. "When did this come in?"

"Um." The woman frowned at it. "This morning while you were in the meeting, I think?"

"Did you see who dropped it off?"

"No, I popped to the loo and it was on my desk when I got back. But a lot of locals just drop things by. Quicker than posting, you know?"

"Right. Thank you." Alice turned back to the doors, and almost bumped into Len.

"Hello, Alice. Still here?"

"So it would seem."

"Are you alright?" He examined her. "You look a bit peaky."

She gave him a cold look, and raised the envelope. "Do you recognise this?"

He looked at it for a moment too long, then said, "No. Can't say I do."

"Are you sure?"

He met her eyes. "It's an envelope. What's to recognise?"

"This one has some unexpected contents."

"Does it, now?" He leaned past her to take his mail from the receptionist, who wasn't making any pretence not to listen to them. "What sort of contents?"

"I imagine you know."

"I said I didn't recognise it."

"Do you think I don't know when a man's lying to me? I've seen it plenty of times." Alice kept her voice steady, but it took an effort.

Len headed for the door, shuffling through his mail. "I have no intention of listening to this."

Alice followed him, not speaking again until they were on the steps outside. "I think everyone on the council's had a letter like this."

He looked at her finally. "Yes. I think probably. The smart ones among us only got one letter. The ones that got more …? Well. You don't want to be getting more, Alice." He smiled at her, then marched down the steps and across the road, not looking back.

Alice watched him go, then took out her phone again and pulled up DI Adams' number. Certain things she could handle alone. This, she couldn't.

16
MIRIAM

Miriam's phone was ringing in her bag, but she didn't reach to answer it. She didn't so much as *look* at the phone when she was driving her own car, let alone someone else's. And Betsy, her little old (but perfectly maintained) VW Beetle, was much more sedate than Alice's SUV. Every time she put her foot on the accelerator the car lunged forward like a dog after a rabbit, and she'd stalled in fright three times already. She certainly wasn't about to answer any phone calls.

She indicated around the mini roundabout and turned onto the road that ran down to the skinny bridge over the river. It was one-way over the bridge, the traffic coming toward her, but she was going to turn into the car park on the right before she reached it and leave the car there. Someone would have taken her spot near the town hall by now, and it being market day she probably wouldn't find another parking space in the centre of town. She'd just park up here and call Alice to let her know. It wasn't more than a five-minute walk, anyway.

She put the indicator on and coasted down toward the bridge, the hill short but steep, feeling a little better now she was almost there. Driving Alice's car always made her terribly nervous. Well, the one time before this had, and this one was as well, so she figured that was a pattern.

A car came over the bridge and started up the hill, and Miriam tapped the brakes to slow down so she could turn after it passed.

The SUV kept going.

She pressed the brake pedal down with a little more authority.

She was gathering speed, heading for the bridge and the next car crossing it. She stomped the brake down as hard as she could.

The SUV didn't even hesitate. It kept rolling, and now she was past the car park entrance with no chance of turning, into the start of the one-way street, and the car approaching her braked hard, a woman in the front waving wildly, shouting something Miriam couldn't hear over the scream of blood in her ears. There was another car behind the woman, and another behind that, and the woman was trying to back up but she couldn't. There was a second one-way road that fed into the one-way section, not far before the bridge, and Miriam jerked the wheel over, hard, still pumping the brakes uselessly. She was going too fast, the SUV's momentum piling up, and the wheels skidded and bit, giving the car a horrible little tottery motion that set her heart scrabbling for escape in her throat.

Another car loomed up, coming out of the road that had been her one escape, turning toward her, not checking in her direction because *of course* no one would be coming down this way, and there was a small boy in the front seat and she could even see him saying *Dad, look,* and she pulled down on the wheel even harder. She flailed for the handbrake, realised there wasn't one, and stabbed the electronic handbrake lever as the man in the car shot into reverse.

Nothing happened. She was still trundling down the hill, but now the other car was fishtailing away from her up the side road, and she grabbed the gear stick, hoping this was even possible in an automatic and wishing fervently for Betsy. She slammed the car straight into reverse and hung on.

Again, nothing, and the cars at the bridge loomed closer, and she just hauled the wheel over, hard as she could and never mind if the damn thing rolled, because then at least she'd *stop*.

For one awful, stomach-clenching moment she thought the SUV really was going to go over, then she was into the side road, only the car was sliding and staggering, and she collided with the wall in a sickening snarl of metal on stone and shattering headlights. The other car had stopped backing up, halted by someone else pulling into the lane behind him, and the SUV was still moving, the stone wall of the bridge screeching against the side as its weight and momentum carried it forward. Miriam muttered an apology to Alice and heaved the wheel toward the wall as hard as she could force it. The screeching intensified, punctuated by a very pricey-sounding crunch, and the car stopped. Miriam stayed frozen where she was, both hands on the wheel, sweat prickling her sides. She was panting, and her phone was ringing, and people were shouting outside the car, running toward her. She lowered her forehead very carefully to the wheel and wished she'd just stuck with knitting.

DI ADAMS' Golf drew up next to the SUV with a growl of its powerful engine, and Colin threw his door open before she could even put the handbrake on.

"Auntie Miriam!" he shouted, his normally red face pale. "Are you alright?"

Miriam was sitting on the tailgate of the ambulance with one of those crinkly foil blankets over her shoulders despite the sun, wondering if they carried tea for these sort of mild emergencies. Well, mild for her. Not so much for Alice's poor car. "I'm quite alright, dear," she said. "Not even a scratch. Really. It's such a fuss." She waved vaguely, taking in the ambulance, and the uniformed officers cordoning off the road, and the people standing around staring. She almost felt like she should actually be hurt, just to make all this worthwhile.

"Thank heavens for that." He sat beside her, the ambulance's suspension dipping under his weight, and hugged her. "You gave us an awful scare."

"It was quite a fright," she agreed. "But telling Alice is going to be worse. Look what I did to her car!"

"You did do a number on it," DI Adams agreed, examining the SUV.

"Adams," Colin said.

She looked around, eyebrows raised, then said, "Oh," in a rather different voice, and added, "But she'll just be happy you're okay."

Miriam had doubts about that, but she just looked up at her nephew, still sat with one arm around her and a frown on his face, and asked him, "Can I get some tea? I could really use some tea."

Colin looked at the paramedic, who nodded and said, "She's fine. Bit of a fright, is all. Could have been a lot worse." She patted Miriam's arm. "Just take it easy for the rest of the day."

Miriam nodded, and said, "I like your hair."

The woman, who had long blue hair tied back in a ponytail, touched it and smiled. "Thanks. It tends to distract people."

"Yes. Well done." Miriam frowned. "I think it works."

The woman laughed softly and said, "Well, good."

"I think that's enough driving for you today," Colin said, and helped her up. "Do you need anything from the car?"

"My bag," Miriam said, and was about to ask what they were going to do with the SUV when a patrol car pulled up. Alice was in the front seat, as impatient to get out as Colin had been. "Oh *no!*"

"Miriam!" Alice exclaimed, hurrying toward her. "Are you—"

"Alice, I'm so sorry!" she wailed, clutching the foil blanket to her chest. "Your poor car! I don't know what happened! Everything was fine, and then I just— I don't know what happened!" She was surprised to find herself on the verge of tears. That was no good. Alice didn't approve of tears. "I'm so, so sorry!"

Alice just stared at her for a moment, then put both arms around her and hugged her hard, tears and crinkly foil blanket and all. "You silly thing," she said, and Miriam was startled to hear a tremble in the older woman's voice. "As if I care about the car."

Miriam gulped, and found the tears were going to make their presence felt, whether she liked it or not. She still tried to hide them, until DI Adams, who had retrieved her bag from the SUV, found a packet of tissues and handed them to her. Then she bawled in a most undignified way, and Alice didn't even let go of her.

It was a little unnerving.

❧

MIRIAM STARED at the letter sitting on the table, the bold black print unnecessarily stark against the heavy paper. She still felt shaky and unsure of herself, and the letter wasn't helping. She added some extra sugar to her tea. That was meant to be good for shock, she was sure of it.

There had been two sheets of paper in the envelope. The first one, the one Alice had seen as soon as she opened it, said simply, *Consider today a warning*, and under it was her car registration. The second one was more detailed.

Alice Martin, it said, and listed her address, her phone numbers, her National Insurance number, even her bank account details and her favourite tea (although, as Alice pointed out, it was Yorkshire Tea, which was hardly a stretch to guess). All of which could be found by someone who knew how to look. But it also listed the trips she'd made in the last week, who she'd been to see, and when she'd seen them. It even mentioned the detective inspectors, who were sitting there frowning at the letter too. DI Adams said it didn't much matter if they were seen together anymore, as Alice was obviously under surveillance, and now she was going to be under police protection, too.

Alice hadn't said much to that bit.

Underneath the list of facts and figures, the letter said simply, *We know you. This can be easy and profitable, a business arrangement to suit all parties. Or not. Your choice.*

It wasn't signed, of course.

Miriam took a sip of tea and wrinkled her nose at the over-sweet taste.

"Alice, this is serious now," DI Adams said.

"I know." Alice rubbed her forehead, as if there was a small headache starting there. Or a big one. Miriam thought that if she were prone to stress headaches, she'd have a monster now. Instead she hiccoughed, and grabbed her glass of water.

"Here we are," a waiter said, appearing at Miriam's shoulder so suddenly she yelped and spilled water down her top. She looked at it in dismay, and hiccoughed once, rather loudly.

"Oh dear," the waiter said. "Let me grab you some more napkins." He set Miriam's baguette on the table and hurried away again as she tried to mop the spill up. Alice unrolled the napkin from her cutlery and passed it over.

"He sneaked up on me," Miriam said.

"He did," Alice agreed, then added, "Put your glass down, dear. He's coming back."

Miriam put the glass down obediently. After the crash – she shuddered. *The crash. Her* crash. She still couldn't quite believe it, but the sound of metal on stone seemed to be carrying on incessantly, just on the edge of hearing, even here. But, after the ambulance had driven off, anyway, DI Adams had bundled them into her car. She'd wanted to take them to the police station, but Alice had insisted Miriam needed a cup of tea, so they were here, in the beer garden of one of the pubs in town, the river running quietly just beyond the wall and umbrellas sprouting from wooden picnic tables all over the tiered grass. It was early for lunch, and the only other people in the garden were an elderly couple sharing a pot of tea and holding hands.

"Are you feeling any better?" Colin asked.

"Oh yes," she said, going for brave but coming up a little on the squeaky side. But it was at least a little true. She knew why she'd crashed now, if nothing else. She'd crashed because she'd been driving Alice's car. The one whose registration was printed on the paper in front of her. She hiccoughed again, and managed not to spill the glass as the waiter materialised, putting a bacon butty down in front of Colin.

"Can I get you anything else?" he asked, grinning so widely it made Miriam's cheeks hurt.

"We're good," DI Adams said.

Miriam nodded, inspecting her haloumi and salad baguette. She suddenly wished she'd gone for a bacon one too. This was not a day for half measures.

"Chips?" Colin said hopefully.

"Oh, right, yes. Coming up." The waiter rushed off, and the little group looked at each other. Miriam tried holding her breath in the hope of banishing the hiccoughs, but she could feel another one building. She desperately wanted Beaufort to materialise out of the bushes and make the whole thing seem much more reasonable, but he wouldn't. Not here, so close to Skipton.

She sighed, and said, "Is Dandy around?"

DI Adams looked up from the letter, which she'd slid into a plastic bag. "He's, uh." She blinked at the river. "Swimming, apparently."

"Wet invisible dog," Colin said. "Great."

"At least someone's around," Miriam mumbled. Although a wet invisible dog was less reassuring than a warm, visible dragon.

DI Adams tapped the letter and said, "Where's the envelope?"

Alice looked in her bag, then shook her head. "I must have dropped it."

DI Adams frowned at her for a long moment, then said, "Right. Alice, this is you done. No argument."

To Miriam's astonishment, Alice nodded. "I quite agree," she said. "When I saw that note and realised Miriam was driving my car …" she trailed off, uncharacteristically hesitant, then shook her head. "Not worth the risk."

Both inspectors seemed rather taken by surprise, too. "Um, right," DI Adams said, and scratched her jaw as if not sure what to do next. "Good?"

"Good," Colin echoed, and looked from one woman to the other. "Are you sure? This isn't one of those 'Let's tell the police what they want to hear while we rush off and raise the W.I.'?"

"Not this time," Alice said. "I've kept the rest of the W.I. out of it, anyway. And this is just too risky." She reached out and took Miriam's hand, and Miriam's hiccoughs resurfaced. Could people be possessed? If there were dragons and goblins and talking cats, perhaps that was a thing?

"I really am fine," she said.

"Of course you are," Alice said, releasing her and examining a rather uninspired-looking salad. "And we shall keep it that way." She moved a lettuce leaf around and added, "Are they rationing dressing around here?"

LUNCH WAS ODDLY pleasant after that. The sun was warm enough for it to almost be uncomfortable (Miriam wasn't sure how DI Adams was coping in her suit jacket), and her haloumi baguette was reasonably good. Colin's chips were even better. DI Adams made Alice show her the resignation email she was sending the council, and hit send herself, then warned her not to go back on her word. Alice just shook her head.

"I will not put my friends at risk," she said. "Not ever."

Miriam thought of confronting goblins in the middle of the night and tracking down murderers in spring storms, but didn't say anything. If Alice was stepping out of the investigation, she wasn't going to argue. Not at all.

Colin complained loudly because half his bacon butty vanished from his plate, replaced by a puddle of water and some saliva, but Miriam gave him half her baguette in exchange for the chips. It was too big, anyway, and her stomach was still tight and nervous, still singing that song of crumpling metal. And Alice seemed very *adamant*, but she'd known Alice too long to think she'd let go of anything that easily.

"Alright," DI Adams said as they walked back to the cars. "Let me know if you see anything odd, okay?" She raised a hand to a woman in jeans and a short-sleeved shirt, leaning against the side of a slightly decrepit-looking estate. "DC Smythe will take you home. In theory, you should be alright now you've done what they asked, but no point taking chances."

"Okay," Alice said, suspiciously agreeably in Miriam's opinion.

DI Adams looked like she was entertaining doubts, too, but as she started to say something Colin shouted, "*Hey!*" He leaped away from the little group, waving one arm around wildly and swiping at his jeans at the same time. They were splattered liberally with water, and he glared at DI Adams. "Really? *Really?*"

"I think it means he likes you," she said.

"Well, I do not like him."

"Colin!" Miriam said. "That's mean."

He waved at his jeans. "I'm soaked! And I bet I smell of invisible dog."

"I suppose it doesn't matter if one can't actually smell it," Miriam offered, and he snorted.

"I still know."

"Well, at least he doesn't talk," Alice said, and crossed to the car while DC Smythe looked past them curiously at the scowling Colin. "Come on, Miriam."

Miriam gave the two inspectors a nervous little wave and clambered into the back of the estate. Alice climbed into the front passenger seat, and DC Smythe said, "Do you need to go anywhere in town first?"

"I think we just need to go home," Alice said. "It's been quite a day."

"Right you are," the detective constable said, and they drove in thoughtful silence all the way back to Toot Hansell.

❧

"ALICE," Miriam said, one hand on the front door of her cottage. "You're not going to do something silly like investigate on your own, are you?"

"Of course not," Alice said. She'd accompanied Miriam to the door, but turned down a cup of tea, which seemed just as suspicious as her agreeing with the inspectors. "I was scared today, Miriam. I wouldn't know what to do without you."

Miriam gave a funny little hiccoughing burp. "Well, okay, but you can't be leaving me out of things!"

"I won't. Don't worry, Miriam. I'm not putting you in a situation like that again. You just have a nice afternoon."

And as that was as clear a dismissal as Miriam had ever heard, she opened the door and stepped inside, watching as Alice went back to the car and they drove off down the lane. The way Alice was acting niggled, like that one seed stuck in your teeth that won't come out, but surely Alice wouldn't lie? Not to her. She sighed, and poked at the climbing roses trying to force their way inside. She'd do a spot of gardening. That would make her feel better.

As it happened, it didn't make her feel all that much better, but by the time she'd attacked the weeds that were threatening to block out all light to the veggie garden, and dead-headed all the flowers in the borders, and run her lawnmower (set at the highest setting, so as still to allow plenty of cover for bees and other critters) around the uneven lawn, cursing at the mole hills and apologising to the daisies, she was at least tired enough to feel she'd earned a cold drink and a rest. She packed away her gardening tools and fetched a pint of homemade lemonade from the fridge, then pottered out to her rickety wooden table and sat down with a sigh.

She sat there listening to the garden purring with busy life around her, wriggling her green-stained toes and wondering what to do. Maybe she should make some dinner and take it around to Alice's, say she needed company. Or maybe she could just sneak into Alice's garden and keep an eye on her, make sure she stayed there. No, that's what the detective constable was for, and besides, it'd probably get her accidentally arrested or something, the way her day was going.

She was still thinking about it when she heard the back gate creak open, and the clatter of scaly bodies passing through. She smiled, her shoulders dropping and her heart suddenly finding a better rhythm. The dragons were here. If anything in the world could make her feel safer, that would.

"Over here," she called, as Beaufort led the way past the crouching apple tree toward the house.

"Miriam!" he shouted. "You've been gardening!"

"I have," she said, seeing Mortimer padding after the High Lord. His scales were an anxious grey, which seemed a bad sign, and unease wormed into her heart again.

"It looks marvellous," Beaufort declared. "And the smell! Cut grass. Just wonderful."

"Ye-es." Miriam watched Amelia and Gilbert appear. The youngest dragon had furious purple spots on his cheeks, and Amelia virtually radiated outrage. "What's going on?"

"Well. We may have a slight problem," Beaufort admitted, and Miriam set her glass down before she could drop it.

She hiccoughed, sighed, and said, "Cake?"

Because even if nothing else was right, tea and cake always was.

17
DI ADAMS

"Do we believe our contrite Ms Martin, then?" DI Collins asked, as they let themselves back into the poky office they shared.

"Not particularly," DI Adams said. "I mean, I believe she's upset about what happened to Miriam, but this is Alice."

"I still think she was a spook. I can just see her poisoning a foreign enemy with a blow dart then escaping off a skyscraper using a parachute fashioned from her cocktail dress."

"Just how much time have you spent thinking about this?"

"I don't sleep well."

"I wouldn't either, if I was thinking about Alice armed with blow darts." DI Adams sat down at her computer and switched it on, watching a puddle spread around Dandy where he'd flopped to the floor.

"Speaking of venom, the lab report's back on Charles Morgan," Collins said, clicking open an email.

"Can we hope for cocaine?"

"*Hmm.* No. They were able to recover some of the cupcake still in his oesophagus, and there were generous amounts of dried shrimp powder in the icing." He made a face. "That's just nasty."

"Any chance it was an accident?"

He scrolled down a little further. "Unlikely. Apparently it's not used as a colouring or anything like that, so you really wouldn't put it in a cupcake. And Lucas also says that he'd have been able to do further tests and potentially trace the box if it hadn't vanished."

They both gave Dandy an accusing look, although DI Adams supposed Collins was just staring at the damp patch hoping he was in the right area.

"Alright." They'd stopped to retrieve the brochure and letters Dandy had discovered last night from the evidence room, and now she laid the letters out on the desk next to the ones Alice had received. It was impossible to be sure without an expert looking at them, but to her the paper looked and felt the same, the print the same size and font and layout. "Do you think it's time to pay a visit to BelleVue?"

DI Collins was still working his way through his emails, and now he looked over at her with a grin. "Yes, but you might want to wait while I make a phone call."

"Who to?"

"The tech's tracked down the owners of that farm."

THE EMAIL WAS RATHER heavy on the details regarding how difficult it had been to find a contact number, and just how late Jules (the tech) had been up last night, and just how early she'd got up this morning. There was also a lot of detail about exactly how she'd done it, all of which DI Adams skimmed, leaning over Collins' shoulder. The landline and all the mobiles for the Elliot family had been disconnected. There was no forwarding address. Not even their customers or suppliers seemed to know where they'd gone – although they had paid off all their accounts before they went, which to DI Adams' mind rather suggested they were hoping they'd be back. Jules hadn't been able to get hold of anyone on the neighbouring farms, which seemed a little odd, but from the phone records she had eventually turned up a worried best friend, who told them the family had just packed up and moved to Spain. "It doesn't seem right," she'd said. "Sara hates paella."

And she had Sara's Spanish number.

Now DI Adams tapped her pen against her notepad as she leaned over the phone. She'd argued that Sara might be more willing to talk to a woman, and after some grumbling about people skills Collins had given in and settled back in his chair to listen.

"And you don't know what the buyer wanted the farm for?" DI Adams asked. She could almost see the woman, standing in a quiet spot well out of earshot of her family, in some Spanish town where whitewashed walls glowed in the sun and bougainvillea splashed purple across the courtyards, and the earth was baked terracotta.

"No," the voice said over speakerphone, her tone low and subdued. "But you can't run a farm without livestock. And we couldn't afford to replace them. The offer came just in time."

"And was it the first offer they'd made?"

A moment's hesitation, so small that if DI Adams hadn't been looking for it, she'd have missed it. "Yes, first time."

"That was lucky."

"Yes."

"And when you said you lost the livestock, how did that happen?"

"Some contaminant got into the water troughs. It was quick. We just woke up one morning and ..." her voice caught, then she continued. "We lost about a quarter of our sheep. We were trying to claim on insurance, but you know what they're like. They were insisting it was a man-made, introduced substance, and that we'd done it ourselves." Another pause, and DI Adams looked at Collins across the desk. He had his fingers wrapped around his mug, his face serious. "Anyway, we were still trying to deal with that when we lost fifty more."

"Fifty?" DI Adams wasn't quite sure how many sheep a place like that had. Collins mouthed, *that's a lot.*

"Yes."

"Poisoned again?"

"No. They … something ate them."

"Something ate fifty sheep?"

"We thought it might be feral dogs, but they were really eaten. Dogs usually just savage them."

DI Adams scrawled a couple of notes on her pad, her writing messy and spiky. "So you reported it?"

"We …" a sigh drifted across the phone. "We did, but the police who came out couldn't find anything, and the insurance policy didn't even cover being eaten. I suppose that's kind of a rarity in the Yorkshire Dales."

"I suppose."

"And then we lost the rest."

"What, all of them?"

"Right down to the old girl who was in the barn because she'd gone lame."

"How?"

"They were just gone. And our dogs as well."

Collins shook his head, lines creasing his forehead.

"Were they stolen?" DI Adams asked.

"That's what we thought, but how do you get a couple of hundred sheep into trucks in the middle of the night without anyone noticing? Without the dogs barking? How does that even happen?"

"You heard nothing at all?"

"No. We just woke up the next morning and the fields were empty. It was like some *Twilight Zone* thing."

"Did you report that?"

A longer pause this time. "No. We were just … shell-shocked, you know. In less than a month we lost everything except the land itself. We couldn't even think straight."

"I'm so sorry," DI Adams said, and she was. She couldn't imagine that sort of loss.

"And then the offer arrived. And they only wanted the land. So we took it."

"The insurance claim is still ongoing?"

"We gave up. The offer was good enough that we just cancelled everything and told the insurance not to bother. Fat lot of good they were anyway."

"And was this offer through an agency or private?"

"Private."

"Can you give us a name?"

"No. No, I can't do that."

DI Adams made a quiet fist on the table. "Okay. Any particular conditions on the sale?"

Silence, then the woman said in a low voice, "That we left, and we didn't talk about it. They even gave us … they called it a property swap. But I just … the timing's all wrong, you know?"

"I know," DI Adams said quietly. "Thank you for talking to us. It won't go beyond this room."

"Alright." The woman paused again, then said in a very soft voice, "I want to go home."

"We want that for you. Is there anything else you can tell us? Anything at all? Even if you can't give us a name, anything that might help us look in the right place?"

"No."

"Mrs Elliot—" DI Adams could hear kids shouting in the background, excited holiday shouts.

"I have to go."

Then there was nothing but the dial tone, and DI Adams

scowled at the phone as she hung up, suddenly wishing she'd had more for lunch than a salad. This sort of thing called for more substantial fuel.

There was silence for a moment, then Collins said, "Jules put a note at the end of the email."

"What's it say?"

"Sara called Thomas Wright twice the week he died."

DI Adams rubbed her mouth. "Interesting."

"I suppose we need to find out who owns all that land now."

"I can guess."

"So can I." He thought for a moment, then added, "I don't understand how they heard nothing, though. You can't exactly muzzle a couple of hundred sheep."

"You think she was lying?"

He shook his head. "It didn't sound like it. But it does sound very *Twilight Zone*-y."

"Or, you know. Other stuff."

He raised his eyebrows at her. "Magic stuff?"

"There has got to be better way to put it."

"Says the woman with the invisible dog."

DI Adams waved at him dismissively, and he snorted, then added, "I'd also like to know what can eat fifty sheep in a sitting."

"Well, if we're talking other stuff, I can think of two kinds of creature. One I'm pretty sure is innocent."

Collins stopped with his mug halfway to his mouth. "Not goblins. I did *not* like goblins."

DI Adams wondered if it was wise to hope for more than two varieties of large, magical, and carnivorous creatures to be living in one of the most popular tourist areas in the UK. She supposed not.

SHE WAS JUST HEADING out of the office with her car keys in hand when the tech appeared, hands in her pockets.

"Want to see it?" she asked

"See what?" DI Adams asked.

"The thingy that popped the brakes on that SUV."

"Is 'thingy' tech-talk for some kind of explosive device, Jules?" Collins asked from inside the office.

"Yeah. Pretty much."

"So no chance of an accident," he said, joining them at the door.

"Not unless someone accidentally stuck the thingy to the exact spot where they could destroy the braking system by detonating it remotely at whatever time suited them. Accidentally, of course."

"Seems unlikely," DI Adams said.

"Yeah. Wanna see?"

"I'll come see," Collins said.

DI Adams checked the time. It was already after 3 p.m., and if she wanted to get down to the Manchester offices of BelleVue and have a chat to anyone she couldn't leave it much later. It was an hour and a quarter even in good traffic. "I'll pass."

"Sure? It's interesting."

"I believe you. Send photos." She headed for the door, Dandy loping happily behind her.

SHE WAS JUST OPENING the car when a familiar voice shouted, "DI Adams! Inspector!"

She groaned, considering just jumping in and making a run for it, but Ervin was already jogging across the street.

"I was just coming to see you," he said.

"I'm busy, Ervin."

"I'll be quick. I wondered if you'd heard about all the cars that had their tyres slashed near Toot Hansell last night?"

DI Adams frowned. "No. Vandals?"

"Maybe, but it was on a walking track. Pretty weird, right? And Toot Hansell again!"

She leaned on the car. "Where were they parked?"

"Near the woods to the northwest of town. A sunset ramble, apparently. The ramblers all came back and there wasn't a single tyre left whole. Weird, right?"

Northwest of town. The dragons had their mount somewhere around there, as far as she knew. Not even the W.I. had actually seen the place, but she knew that was where the ground got rough and the woods impassable. And, of course, dragons had been sneaking around farms in just that area. *Empty* farms. She sighed. "Maybe it was an angry rival rambler group."

Ervin snorted. "Yeah, we all know how competitive those ramblers are."

"What do you want, Mr Giles?"

"For you to stop calling me Mr Giles, and also tell me if you've looked into BelleVue at all."

"I can't comment on an ongoing investigation."

"Not even a little? I did give you everything I knew."

DI Adams folded her arms and regarded the journalist with narrowed eyes. Dandy had given him a good sniff, paying particular attention to his satchel, then gone to lie in the middle of the road, flopping down like a very old and rather dirty rug. DI Adams wondered if invisible dogs could still get hit by cars, or if he had the same casual relationship with them as he seemed to have with doors and walls.

"Fine," Ervin said. "I hope I get an exclusive at the end, at least."

"Alright," she said. "Not saying this is related to anything, but you might want to look into a farm in that sort of area. Maybe more than one," she added, thinking of the tech's note saying she hadn't been able to reach any neighbours.

"What about them?" If he'd been a dog, she was pretty sure he'd have been quivering. "More slashed tyres?"

"You're the investigative journalist." She pushed herself off the car and opened the door.

"Right, so I just go wander onto some farms and hope no one sets any dogs on me for trespassing?"

"I pretty much guarantee you'll be safe from that."

"Pretty much? I'd rather a more categorical guarantee."

DI Adams watched Dandy put himself in the passenger seat, apparently without actually climbing in the door. She could never quite tell how he did it. "Well, I wouldn't like to overstretch my boundaries. One never knows, after all." She swung into the car and added, "Let me know what you see."

"Oh, well, *that's* a fair exchange," he said, but she was already pulling out of the space, powering the passenger window down so Dandy could stick his head out, dreadlocks flopping wildly and his eyes that uneasy LED red that had somehow come to seem entirely normal. In the rear-view mirror, she saw the journalist jog to his car, and she smiled. She didn't think there would be anyone at the farms for the journalist to worry about, and if there were, she had a feeling he was the sort of person who could wriggle out of almost anything. And maybe a little extra pressure was just what BelleVue needed.

A BIT OVER AN HOUR LATER, she found herself being swallowed by a black leather sofa that was too hard on the edges and too soft in the centre, while a young man at a glossy black desk whispered into his phone and Dandy roamed around the stark room sniffling at the walls. She wished she knew what he was thinking. He seemed to regard everyone from Miriam to the car thief she'd arrested on her last case with the same distracted interest, which struck her as very undiscerning and not very useful. He certainly didn't live up to Thompson's dire predictions about devil dandy dogs. Unless he was secretly sacrificing chickens in the bathroom while she was sleeping or something.

The young man put the phone down and said, "You can go in now."

"Thanks," DI Adams said, peeling herself out of the sofa with some difficulty.

"Tea, coffee?" the secretary offered. He seemed to be having some trouble looking directly at her, and she wondered if she had biscuit crumbs on her nose.

"No, thanks." She didn't wait for him to show her in, but opened the door and walked into an office with two glass walls that overlooked a slightly rundown area of canal. It was a grey sort of day down here, not as sunny as it had been when she'd left Skipton, and the dull sky was reflected in the marble floor.

"Detective Inspector," the man behind the desk said, getting up hurriedly and extending a hand. "Welcome."

"Thank you," she said, shaking his hand and seating herself without being asked.

"Has Tom offered you a drink?"

"I'm fine, thanks."

"Right, right." The man sat, smoothing the hair at the sides of his head. "To what do I owe the pleasure of a visit from the Skipton police?"

"Mr Butler—"

"Please, call me Gary."

"Mr Butler," she repeated, watching Dandy sniff the man then wander to the windows and stare out, apparently transfixed by the view. Useless animal. "What can you tell me about your company's plans for building in the Skipton area?"

"Ah, yes. We have a most excellent range of executive homes

currently under construction. Two, three, and four-bedroom duplexes with——"

"I was aware of those, yes. How about any other projects?"

He frowned. "No, none."

"Nothing, say, in the region of Toot Hansell?"

"Toot where?" He grinned. "Is that a real name?"

He was either an excellent liar or he really knew nothing about it. Which wasn't out of the question. "Alright. Why did BelleVue host a cocktail party for the Skipton council members?"

"A combination of market research and, shall we say, greasing the wheels?"

She made a quick scribble on her pad. "A bribe, in other words?"

"No! No, of course not. But it doesn't hurt to wine and dine those who might be approving planning permissions, or indeed might become buyers. It's just business."

"*Hmm.*" She scribbled again, less a note than a doodle. "Did you meet Gavin Peabody, Thomas Wright and Charles Morgan?"

He frowned, rolling a pen in his fingers. "I think so. Councillors?"

"Yes. All recently deceased."

He stopped rolling the pen. "Oh dear. I'm sorry to hear that."

"There's been a lot of upheaval at the council since your cocktail party. Two retirements. Three deaths."

"I hope you're not suggesting BelleVue had anything to do with it."

"An excellent question." DI Adams said, even though it hadn't been a question. She took a moment to scratch on her notepad, and Gary craned his neck to try and see what she was writing. "I've looked into your company. There have been complaints made about your methods of acquiring property."

"Unfortunately people sometimes regret selling, even when

they get an above-market price. Their claims have always been groundless. Nothing has ever made it to court."

"Some environmental groups have been less than happy, too." This she'd found with a quick Google search the night before. Protests at development sites and concerns about construction techniques.

"Well, yes. But, again, we were never found to be at fault. All our works have been fully approved by local councils. Progress is disruption, I'm afraid." Gary clasped his hands on the desk, his face smoothing, and DI Adams wondered how many times he'd said those words. They had the hollow ring of the well-rehearsed.

"I guess that depends on your perspective," she said, and scribbled in the notebook again. It was making him wonderfully uneasy. "What do your developments normally look like? Housing? Shops?"

"It really depends on the area. We do tend to work with mostly residential, though. High quality builds and secure, well-landscaped neighbourhoods."

She frowned. "Like gated communities?"

"Yes, exactly."

DI Adams tried to imagine a gated community springing up next to Toot Hansell. Somehow, it seemed as impossible as a cluster of skyscrapers. This was a village that didn't even bother to lock its doors. A gated community felt more than disruptive. It felt insulting, somehow. "And there's a lot of demand for that?"

"Oh, definitely. Everyone wants safety. Everyone wants that exclusive, American-style home, with large square footage and a big yard. It's the dream."

DI Adams wasn't quite sure whose dream it was, but she was pretty sure it wasn't everyone's. "I see."

"We offer a new way of living. Real security, happy environments, reliable neighbourhoods."

"Reliable neighbourhoods?"

"Yes. Ones where you really feel safe connecting to your neighbours, because they've got the same values as you."

DI Adams wished she could imagine that he was talking about sharing similar tastes in fence paint, but she rather doubted it. "So we're not talking affordable housing here."

He made a startled little gesture, as if to push away the very idea. "No. Not our area."

DI Adams nodded, glancing at Dandy. He was on his back in the middle of the office, wriggling enthusiastically while dust rose off him in a cloud. "I see."

"Well, it's a question of appeal, isn't it? People who want the sort of houses we sell don't want to live next to ... those sorts of people."

DI Adams smiled. "Those sorts of people." She expected she bore a strong resemblance to what Gary would term *those sorts of people*, with her skin and her hair and her TK Maxx clothes.

"Umm." Gary's face had taken on a suddenly florid tone, and he looked at his watch rather desperately. "Is that the time? I'm terribly sorry, but I'm going to have to cut this short. I have an appointment. That I have to go out to."

"Of course." DI Adams stood up. "I'll walk you out."

"Oh no, I mean, I have to get the paperwork together first." Gary waved at his empty desk, and nodded. "Yes, paperwork."

"Terribly busy, all this exclusive housing stuff."

"It is. Yes, it is."

"I wouldn't mind a brochure," DI Adams said.

"Of course. Yes! An officer of the law. Perfect. Perfect." Gary stared at her as she waited expectantly, then said, "Ah, give your details to Tom and he'll email you a prospectus."

DI Adams smiled, and held out her hand. Gary grabbed it, his palm slick against hers. "Wonderful," she said, and held on just a little too long.

"Always a pleasure to help the police," Gary said. His face had gone a strange blotchy colour, and she wondered about mentioning the letters. But she thought he was just snobby, rather than guilty. She'd keep that card a little longer.

"Thank you for your time," she said, and headed for the door. Dandy lingered a moment longer, and when she glanced back he was weeing on the plastic palm in the corner. She thought she might buy him a bacon butty of his very own for that gesture of solidarity.

❧

SHE CALLED Collins as she eased her way out of the city, just on the edge of rush hour traffic.

"Any news?"

"Spoke to the councillors I could get hold of. No one's saying anything about BelleVue."

"What about Alice's buddy Len and that whole 'we all got envelopes' thing?"

"Denying it entirely," Collins said. "Says she's an old busybody sticking her nose into what doesn't concern her."

"Well, it's accurate, if a bit harsh."

He snorted. "How about you?"

"Not much to report, except that social divides are alive and well, and Dandy disapproves strongly."

"Good dog," Collins said. "Fancy a curry tonight?"

DI Adams glanced at the time. It'd be getting on for seven by the time she got back, and she really couldn't be bothered with shopping, especially at that time. "Is it any good?"

He made a sound that could only be described as a scoff. "You southerners know nothing about curry. *Nothing*. Give me a shout when you get back and I'll pick some up."

"Deal." She hung up and settled back into the seat, nudging the cruise control up slightly. She was oddly eager to get away from the mass of cars, the hulk of the buildings. The green hills, already visible to the north, looked wild and alive and full of promise, and she suddenly craved the silence. "Oh bloody hell," she said, and looked at Dandy, sitting bolt upright in the passenger seat. "Do you think this place is catching?"

Dandy *whuff*-ed softly, and she wondered if she'd maybe not had enough coffee today. She couldn't actually like it out here. Despite the lick of new paint, the office looked like it hadn't been done up since the seventies, and the rooster was still living in her backyard, and the place had an annual *sheep festival*. It wasn't her sort of place at all.

Although it was nice to run without thinking about how much air pollution she was breathing. And to be able to sit on her back step with a cup of coffee and hear birdsong. Even to see that hulking fell beyond town every time she turned around, like an anchor to the land. Of course, the flip side of that was Collins spent half his time chasing sheep, which wasn't what she'd joined the police to do. Not that she could accuse the Skipton police of being slow or behind the times when it came to actual cases. They were terribly efficient, in fact, but in the most relaxed way possible. It was annoying.

She sighed, turned the radio up, and said to Dandy, "I think it *is* catching."

He snorted and looked hopefully at the window.

18

MORTIMER

"The dryad was *super* worried," Gilbert insisted. He had a slice of carrot cake in front of him but was ignoring it, which Mortimer considered to be rather a waste.

"But Beaufort's right," Amelia said. "They *are* drama queens, and besides, you can't just go around slashing tyres!"

"They were probably scheming on how best to destroy the forest!"

Amelia made the sort of noise someone does when they've exhausted every argument they have, and would rather like to hit their opponent over the head with something heavy.

"Now, you two," Miriam said. "Gilbert may not have gone about things in the best way, but he's quite right to be worried, in my mind. Two other empty farms?"

"We can't be sure," Beaufort said. "For one thing, dryads aren't exactly reliable. And even if the farms are empty, it might be as simple as someone rebuilding the farmhouses. You know, like on that show." He waved vaguely at Miriam's cottage, presumably meaning the TV inside.

"But what about the animals?" Gilbert asked. "Why would they get rid of them? I'm telling you—"

"You're telling *everyone!*" Amelia snapped. "You know all Rockford needs is half an excuse to go try and eat someone! And that Isobel's no better."

"At least *she* listens to me."

"Only when you're spouting rubbish."

"I don't think eating anyone is a good solution," Miriam said, sounding as if she'd given it some thought.

"Mortimer," Beaufort said. "What do you think, lad?"

Mortimer had just taken a large mouthful of quiche, and he froze, staring at the three dragons and Miriam. He'd been trying very hard not to get involved, which was actually quite easy when Gilbert and Amelia were around. It was, in fact, very easy to stay out of conversation altogether with those two. He swallowed, choked on a pea, and went a rather lovely lilac shade as he tried not to cough quiche all over the lawn. "Um," he managed, once he'd got his breath back, then took a gulp of tea.

"Morts, come on," Gilbert said. "You know this is important!"

Amelia shoved him. "Leave him alone! He can make up his own mind without you nagging him!"

Beaufort gave a sudden, rather alarming growl. "Both of you stop it. If I wanted to talk to squabbling hatchlings I could have stayed back in the grand cavern."

The two young dragons fell silent, and everyone looked at Mortimer.

"Um," he said again, feeling the lilac colour spreading. "Well, obviously we need to avoid any action that might draw attention to ourselves."

"You see?" Amelia hissed at her brother, drawing another growl from Beaufort.

"But," Mortimer continued, "it's not just the potential threat to the mount. The dryads are *our* Folk, just like Nellie. If we can protect them, we need to."

"Hah!" Gilbert said, and Beaufort stood, drawing himself up to his full height, almost as tall as the table.

"I fought *wars*," he told the two young dragons. "I fought against dragons, and goblins, and knights with swords and lances, and I made peace with queens and princesses, who were much more sensible than their counterparts. I have led the Cloverlies to battle and to peace. I have outlived clans and cities and the fall of the Folk. And I've kept the Cloverlies safe for centuries. So would you *please* stay quiet when I tell you to?"

"Sorry," they mumbled together, and Beaufort glared at them a moment longer before sitting down again.

"Do go on, Mortimer."

"Well, that's kind of it. I mean, you know, I can see both sides." There was silence for a moment, and Mortimer could see Amelia and Gilbert looking at each other, both of them obviously desperate to say something, but not daring.

"Well," Miriam said. "You'd make a terribly good politician, Mortimer."

"Would I?" he asked.

"Yes." She clasped her hands together and leaned forward to hold his gaze. "Now what do you think we should *do?*"

Mortimer swallowed hard, wanting to protest. Miriam was meant to be the one person who'd back him up in not doing things! She just smiled at him encouragingly, so he looked pleadingly at Beaufort instead. The High Lord was watching him with bright eyes, and there was clearly no help coming from that direction. This was ridiculous! What did he know about *any* of it? He sighed, then said, "Well, I think we need more information. I think we need to see what's actually happening. I mean, we're just guessing at the moment, aren't we? We haven't seen if the other farms are actually empty, or even checked the first farm properly."

Gilbert was nodding, if a bit reluctantly, and Beaufort grinned at him. This wasn't so bad.

"And, well, I think we do need to be ready to take some sort of action if they're really up to something awful, like putting horrible stuff in the water, or chopping down trees. But that should be a last resort, only if we think we can't get the police to stop them in time. And it should all be things that could be done by humans, like Gilbert slashing those tyres."

"See?" Gilbert exclaimed, unable to stay quiet any longer. He'd gone a delighted orange.

"I didn't say that was a good idea," Mortimer said. This whole speaking up thing was getting much easier the more he talked. "We don't know who that was. But yes, that sort of thing. We could do it to those machines in the shed, so they can't use them. But this is really a human matter, and we should only get involved if we have to."

"Lad, I think you have it," Beaufort said. "Miriam's quite right, you're very good at this."

Mortimer went even more orange than Gilbert. "Well, I don't know about that."

"And I actually meant he was like a politician in that he'd said a lot without really saying anything," Miriam said. "But you're wonderful once you get started, Mortimer!"

"Oh." His orange flush faded slightly.

"Really. Much better than a politician."

"More like a lord," Beaufort said, and grinned again.

Mortimer grabbed his last piece of cake, the orange fading rapidly. He didn't like the sound of that.

"So," Miriam said, "we need to take a look at those other farms, then keep an eye on things."

Beaufort nodded. "We'll talk to the dryad ourselves first—"

"But I already—" Gilbert started, and his sister tweaked his tail hard enough to make him yelp.

"Don't interrupt, you toadstool."

"Ow," he said sulkily.

"Then check the farms," Beaufort continued. "Shall we see if Alice can drive us?"

Miriam wrinkled her nose. "No, I don't really think she can," she said.

"Why not?" Beaufort asked, and Miriam launched into the quite astonishing story of sabotaged cars and threatening letters and corrupt land developers, while Mortimer sank lower and lower to the grass and wished he'd said absolutely nothing about going to look at farms or being defenders of the Folk.

"And so Alice is under police protection, and has no car," Miriam finished finally. Her voice had gone a little shaky as the story went on, and Mortimer had a feeling she'd been able to forget about it a little while dealing with dragonish issues. He put a paw on her knee gently, and she smiled at him.

"How awfully frightening," he told her, and meant it.

She sighed. "It was. I'm not very good at these things."

"Me either," Mortimer admitted.

"You're both quite wrong, of course," Beaufort rumbled. "You're marvellous at this sort of thing. We couldn't do without you."

Miriam frowned at him. "But it's just so silly. Why do these things keep happening to us?"

"Because sometimes that's just the way things work," Beaufort said. "It could have been the next village along. It could have been ten years ago, or ten years from now, and the whole situation could have been different. But it's here, now. With us. So we can stay out of it and hope things will somehow fix themselves, even when we know they won't, or we can try and do better. That's the choice. One that must be made one way or another."

Mortimer looked at his claws, carving small divots out of the soft ground, and wished Beaufort weren't so *right*. But he supposed that was what came of a millennium of watching, of keeping his clan alive through the rise of humanity and the crumbling of the magical Folk. Of not just surviving, but adapting, learning, changing, over and over and over. No one could do that and not learn how to see things clearly.

But it was still annoying.

Miriam obviously thought so too, because she gave an enormous sigh and said, "Well, it's not really a choice, then, is it? If it's do something or risk Folk dying and land being destroyed and these horrible people just getting away with it all."

"You'd be surprised how many people do think that's a choice," Beaufort said, and his voice was so quiet Mortimer wasn't sure if the High Lord was talking to them or himself. He could taste sadness in the garden, like the colour of fading daffodils.

❧

MIRIAM PULLED the kitchen door shut behind her and marched over to the waiting dragons. She'd changed into baggy green combat trousers with flowers on the sides, a jacket and some hiking boots. She was also carrying a cricket bat.

"I'm ready," she announced. There was a new and unusual set to her shoulders. "This is just ridiculous. Alice locked up and me half-afraid to drive, and you all worried? I've had quite enough of it!"

Mortimer had been in a car with Miriam before, and he wasn't entirely unafraid of her driving himself, but before any of them could say anything a new voice said, "Enough of what?"

Miriam squeaked and raised the bat, then dropped it again, going pink. "Hello, Gert."

"Hello, love." She examined Miriam's outfit with her hands on her hips, and said, "Where are you off to, then?"

"Well—" Miriam was interrupted by Jasmine, who popped her head around the side of the house, yelled, "They're here!" and trotted to join them. She had a bag slung over one shoulder that was yipping and growling.

"Wonderful!" Beaufort exclaimed. "All my favourite people in one spot." Jasmine gave him an enormous grin, and now Mortimer could see more members of the Toot Hansell Women's Institute appearing around the house, Rose being towed by Angelus, and Teresa and Pearl doing some strange little skip and dance as they came, singing in not very tuneful voices, *"Pop, goes the weasel!"*

"Please would you stop that?" Priya said. "Honestly, I'm never getting it out of my head."

Teresa burst out laughing, and Pearl said, "I'm sorry. It was the way that nice detective popped out of the car when we got to Alice's. She looked so worried!"

"You've been to Alice's?" Miriam asked. "Is she alright?"

"She was fine," Gert said, squeezing Miriam's arm. "She said you'd had a bit of a hard day, though, and we should come see you."

Miriam frowned. "She didn't want company?"

"No, she said she had a headache," Carlotta said. "Said we'd be better off seeing you and you'd catch us up on everything."

"I hope she's not up to anything foolish," Miriam said. She had rested the cricket bat on the ground and folded both hands over the top of the handle, like a knight with a sword. "That would be just like her!"

"Are *you* alright, Miriam?" Rose asked, squinting up at her. "You look like you want to hit someone with that."

"No," Miriam said, then paused. *"Yes.* Yes, I'm so sick of this! We always end up caught up in these silly things, and I'm always scared, and I'm just *sick* of it!"

Mortimer thought that this was a rather new type of scared for Miriam. She was gripping the bat hard enough to turn her knuckles white, and glaring at the other women as if daring them to challenge her. He thought he'd quite like to feel the same way, but couldn't quite muster anything other than an immense anxiety, and a growing concern for his scales.

"Well, then," Priya said. "You'd better tell us all about it."

IT WAS the most unusual meeting of the Women's Institute Mortimer had ever seen. Of course, Alice wasn't there, which made it strange enough, but there were also no Tupperwares of cake and slices, and no one even put the kettle on. It was all very serious, and he whispered to Beaufort, "Is this wise?"

"I think they're all terribly wise, in their own ways," Beaufort replied, which wasn't particularly helpful.

"And so we were just about to go and take a look at the farms," Miriam concluded, looking at the women gathered at the garden table. There weren't enough chairs to go around, and Rose and Jasmine and Teresa were all sitting on the ground. Jasmine had set her bag on her lap, and every now and then her nippy little Pomeranian, Primrose, pushed her teeth against the mesh in a most alarming way. A very decrepit Labrador had also trailed around the house and flopped down next to Pearl, then promptly started snoring. Miriam was still standing, refusing to let go of her cricket bat.

"What, on your own?" Rosemary asked.

"With us," Beaufort said.

"Some of us," Amelia amended. "Some of us shouldn't be allowed out at all."

Gilbert made a face at her.

"But what are you going to do?" Pearl asked. "Call the police if you find the other farms empty?"

Miriam scratched her shoulder. "Um."

"I'm not sure we need bother the police at this stage," Beaufort said. "Not if it's just an empty farm."

"We need to do something," Rose said, hands on her hips. Angelus was sitting next to her, making Mortimer nervous. Why did he have to be so *big?* "Bloody developers! I bet they haven't even carried out proper research into the wildlife species in the area!"

"But what can we really do?" Jasmine asked. "I mean, even if they start using diggers and so on, it's their land."

"There are regulations, though," Gert said. "It being the national park and all."

"It's not right!" Rose shouted. "Do you know how many times I've seen species wiped out because someone wanted a new car park?"

"Preach!" Gilbert said, and Amelia shoved him into the petunias.

"I do see that," Teresa said, plucking at her leggings. They were patterned with mermaid scales. "But I'm rather with Jasmine here. We can't really stop them."

"We can't let them hurt the Folk, though," Priya said. "That's not right."

"No, we just need to see what's going on," Miriam started, but Rose shouted over her.

"Sabotage! We need to find their machines and put sugar in the tanks!"

"Slash their tyres!" Gilbert cheered, scuttling away from Amelia.

"Easy, now," Beaufort said.

"Yes, we're not doing any of that unless we absolutely have to," Miriam said, but now Rose was shouting about the extinction of some sort of frog, and Pearl was pointing out that if everyone looked the other way all the time people could get away with the worst things, and Teresa was nodding and saying civil disobedience was sometimes the best option, and Amelia was still chasing Gilbert across the garden. Angelus took the opportunity to jump up and stick his nose in Mortimer's face, and Mortimer pushed him away with a yelp of alarm.

"Oh dear," Beaufort said. "And we just got away from this at the cavern."

Miriam slammed her cricket bat into the ground and shouted, "Everyone be *quiet!*"

"And what about the bats?" Rose roared. She was really very loud for someone so small. "There are at least three endangered varieties in these woods!"

"Save the bats!" Pearl shouted, apparently caught up in it all.

"*Quiet,*" Beaufort said. His voice was a rumble Mortimer could feel in his scales, rolling around the garden and silencing the evening birds as well as the women. Angelus dived behind Rose with a whine, and Jasmine's dog kept yapping hysterically from the shelter of the bag, but everyone else looked at Beaufort.

"Ex*cuse* me?" Priya said, and Gert crossed her arms, scowling at the High Lord in a most impressive way.

"Please," Beaufort added, giving Gert an alarmed look. "Miriam was trying to say something."

Everyone looked at Miriam, and she cleared her throat. She was very pink. "Alright, then. Everyone done shouting?" There were agreeable noises from around the table, and a *Ha!* from somewhere in the garden as Amelia finally caught up to her brother.

"So, my – our – idea is that we go and check these other farms and see if they really are empty. And if we see anything that suggests they're up to something dodgy—"

"We attack?" Rose asked hopefully.

"No, we call Colin."

"What if they're up to something now, though?" Gert asked. "Like they've started bulldozing the woods or knocking down buildings?"

"Well, we thought that if we absolutely had to the dragons could slash the tyres, and *then* we'd call Colin."

"I like it," Rose said. "But what if there's people around? The dragons won't be able show themselves. What's the plan then?"

"Oh." Miriam scratched her arm. "Oh, that's a good point. Maybe we could, um, film them?" Everyone looked at her silently. Even Pearl's old Labrador, who'd slept through Beaufort's bellow, lifted her head and stared.

"We stand in front of the machines," Rosemary said. "Do a full protest."

Mortimer gave Beaufort a horrified look. Surely they couldn't let that happen? But the High Lord was just watching, fascinated.

"We could," Miriam said slowly. "That could work! Rainbow and I used to chain ourselves to trees when we were younger."

Mortimer thought Miriam's older sister probably still chained herself to trees, given his last encounter with her.

Jasmine had gone very pale. "That sounds awfully dangerous."

"They won't hurt you, dear," Teresa said, patting her shoulder. "Not with all of us as witnesses."

"Well, obviously we won't do anything that endangers us—" Miriam started.

"I do see one problem," Gert said.

"What's that?" Miriam asked.

"If they have got more than one farm, how do we know where to start?"

"We may be able to help there," Beaufort said.

"Oh no, you have to stay out of sight," Miriam said. "You can come in the car, but you can't go flying about the place."

Beaufort looked startled. "But of course we can."

"Look at that sky," Pearl said. "Perfectly clear. No, that's a terrible idea."

"Oh," Beaufort said, and looked at Mortimer. "Really?"

Mortimer gave a funny little shrug that he hoped indicated that he didn't think anyone should be doing any of this, but that he also agreed flying around in the evening light was a bad idea.

"Pre-emptive strike," Rose said. "I really think it's the only option."

"I don't think it's a very good option," Jasmine said, hugging her dog bag a little closer. "I mean, that's vandalism."

"What they're doing to the woods is devastation!"

"If they're doing it," Miriam reminded her.

There was silence as the ladies of the Toot Hansell Women's Institute considered their options, then Carlotta said, "When I was young—"

"In the old country?" Rosemary interrupted.

Carlotta glanced at her and said, "Manchester, actually. I may have learnt a few things regarding how to disable vehicles without actually damaging them."

"What, like removing batteries?" Priya asked. "That's quite heavy work."

"No, wires, mostly," she said, and Rosemary nodded.

"And here I thought you were going to suggest leaving a horse's head on the seat or something."

Carlotta snorted. "You're racist, that's your problem."

"Against Lancastrians? Completely."

Miriam said, "That's all very well, but there's something else as well. The last time we went to a farm someone showed up almost immediately, and he wasn't very nice."

"Danger keeps you young," Rose said.

Miriam shook her head. "These could be the same people that sabotaged Alice's car, remember. It's not like they're just going to scold us and send us away. It could be dangerous. I can't ask you to come with me."

The ladies of the Toot Hansell Women's Institute stared at her, then Rose started laughing. Gert joined in, and within a moment the only ones not laughing were Miriam and the dragons. Miriam had gone very pink.

"I had to say it," she pointed out.

"You are silly," Pearl said, still giggling.

"Well," Gert said, "Miriam, you know more than any of us. We're going, and you take the lead."

"Really?" Miriam squeaked.

"Yes," Gert said, and looked around the table.

Everyone nodded, still wiping eyes and laughing a little, and Mortimer sagged to the ground and took a deep, wobbly breath of air. He'd been half-convinced the Women's Institute were about to add guerrilla warfare to their skill set, but with Miriam in charge they should be safe.

"Alright," Miriam said, then took a deep breath and stood up straight. "Alright. We go, we observe without getting too close, and if anything happens we call the police and protest peacefully."

"Boo," Rose said, but without any real vehemence.

GETTING four dragons and one woman into an old Volkswagen Beetle was complicated, to say the least. Mortimer rather thought that they should have waited for one of the other ladies to come back with their car, and he was starting to regret insisting that they shouldn't fly.

"*Ow!*" Amelia yelped. "Gil-*bert,* that's my tail!"

"So? You've got your elbow in my ear!"

Both younger dragons pushed into the car further, and Mortimer was so squished against the side all he could do was squeak. Beaufort tucked Gilbert's tail in, then climbed onto the front seat and looked at Miriam expectantly. "I think we're all in."

"Speak for yourself," Mortimer mumbled to the window.

"Are you alright there?" Miriam asked. "Can you breathe?"

"Just."

"Good." She shut Beaufort's door and went around to the driver's side. "She's sitting very low. I hope the suspension can take it."

Mortimer hoped so too, and as they pulled away from the kerb he wriggled around, trying to create a little space. "Have you told Alice?"

"No," Miriam said. "I don't want her worrying."

"This is most unlike you," Beaufort said, regarding Miriam with enormous interest.

"I suppose so," she said. "But sometimes one just has to do what one can, isn't that what you said?"

"I did indeed," Beaufort agreed, and sat back, making Gilbert yelp as the front seat settled. "I'm glad someone listens."

19
ALICE

Alice wondered how Miriam was managing, explaining the whole thing to the W.I. She hoped no one was getting too overexcited about it all. She probably should have done it herself, but she hadn't wanted to deal with answering questions and calming fears right now. She hadn't wanted to sit there being completely unruffled and steadfast, because she didn't feel much of either. It was the envelope that was annoying her, more than anything. That feeling of utter distaste that had washed over her at the very touch of it. It made no sense.

When she had arrived home she had made herself a cup of tea and sat for a long time with the envelope – the envelope she had told DI Adams she'd dropped – and a photo of the letter itself open on her phone, looking from one to the other and trying to decide just what it was that was so disturbing about it. Her tea had grown cold and she'd made another, then gone back to staring at the envelope, interrupted only by the arrival of the entire W.I., which seemed to have alarmed DC Smythe rather a lot. Alice had sent them away and gone back to staring, but still, nothing. Just the feeling that she was missing something, that all these pieces – the empty farms, the bribes, the deaths – were all connected in a way that would be so obvious once she found it. But she wasn't at all sure how she was meant to do that.

Eventually she decided food might help, and with rather more indecision than usual she fished some pasta and chicken out of the fridge and set herself to chopping and frying and simmering. It wasn't a distraction exactly, but it was at least something to do.

She seared chicken in a pan then tipped it onto kitchen roll to drain while she cooked off garlic and onions in the same pan. When they came back together she added white wine, pouring a decent glass for herself. She was a firm believer in cooking with the same quality of wine one would drink. Not only was there less waste, it made cooking rather more pleasant.

Once the dish was made, pesto and basil and peas tossed into the sauce and the whole lot mixed into a pot of tagliatelle, she dished up a generous serving and popped it on a tray with a glass of sparkling water and some cutlery, then took it out to the detective constable. DC Smythe was staring at a very soggy-looking tomato sandwich when Alice leaned down to offer her the tray.

"Since you can't come in," she said, hoping it conveyed the fact that she wasn't extending an invitation in the event that the DC could come in.

"Oh! Oh, thank you. That's lovely." DC Smythe put her sandwich down hurriedly. "I—"

"Can't have you starving." Alice turned and marched back to the house, wondering whether to eat at the kitchen table as usual or whether to be slightly decadent and eat in front of the TV. She let herself back inside, locked the door, and decided on the kitchen table. Just because it had been a tough day was no reason to let standards slip.

She walked into the kitchen to find Thompson with his paw in the pan.

"Stop that!" she snapped. "Why do you insist on putting your paws in everything?"

"Would you rather I stuck my face in it?"

"I'd rather you waited until it was served to you, like the civilised creature you obviously believe yourself to be." She examined the pan. "Which bit did you touch?"

"All of them," he said, and if a cat could grin, Alice was quite sure he was doing just that.

She huffed, and scooped out a piece of chicken, putting it in a saucer. "If I get some hideous disease and turn into a cat lady, I'll know why."

"Cat ladies are mostly just people who see Folk," Thompson said. "It does make you a bit odd."

"I am not odd," Alice said, even though she'd found herself picking up a scarf covered with tiny cat paw prints the other day. Insidious creatures.

"Do you know," the cat said, examining the chicken, "this is entirely unlike a scallop."

"Yes, well. I didn't get to the fishmonger today."

"Way to let the side down, Alice."

She resisted a very strong desire to bop the cat on the nose. "For your information, someone sabotaged my car, and Miriam was very lucky not to be injured."

"Whoa." The cat scratched his chin with a back foot. "Couldn't you have gone afterward?"

"Eat your chicken, you ungrateful stray."

"Kidding, kidding." He looked at the plate. "Can you at least scrape that green stuff off?"

Alice poked him in the side, but she picked up the chicken and wiped the pesto off with some kitchen roll, then fished a few more pieces out of the pan and did the same to them. Then she put the saucer on the floor. Thompson glared at her, tail thumping, and she put it on the table instead. "You're insufferable," she told him as she dished up pasta for herself.

"But adorable."

"No." She took her wine and pasta to the table. "Mostly just insufferable."

Thompson snorted and jumped up next to her as she sat down. "So, other than the attempt on your life, how's your day been?"

"I have no car and am being guarded by a police officer."

"Living to the max." He gnawed on a piece of chicken. "You want to know what I found out?"

"Enlighten me." She took a mouthful of pasta and tested the sauce. It could have done with some fresh spinach, but she hadn't had time to get that either. Never mind. The basil from the garden was excellent.

"So I couldn't find so much as a whisper through the official channels about vanishing livestock and so on."

"Well, that's helpful."

Thompson narrowed his green eyes at her. "We need to get you another car immediately, if this is what you're like without transport. You call me insufferable?"

"Well, you aren't exactly telling me anything useful, Thompson."

"Listen and learn, impatient human."

They glared at each other, then Alice nodded. "Fine. I shall be quiet."

"Good." Thompson made a show of eating another bite of chicken, then said, "So I've got an in with the shadow Watch—"

"The who?"

He licked sauce from his chops. "You're doing excellent at the keeping quiet thing."

"I may be missing vital information here."

"Gods. Okay, look. You know how every organisation has a department that keeps it on the straight and narrow?"

"Like internal affairs?"

"Yeah, along those lines. So, the Watch being what it is, we don't officially have anything like that. We know we all work for the common good, which is to keep Folk and humans apart. Who'd go against it? Plus, cats. We don't like being questioned."

"I see. You must have a lot of faith in each other."

"Eh. Not all of us. So there's a shadow Watch, even though we all pretend there isn't. It makes sure that the Watch doesn't get too enthusiastic. You know, cleaning up problems that just need tidying, so to speak."

Alice didn't know, but she got the gist. No matter what the species, it seemed certain people were always inclined to err too far on the side of caution. "I'm still not sure how you do that."

"Remember the journalist at the manor house? How I told him he'd seen nothing, and that was it? He forgot me, the bollies in the walls, everything?"

"I do." It had been most odd. Thompson had still been in front of the man, and all he'd seen was a normal, un-talking cat. If that actually was a normal cat. Alice had doubts these days.

"So that's a thing we can do. Another thing we can do is vanish people. Some cats get so they use one when they should be using the other, because they want to be *sure*."

Alice nodded, and took a sip of wine. She'd known people like that. She still did, she supposed, only they didn't wear uniform anymore. They wore suits and preached immigration and jobs instead of national security and air space.

"Anyhow, the shadow Watch is unofficial, and secret. They monitor the Watch, and they know things the Watch hasn't stumbled across yet. Often they sort things out before the Watch can even get wind of it. Even they hadn't heard about the vanishings, but they were most interested."

"And did they have any theories?" Alice asked.

"Not so much. Even werewolves don't——"

"I'm sorry?"

"Werewolves. You know, part human, part wolf. *Rah.*" He pulled his lips back from his teeth and pawed at the air. Alice stared at him, wondering if he was joking, then wondered why he would be. After all, given the other creatures they'd come across, it was hardly unbelievable.

"It may have escaped your notice," she said, "but it's not full moon."

Thompson snorted. "You lot make fake sunlight. Do you really think there isn't fake moonlight too?"

"But how do they stay changed? Do they have to carry the light around with them?"

"No. The light triggers the change to wolf, but the change back is optional. Some of them turn once and that's it – wolves forever."

"They get stuck?"

"They prefer it."

"Ah." Alice considered that. Yes, she'd known people like that, too. "But you don't think it's them?"

"It's not impossible, but it's unlikely. Most werewolves are pretty good sorts, keep to themselves. And even the ones that don't aren't usually sheep rustlers. They just tear into the animals right there and then rather than stealing them off."

Alice put her fork down and rubbed her forehead, watching the cat chewing on a piece of chicken with every evidence of enjoyment. "So we're no further on than we were before."

"No. Sorry."

She sighed, and took another sip of wine, and Thompson looked up at her with his flat green eyes, then wandered across the table, tail twitching.

"Don't shed in my food," she told him, but when he rubbed his face on her arm she didn't push him away.

"Don't be so precious," he said. "You can't be a cat lady with that sort of attitude."

She huffed at him, and scratched between his ears, setting him purring. "You're impossible."

"Yeah, yeah."

THOMPSON HAD GONE BACK to his chicken, and she was picking at her pasta when she said, "I had a letter from them today. The people that sabotaged my car."

He looked up, eyes bright. "Yeah? What'd it say?"

"Lots of details about me. Where I'd been, who I saw. It was a threat."

"Well, it was hardly going to be a party invitation, was it?"

She ignored him. "Something's been annoying me about it. I just can't quite figure out what."

"Something's been annoying you about the threatening letter that proved you were under surveillance and in danger? Dear me, I can't imagine what it could be."

"Don't be a pain. I mean something seemed ... familiar. It's why I didn't want anyone around. I thought maybe if I could just let my mind wander I might stumble on it." She sighed, and took a sip of wine. "But there's nothing. I even kept the envelope back from the inspectors so the dragons could have a sniff at it, but of course they're not here."

Thompson sat back from his empty plate. "I'll have a sniff."

Alice frowned at him. "You can't smell like dragons can."

"No, but let's have a look anyway. Can't hurt, right?"

"I suppose it can't." She got up and fetched the envelope from the counter, dropping it on the table in front of him.

Thompson leaned forward then instantly recoiled, one paw in the air as he wrinkled his nose. "Phew. Your enemy likes his cologne, doesn't he?"

Alice looked at the cat sharply. "Cologne?"

"You poor humans and your silly little noses. Have a sniff." He pushed the envelope toward her with one soft paw, and she picked it up, her stomach suddenly, unaccountably tight.

"I'll go in the hall where I can't smell dinner," she said, her voice calm, and walked away from the table with the envelope pinched between her fingers. In the hall, she inhaled the warm clean scents of the house, anchoring herself in them. She kept her back to the cat, aware her hands were shaking just slightly as she brought the paper to her nose. She breathed in deeply, and could still smell the familiar, comforting scents around her, but she could smell something else too. She must have caught the faintest whiff of it before, and that was what had been niggling at her. Her heart had recognised it even if her mind hadn't. She resisted the urge to rip the envelope into pieces and throw it into the Aga, and inhaled again.

There was no mistaking it. He'd had it on his hands when he wrote the letter, when he put it in the envelope, when he dropped it at the desk. Of course he did. He always wore it. Always had.

"Bastard," she said aloud, and finally turned to look at Thompson, standing in the doorway to the kitchen.

"Hey, I know my father. Well, for a couple of my lives, anyway."

"I didn't mean you."

"I know." He examined her for a moment, then said, "What do you want me to do?"

Alice considered it. Her heart was slowing, the sticky sweat that had sprung up on her back at that sick, familiar scent already cooling. She didn't want Thompson here. She didn't want anyone here right now. "I don't know," she said. "I just need some time to think."

"To think."

"Yes. Alone."

Thompson kept those steady green eyes on her, then said, "If you say so." He looked like he wanted to say more, but instead he just nodded, and stepped sideways into nothing, leaving the doorway and the house suddenly empty.

Alice stayed where she was for a moment, fighting a see-sawing nausea in her belly, wondering if she should be calling the inspectors or the W.I. or Miriam or a hitman. Not that she knew any hitmen, but the thought still crossed her mind. Then she straightened the front of her blouse, ran her hands through her hair, and went back into the kitchen to tip her dinner into the bin and her wine down the sink. She made a cup of tea, still thinking, then sat back down at the table, and picked her phone up. No. No police. She didn't know enough yet. One whiff of a cologne that was hardly rare wasn't enough to be certain. Not even when combined with dodgy real estate dealings. But, if she was right, there was a way to be sure.

The phone rang three times before it was answered, the voice at the other end cheery. "Lily speaking."

"Hello, Lily. It's Alice, from the cou—"

"Alice! How lovely to hear from you! Are you okay?"

Alice frowned at the empty kitchen. "Why wouldn't I be?"

"Oh, well. You just didn't strike me as the sort of person who made phone calls after dinnertime."

"Is it too late?" Alice asked, managing to loosen her grip on the phone a little.

"No, no! I just— You know, you just struck me as that sort of person."

"Right. Of course. Lily, I've had a little bit of a bad day—"

"Oh no! What *happened?*"

Alice thought that, if she was wrong, this was about to be a most trying evening. "I'll give you all the details later, but the thing is, I need a favour."

"Oh, of course! Anything you need."

"I don't feel very safe at my house, and I'm not sure my friend's houses are any better. I was going to get a hotel—"

"No! No, don't do that. You *must* come here."

"Lily, you are *wonderful*. Thank you so much."

"Don't be silly! I knew we were going to be the most wonderful friends as soon as we met!"

Alice thought that either Lily really wasn't involved, or she was laying it on very thick. "I find myself temporarily without transport, but I'll call a taxi—"

"Nonsense. I'll come to you."

"*Hmm*. That won't work. I have the police watching my house, and I don't want them to ask where I'm going." She lowered her voice. "I'm afraid they may be involved." She must remember to go and fetch the plate from DC Smythe so that she didn't knock on the door with it later and wonder where Alice was.

"Ooh! *Really?*"

"Maybe. You're the only one I can trust, Lily." Now she was the one laying it on too thick, but so be it. "I'll meet you in Toot Hansell. Do you know the village?"

"I've been a couple of times."

"Come to the square. I'll meet you there."

"Alright," Lily said. "Please, Alice, be careful!"

"I will," Alice said honestly, and hung up.

TWENTY MINUTES LATER, she slipped out the back door and padded down the path, her feet light in trainers and her black cane with the silver dragon's head handle in one hand. Her bedroom light was on, the curtains drawn, the house locked. Her hair was held back by a black headband, and she was carrying a small overnight bag slung over one shoulder. She let herself out the gate that gave onto the woods behind the house, easing it gently shut behind her, and slipped into the cover of the trees. She had a torch in her bag, but sunset came late to the Yorkshire Dales in summer, and even on the skinny path that wound between the tree trunks there was enough light to see by. She rejoined the road beyond the entrance to her cul-de-sac and headed for town, the street lights still not on and the sky deep blue above her.

The pleasant detached bungalows gave way to equally pleasant semis, and then she was slipping past the stone walls of terraced houses, the town quiet and at peace around her. Blue light from televisions bled out through uncurtained windows, and here and there voices floated from backyards, relaxed and jovial. Her own shoulders were tight, but she moved quick and sure, barely using her cane. She kept to the shadows as she entered the square, and spotted the car outside the bookshop.

She paused, and took a deep, steadying breath. She could have just asked Lily to meet her for a drink, of course, but that would seem very curious when she had her own friends in the village. No, staying with Lily was the only option. It'd be easy to bring her around to the subject of her businessman husband. And maybe she wouldn't even need to. If she was wrong about the husband, there'd be photos in the house. And if she was right, she'd get it out of Lily somehow. Then, once she was sure, she could text DI Adams and tell her she knew who was behind it all. Yes, it was risky, but despite the car incident she didn't think there was any real danger. They wouldn't be sure who knew she was meeting Lily, or if she was being tailed. No, the worst that would happen would be she'd find out nothing, because the house would be clean and Lily would try to mislead her. *Try to* being the operative word.

She shifted her bag to the other shoulder and started across the square. Lily scrambled out of the car and rushed to meet her.

"Alice! Are you okay? What's *happening?*"

"Hello, Lily. Thank you so much for coming." Her shoulders seemed to be getting tighter by the second, as if they might snap under the weight of expectancy.

"Well, how could I not? You sounded so upset!" She took Alice's hand and towed her toward the car. "Let's get home and have a nice drink. Get in, get in!"

Alice stopped, the hair at the back of her neck suddenly standing to attention, and pulled her hand away. "Lily, is your husband home at the moment?" The smell – was it the memory of it, the fear of it?

"No, why?" Lily asked, and Alice took a step back at the suddenly shrill note in her voice. She hadn't expected this. It wasn't his style. He was a conman, a dodger and dealer, but he never liked getting his hands dirty. He was always one step back from the action, never quite able to be blamed. So he wouldn't—

"Hello, Alice," a familiar voice said, and a hand closed firmly over her shoulder, accompanied by the prick of a needle against her neck. "Get in, please."

She considered running, but there wouldn't be time. If he'd been prepared to come out and meet her in public, he'd be prepared to press the plunger in the needle home. And, in the end, wasn't this why she'd called Lily? To know?

She put one hand on the car door and said, "I was planning to."

20
MIRIAM

By the time Miriam pulled carefully into the lay-by near the farm, the shadows were deepening under the trees, and the fields where the lowering light touched them were rich and gold-edged. A shabby van that seemed mostly made of rust held together by stickers was pulled up at the far end of the lay-by where the walking track started, and there were folding chairs and bean bags outside it. Someone was cooking sausages over a very cheap-looking barbecue, and Gert was just climbing out of her car, accompanied by Jasmine with Primrose still in her carrier, and Priya looking most unusual in running shoes and leggings.

Miriam looked at the dragons and said, "You should probably stay here."

"Miriam, is that your sister?" Beaufort asked. "The one with the tree?"

"Yes," Miriam sighed. "It is indeed my sister with the tree." She'd called her earlier, while the W.I. were getting organised, and she was already regretting it. Rainbow (who wasn't really called Rainbow at all, but got very upset if anyone called her anything else) had made a career out of protesting, and rather objected to the fact that Miriam had given it up after her younger years. She'd been defending a fallen tree when the dragons had encountered her in the spring, and she seemed to have much the same group with her now. Harriet from the bookshop, Ronnie, apparently wearing the same camouflage suit he'd been wearing then, a slim young woman with artful dreadlocks, and–– "oh no."

"Oh dear," Beaufort agreed. "No one move. Maybe he won't see us."

But a skinny bearded man had bounded out of his seat and run across to the car, ignoring Miriam entirely. He was barefoot and wearing nothing but a piece of cloth, although that was an improvement. Miriam had seen him running around in less, and she had no desire to see it again. "Spirits!" the man shouted gleefully, and hauled the car door open, leaning into the passenger seat. He grabbed Beaufort's face in both hands, and the High Lord stared at him in alarm. "Earth spirits! Air spirits!"

"Should we be worried?" Amelia asked, muffled by Mortimer's wing.

"Yes," Mortimer said, and Miriam sighed.

"You're sure about this?" Rainbow was saying. "They're planning to clear this glorious wood?"

"I don't know, exactly," Miriam said. She'd tried to drag the over-friendly Barry away from the car, but she'd been making more of a scene doing that than leaving him, and the rest of the W.I. were arriving. She hadn't wanted to leave them alone with Rainbow. "All the people are gone from the farms, and all the livestock as well."

"I noticed that," Harriet said. "It's weird."

"We should go check out the farms," Ronnie said. "See if they've got any machines hidden over there. Then, boom, you know."

"No, don't do that," Miriam said. "You don't want to get arrested for trespassing."

"Hazard of the job," Rainbow said, folding her arms. Her hair bushed out wildly from her head, although she had tamed it under a pink scarf. "You want our help, we do it our way."

"You asked for their help?" Gert demanded. "Oh, that's going to keep things really low-key, Miriam."

"I thought more people might be helpful," Miriam said. "And, you know, Rainbow's very good at this sort of thing."

"Good at being a pain in the bum," Gert mumbled, and Rainbow glared at her.

"Look, if you get arrested, who'll protect the woods?" Miriam asked hurriedly.

There was a silence, then Harriet said, "She's quite right."

"I'll go take a look," the young woman with the dreadlocks said. "They'll never see me. I'll be too quick."

"No, really," Miriam said. "It'll need all of you, anyway, if they start. To stand in front of the bulldozers and that sort of thing."

"So, you want us to protest this for you. Where're you lot going to be?" Rainbow demanded. "Home on the sofa, watching the soaps and twiddling your thumbs?"

"Would we be here if that was the case?" Rose demanded. She'd changed into black trousers and a black fleece, and had a black woolly hat on her head, the bobble sticking straight up.

"Well, you're hardly going to *do* anything, right?" the young woman with the dreadlocks asked. She was called something terribly posh. Jemima, Miriam thought. "This isn't a damn tea party."

"Mind your manners," Teresa said. "You don't know who you're talking to."

"The Skipton Bridge Club?"

"The Toot Hansell Women's Institute," Teresa said. "And you have no idea what we're capable of."

Jemima opened her mouth, probably to say something rude, and Gert took a step forward, folded arms heavy and muscular, a rather alarmed mermaid bobbing on one. Jemima sniffed, and subsided.

There was a moment's silence, then Pearl said, "Does anyone want a cuppa? I brought a thermos."

"Oh, that'd be nice," Rosemary said. "I've got some parkin."

"Is this a picnic to you?" Ronnie demanded. "This is war!"

"An army marches on its stomach," Carlotta said.

"Homemade parkin?" Harriet asked.

"And flapjack," Rose said. "Easy to eat on the move."

"I suppose we could be waiting a while," Rainbow said, eyeing the Tupperware containers and thermoses emerging from bags and cars. The W.I. did not travel without provisions.

Miriam took a moment to hurry back to the car, feeling a bit queasy. She should have stopped to have a proper dinner, rather than just cake.

Barry was still in the car. Beaufort had clambered across onto the driver's seat and was wedged against the door, trying to stop Barry stroking his back.

"Nice earth spirit," Barry crooned. "So nice!"

"I should like this to stop now," Beaufort said, as Miriam opened the door. "Can we get out?"

"Yes," she said. "Barry's the only one out of Rainbow's lot that sees you, anyway." *And he probably also sees little green men living in his ears,* she added to herself, then wondered if there actually was any such thing.

Beaufort patted Barry on the head. "Nice human," he said encouragingly. "Off you go, now."

"I don't have anywhere to go." Barry started inspecting Beaufort's wingtips.

Miriam tugged Barry's arm. "Get out of the car."

"But look at all the nice spirits!"

Miriam tugged harder. "You can look at them later. Get out!"

"Aw." Barry reluctantly allowed himself to be removed from the car, and sat down cross-legged to watch.

"Gilbert's going to have to walk home," Amelia said, with not a little satisfaction in her voice.

"Are we going home?" Gilbert asked, his voice muffled behind the seats. "Why?"

"You can come with me, Gilbert," Beaufort said. "We'll have a word with the dryad, scout around a bit."

Gilbert made a small sound that Miriam didn't think exactly exuded enthusiasm.

"What about us?" Amelia asked. She was red with excitement. "Do we attack? Slash tyres? Push tractors into ditches? Set their roofs on fire?"

"No," Beaufort and Miriam said together, both glaring at the tangle of dragons on the back seat.

"No," Miriam repeated. "This is a peaceful, *human* protest, remember."

"And the most important thing is that the Folk are not exposed," Beaufort said. "No matter how much we want to stop the humans, we cannot endanger that. Mortimer, you're in charge."

"Yes, sir," Mortimer whispered, and Amelia made a dissatisfied noise.

Beaufort reached out to pat Mortimer on the shoulder, but couldn't quite find him, so he just said. "You'll be fine. Come on, Gilbert." And he hopped out of the car and trotted away, leaving the three younger dragons still trapped in the back seat.

Miriam leaned in and flipped the seats forward, sending Gilbert sprawling half out of the passenger's side. "Good luck," she said.

"You too," Mortimer replied, and she gripped his forepaw for a moment, then stood back to let the dragons out of the car.

"Spirits!" Barry shouted happily.

Miriam leaned back against the bean bag she was sharing with Priya and looked up at the high arc of sky. Dark was still a while off, but the light was rich and the deepening blue above was scraped with orange and apricot clouds. Things had calmed somewhat as cake was shared and tea was poured, and the W.I. settled in for a night of potential protest. Rosemary had brought her knitting, and the needles clacked peaceably, audible even over the snoring of Pearl's Labrador. Jasmine hadn't let Primrose out of her carrier, which was a relief. The dragons would still be around somewhere, and Beaufort was horribly allergic. Miriam imagined more than one forest fire had been started by a sneezing dragon.

"Tofu sausage?" Harriet asked, offering Miriam a pitta bread with the sausage sticking out of it like some strange stamen from a flower.

"Thanks." She took it and wriggled herself around until she could see Rainbow. "Is this really everyone?"

Rainbow shrugged and took a bite of her pitta, leaning forward so the salsa dripped on the ground. "People only seem to like the glamorous protests these days," she said around a mouthful of food. "You know, the ones that get on the telly and don't involve having to sleep on site."

Miriam thought people had a point regarding being able to sleep in their own beds. She was rather impressed that the W.I. had rallied so quickly, even given the fact that most of them had come armed with deck chairs and folding tables. "I'm just worried there won't be enough of us. You know, if there are a lot of machines."

Rainbow sighed. "There's never enough," she said. "But one has to keep trying."

Miriam tried a bite of pitta, discovering tomatoes and spice and a hint of herbs against the tofu and bread. One did have to keep trying. She took another bite. It was surprisingly good.

MIRIAM WAS THINKING that she should go back to the car to retrieve her phone, and to maybe call Alice and see how she was doing, when Ronnie hissed, "Car!"

Everyone looked at him. He'd slid off his beanbag, pulling his hat down to hide his eyes. "Don't let them see you!"

"Who?" Pearl asked.

"Them!"

Miriam wondered if camping in a lay-by was actually legal. She didn't fancy getting arrested before they'd even got around to doing anything *il*legal. She could hear the car now, slowing as it approached. "Is it coming here?" she asked no one in particular.

Jemima ran to the road. "No! It's going up the farm track! It must be them!" She had binoculars around her neck, and now she peered through them, then waved to Miriam. "Here! Hurry!"

Miriam ran to the young woman as quickly as she could, not sure why she was being singled out, and feeling a little like she was back at school, when the popular girls only talked to her so they could laugh at her. Jemima thrust the binoculars into her hands. "Look!"

Miriam looked, struggling to find the car at first as she swung the binoculars wildly across the fields. But then she got them pointed in the right direction, squinting as she tried to make out details while the car jounced down the track to the farm and the binoculars didn't seem to be focused quite right on anything. There was a man in the back and a … she leaned forward, as if that'd make the view clearer. In the front was … someone. Soft grey hair falling almost to squared shoulders, the pose stiff, the gaze straight ahead, and it was all so *familiar*, but it was impossible to tell features from here, really. Wasn't it?

"Is it them?" Jemima asked. "The developers?"

"I … I don't …"

The man leaned forward, saying something, and the woman in the front seat lifted her chin. It was a small movement, that anyone could have made, but it wasn't anyone. Miriam couldn't have said how she knew, but she did.

"Is it them?" Jemima repeated, and Miriam ignored her. She ran to the Beetle, digging in the pockets of her jacket, dropping her keys, snatching them up, getting the car open and scrabbling around inside until she found her bag, shoved under the seat by dragon feet.

"Miriam?" Beaufort whispered from the trees, but she ignored him, unlocking her phone and hitting dial with fingers that felt stiff and unnatural.

"What's going on?" Gert called.

The phone rang, and rang, and clicked. "You've reached Alice Martin. Leave—"

Miriam hung up, staring at the phone screen. This wasn't how things were meant to happen. This was *never* how things were meant to happen. She looked up at the little group, leaving their seats and drinks and all looking at her, waiting for her to say something, expecting something of her, and for one moment she considered just getting in the car and driving away.

But she couldn't.

She tried to speak, found the words stuck in her throat, cleared it again, and said, "That was Alice."

"Alice?" Jasmine asked. "But she's under house arrest."

"House arrest?" Ronnie said. "Oh, nice. What'd she do?"

Miriam shook her head. "Not arrest. Protection."

"Oh." He lost interest, watching the car puttering up the lane to the farm. "What's she doing there, then?"

"I don't think she's there willingly."

"What?" Gert demanded, and a ripple of unease passed through the W.I. "What does that mean?"

"She … I don't know. She wasn't meant to leave the house. She was under police protection. I think she's been kidnapped." The words sounded unreal.

"She was *kidnapped?*" Priya asked.

"I think maybe."

"Who was with her?" Gert asked.

"I don't know. A man, but I didn't recognise him. And I couldn't see the driver."

There was silence for a moment, then Rose said, "Two of them. Thirteen of us. Well, fourteen if you count Barry, and I'm not sure you really can." They turned as a group to look at Barry, who was weaving twigs and weeds together to make a crown. Miriam thought it looked dragon-sized.

She looked back at Rose. "Yes, but we don't know what's going on. We can't just rush over there."

"We need to call the police," Jasmine said.

"Pigs," the protesters chorused, although Harriet rather whispered hers.

"My Ben isn't a pig," Jasmine protested.

"Pig-lover," Jemima said, looking like she was enjoying herself rather too much.

"At least I take a shower now and then," Jasmine retorted, and Primrose snarled from the bag.

"Dreadlocks aren't dirty! That's just ignorance!"

"This is really unhelpful," Miriam said, although she wasn't sure what would actually be helpful.

"So what are we doing?" Gert demanded. "Calling the police or getting over there?"

Miriam looked back over the fields. The car had stopped at a gate, and she could see someone getting out to open it.

"The police'll take ages to get here," Rose said. "No one'll be nearer than Skipton."

"Useless pigs," Rainbow said.

Miriam rubbed her forehead. "I wish you wouldn't say that. Colin's a wonderful detective."

"I still can't believe a son of mine became a pig," Rainbow said.

"Traitor," Ronnie added.

"Oh, stop it," Teresa said. "We can't just stand here arguing when Alice is being taken off to some criminal's lair!"

"I say we go in," Rose said, bouncing on her toes. Angelus bounded to his feet and started dancing around her. "We can disable the car. I brought sugar."

"Hell, *yes!*" Ronnie exclaimed. "Stick it to them!"

"I don't think it'll be that easy," Miriam said. "We don't even know who else is there. Or what they might do."

"We'll have to be careful," Gert said. "Quick and quiet."

"Like ninjas," Pearl added.

"I'm not sure my knees are up to ninja-ing," Rosemary said.

"You should drink olive oil," Carlotta told her.

"Like in the old country?"

"No, like on the diet programme."

"There could be anyone in there!" Miriam insisted. "We could make it worse!"

"I'm not hanging around if you call the pigs," Ronnie said. "They'll probably arrest us and let *them* walk free, especially if they're developers. It's all about the money and the influence." He spat on the ground, and Priya slapped his arm.

"That is *disgusting*."

"Miriam?" Gert said. "We have to do *something*."

They were all looking at her again. Why did they keep looking at her? What did they want? And why did they want it from *her?* She was the last person in the world anyone should be looking to. She'd spent half an hour deciding between laundry soaps the other day because her usual brand wasn't there. "Um ..."

"Spit it out, Miriam," Rainbow snapped.

Miriam looked at the ground, trying to ignore the bouncing

Angelus and the yapping Primrose, and everyone still talking very loudly and voicing lots of different opinions, and tried to imagine what Alice would do. But that was no help. She wasn't Alice.

She looked up and said, "Vote. *Vote!* We go to the farm, hands up. We call the police and stay here, hands down."

Rainbow, Ronnie, Harriet and Jemima put their hands up. So did Gert, Rose, Pearl and Teresa. Carlotta and Rosemary looked at each other, then put their hands up too. After a moment's consideration, so did Priya. Jasmine looked at Miriam. "I'd like to do both," she said in a small voice.

"Excellent idea," Miriam said, even as Rainbow opened her mouth. "I will text DI Adams so she can't tell us not to do anything, and we will go to the farm."

"Pig—" Jemima started, and Miriam jabbed a finger at her.

"You be quiet. You've no call to be so rude, and I don't think you're such a bad person. Stop acting like it."

"But—" Rainbow began, and Miriam shook her head.

"No! Decision made! I'm going to text the DI, and we're all going to go in your van. And that's all there is to it." She folded her arms and glared at everyone, and after a moment Ronnie put his hand up. "Yes?"

"I don't think we're meant to carry that many people in the van?"

She just looked at him, and he nodded.

"Right. Right, I'll, um, take all the stuff out of the back then." He turned and scampered away.

Miriam nodded stiffly, and walked to her car, her face so hot she wasn't sure if she was about to cry or faint. She sat down in the passenger seat while she tried to figure out what to say to the DI, and after a moment Beaufort said, "Are you alright?"

Miriam squeaked, and dropped her phone. "Ooh, you do camouflage well, don't you?" she said, peering into the shadows under the trees.

"A necessary skill," Beaufort said. He had his paws tucked under him like a cat. "What's happening?"

"Right, well." She took a deep breath and squared her shoulders. "We're off to the farm."

"Why?" Mortimer demanded, peering around a tree trunk. "You were going to just be ready to defend the woods! Peaceful protest, that's what you said!"

"Told you," Amelia said. "We're being out-dragoned by the Women's Institute."

"What on earth are you doing?" Beaufort asked. "Why?"

"Well, it looks like Alice has been kidnapped. I wanted to wait for the police, but there was a vote," Miriam said. "I lost."

Beaufort scratched his chin. "I may have to rethink my views on democracy."

"This could be terribly dangerous," Mortimer said. "Anyone could be over there. Any*thing!*"

"I know," Miriam said. "I do know. But they're right, as well. The police could get here too late."

"Well," Beaufort said. "We shall just have to accompany you."

For one moment Miriam wanted to just say *yes, yes, do,* to have the security of the dragons beside her, to know that nothing could really go wrong with them there, but she couldn't. She couldn't risk them as well. "You can't. It's too dangerous. I know Barry sees you, but the others don't. They just think he's dotty." She paused. "He is dotty."

"Alright," Beaufort said immediately, and Miriam had a sneaking suspicion it was an Alice sort of alright, where one went on and did exactly what they wished anyway. And she had neither the energy nor the desire to argue with him.

She rubbed her face with one hand and said, "Have you found anything?"

"No," Beaufort said. "We haven't found the dryad yet, and you were quite right – it's still too light to fly, so we can't get to the other farms just yet. We'll go as soon as we can."

"That's sensible," Miriam said, as firmly as she could, then sighed. "I suppose I'd best go."

"You had," the High Lord agreed. They looked at the van, where Rose was arguing that she and Angelus together only made one Ronnie, so *of course* the dog was coming.

"Be careful," Miriam said.

"You too," the High Lord said, and she ran to find a seat in the increasingly crowded van, wedging herself in next to Rosemary and trying not to step on Martha, Pearl's Labrador, who was awake and helping herself to the last of the tofu sausages.

21
DI ADAMS

The fields to either side of the road were richly green, the stone walls glowing in the low warm light, and DI Adams had to stop herself taking a deep breath as she left the motorway behind. It wasn't like the air was any different here to what it had been for the last few miles of driving, but something about the way the houses melted away and the hills crept in made it feel as though you should pause to savour each breath, somehow. She took a takeaway coffee cup from the holder and had a last sip, making a face. It wasn't even vaguely warm anymore. She went to put it back, and Dandy stuck his nose against her hand.

"What? You want it?"

He took the cup delicately, and the whole thing vanished into his mouth. There were a couple of crunches, then he panted coffee-scented breath at her.

"Wow. I think you have a caffeine problem, dog."

His tail thumped against the seat, and he peered out through the windscreen at the fading day.

"I should have some treats in the glovebox. You hungry?"

He looked at her, then looked away again, and she shrugged.

"Suit yourself."

Her phone burred through the car's speakers, Collins' number flashing up on the dashboard, and she hit answer.

"Hey, Collins. I shouldn't be more than half an hour. I'm just–—"

"Adams, listen. You need to get to Toot Hansell."

DI Adams' belly bottomed out somewhere around her boots, and she nudged the car a little faster. "What's happened?"

There was a moment's hesitation, then Collins said, "I'm not sure yet."

"Alice?"

"Yes. She's gone. The DC thought she'd gone to bed, but Thompson's here and he says she's not there."

"Has the DC checked?" Although she supposed the cat would know.

"Yeah, she checked. No sign."

"But *where?* Where's she gone? What the hell's she playing at?"

"Your guess is as good as mine. Thompson won't say."

"I don't *know!*" The rasping tones of the cat came over the phone suddenly. "Honestly, what am I – her keeper?"

"Get off!" DI Collins said indistinctly, then more clearly, "I can't reach Auntie Miriam, either. She's not answering her mobile or her home phone."

"Why does that not surprise me? They're probably off making an armed assault on the offices of BelleVue as we speak."

There was silence, then she heard the cat say faintly, "I know she's exaggerating, but has anyone checked?"

"I'm sure policing was simpler before dragons," Collins said. "And involved less of my family."

DI Adams snorted. "Other than your mum."

"Hey, she's only a protester. Auntie Miriam keeps getting caught up in actual investigations."

"Well, give it time. Maybe it'll become a whole family affair. Meet you at Alice's?"

"I'm on my way out the door. Oh, and Adams? The cat says there are werewolves."

"I knew that."

"I didn't. But he also says although werewolves don't generally steal sheep, they may have eaten them."

"Oh, good." DI Adams clicked the phone off and switched her blue lights on as she accelerated, thinking with some regret of the promised curry. But it wasn't as if she'd actually expected anything to go smoothly – or for anyone to do as they were told – when it came to Toot Hansell in general and Alice Martin in particular.

HER GPS LED her through narrow lanes and around blind corners where there wasn't even room to pass another car, finding the shortest, although maybe not best, route to the village. She still considered all the roads around here to be indecently small, but with her blue lights on, hopefully any other cars would see her coming. She kept the speed up as much as she dared, crossing her fingers that she didn't encounter any unexpected sheep. Dandy pawed the window until she rolled it down, and they roared down the wall-pinned lanes with his dreadlocks streaming in the wind and her lights painting colour across the abandoned stone sheds and leaning trees.

She slowed as she drew into Toot Hansell, rolling over the arch of a bridge and sliding in among the houses. She switched her lights off so as not to draw attention to herself and headed for Alice's. Collins wouldn't be here yet.

She pulled in behind the beaten-up estate, and the detective constable scrambled out and hurried to meet her.

"Hey," DI Adams said as she got out of the car. "What happened?"

The woman's cheeks coloured. "I don't know. She brought me some dinner, and then came and took the plate away and said she was feeling tired after all the fuss – that's what she called it, all the fuss – and was going to have an early night."

DI Adams sighed. "And no one came by?"

"Um. Well, earlier some people did. A whole group of ladies."

A whole group of W.I. ladies, she imagined. "Did they stay long?"

"No. I accompanied them to the door, to make sure Alice knew them, and she did, but she didn't let them in. She said she was tired and didn't want to see them, and that they should go and see Miriam instead."

"And did they?"

"I guess so? They all left together again."

"And then she said she was having an early night."

"A bit later, yes. When DI Collins called, I thought he was just checking in, but when he asked me to make sure she was in there I banged on the door and even threw rocks at the window, and there was nothing."

"Did you go in?"

"Um, yes." She turned so red that DI Adams was worried for her blood pressure. "I kind of had to break a window."

"Needs must. Any sign of struggle?"

"Not that I could see."

"Alright." DI Adams started up the path to the house, then hesitated and turned back. "Um, well done. No one expects someone to run off when they're under protective watch."

The DC nodded enthusiastically. "And she's kind of old. I never thought she'd sneak off through the woods or something!"

DI Adams thought that she, personally, seemed to be constantly re-evaluating both the definition of "old" as well as just what the bearers of that label were likely to get up to, but she just said, "Exactly," and continued up the path.

The DC called after her, "I got in around the back, but I locked up again. Do you want me to come?"

DI Adams waved her off and hurried to the back door, where she found the window over the sink missing a pane of glass. "Well, that's convenient," she said, and took her jacket off to cover the shards still remaining in the frame. She pulled herself through the window, wriggling around the high kitchen tap and muttering dire things about using common sense and weren't there any better windows about the place, and if you'd already broken it why wouldn't you leave the door open? Then she was in, and she rolled over so she could swing her legs off the counter and onto the floor.

The house was definitely empty. She could feel it. She looked down as something nudged her leg, and glared at Dandy. "So, if you could get in, why couldn't you let me in?"

The dog looked at his paws as if to indicate the distinct lack of opposable thumbs, then padded off to nose around the table. DI Adams ignored him and went to check upstairs.

Alice's bed was un-slept-in, the lamp on her bedside table washing over the neatly turned down bedspread and the book beside the lamp, which had some sort of sea monster on it. Fascinated, DI Adams moved the book so she could see the one underneath. The cover of that featured hearts and quirky writing, and the next book was an analysis of military strategies of Ancient Egypt. They all had bookmarks poking out of them.

"Okay," she said, and straightened the books up again. "Why not." She left the bed and checked Alice's closet, but nothing in particular seemed to be missing. The bathroom down the hall was empty, as were the two spare rooms, one fitted with the obligatory dresser, chair, and a bed with a quilted bedspread, the other set up with what DI Adams recognised as bars and straps for physical rehab. That room also had three fencing swords on the wall, thick rubber matting on the floor, a small selection of weights, and a large telescope on a stand, positioned by the window. DI Adams had a peek through it and found herself staring at a circle of dimming sky, waiting for stars to arrive. She didn't touch the settings, feeling like a voyeur for the first time in her career.

Downstairs, the living room was empty, and what would have once been the dining room housed instead two slightly tatty chairs, a fancy chaise longue, and bookshelves that lined the walls from floor to ceiling, but still couldn't contain the volumes that crept onto the floor and stacked up on side tables, hardbacks and paperbacks and coffee table books and even a rather ancient-looking encyclopedia set. There was a ferociously clean utility room beyond the kitchen, and a cellar that the inspector investigated with some trepidation, hoping she didn't find some sort of survivalist stash of weapons and rations and gas masks.

But there was nothing down there except folding chairs and tables stacked neatly and covered with tarpaulins, as well as some half-empty tins of paint and spare brushes and rollers still in their packets. Dandy bounded around on the stone floor, chasing shadows, and DI Adams said, "You're not much use, you know. Can't you track her?"

Dandy stopped mid-bound and looked at her, eyes glinting behind his dreadlocks. Then he looked up the stairs, *whuff*-ed, and ran for the door. DI Adams followed.

Collins had his head and shoulders in the window, and was saying to Thompson, "Can't you just open the door?"

The cat, sat on the kitchen table, inspected a paw and said, "Do you see any thumbs?"

"These smart animals are useless when it comes to hardware," DI Adams said, turning the cellar light off and shutting the door. "Dandy did some magic thing to get in, but I've got a jacket full of glass now because I had to do it the hard way."

"I hope you're not suggesting that *thing's* as smart as I am," Thompson said. Dandy huffed at him.

"He talks less. I take that as a sign of intelligence." DI Adams opened the back door and let Collins in.

"They can't talk at all! They're just nasty stinking mutts!"

"You're so repetitive."

"Anything?" Collins asked, looking around the kitchen.

"Nothing. Except the swords, but there didn't appear to be any missing, which I take as a good sign."

Collins rubbed the back of his head. "Why am I not surprised that Alice Martin has a sword collection?"

DI Adams pointed at Thompson. "You seriously have no idea where she went?" Dandy *whuff*-ed from the door, but she ignored him.

"Look, she's an adult. All I know is she took a good sniff of that envelope, and that was it. She said she wanted to be left alone, so I popped away for a bit, and when I came back she was gone. And I thought you should know, given that you're meant to be protecting her and all."

"What envelope was she looking at?" Collins asked, and Dandy whined.

"That one," Thompson said, tapping it with one paw. "Doused in some stinky cologne. I think she recognised it."

Both inspectors stared at the envelope as the dog pawed the door behind them. "That matches the letter," DI Adams said.

"She said she lost it," Collins said. "I guess she found it again?"

DI Adams snorted. "Sure she did. Dandy, what?" Because the dog had taken her hand and was tugging her toward the door. "Have you got a scent?" He gave a low, rumbling bark, and trotted out the door, waiting on the path.

"Jeez, look, it's got a nose," Thompson said. "Genius! He's figured out she left by the back door, not by tunnelling under the house or parachuting off the roof!"

"Alright then," DI Adams said. "I know you can track us with your teleporting thing—"

"Shifting. It's called shifting. It is *not* teleporting. That is science fiction, which is rubbish. This is magic, which is real."

"Leaving aside the talking cat telling me sci-fi is rubbish, back to my point – can't you find her?"

Thompson shuffled his paws. "Um. I did have a go before I came to find you."

"And?"

"Well, magic's not all-powerful. The right runes and we can't see things. The right combinations mean we can't even shift into a protected area. Like the dragon's mount. I can't get anywhere near the place except on foot, and I can't tell who's there from the trails they leave, either."

"Awesome," Collins said. "Like a forcefield."

"It's not science bloody fiction!"

"And not awesome, if we can't find Alice," DI Adams said. "What about Miriam?"

"No luck there, either."

"Any chance the dragons could have taken them to the mount for safety?" Collins asked.

The cat shrugged. "Maybe. But walking there from the edge I can shift to will take me the best part of an hour. I've only got little legs."

Collins pulled his phone out. "Well, sod all this magical stuff." He hit dial and a moment later said, "Tracy? Can you get me the tracking on two phones? Yeah, I'll text them through now. Cheers." He hung up again and looked at DI Adams. "I could murder a cuppa."

DI Adams looked around the kitchen. "You do it. I might put the spoon back wrong or something." She sat down at the table and Dandy came over to flop at her feet with an exasperated air.

She tapped her phone against the table a couple of times, then said, "Werewolves."

"Bloody hell, I almost forgot about them," Collins said, checking the cupboards. "She doesn't have teabags. It's all loose leaf."

"You think they were at the farm?" DI Adams asked Thompson.

"Well, I'd kind of dismissed it, but big man there told me about the eaten-up sheep. That sounds like their style."

"And the stolen ones?"

"Maybe. It's not normal, but they could be saving them for later."

DI Adams put the phone down and stared at it. "Any chance they could still be on the farms?"

"It's possible."

"Dammit."

"What's up?" Collins had found a teapot and was examining it dubiously. "Is it one spoon per person and one for the pot?"

"Don't forget to warm the pot first," the cat said.

"The journalist," DI Adams said. "I tipped him off about the farms, said he should take a look around."

"Ah." Collins put the kettle on to boil. "I mean, I don't much like journalists, but being eaten by a werewolf seems a bit harsh."

DI Adams found Ervin's card tucked into her phone case and dialled, leaving the phone on speakerphone. There was no ring, just a click, and the automated message. "Hello, you've reached Ervin—" She hit the disconnect button and looked at Collins.

He put the teapot back in the cupboard. "Skip the tea, shall we?"

"Probably best. Add that number to your tracking request, will you?" She turned the phone toward him and got up, stretching and hearing her joints creak. "So, werewolves. Silver bullet through the heart and so on?" It sounded so perfectly surreal that she couldn't be serious about it, even given the existence of dragons.

The cat yawned. "You shoot anything in the heart with any sort of bullet, it's not exactly going to go skipping over the hilltops, is it?"

"So, just ordinary bullets'll do it?"

"Do you have any of those?"

Collins hit send and put his phone down. "No. And going back to Skipton to tell them we need to check out a couple of shotguns because we have a werewolf problem isn't exactly going to play well. We need another plan."

"Dragons?" DI Adams suggested. If they were going to embrace werewolves, they may as well do it with the help of fire-breathing, winged backup.

"Sure, got their mobile number?"

"Well, you can stop hanging around the cat and all." She headed into the hall. "I'm not going out there empty-handed."

She ran up the stairs two at a time and ducked into Alice's workout room, choosing the two heaviest-looking fencing blades. She bounced them, one in each hand, then turned and trotted back down the stairs.

"Tracking's in," Collins shouted from the kitchen. "Alice is in the village, apparently."

"That seems unlikely," she called back.

"Yeah. The journalist and Auntie Miriam are both at the farm, though."

"Good," she said, walking into the room with a sword in each hand, the tips of the blades pointing at the ground. "Let's go deal to some werewolves."

Collins just stared at her, and the cat said, "Holy fricking hell. It's the return of Zorro."

22
MORTIMER

Mortimer's nose was perilously close to some nettles, which he wasn't happy about. He wasn't quite sure just how resistant his scales would be, considering all the stress-shedding. Amelia lay to one side of him, wriggling around restlessly and craning to see better, and on the other side Beaufort was stretched out, a perfectly mottled blend of greens and greys that was smoking slightly. The dew was settling on his scales and evaporating, and if one wasn't expecting dragons, Mortimer rather thought he probably looked a lot like a pony-sized shrub on the verge of spontaneous combustion.

There was an awful lot of shouting and waving going on at the van still, but at least all the dogs were inside. They made him nervous. Angelus was bigger than he was, and Jasmine's dog had a tendency to bite things, even dragons.

"I can't believe they're going to the farm while we're just lying here," Amelia said. "We should be helping them!"

"What, like Gilbert did, slashing all those tyres?" Mortimer asked, although he felt a bit uncomfortable about the whole thing too.

"Hey, he was trying!"

"They were *ramblers!* And you said it was a bad idea, too. He could have exposed us all!"

"At least he *did* something," Amelia said. "We're just hiding in the bush like rabbits."

"Right, well, this rabbit feels like it's less likely to get eaten at the moment," Mortimer retorted.

"Lucky, because I'm hungry."

Mortimer made a rude noise and Amelia shoved him, sending him falling into Beaufort, which was rather like falling into a warm, round wall.

"Easy, lad," Beaufort said.

"It wasn't me," Mortimer pointed out, righting himself.

"Tattletale."

"Quiet," the High Lord said, his voice a low grumble that stilled the scuffling dragons. Mortimer peered out into the lay-by as the back door of the van slammed and Ronnie ran to the passenger side. Rainbow turned the key and the engine groaned and clattered, then roared into life, belching black smoke over the short grass and bushes as she revved the engine. She shoved it into gear, and the van lurched, threatened to stall, then coughed its way out of the lay-by and onto the road, leaving a layer of smog behind it.

Someone coughed rather pointedly, and Mortimer looked up to see the dryad swinging her legs above them. "They're the saviours of our environment, are they?"

"They mean well," Beaufort said, getting up and trotting out into the open to give his wings a shake. Mortimer followed more cautiously. It might be late, and they might be on a little side road, but it didn't mean there weren't going to be cars about.

"Hey, where's the heavy metal dragon?" the dryad asked. "You know, the one with all the stuff in his tail."

"There," Amelia started, nodding toward the bushes, then frowned. "Well, he was there."

"I didn't see him," the dryad said.

"He's probably sulking somewhere," Amelia said, peering into the trees.

"Why?"

"He's in disgrace."

"What, for the cars?"

"It was very foolish," Mortimer said.

"It was very funny," the dryad replied. "You should have seen the humans. They were just beside themselves. All running around trying to figure out what to do." She snorted, and plucked a wood louse out of her chest moss, popping it in her mouth.

Beaufort looked up at her and said, "That sort of thing attracts a lot of attention. We don't need that. Any of us."

The dryad shrugged. "Sure. I don't do anything except keep them out of the deeper woods. We're not picking fights." The trees shivered as she spoke, and Mortimer glanced around. Even for dragons, dryads are difficult to spot, rising out the trees and fading back into them just as quickly. She could be alone out here, or there could be a hundred of her sisters just behind her. Not that there were a hundred of them left, he thought sadly. Probably not in the whole country.

"As it happens," Beaufort said, "we were looking for you. Have you seen much going on at the farm?"

The dryad was hunting for more wood lice. "Not a lot. They put some machines about the place, but didn't do anything much with them. A bit of digging, all well away from the trees."

Mortimer swallowed a sigh. It really was hard to get a dryad to worry about anything other than trees.

"And you mentioned there were other empty farms to Gilbert?"

"Gilbert?" The dryad had given up on her chest moss and was inspecting the tree.

"The young dragon with the piercings."

"Oh yes. No, those farms are leaving the trees alone, too."

"Well, that is good news," Beaufort said. "We shall endeavour to keep it that way."

The dryad stared at him, chewing something that crunched unpleasantly. "Yeah," she said. "Good-oh." And then she was gone, the way dryads do. Not vanishing like a cat, but simply stopping being there, so one was never quite sure if they had been there at all, or if it was just a trick of light and shadow and leaves.

Mortimer didn't think she'd been particularly helpful, but Beaufort nodded to himself, and said, "Come along, then. We'll head straight across the fields to the house. It's still a bit too light to risk flying."

Mortimer sighed. It was a bit too light to be running about the fields, too, but what else were they going to do? Leave the W.I. to it?

Amelia scratched her cheek and said, "Where *is* Gilbert?"

"Gilbert?" Mortimer called, but not too loudly. There could still be ramblers about the place. There was no reply, just the quiet noises of the woods, leaves against leaves and small lives playing out old dramas.

"Oh dear," Beaufort said, not sounding very surprised.

"He can't just be *gone*," Amelia said. "He wouldn't! Well, he might, but this whole farm deal was kind of his thing. Why would he run off now?"

Mortimer had a horrible feeling he might know why, but he wasn't about to say. He might be wrong, and anyway, the other two knew Gilbert just as well as he did. They'd probably already guessed what a young, protest-minded dragon would do when he didn't feel things were happening fast enough.

"Well," Beaufort said. "I rather think we shall just have to manage without him."

"He's not even a toadstool," Amelia muttered, trotting after the High Lord. "He's a sneaky little earwig."

Mortimer followed, thinking that he wouldn't mind sneaking off, as far as that went. But he couldn't. Not with the W.I. out there. Not when Alice had been kidnapped and Miriam had been in a car crash. What hideous sort of people would do something like that?

Like it or not, they weren't the sort of people you sneaked away from. They were the sort of people you sneaked *up* on.

THEY SLIPPED across the empty road and over the drystone wall on the other side, landing softly in the long grass and padding in the direction of the farmhouse. Mortimer felt horribly exposed. Even with the sun dipped below the hills, the sky was still high and pale above them, and every dimly seen bird made him want to cower down among the wildflowers. The grass was strangely long in the absence of livestock, grown high and full of blooms that were still attended by the odd sleepy bee. The green parted around the dragons like a viscous sea, and they left trails of crushed and fragrant vegetation behind them.

It was quiet, too, without the bleating and rumble of the sheep, the clatter of their hooves on stone. A bird cried somewhere, and Mortimer shivered hard enough to make his scales clatter. He really wasn't cut out for this sort of adventuring and intrigue. What if the whole place was protected by armed men? What if they rushed out shooting? Were dragon scales resistant to bullets? He didn't imagine anyone had ever found out. And what if they had tasers? Or just ran them down with the earthmoving machines? He supposed they could take flight if it came to that, but what if the men shot holes in their wings? And who would be left to look after the W.I. then? It could happen!

He almost yelped as Beaufort stopped in front of him, raising his nose over the next wall to check the field beyond. "All clear," the High Lord said. "And I can see the van. They've stopped for the gate."

"They're going to get there before us if we keep going this slowly," Amelia said.

"I'm sure it'll be fine." Beaufort scrambled over the wall and padded off into the next field, and the two younger dragons followed him. The grass wasn't as long in this field, soft under his paws, and Mortimer examined it as he walked.

"Has this been cut?" he asked.

Beaufort and Amelia looked at him, then at their feet. "I think you might be right, lad," the High Lord said after a moment. "How curious!"

"You think that's curious," Amelia said. "Look."

They followed her pointing paw down the length of the field, to where the earth had been gouged and torn, piled up in a dark raw wound. A bright red digger had its front wheels on the piled dirt, like a victorious hunter. Mortimer ducked, then realised there was no one there. They looked at each other, then trotted down the field. The digger and its earth sat unmoving, an odd little still life, and they sat in front of it for a moment. One of the drystone walls had been knocked over, the rocks piled into a messy cairn as well as scattered on the cropped grass. But the scatter was wrong – there was no crushed grass to mark the path of the rolling rocks, and they were placed in a pattern that wasn't nature's. Stones just didn't fall so tidily.

"This is strange," Amelia said. "What're they doing?"

Beaufort put his head on one side. "Do you think it's art?"

"It kind of feels like it," Mortimer said. "But why kick everyone off a farm to make art?"

"Maybe it was the farmers'," Amelia suggested.

"No, it's new," Beaufort said, and got up. "Come on. They really will be getting away on us now." He trotted through the broken wall and padded down the gentle slope of the fields to the next gate, and, with a final dubious glance at the digger, Mortimer followed him.

There was another machine in the middle of the next field, the grass here left long so it half-obscured the big tyres and whispered against the thing's glossy body. There was a faint path to mark where it had been driven onto the field, the long grasses already recovering.

"Humans are so weird," Amelia whispered.

"Not all of them," Mortimer felt obliged to point out.

"The ones who did this are."

That he couldn't argue with.

Beaufort skirted the machine and waded through the grass to the next gate, standing on his hind legs with his front paws on the heavy wooden crossbars. "Oh dear," he said.

"Oh dear?" Mortimer echoed, looking up from the machine. "*Oh dear?* What? What's *oh dear?*" He broke into a trot.

"Oh dear," Amelia agreed. She'd followed Beaufort, and had scrambled up a couple of rungs of the gate to see over the top.

"What? What're you talking about?" Mortimer could hear panic in his voice, and swallowed hard. Both of them were just standing there, which seemed to indicate they hadn't spotted men waving shotguns or enraged tractors charging toward them across the next field. He took a deep breath and scrambled up next to Amelia as the gate groaned warningly. "*What?*"

"They seem to be stuck." Beaufort nodded at the lane, downhill from their vantage point and off to the right of the fields and the farmhouse ahead. It had rained since they'd come up in Alice's SUV, and her car had been much better equipped – and less heavily loaded – than the ancient van. It had come to a standstill in the centre of the path, and as they watched the engine roared, and with a lurch it slewed sideways and buried its nose in the bank.

"We could help," Amelia said.

"Too risky." Beaufort folded one front paw over the other,

watching with interest. Ronnie had run around to the back and opened the rear doors, and everyone was spilling out, milling about excitedly. They seemed to have armed themselves with various garden implements and branches, and Angelus was bounding about the place, barking in delight. Pearl's Labrador wandered a little further down the path and flopped down on her belly, promptly falling asleep. Primrose was yapping steadily. "They may have lost the element of surprise."

There was a lot of arm-waving going on, and people trying to shush the dogs, then everyone huddled behind the van. There was a pause, then the engine revved and the mass of people surged forward. Three promptly vanished onto the ground, and the van's wheels spun and spat dirt at everyone else. Amelia snorted laughter.

"Oh dear," Beaufort said, and there was a tremble in his voice. "That's not good, is it?"

The van roared again and lurched forward, sending four more people stumbling to their knees, then stalled and settled further into the mud. One of the figures hauled itself out of the muck and started waving furiously, and now Mortimer could catch scraps of argument as their voices started to rise.

"—couldn't organise … ridiculous—"

"Surprise? What surprise?"

"Anarchists? More like—"

"—waste of—"

One of the larger figures, probably Gert judging by the fact she was wearing a mud-caked sundress, lunged at a pot-bellied figure that could only be Ronnie and chased him around the van, and Mortimer surprised himself with a snort of laughter. It just bubbled up out of nowhere, overtaking his worry for Alice and the W.I. in general, and he clasped his paws over his snout in horror. Beaufort glanced at him, the corners of his mouth twitching to expose old yellow fangs.

"Seriously. Humans," Amelia said in a tone of wonder, and the terrible hilarity rose like a wave. Mortimer had to drop to the ground and shove his nose into a tussock to keep from bursting out laughing.

"Are you alright there, lad?" Beaufort asked, but his voice was shaking with half-contained laughter, and Mortimer gave a guffaw that scared a small family of shrews out of the tussock and sent them bolting across the field. Somehow that was even funnier than the mud-caked W.I., and Mortimer squeezed his eyes shut, horrified by his own laughter and yet unable to stop.

Amelia looked down at him and added, "And you're pretty weird too," and that set Beaufort laughing so much he had to sit down.

"THEY'VE GIVEN UP," Amelia announced.

Mortimer sniffled and sat up, his cheeks hot and steaming with laughter tears. Something else seemed to have been pushed out with the tears, too, some desperate tightness lifted from his chest. The long dusk looked golden rather than threatening. "What're they doing?"

"Heading this way." She jumped off the gate. "What do we do?"

"We wait," Beaufort said. "But come away from there." He loped toward the far corner of the field and they ran after him, hunkering down in the long grass just as Barry came vaulting over the fence in purple cycling shorts and nothing else. He didn't spot them, just kept running, grabbing the top of the gate at the bottom of the field and flinging himself over it with a quiet whoop of joy. A moment later Jemima scrambled over the gate and sprinted after him, shouting as quietly as she could, "Barry! Barry, stop, dammit!" She vanished out of the field in pursuit, and for a moment all was still.

Then Teresa swung over the gate with stiff, long-legged grace, lowering herself into the field. Rose scrambled over next as someone boosted Angelus up after her, and now Mortimer could hear Rainbow hissing, "Fan out, fan out!" Rose jogged across to the dragons and flung herself down next to Amelia while Angelus raced around the field with his eyes rolling in excitement, darting at the dragons and tearing away again. Mortimer blinked at Rose. She had used mud to draw stripes on her cheeks and was clutching a pair of gardening shears.

"Hello you lot," she whispered. "Ready for the assault?"

The dragons looked at each other. Rosemary and Carlotta were still helping each other over the gate when there was a quick, two-tone whistle, and Rose jumped up again.

"Advance! That means advance!" She raced back to the gate she'd just come over, Angelus sprinting to catch her. Rosemary was still clinging to the top, wobbling precariously, and she gave a little squeal of fright as Rose helped Angelus scramble over. Carlotta stopped trying to boost Rosemary up from the other side and started trying to find somewhere for her to put her feet instead.

"I don't think the gate's locked," Amelia said, frowning at the women. "I didn't see a lock on it."

"I didn't see them check," Mortimer said.

"Why wouldn't you check?"

Beaufort ignored them, getting up to peer over the wall. He stayed where he was for a moment, then beckoned them forward. Mortimer stood on his tiptoes to peek through a gap in the crowning stones and watched as the ladies of the Toot Hansell Women's Institute (other than the missing Alice, obviously, as well as Rosemary and Carlotta, who were still having trouble with the gate), elbow-crawled across the short-cropped grass of the next field with varying degrees of effectiveness.

"Ew!" Jasmine yelped. She'd finally abandoned her dog carrier

and had let Primrose out, which seemed to Mortimer a rather bad idea. The yippy little monster was currently worrying at Ronnie's leg as the man tried frantically to kick her off. "That was a cow pat!"

"Oh, I don't think so, dear," Pearl said. "This is a sheep farm."

Angelus bounded from one woman to another, convinced it was all a game for his benefit, and rammed his head so hard into Gert's side that she squawked and rolled into a thistle. Martha was, presumably, still asleep in the lane. Mortimer looked up at Beaufort. "What do we do?"

"I really have no idea," the High Lord admitted.

"Humans," Amelia said again, with such wonder in her voice Mortimer almost started laughing again.

23

ALICE

Alice pressed her hands against the constriction of the cable ties and said, "Is this really necessary?"

"Don't think I've forgotten what a sneaky old bag you are," her missing-presumed-dead husband said. He was leaning against the wall of the farmhouse bedroom in what he obviously felt was a very louche manner, his arms folded over the small hint of a pot belly.

"Well, that's a little harsh. Just because some of us haven't been keeping the plastic surgeon in holiday money."

He snorted. "I needed a fresh start after you drained me of the very will to live."

"By propping up your failing businesses and keeping a roof over your head?" She looked at Lily, who was perched on the edge of the bed with her arms folded, scowling at both of them. "I hope you didn't give him all the money from your shops. He's not very good with it."

"You wouldn't know a good business idea if you fell in it." Harvey pushed dusty-blond hair out of his face. It had been glossy, grey-streaked brown when she'd last seen him, and his nose had been a slightly different shape. She was also fairly sure that he had less crow's feet now than he'd had eleven years ago, so that was just vanity rather than necessity. Silly man.

"Do you mean the car dealership selling stolen cars? Or the antique shop selling fake antiques?"

"You didn't tell me about those," Lily said. "And why's she calling you Harvey?" Alice couldn't quite tell from her body language who Lily was upset with, but she was definitely upset with someone. That seemed a good sign.

"She's full of crap. Silly, superior cow. Always the same. Always looking down at me. I had to change my name just to get away from her."

"I was mostly upset with myself for marrying him," Alice said to Lily. "I may have taken it out on him a little." The words tasted truthful, and bitter. She was still angry at herself. It wasn't even as if she'd been young and silly at the time. Hearts were so *ridiculous*.

"You're lying!" Harvey shouted, jabbing a furious finger at her. "You're just upset because I left!"

"Oh no, that was fine. I didn't want to have to pay divorce lawyers and settlements and so on anyway. Although leaving without so much as packing your toothbrush did have the police asking me some awkward questions."

Lily had been looking back and forth between them like a spectator at a slow but exceptionally interesting tennis match. Now she said, "No! Really? That was *him?*"

"Lily, focus," Harvey snapped. "She's just trying to distract you. We've got work to do."

Lily frowned. "I want to know about this. You never told me any of it. You said your first wife was a horrible person who took all your money and threw you out."

"Oh, I wasn't his first wife, dear," Alice said, before Harvey could answer. "She was very nice, though."

"Shut up," Harvey snarled, but Alice ignored him.

"I looked her up after Harvey vanished. She knew him as ... was it Frank, Harvey? Do you remember? Or are there too many names to keep track of?"

"I swear I'm going to gag you."

"You're not doing anything of the sort," Lily said.

"I am quite interested to know what you do plan to do, though," Alice said. "Induce a heart attack via cocaine overdose, I presume?"

Lily gave a horrified little gasp, and Harvey took a step toward Alice, raising one fist. "Shut. Up."

Alice stared up at him, holding her face in calm lines. Harvey's hands were shaking. "This isn't like you," she said. "If I remember, you preferred to run from your problems, not get your hands dirty."

"You don't know me," he hissed. "You never did."

"That became quite obvious when you disappeared."

"Can't shut up, can you? You never could!"

"Stop that," Lily got to her feet. "You leave her alone, Derrick."

"Derrick?" Alice said, unable to stop herself. "Dear me, you're not very inspired in your name choices, are you?"

"I told you to shut up," Harvey/Derrick snapped, and fished the syringe out of his pocket. He'd put the cap back on once he'd tied her up, and now he shook the thing at her. "I should just stick you with this and be done."

"Put that down," Lily snapped. "What does she mean, induce a heart attack? And what are we doing here, Derrick? What do you think you're going to do?"

There was a very long moment of silence, then Harvey said, "What I should have done when I left."

"You hated me that much?" Alice asked. She was surprised that could hurt. She thought she'd got over being hurt a long time ago, maybe even before he'd actually vanished.

"You never believed in me, ever. Neither did Dierdre. Both of you just so full of yourselves and sure of yourselves."

"You cleared out her bank accounts," Alice said. "She told me that, when I contacted her."

"She had investments. She was fine."

"No," Alice said quietly. "She wasn't. Neither was I. The police thought I murdered you. Still do, I imagine."

"I'm sure you got out of it easy as you like. RAF hero and all."

"I managed," Alice said. "But it didn't stop how angry I was at myself. How stupid I felt at being taken in by you. How helpless to do anything while police officers tore my home apart. It still leaves marks, Harvey." There was a tight spot in her chest, but she kept her voice level.

"You did that?" Lily asked. "And to Dierdre as well? Just vanished? Let them think you were dead?"

"Aw, honey," he said, turning to her and flashing an unnaturally straight, white smile. "They made my life a misery! I'd never do that to you."

Lily just looked at him, not smiling, her chin lifted. "I bet they didn't think you'd do it to them, either."

Harvey lifted his hands in the air in mock surrender. "Okay, okay. I was young and misguided. I couldn't face letting them down."

Alice wrinkled her nose. "Eleven years ago made you fifty, if I remember right. Not so young."

"What did she mean about the heart attacks, Harvey? You said you were just greasing the wheels when I joined the council for you. You didn't say *anything* about hurting people or kidnapping your ex-wife."

Alice wondered how exactly one would put that into conversation, although she approved of the way Lily's thinking was going.

"Lily, honey—"

"*Tell me.*"

"She's obviously gone a bit old and dotty—"

"*Derrick,*" Lily said.

Alice gave a *hmph* of disapproval. "Says the man wearing white trousers and tasselled loafers in a Yorkshire farmhouse."

"You shut up. I didn't expect to be spending much time in bloody Yorkshire."

"I live here!" Lily exclaimed, putting her hands on her hips, and Harvey pressed a fist to his forehead.

"Look," he began, and at that moment there was a knock at the front door. They looked at each other, startled, and Alice considered shouting. Then she looked at the syringe still clutched in Harvey's hand and decided there was no point. He wouldn't risk being found out. Lily was her best hope, not getting someone else caught up in this mess.

The knock came again, heavier, then the creak of the door being pushed open, and someone shouted, "Hello? Anyone home?"

There was something vaguely familiar about the voice, and Alice frowned at the ceiling, rubbing her fingers together to try and get some feeling into them.

"You didn't lock the door," Harvey hissed at Lily.

"You went back to the car for your phone," she spat back.

Harvey put a finger to his lips and stepped across to Alice, taking the cap off the syringe and holding it warningly in front of her.

They waited.

ALICE ROLLED her shoulders as if to ease stiffness, but it was more to put pressure on the chair. It creaked softly, and she put her weight against one arm, then the other. It wasn't one of the heavy old dining chairs from downstairs, but one of those small chairs with spindled backs that always seem to exist in guest rooms and bathrooms. They were never really made for sitting in, and always seemed to become homes for embroidered cushions that didn't belong anywhere, and discarded clothes. She pressed her feet into the floor and rocked back and forth minutely.

"Stop it," Harvey hissed.

"Hello?" the voice called from downstairs again. "Anyone home?" The familiarity of it annoyed Alice. She kept shifting gently in her seat, arm to arm and foot to foot, the chair protesting gently. Harvey scowled at her and waggled the syringe, but she didn't entirely believe him. If he jabbed her she had nothing to lose from screaming the place down.

There were footsteps in the hall as the intruder wandered a little further into the house, then silence. Alice could almost see him, gazing around at the silent rooms, stripped of paintings and trinkets and toys and life, but with the furniture still crouching, dusty and abandoned, against the walls. The footsteps started up again, heading back to the front of the house, and a moment later they heard the door close.

"Call the boys and tell them to let the dogs off," Harvey said to Lily. "That'll get him moving."

Lily looked at Alice, and Alice tried to read her expression. Doubt? Guilt? Resignation? She couldn't tell. "Fine," Lily said. "But what if they're police? They'll just come back."

Harvey waved dismissively. "They'd have said if they were police. Besides, we'll be gone by the time they get back."

Lily didn't answer, just took one last look at Alice then slipped out the door. Alice heard the stairs creak as the other woman padded down them, and she kept up the steady pattern of testing her arms and shifting her legs.

"What the hell are you wriggling around for?" Harvey demanded.

"I should like to use the facilities," Alice replied.

"Well, that's just too bloody bad then, isn't it?"

"What *are* you planning, Harvey? What are you doing with these farms? Even if you got permission from the council, the public outcry over building some sort of complex in the national park will slow you up for years, if not shut you down completely."

He grinned. Between the teeth and the hair and those clothes, if he was going for the ageing Ken doll look he was succeeding rather well. "Ever heard of that guy who sold London Bridge to some American?"

"Ah. I see." Alice tested her weight on her legs. The pins and needles were almost gone. "It's just another scam. Like your bakery that burned down a week after you upped the insurance on it. Or the boat in Greece that sank within the month." By the time she'd known about those, the whole sham had been all but over. Yet she'd not done anything. She still couldn't understand why. He'd been charming all the way through, of course. Flimsy, but charming. Had it been that simple?

Harvey shrugged. "Was I ever found to be at fault? No. An unfortunate accident with wiring. Some less than scrupulous Greek business partners. I just had such terrible bad luck." He put the cap back on the syringe and pocketed it, wandering across to the window. "And all such small stuff, anyway. Practice runs. *This*" —he waved at the window—"this is the real deal. Three farms, sold to four international businessmen who believe they're going to own their own slice of the Yorkshire Dales with full development potential."

"But why even bother buying them if it's just a scam?" Alice asked. "Why force the farmers off or bother with bribing the council and all the rest?"

"Because certain things need to happen to give it an air of legitimacy, and for the money to keep coming in." He posed, one hand on his chin and the other miming a phone. "Yes, sir, of course you can come and visit the site. Yes, I will arrange a meeting with the councillors. Of course, they're not all in favour, but perhaps if I could grease the wheels a little more ..." He shrugged. "You can't fake all that. It doesn't end well." He rubbed his chin, and she wondered how many scams, how many new faces and identities he'd been through since she came home and found him gone. Everything had still been there, even his shoes still lined up in the hall, but he'd been gone anyway. She'd known straight away, and it had seemed so inevitable that all she could feel was anger at herself for not being the one that left.

And she'd put up with it all, with the police and the questions and the accusations and the cold hard walls of the interview rooms, and she'd said nothing. And she still wasn't sure why. Looking at him now, she couldn't *imagine* why. Although she had a niggling feeling that it had to do with not wanting to admit how well he'd deceived her. Which felt like a rather sorry excuse, now she was here.

"I had hoped to run with this for another six months," Harvey said. "Get the money in from the investors, cash the machines in, then get out. But it's just my luck to run across you, isn't it?"

"The luck's all mine," Alice said, and he snorted.

"You never could just listen and not be smart, could you? Always so *smart*." He sneered the word, starting to turn back to her, then stopped. "What the hell?" He leaned closer to the window. "What's going on out there?"

It was the best chance Alice was likely to get. She gripped the chair spindles she was lashed to, surged to her feet, and spun, smashing the rickety chair into the wall. The shock jarred up her arms, and her back made a most alarming crunching sound, but she felt the chair collapse into the impact.

"Hey!" Harvey bellowed, turning back to her and holding a hand up like a policeman shouting *stop*. "Don't be stupid!"

Alice gave up on the wall and charged Harvey with the wreckage of the chair still clinging to her back. He scrabbled in his pocket for the syringe but she was too close, dropping her shoulder and driving it into his midriff. He yelped as they slammed into the wall together, then shoved her off. Alice staggered back, struggling to keep her balance, then stepped forward and pivoted hard, slamming the chair into him just as she had into the wall. He was spitting curses at her, and this time when he threw her off she felt the chair come apart. She sprawled to the floor on her belly, pulling her arms free and rolling onto her back to see him standing over her with the capped syringe in one hand and one of the chair legs raised in the other. She stopped.

"You just couldn't leave it, could you?" he snarled. There was blood on his chin, Alice noted with a small curl of satisfaction. "I gave you a warning. An offer, even. I mean, I knew you wouldn't take it, not you. Always poking, poking, being oh so smart. But I thought maybe, if your friend was threatened. But you don't care, do you? You don't care about anyone. No, you just care about being *smart*. You figured out it was me, and you've ruined this whole operation."

Alice pushed herself onto her elbows. "Is that what Thomas did? Charles? Figured out it was a scam?"

Harvey shrugged. "Thomas was talking to the farmers and was going to file a suit against BelleVue on their behalf. Gavin Peabody wanted more money. And Charles was going to go to the press about the bribes." He waved the syringe at her, a nasty little smile that she'd never seen before curling the edges of his lips. "I'm going to drop you in some back street in Leeds. Let everyone think you were out having some dirty fun when it all got too much for your poor old heart."

Alice licked her lips. "Did you know I was here, then? Did you set this up?"

"Don't flatter yourself. How the hell would I know you'd moved to this crappy sheepfold of a place?" He was trying to pull the cap off the syringe with his teeth, but it seemed to be stuck.

"So just bad luck, then?" He was still doing battle with the syringe. If she was going to do anything, she needed it to be now.

"You brought it on yourself, Alice. Poking your nose in and

being so smart. Dammit." He dropped the chair leg so he could use both hands on the syringe. "Hold still."

She spared a moment to wonder if anyone actually did hold still in a situation like that. Then she rolled onto her belly, grabbed his ankle with both hands and *heaved,* bringing her knees under her at the same time and turning the pull into a lift. Harvey yelped, staggering, and as his weight hit his back foot she flung his leg up and away, sending him crashing into the window with the sound of shattering glass. She snatched up the chair leg he'd dropped and started to scramble to her feet, but her bad hip betrayed her, and she spilled to her knees with a little cry.

Harvey charged back from the window and aimed a kick at her stomach, and she flung herself sideways, landing hard and setting her hip complaining again. Harvey grabbed the back of her jacket, hauling her half upright, and she let herself be pulled up. She still had the chair leg and she jabbed for his belly, but the angle was all wrong, and he gave an *oof* of pain but didn't let go. She dropped the chair leg and grabbed his free arm instead as he stabbed the syringe toward her neck, giving a little mewl of alarm as he forced her back. He let go of her jacket, using both arms to drive the syringe down. Her knees gave way, and now he had height as well as weight, the needle coming closer and closer.

"Brought it on yourself, Alice," he hissed, and a horrible coldness clawed its way up her spine as she realised she couldn't stop him. She pushed harder against him, but it was no good. He was heavier and younger than she was, and the needle was too close to escape. And no one knew she was here.

Then there was movement in the corner of her eye, and a yellowing plastic kettle bounced off the side of Harvey's head with a hollow clang, more startling than painful. He yelped, turning to see who it was, and Alice drove her head straight forward into his belly. Well, lower belly, since she was kneeling. He howled, dropping the syringe and clutching his injured parts, and Alice scrambled to her feet, retrieving the chair leg on her way up. She smacked Harvey on the side of the head with it, and he pitched into the wall, bounced off and went to his knees. She hit him again, and he went to the floor, still holding his injured dignity, his howls becoming wails, and Lily picked up the kettle and hit him again. He whimpered into the carpet, and Lily hit him a third time, splitting the kettle down the side. She discarded it, took Alice's chair leg, and gave the gasping Harvey a final whack that silenced him entirely.

She looked at him for a moment, then at Alice. "That felt good," she said.

Alice rubbed her complaining hip and examined the kettle. "Well. No tea, then."

"No," Lily agreed, and walked to her handbag, lying on the dresser. She drew a quarter bottle of whisky out. "I was feeling more in the mood for this, anyway."

Alice nodded, and nudged Harvey with the toe of her hiking boot. "You want to give him to the police?"

"Do you?" Lily asked.

Alice smiled. "I have a better idea, as it happens."

Lily smiled back. "Do tell."

24
MIRIAM

Miriam pulled herself forward a little further, trying to avoid the sheep droppings, and put her hand in a thistle. "Ow!"

"Gloves," Rose said, crawling past her. "You really should be better prepared."

Miriam made a face at Rose's retreating form and fended off Angelus, who had decided that any talk meant he was invited to lick the speaker enthusiastically and generously. They had almost reached the farmyard. One more fence to scale, one more field to cross, then there'd be only one wall left between them and open ground. There hadn't been any sign of movement yet, but it was still far too light out here for her liking. If Alice's kidnappers looked out the window, there'd be no hiding, she thought. Although, she also rather thought they were unlikely to strike fear into the heart of hardened criminals, unless they were particularly alarmed by women of a certain age.

"Car!" The hiss came from Jasmine, who grabbed Primrose and clamped a hand over the dog's mouth to stop her yapping. It was quite the improvement.

Miriam flattened herself to the ground, damp seeping into her trousers. Her knees hurt and her shoulders ached from all the crawling about the place. She wasn't built for this. And given that they had been about to drive up to the house before the van got stuck, she wasn't entirely sure why they were trying to be stealthy now. Ronnie just kept talking about the element of surprise and throwing sheep droppings at anyone who tried to walk about normally. Well, he had been until Carlotta threw some back and high-fived Rosemary when she got him in the mouth. Rainbow and Harriet were crawling about in combat jackets with bandanas on their heads, and Barry and Jemima still hadn't come back. Miriam imagined they were doing rather less crawling through thistles and sheep droppings, and felt vaguely jealous.

The car came to a stop somewhere on the lane, and after a moment someone shouted, "Hello? Anyone about?"

Priya had scuttled over to the wall that bordered the lane, and now she peeked over the top, then sat down again. "He can't get past the van," she whispered.

"What's that?" Teresa asked, a little too loudly, and Pearl shushed her.

"Hello?" the man called again, and a car door slammed.

Priya took another peek. "He's walking this way!"

"Sit down!" Ronnie hissed, waving at her wildly. "Everyone quiet! He could be a pig!"

Miriam thought he'd be better being quiet himself, rather than carrying on about pigs, but the women stayed silent, clustered near the walls and flattened against the ground. The walls to the lane were high, so unless the man came right up and peered over, he wouldn't see them. Rose and Gert were both holding Angelus still, and Miriam could see the dog shivering with excitement.

Boots crunched on the gravel drive, heading for the farmyard, and when Miriam sat up she saw the man's head bobbing toward the house.

"That was close," she whispered to Jasmine, and the younger woman nodded furiously. She had a smudge of dirt on her forehead and her pink fleece was barely visible under the mud.

"Do you think he was a thug?" she asked.

"A thug?"

Jasmine shrugged. "You know, a heavy hired by the developer."

"I don't know. He didn't sound like a thug." Not that she was sure what a thug sounded like. Maybe like someone in one of those London movies full of gangsters.

"Stop gossiping and get moving!" Ronnie crept past them, walking bent over and clutching a tire iron like a rifle.

Miriam gave him her most Alice look. "Stop talking so much. The rest of us don't like your voice as much as you do."

He gaped at her, and Jasmine giggled.

"Come on, Jas, dear. This is ridiculous." She led the way across the field on her hands and knees, dragging her cricket bat with her, slipping as she got to the muddy area by the gate and gouging herself on inopportune pebbles. She peeked into the last field, with its soft long grass and wildflowers, then opened the gate and led everyone through except Rose and Teresa, who had already climbed over.

"Cheat," Rose said, and Miriam stuck her tongue out at her.

They hurried across the last field in awkward crouches, Miriam fighting the urge to sneeze as pollen and seeds rose around them in a cloud. She glanced around, checking for the dragons, and saw them watching over the wall from the field behind them. It made the tightness in her chest ease a little, just knowing they were there, even if she'd said they shouldn't be. Some directions weren't meant to be listened to. She looked back at where she was going in time to avoid being knocked over by Angelus, who was bouncing around the field like a kangaroo on all fours. She joined the others as they lined up behind the stone wall, Rose just able to see over the top by standing on her tiptoes, Teresa in an uncomfortable crouch that made Miriam's knees hurt just looking at it. The house was directly across the yard from them, the front door open, and someone had turned the light on in the hall. Ronnie raised his hand with his fist clenched, and the ladies of the W.I. looked at each other, then at Rainbow and Harriet.

"He can't help himself," Harriet said apologetically.

"Army?" Carlotta asked.

"Couldn't get in. Bad hips," Rainbow said.

"*Shh!*" Ronnie said, glaring at them all.

They went back to staring at the house. They waited long enough for Miriam to see Beaufort, Mortimer and Amelia had crept into the field to their left, and were padding down to the farmyard wall. Amelia waved, and Miriam gave a nervous wave back.

"Someone's there!" Rosemary whispered.

There was movement beyond the door, and a moment later a man stopped in the doorway, frowning out at the yard. He'd put the outside light on too, and it washed over his curly dark hair and lit his face.

"It's the journalist!" Miriam exclaimed.

"The one with the dimples," Carlotta said.

"You would remember those," Rosemary said, then gave a muffled *oof* as Carlotta elbowed her.

"*Duck!*" Jasmine squeaked, and the eleven women – and Ronnie – dropped behind the wall as the journalist scanned the yard. They stayed crouched there, looking at each other.

"What's he doing here?" Miriam asked.

"He must've found out about the farms," Rainbow said. "We should use him."

"No, no. We can't talk to him," Gert said. "He's an annoying little hack."

"We definitely shouldn't talk to him," Miriam agreed. Especially not with the dragons in the other field. He might end up *seeing* them, and they had more than enough to deal with, what with kidnappings and murders and car crashes.

"But it's good to have the press on our side," Harriet said. "He could write a whole piece about it. It could really help!"

"We don't know who else is there," Priya said. "We can't just shout, hey, come join us!"

There was a murmur of agreement among the group, then Miriam got to her knees. As if it were a signal, everyone else scrambled up, and they peeked over the wall together, only to find the journalist standing in the yard looking back at them.

"Hey," he said.

Miriam glanced around. Everyone else had ducked back to safety, leaving her staring at the journalist. She considered following them, but there didn't seem to be much point. "Um, hello," she said.

They looked at each other for a moment longer, then the journalist said, "What're you doing there?"

Miriam licked her lips. "Rambling?"

"Rambling? In a farmyard?"

"Well, *we're* not actually in it, you are. We, um, we're looking for the footpath."

The journalist took a step closer. "I know you."

"Really?" She'd been hoping he might not recognise her with all the mud on her face and, she had a feeling, foliage in her hair.

"Yes. From the manor house. Ms–– Ms Ellis, right?"

"Um. Yes, actually."

"Don't tell him your name!" Jasmine squeaked from somewhere around Miriam's knees.

"But he already knows who I am," she said, looking down at the younger woman.

"I'm Ervin, Ervin Giles," the journalist said.

"I know," she admitted, turning back to him.

"Okay." He gave her a really quite lovely smile. "So what're you actually doing here?"

"Protesting!" Rainbow jumped up next to Miriam, making the journalist take a step back. "We won't stand for our beautiful land to be flattened and pulverised in the name of corporate greed!"

"Quite," the journalist said, taking his phone from his pocket. "Do you mind if I record this?"

"No! I'll shout it from the rooftops!"

"No need for that." He squinted at her. "Wait – I remember you! You blocked the road with that tree."

"Mother Nature did that. We merely protected the tree."

Ervin nodded. "Fair enough. Look, how many farms are involved in this? I've been to two others already that were empty."

"It's a conspiracy of the highest order," Rainbow declared, lifting her mud-spattered chin. "An age-old tale of greed winning out against the rights of the little people!"

Ervin gave an agreeable nod. "Okay, so tell me what's going on. What are your plans for the protest, exactly?"

Miriam stared at Rainbow as she launched into a grand description of how they'd form human barricades and sleep in the trees for months rather than allow the land to be destroyed. She was quite fuzzy on the details of what, exactly, the developer's plans were, but so passionate it was quite easy to miss that omission. Certainly Ervin didn't seem too bothered. He just kept nodding and making encouraging noises. Miriam wondered if it could actually have been this easy. If they could have just gone to the press and put the story out in the open, and the farms would have been safe, and so would Alice. Then she remembered the terrible, heart-freezing realisation that the brakes weren't working, and the sight of the other cars coming toward her, and the impact of car on wall, which could have gone so much worse than it did. No, she wasn't sure it ever could have been that easy at all. And Alice was still in there somewhere.

"I'm not sure we should do this right now," she started, and at that moment there was the sound of smashing glass from the house. Ervin spun around, and the W.I. popped up from behind the wall, staring at the house. A man staggered away from the shattered window, and Miriam whispered, "*Alice.*"

"I *knew* there was someone in there!" Ervin said, and started across the yard, just as a door slammed open somewhere out of sight around the sheds.

"Wait!" Jasmine shouted. "There's someone else out here!"

Ervin hesitated, and someone whistled, a sharp shrill noise that sounded awfully authoritative to Miriam.

"I think you should get over here," she said to the journalist.

"No, I need to see what's going on." But he didn't make any move toward the whistle. Miriam peered up at the window, looking for movement or a swirl of silver hair, but there was nothing. She wondered what the breaking glass meant. It couldn't be anything good.

A man appeared around the corner of one of the sheds, and stopped when he saw the journalist in the yard and the women peering over the wall. He was wearing black trousers with far too many pockets and a black jacket that looked very shiny and sleek. He stared at them for a moment, then said, "What the hell are you lot doing here?"

No one replied for a moment, then Ervin said, "Um. Rambling?"

"That seems a bit bloody unlikely."

"We're lost," Miriam said, her tongue too dry in her mouth.

"Got that right," the man said, then, raising his voice just slightly, called, "Rich?"

There was a pause, and Miriam hissed at the journalist, "*Get over here!*"

"I might, actually." He took a step toward to wall, and the man clicked his tongue sharply.

"Stay," he said, and raised a hand, levelling it at Ervin. Miriam stared at his hand, wondering if it was a prosthetic. Gloves didn't tend to be so hard and metallic looking. So—

"Oh bollocks," Ervin said, sounding a little breathless.

"Down!" Rainbow bellowed.

Miriam tore her gaze off the man's hand in time to see the tall, bearded man they'd met before come around the corner of the shed, then Jasmine had hold of her and was hauling her to the ground.

"That was a *gun!*" Jasmine gasped, her hands shaking. Angelus was barking, big booming *arfs* that seemed to echo off the walls and ring in Miriam's ears, making the world around her swim. *"Miriam!"*

She shook herself, trying to dislodge the noise. "Are you sure?"

"Definitely," Gert said. She looked uncharacteristically pale.

"But why— why would they have *guns?*" Miriam whispered. And not practical old shotguns for rabbits or anything like that. Whatever he'd been holding had been short and fat, a nasty ugly thing made for hiding and hurting. "They shouldn't have guns!"

Rose started to say something regarding the man's ancestry and possible relation to non-humans, and from over the wall, they heard the man say, "Hold it right there." Miriam supposed Ervin was making a break for it, and started to climb to her feet, not sure how she could help, but sure she should do something, then there was a horrible *bang*.

Miriam felt something reach inside her and squeeze her heart so hard she thought it might stop. Pearl gave a small scream, and Carlotta clutched Rosemary to her like she would a child. Then there was echoing silence.

Jasmine touched her ear, then said in a shaky voice, "Is everyone okay?"

There was a general murmur of agreement, and Miriam took a deep, wobbly breath. No one seemed inclined to move, just exchanging anxious looks and little touches, a way of assuring each other they all still existed. She pressed her trembling hands together, counted everyone again, then said, "Was— what about Ervin?"

Rose lifted herself onto her knees carefully, while Priya tried to drag her back down. Rose pushed her gently away, took her hat off, stuck it on the end of her garden shears and lifted them so the hat stuck up over the wall. There was no response, no more shots, so Rose climbed to her feet and peeked cautiously into the yard. "I don't see anyone."

"What? They were right there." Miriam scrambled to her feet, took a deep breath, and lifted her head over the stones, flinching from a shot that never came. The yard was empty. "Where's he gone?"

"Well, he wasn't shot, at least," Gert said, standing up next to Miriam. "We'd … well, we'd be able to see if he had been."

"They must have taken him prisoner," Pearl said, her eyes wide.

"Are we going back?" Jasmine asked in a small voice. She was hugging Primrose to her, the dog wriggling and whining. "They've got *guns*."

"I think that's wise," Priya said, and everyone looked at Miriam. She tried to ignore them. Why did they insist on looking at her? She wasn't the sort of person people looked to for leadership in a crisis. Or outside of one. But even Gert was waiting to see what she said.

She took a deep breath, thinking that she'd really like to be home, in her pyjamas, watching something terribly cheesy and mindless and probably involving sequins and dancing on TV, rather than standing in a field covered in mud and sheep effluent while someone took potshots about the place.

"We could wait for the police," Rosemary said. "You know, just keep an eye on things."

The police. "Um," Miriam said. She'd had her phone out to text them, of course, and she'd sat in the car, yes, then Beaufort had surprised her, then … "Oh dear."

"Oh dear?" Gert said. "As in oh dear, I didn't call them?"

"Maybe?" Miriam said, then wilted as everyone glared at her. "I was going to, I was! But everyone was rushing, and the …" she caught herself before she could say *dragons*, because Rainbow and Ronnie and Harriet were here, and they still didn't know "… I forgot."

"Well, damn," Gert said. "That's inconvenient."

"We'll just call them now," Rose said. "Who's got a phone?"

There was a rustle of movement as everyone checked their pockets, then silence other than Angelus' steady barking. Everyone looked at Ronnie, who was unusually quiet and pale.

"You made us leave them all behind," Priya said. "No room for them on a covert operation, you said. You silly man!"

"To be fair," Teresa pointed out, "I can never find clothes with a good phone pocket."

"Buy men's," Jasmine said. "They're much better for that sort of thing."

"So sexist," Rose said. "Typical!"

They all glared at Ronnie, who tried to hide behind Rainbow.

"Well," Miriam said, "Someone has to go back for the phones." She looked at the house, looming grey and uninviting across the yard, and the sheds crouched together as if they held monstrous secrets. Which they did. They held at least two men with guns, and who knew what else. "I'm going after Alice."

No one spoke, until Jasmine said, "They *shot* at the journalist."

"But they didn't hurt him." She hoped. "We need to get Alice out of there." Miriam was almost certain that a last hold-out of common sense was jumping up and down in the back of her mind and screaming, but she ignored it. "I can't just leave her."

Silence again, and this time it was Rose who broke it. "Well, damn." She'd managed to get hold of Angelus and stop him barking. Now he was just growling steadily, like some massive engine. "Let's go, woman!"

"I'm in," Rosemary said. "How do you deal with kidnappers in the old country, Carlotta?"

Carlotta looked thoughtful. "I think it involves missing limbs. Or eyes. We may have to improvise."

Priya climbed to her feet. "I'm in, then."

"Me too," Pearl said. "Obviously." Teresa gave her a quick, one-armed hug, and Jasmine put Primrose on the ground, where she growled at everyone.

"I'm coming. We can set Primmy on them."

The women mumbled agreement, although Miriam imagined they all thought much as she did – that with any luck the dog might run away and never be found again, and that she was more likely to bite one of them than the gunman. But it was the thought that counted.

"You're all mad," Harriet said. "I'm a protester, not a commando."

Rainbow fidgeted for a moment, then said, "Fine. *Fine*. But only because I can't stand for anyone shooting at my little sister." She looked at Harriet. "Can you go call the police, and take Ronnie with you?"

"That I'll do." Harriet helped a trembling Ronnie to his feet and they crept off down the field, bent low. He clung to her, reciting numbers and making little squeaking noises every time he tripped on a stone.

"What's wrong with him?" Gert asked.

"He's not very good in high pressure situations," Rainbow said. "He was a stockbroker when he was younger, and now if the stress gets too much he just shuts down and starts reciting stock prices." She looked at Miriam. "Alright then, little sister. What's the plan?"

Miriam managed to swallow her own squeak, and reminded

herself that, at the very least, she wasn't haunted by stock markets. That sounded dreadful. "Well," she said, "I think—"

"Can you hear that barking?" Rose interrupted.

"What barking?" Teresa asked.

"I hear it." Jasmine put her hands on the wall, peering into the darkening yard. "It sounds like it's in one of the sheds."

"Or not," Rose said, as Ervin bolted into the yard, arms and legs pumping desperately, followed by a wash of men's laughter and the deep-throated baying of dogs. He sprinted for the nearest wall, flung himself at it so hard the women gave a collective wince, and tumbled over the top into safety as at least a dozen frankly enormous dogs thundered into the yard.

"Well, at least he's not hurt," Pearl said.

25
DI ADAMS

DI Adams swung the Golf into the farm lane, the engine snarling as she pushed as fast as she dared, the surface a mix of rock and mud that wasn't designed for speed. Collins had one hand on the door, the other on the dashboard, and Thompson was clambering over him as if he were one of those carpeted towers people buy for their cats to ignore.

"There's definitely a block on this place. I can smell it. I bet it's werewolf runes." He stepped rather heavily on Collins' lap, and Collins yelped.

"Watch it!"

"How's that tracking looking?" DI Adams asked, trying to see beyond the stone walls to the house.

"The journalist and Auntie Miriam are both here."

"We just have to hope Alice is, too." By the time they'd left the house the little blip that showed Alice's phone had vanished entirely from somewhere around the middle of town, and DI Adams had a sneaking suspicion that the culprit was the well in the centre of the village square. But even in a village as quiet as Toot Hansell it seemed unlikely anyone had stuffed a body down the well when it was still light out, so they'd left it and gone in pursuit of Miriam and Ervin.

Dandy *whuff*-ed in her ear and she shoved him away with one hand, then grabbed the steering wheel and brought them to a sliding stop that sent the dog pitching between the seats in a sea of grey dreadlocks.

"Get it off!" the cat wailed. "Gods, the stink!"

"Stop making such a fuss. He doesn't smell."

"Your noses *suck*."

DI Adams managed to get the handbrake on under the overexcited Dandy, then joined Collins as he climbed out of the car. They left the doors open, and the visible cat and invisible dog followed them.

"What d'you reckon?" Collins asked. There was a car stopped in the lane just beyond the gate, nose not far from the tail of a van that was slewed across the lane and leaning at a rather sad angle into the mud.

She squinted at the car. "Might be Ervin's."

"Ervin now, is it?"

She gave him an unimpressed look. "Don't know the van."

Colin scratched his head. "I might."

"Really? Whose is it?"

"My mum's."

"Oh, good," DI Adams said, thinking of her first encounter with Rainbow and her entourage. "Shall we prepare for assault with table condiments?"

"Possibly."

DI Adams leaned into the car and got out the swords. "Want one?"

He frowned at her. "I feel ridiculous carrying that thing around."

"You look pretty ridiculous, too," Thompson said. "It's not like the sword makes that any worse, though."

Dandy took a couple of steps forward and gave a sudden, low growl. "What is it?" DI Adams asked.

"What's what?" Collins asked.

"Dandy's growling."

"That can't be good." He held out his hand. "Give me a sword."

DI Adams passed him one of the fencing blades hilt-first, and as he grabbed it there was an eruption of sound from the direction of the farmhouse, great bellowing barks that sounded like the Hound of the Baskervilles had built itself an army.

Dandy snarled, and every hair on DI Adams' skin tried to abandon ship at the sound. It shook something old and primal and frightened in her, and she swallowed hard.

"Was that Dandy?" Collins whispered.

"Yeah." She had to lick her lips before answering. "You heard him?"

"Yeah, and now I'm glad I can't see him."

"Let's go." She started forward at a jog, obscurely sure that if she didn't move fast enough she'd grind to a halt. Sure, they had a devil dandy dog, but if Thompson was right, there was what sounded like a whole battalion of werewolves up there.

"I might just hang with the car," Thompson called after them, and no one answered.

DI Adams squeezed past the back of the van, scraping her side on the wall, and spotted something lying on the lane a little further ahead. She ran toward it, then pulled up short as she got close enough to see a Labrador sprawled across the rutted lane. "Oh no," she said as Collins joined her. "It's not dead, is it?"

"I don't know." He edged forward and crouched down next to the dog. It didn't move. "Ah, poor thing." He put a hand on its side, and the Lab gave a shuddering snore, thumped its tail a couple of times, rolled over and went back to sleep. He looked at DI Adams. "Narcoleptic, maybe."

"That one stinks too," Thompson said from the safety of the wall.

"I thought you were staying behind," DI Adams said.

"Yeah, well. I've got you lot this far, I can't abandon you now. You'll need all the help you can get."

"I'm so reassured," Collins said, and the two inspectors started up the lane again.

"Don't run with swords," the cat shouted, pacing them along the wall. "See? Hopeless!"

DI Adams felt ridiculous. She was running up a country lane in the dusk of a Yorkshire summer with an invisible dog, an insulting cat, and a sword grasped in one hand, preparing to confront werewolves and hoping for dragons. She was not at all sure what had happened to her life, but she could pinpoint exactly *when* it had happened, as well as who was responsible, as it all came back to her first encounter with the Toot Hansell Women's Institute. She felt rather like stopping right where she was and shouting at the universe, "No one told me about this!"

But she didn't. She kept running for the house and the floodlit yard, toward the baying of the werewolves. She had thought they'd sound more *wolf*-y, but maybe that was a Hollywood thing, like the silver bullets. They just sounded like big, bad-tempered dogs, and as they rounded a last turn in the lane and saw the gate lying half-open into the yard before them, she rather thought the enormous creature that dropped its front paws down from a wall and started thundering toward them *looked* like a big, bad-tempered dog.

"Over the wall!" Collins bellowed, and she stopped worrying about the details and bolted after him. They scrambled over the wall to the right of the lane, knocking the loose stones on top flying, crashing down into a sea of fragrant mud. "*That's* a werewolf?"

"Eh," Thompson said. He was still on top of the wall, staying just out of reach of the dog as it lunged at him, spittle flying and barks shaking its chest. "I think this may be a Rottweiler, actually." He bopped the dog's nose as it got too close, and the dog snarled, lunging hard enough at the wall to send both the cat and the topmost stones tumbling into the field. Thompson jumped clear, landing lightly on the mucky ground, and shook a paw out distastefully. "This is a bit yuck."

"It's a Rottweiler," DI Adams said.

"Yeah. Or some mix, you know. Big. Stupid. Hungry."

"Well, that's just great," Collins said. "I can't stab a bloody *dog,* can I?"

"Oh, but a half human, half wolf you were fine with?" the cat asked.

"I guess we need the RSPCA," DI Adams said.

"And a stronger wall," Thompson suggested, as more rocks tumbled into the field next to them.

"Bollocks." Collins jumped up and waved his arms at the dog. "Bad dog! *Bad dog!* Um – sit!"

The dog bellowed more enormous barks at them, and kept up its attack on the wall.

"Try German," the cat said. "They're German, aren't they?"

"Come on," DI Adams said. "We'll go through the fields." She headed off at a run, Dandy pacing her easily. He seemed bigger.

"*Nein?*" Collins suggested to the dog, then ran after her.

THE DOG BOUNDED along the other side of the wall, still baying, and as they reached the corner of the field it discovered a gate which it promptly started trying to scramble over. It looked as if it was going to be a little too successful, so DI Adams clambered over the wall into the next field. Collins followed her just as the dog crashed over the gate behind them, and he shouted, "Into the yard! We can make it to the house!"

DI Adams didn't bother answering, just hauled herself over yet another stone wall into the yard, wondering why no one around here went in for nice, easy to climb wooden fences, snagging her trousers on the way down and hearing them tear. She stumbled as she landed, bounced to her feet, and sprinted for the house. Two dogs, different breeds and even bigger than the Rottweiler, came barrelling out from behind one of the sheds. They weren't barking, just growling steadily as their enormous legs tore up the farmyard, and she turned to scramble back over the wall, shouting, "Go back!"

Collins was straddling the wall, the Rottweiler on one side and the dogs on the other, and he tried to haul DI Adams up, but drystone walls weren't made for climbing. The top crumpled, sending them both spilling to the ground, and Dandy surged over the wall and grabbed the Rottweiler by the scruff of the neck as it lunged for the inspectors. He flung it like a terrier would a rat, hurling it into the other two dogs, then lowered his head and *growled.* The noise shook DI Adams' bones, and Dandy towered above them, his teeth yellow and glistening in the low light.

The dogs had been knocked sprawling, and now they climbed to their feet, lips drawn back from their teeth as they answered Dandy's growls with their own. More dogs were emerging from around the sheds, twelve, fifteen, more, and people were shouting on the other side of the yard.

"Adams?" Collins said.

"Yes?"

"I'm guessing Dandy's doing his thing?"

"He's sort of standing over us."

"Okay. Should we run?"

"I think probably." She got her feet under her and stood slowly, keeping her eyes on the dogs. They were spreading out, trying to surround them, but most of their attention was on Dandy, who looked the size of a horse in the fading light. Slobber was dripping from his jaws, and his eyes burned through the dreadlocks. He took a slow step forward, snarling, and the dogs backed up. DI Adams grabbed Collins' arm. "On second thought, don't run."

"I really want to."

Dandy advanced again, and DI Adams followed, pulling Collins with her. The dogs spread out further, their circle cutting back toward the wall.

"We're going to be surrounded in a moment," Collins said.

"We're okay while we're with him," she said, hoping she was right. Dandy was still moving forward, and she reached out hesitantly, putting a hand on his flank. His head twitched toward her, then he went back to concentrating on the dogs. His skin was hotter than it had any right to be, making her think of dragons as much as devils. After all, she knew dragons existed.

They were halfway across the yard when the first of the dogs broke rank. It bolted up behind them, nipping at Dandy's heels then retreating. Dandy spun so fast he knocked DI Adams into Collins, and they sprawled to the ground as the circle of dogs lunged at them. Dandy spun back again, but now more dogs had taken up the attack, darting in and retreating, snapping at his legs, distracting him and making him dance. One lunged for the inspectors, and DI Adams slapped it with the flat of her sword.

"Run now?" Collins suggested.

"Not unless you're faster than they are."

"Dammit." They were back to back instinctively, turning and lashing out as the dogs closed in. Dandy had fallen silent and was fighting with a horrible efficiency, but the dogs had banded into a ruthless pack, some attacking his hindquarters while others kept his teeth busy. The growls and snarls bounced off the walls of the sheds and farmhouse, and DI Adams' heart was tight in her chest. She didn't have to know much about dandies to know they could be hurt. There was already blood on Dandy's flanks as well as his jaw.

She swung the sword at a massive brindled dog and said, "We have to get out of this bloody yard somehow."

"I know— Hey!" Collins shouted suddenly. "Hey, you! We're police! Call your damn dogs off!"

DI Adams craned around to see a dozen men in heavy black trousers and fitted jackets walking across the yard. One of them said something to the others, and they laughed.

"Police!" Collins bellowed, and one of them gave a little finger wave. The others laughed again, but the laughter collapsed into yelps as a rain of rocks flew out of the nearest field, most pattering down harmlessly but a few making contact. The men looked at each other, words inaudible over the sound of the fighting dogs.

This time DI Adams was watching when the heads popped over the wall and the rocks were unleashed. One caught the tallest man on the cheek and he staggered, and a cheer went up from beyond the wall. "Oh, bloody hell," she snapped, and caught a dog a solid blow with the side of the sword that sent it scampering away. "Bloody W.I."

"Dammit," Collins said, and as he spoke the men ran for the wall, ducking the next shower of rocks easily. Light caught metal in the men's hands.

"Gun!" DI Adams shouted, and bolted. She heard the enormous *whuff* of Dandy's displeasure behind her, heard Collins shout her name, but she ignored them all and just *ran*. The dogs were barking behind her, and she heard the thunder of quick feet on gravel, too close and too fast, and all she could hope was that Dandy was following her, and she could reach the wall in time. Something snagged her heel, sending a flare of pain up her leg, and she stumbled, yelping as furry bodies surged around her.

"Adams!" Collins shouted, and Dandy gave a howl of fury, but they were both too far away to help. She caught her balance, bringing the sword up in time to fend off some enormous beast that seemed to be channelling Cujo, and Thompson sprinted across her path with his tail the size of a bottle brush.

"Stinking mongrels!" he shrieked as he ran. *"Catch me if you can, you mutts!"*

A volley of confused barking erupted around her, and she broke for the wall again, and now the only footfalls were hers and Collins' as he overtook her. He hit the gate and scrambled over it just ahead of her, stopping at the top to offer her a hand, but she boosted herself up and over in one quick motion.

Mud-encrusted figures were fleeing across the field, and the men had spread out after them, moving much faster. One put a shot into the air and shouted, *"You're trespassing! Stand down!"* There was a chorus of yelps and imaginative cursing, but no one stopped. A few of the figures turned and started pelting the men with more rocks, and others were diving through the gate into the next field.

DI Adams sprinted through the long grass, ignoring the pain in her leg, and reached the nearest man just as he raised his gun. She didn't know if it was going to be another warning shot or not, and she didn't particularly care. She brought the flat of the sword down hard on his wrist, and he released the gun with a yelp of pain. He spun toward her, and she whirled the blade, smacking him on the side of the head and sending him to the ground, momentarily grateful that she'd remembered to use the flat and wasn't going to have to write up a report explaining how she'd come to decapitate a suspect.

"Adams, duck!" Collins bellowed behind her, and she dropped to the ground as a gunshot went off, alarmingly close, and all the light went out of the world.

The man was moving underneath her, so she punched him hard enough that he gasped and lay still, then she sat up. Dandy hulked above her, blocking out the last of the sun, holding one of the black-clad men's arms in his jaws. It was still attached, fortunately, and he'd dropped the gun. She looked around to see dragons pouring over the wall at the top of the field, wings flung wide as they protected the W.I., who seemed to be taking advantage of the cover to throw more rocks at the men rather than retreat. The men were looking rather less hardened than they had a moment ago and were, for the most part, legging it enthusiastically back across the field. There was a large dragon with very baggy skin sitting on top of one of the stragglers, examining a gun with great curiosity, and another man was on his knees with his hands clasped behind his head, eyes shut as he prayed very loudly and enthusiastically. A sleek purple dragon was holding a man face down in the grass rather casually as he thrashed about in panic, and she shouted at a dragon with multicoloured spines, "No flames!"

DI Adams shook her head slightly, and found her handcuffs as Collins jogged up, face pale.

"Are you alright?" she asked him, but he wasn't looking at her. He was looking directly at Dandy.

"Is that …?" he managed.

DI Adams looked at the dandy, who looked back at her with those red eyes. He was unnaturally still, and the man he had hold of was whimpering steadily. "You can see him?"

"I think everyone can see him. How the hell does he fit in the car?"

"He's not normally this big." She nodded at the man she was kneeling on. "Cuff him, will you?" Collins grabbed the man's arms as she stood up and put a hand on Dandy's shoulder. She almost had to go on her tiptoes to do it. "Put him down. Drop him, there's a good boy."

Dandy looked at her for a moment, then let the man go. He crumpled to his knees, clutching his arm with his good hand. It was bleeding, but not badly. "What is that thing?" he shouted at the inspectors. "What *is* it?"

DI Adams patted Dandy. "He's a *very good boy*."

Dandy wriggled with pleasure and licked her hand, and Collins said, "Oh. He's gone again."

The man on his knees said, "Drugs, right? You gave us drugs. Damn pigs."

❧

DRAGONS AND WOMEN were still running around the field, chasing down the rest of the men, who had made it as far as the gate before Thompson came flying over it, shouting, "*Incoming!*" The dogs hit the gate just behind him, their combined weight tearing it from its hinges and spilling the pack into the field. The men swerved and scattered, running silently with their heads down and their legs pumping, and the dragons swept onto the field with their bellies alight and their wings thundering.

"Lord Walter!" Mortimer was coming in low over the wall, angling toward the dogs. "Lord Walter, no eating the humans, please!"

"In my day," the old dragon with the saggy skin began, poking the man he was sitting on, then was cut off by the purple dragon.

"Rockford, that means you too!" she bellowed.

"Aw," a rather chunky dragon said, wheeling overhead. "Really?"

"Round up the dogs!" Amelia shouted, galloping past the inspectors in pursuit of a couple of German Shepherds.

"*Ew*. I bet they taste gross," the chunky dragon said.

"Rockford!" Mortimer snapped. "No one said you could eat them!"

"Oops," Walter said to no one in particular, and put Primrose down. She promptly bit his tail, but he didn't seem to notice.

"Colin! DI Adams!" A muddy figure ran across the grass to them, clutching a cricket bat like they meant business. From the bushy hair, it could only be Miriam. "Are you okay?"

"Auntie Miriam! What on earth are you all doing here?"

"Oh." She hesitated. "Well, initially it was just a peaceful protest, then we figured out Alice had been kidnapped, so now I suppose it's a rescue mission?"

"Right," Collins said, as DI Adams pinched the bridge of her nose and wondered what normal W.I.s got up to of an evening. "At any point did you consider calling us?"

"I did, but then I got distracted. I'm sorry. I did mean to." She waved at the house. "But we think Alice is in there. And there was fighting!"

"Fighting?" DI Adams asked.

"Yes, the window broke and everything." Miriam shook the cricket bat impatiently. "Go on! We've got this."

DI Adams raised her eyebrows and looked at Collins, who shrugged. "They do seem to kind of be on top of things."

DI Adams watched a man struggle to get what looked very much like a not-at-all-legal taser out of his belt, at which point Mortimer shrieked and hit him so hard with his tail the man face-planted into a large clump of nettles, the weapon flying into the long grass.

"I told you!" Mortimer shouted, to no one in particular. "I *told* you tasers were a problem!"

DI Adams wondered where Beaufort was, but between the sleek purple dragon and Mortimer, things did seem to be under a rough sort of control. "Alright," she said. "So long as no one gets eaten."

"We're not planning on it," Miriam said.

DI Adams thought that seemed less than reassuring, but she

headed for the gate at a jog, trying not to trip on panicked dogs or excited dragons. Collins followed her, Dandy loping along with them at a more manageable size.

"Be careful!" Miriam shouted.

They were at the gate before a man scrambled to his feet. He'd been hiding among some fallen stone, and as he lunged for DI Adams, Dandy stepped forward with a growl. DI Adams grabbed the dandy, pushing him back.

"Ervin?"

"DI Adams. I have, um, questions." He waved at the field as a dog ran yelping through the gate, chased by Gilbert, who was shouting, "I'm a pacifist, really, but you were trying to eat my friends!"

DI Adams nodded. "I imagine you do. I have a colleague called Thompson who'll come talk to you in just a moment. Stay put."

They left the journalist videoing the melee and ran across the yard, pushing through the gate to the house without checking for ambush. If anyone was in there with a gun, they'd had plenty of time to take shots at them as they crossed the yard. DI Adams knocked hard and called out, "Police! Open up!" as Collins ran around to the back door.

No one replied, and after a moment she tried the handle. It was open, and she let herself in, pausing on the threshold as she peered into a cool, dark hallway. She flicked the lights on, and called out again, "Police! Anyone here?"

"In the kitchen, Detective Inspector," came back to her, and she frowned.

"Alice?"

"Come in, dear."

The living room was empty and silent to one side as she slipped down the hall, Dandy panting behind her and shouts drifting in from outside. The dining room was a still life of table and chairs and sideboard drawn in shadows, and stairs wound up into darkness at the end of the hall. Light washed out of one door, and DI Adams followed it, finding Alice and Lily sitting at a scarred wooden table with a quart bottle of cheap whisky between them and chipped mugs in their hands. DI Collins was just letting himself in the back door, looking uneasy.

"Hello, inspectors," Alice said. "This is Lily Dean."

"Hello," Lily said. Both women looked a little pink, as if they'd just been working very hard at something.

"Hello," DI Adams said. "Is everything alright here, Alice?"

"Quite," Alice said. "Lily has had the misfortune to be married to a very unpleasant man, who was up to many awful things, but that's alright now."

"It is?" DI Adams asked. "You vanished from your house, your phone disappeared somewhere in the village square, and now you're having happy hour in a farmhouse while the W.I. does battle with some very unsavoury sorts out there."

Alice nodded. "I do apologise for worrying anyone. But I have it on good authority that the situation outside is in hand."

DI Collins nodded at Alice's wrists. "You look like you've been wearing your bracelets too tight."

Alice took a sip from her mug. "I'm quite fine. We were just waiting for the commotion to die down."

"Where's this unpleasant man now, then?" Collins asked.

"Gone, I'm afraid," Lily said.

"Gone where?"

"Well, we were very lucky just to escape," Lily said, her eyes wide. "I'm afraid we didn't see where he went, exactly."

"So he ran?" DI Adams asked.

"Well, we couldn't exactly have held him," Alice said. "I mean, it was just us." She and Lily smiled at each other, the same tidy little smile, then smiled at the inspectors.

It was most unnerving.

26
MORTIMER

The sun was high and hot, one of those summer days where it seems winter might never come, when Dales villages bask under a heat haze and the grey of the high fells is blurred and muted with the fuzz of flowering heather. Birds sang in a way that suggested they were only doing it because it was expected, and it was really far too hot for such things. Sheep clustered under trees and cats slept in shady spots, and Toot Hansell's waterways were full of people paddling hot feet and children in swimsuits pretending it was the Amazon. Even the bees seemed sleepy, and as Mortimer watched Dandy roll over to offer his belly to the sun, he was almost tempted to do the same. It looked awfully comfortable, and possibly quite cooling.

But it also looked very undignified, and probably only suited for younger dragons, so he slurped homemade elderflower cordial and sparkling water from the jar Miriam had given him, snout turning lilac at the sound. "Sorry," he said, although no one was paying attention. He looked sideways at Dandy. The thing looked like it was grinning at him.

DI Adams leaned back in her chair, arms folded across her

chest and legs crossed at the ankles. She'd actually taken her suit jacket off and rolled her sleeves up, and it made her almost unfamiliar. "Seeing much of Lily, Alice?"

Alice nodded, taking her own sip of elderflower. "Not a lot, but I did speak to her the other day. She has a lot to do now her husband's gone."

"Turned out he had some pretty dodgy dealings."

"So I gather." Alice offered DI Collins a plate of round biscuits with little, heart-shaped holes in their middles where red jam shone through. "Jammy Dodger, Colin?"

"Ooh, please." He took two, setting the spare one on the side of his plate, where Mortimer eyed it hopefully.

"We'd have been able to put him away for a long time if we'd got hold of him," DI Adams said. "Got some justice for all those people he ripped off."

"All those very rich people who tried to buy a bit of the national park and turn it into their very own gated estate?" Alice asked.

"And all the people who weren't very rich, but thought he was building them good quality condos in Turkey and Spain."

Alice offered the plate to the inspector. "I'm sure a sort of poetic justice will catch up with him. One can't get away with such things forever."

DI Adams started to shake her head, then sighed and took a biscuit. "I don't really deal in poetic justice."

"Very underrated, poetic justice," Beaufort said. "It's always much more fitting."

"Hit and miss, though," Collins said. "It would've been nice to be sure he got what was coming to him."

"Oh, I'm sure he will," Alice said.

Mortimer flopped onto his belly, letting the soft grass cool him, and considered poetic justice. Would it be poetic justice to be pushed out of the farmhouse, having been beaten half-unconscious by two furious ladies of a certain age, only to be faced with a relatively large, very displeased dragon? To have that dragon twine his talons into the back of your clothes as you very rapidly gained terrified awareness that this was *real*, and to be snatched into the air and borne away by said dragon? Or was it something else? Mortimer wasn't quite sure what exactly had happened at the farmhouse, as he'd been instructed to make sure none of the unpleasant men or dogs were eaten, or any of the buildings burned down, and Beaufort had been oddly reticent about things. But he knew the unpleasant husband had been *dealt with*, whatever that meant. He imagined it had involved a terrifying ride from a certain angry dragon to a very remote tarn and the loss of footwear, and probably a mark left that instructed pixies, gnomes, and other mischief-makers to have at it. He wasn't sure if it was poetic, but it did seem fitting, and Alice looked happy enough, smiling at Miriam as she padded barefoot down the garden to place a plate of egg salad sandwiches on the table.

"How perfect, Miriam!"

"It's too hot to cook," Miriam announced, sitting down and swirling her skirt around her legs to cool them.

"I still have mixed feelings about eggs," Gilbert said. "Do the chickens want their eggs to be eaten?"

"Do you want a clip around the ear?" Amelia asked, and Thompson snorted. He was sprawled on his side under some marigolds, his eyes half-closed in the sun.

"I like her."

"So what will your friend Lily do now?" Beaufort asked, helping himself to a sandwich.

"She wasn't involved with that Derrick's scam at all. She was in the council just to help smooth things over for the actual project."

"She must have known about it," DI Adams muttered. "I can't believe we couldn't connect her at all."

"Maybe she did know, at some level. But sometimes we look the other way when it comes to those we love," Alice said. "Anyway, she's taken on the company and is going to redirect everything into sustainable housing."

"Oh, that's very nice," Miriam said. "What a wonderful idea!"

DI Adams looked like she was rather less impressed, and took a sandwich. "I'll be keeping an eye out for the unpleasant husband."

"Oh, I don't think you need to worry about him," Alice said.

Collins waved a sandwich and said, "Very tasty, Auntie Miriam."

"Thank you, dear." Miriam passed a sandwich to Mortimer, who took it with a happy sigh. This was more like it. Running around fields dodging journalists and chasing men and dogs might be more dragonish, but he wasn't at all sure it was his sort of thing at all.

"And what of our journalist?" Beaufort asked, his thoughts evidently running along similar lines. "Was he ... sorted out?"

"That sounds so sinister," Miriam said with a shudder.

"It'd be more sinister if he hadn't been sorted out," Thompson said. "I got hold of him once the dragons left, then got that Jasmine to clear up his phone. She'd be quite nice if she didn't have that horrible dog, you know."

There was a general mutter of agreement regarding the dog, who had bitten Amelia in the excitement. Amelia was still pointing out how restrained she had been not to bite it back.

"So there's no evidence on it at all?" Alice asked. "Don't they back up automatically or something?"

"Jasmine said she got it all," Miriam said. "She's very good with that sort of thing."

"And he won't remember anything?" DI Collins asked. "Like you gave him amnesia?"

"More like I hypnotised him," the cat said, inspecting one paw lazily. There was a pot of caviar overturned next to him. He'd taken one sniff and batted it away, declaring it disgusting. "He remembers it all, just minus dragons."

"That's handy."

"Yeah, well. I can't keep cleaning his memory every few months. The brain can only take so much."

"This isn't going to keep happening every few months," DI Adams said. "*Is it?*"

"We don't do it deliberately," Beaufort said.

DI Collins pointed at Gilbert, who grinned nervously. "Why were there a load of dragons with piercings running around shouting *down with the humans* when we came out of the house?"

"Why're you looking at me?"

"Because you're a freak," Amelia said. "Also, that was your fault."

"No, I mean, I don't agree with that view."

"It was your fault, lad," Beaufort said. "What I can't figure is how you got to the mount so quickly without flying. You weren't missing for that long before everyone arrived."

"Isobel was already at the lay-by," Gilbert admitted. "She was keeping an eye on the farms in case they started knocking down trees or tearing up the land, and I told her we might need some backup."

"And got *Lord Walter*," Mortimer said. "And Rockford!"

"She just got a bit overexcited."

"Well, I suppose it could have been handy to have dragons in the case of werewolves," Collins said.

"Good point," DI Adams said, and nodded at Thompson. "Where were your werewolves?"

The cat shrugged. "Hey, it was a reasonable assumption. Blocking charm on the house, slaughtered livestock – it sounded like werewolves."

"And instead it was …?" Beaufort asked. He had a dandelion stuck in his teeth, and Mortimer examined his sandwich. No, the High Lord must have eaten it separately.

Thompson huffed. "Brownies."

"Brownies," Collins said. "Like, chocolate cake?"

"Oh my gods. Seriously. No."

"A brownie is a house spirit," Alice said.

"Yes. I'm glad someone around here pays attention to the world of the Folk rather than just their stomachs."

"Less than a year ago, I thought Folk was just a music style," Collins said. "Bear with me."

The cat sniffed. "Well, brownies put blocking spells on their houses to stop other Folk encroaching on their territory. They hate pixies – I mean, everyone does, really – and they don't want to share with gnomes."

"So what about the slaughtered livestock?" Miriam asked. "They couldn't have just set the dogs on them, could they?"

DI Adams nodded. "Looks like it's exactly what happened. We were able to recover emails and contacts from Derrick Dean's phone. He basically hired in a pretty unpleasant security firm. They poisoned the water, set the dogs on the sheep, and stole the rest of the livestock. Put gas through the house to knock the family out so no one heard a thing. We've no idea what happened to the sheep – sold, I suppose. We're still running the firm down. The men are completely uncooperative – say we drugged them and caused hallucinations, and keep threatening to sue us. Not that they'd get anywhere, and lawyers aren't exactly lining up to represent them."

Mortimer watched Miriam's face, seeing the twitch down in the corners of her mouth. It was always so much easier when it wasn't your kind. It was awful to be confronted with what your own people were capable of, to know that they were no different from you and yet chose to do such awful things. He sat up and put a paw on her knee, and she smiled at him.

"And all the machines and so on?" Beaufort asked.

"Ah, now that was interesting," Collins said. "What you thought were drums of diesel were actually hazardous waste. So while he was taking all this money from investors for the land he was supposedly preparing for them, he was also collecting waste from dodgy companies. They were paying him a ridiculous amount of money to dispose of it. I imagine he was just going to bury the lot behind the farm."

"In that trench," DI Adams added.

"Trench?" Alice said mildly.

"There was a trench. Just one. Not terribly big. Very fresh."

"How odd."

DI Adams gave an exasperated sigh. *"What happened to the husband?"*

"I really have no idea."

"I don't—"

"We're not digging trenches up," DI Collins said. There was silence for a moment, while DI Adams muttered something under her breath about untrustworthy older women and Alice cut a Jammy Dodger in two, smiling to herself slightly. Mortimer wondered if things hadn't happened quite the way he imagined, and found he didn't really want to know the answer.

"What about the other ones?" Amelia asked. "The art ones?" Everyone looked at her, and she snorted impatiently. "You know, the ones in the fields."

"Oh, they were very curious," Beaufort said.

"Ah," DI Adams said. "I know. They were for photos."

"Photos?" the dragons asked together.

"Yes. They take pretty photos and put them in a brochure so the actual building process looks very tidy and romantic."

"Well, that's just dishonest," Mortimer said.

"Humans." Amelia shook her head and took another sandwich.

"Of course, they couldn't have actually done much digging, as someone had sabotaged most of the machines." Collins looked pointedly at Miriam, and she flushed, jamming her sun hat down over her ears more firmly.

"We didn't touch them! We didn't have time!"

"You were all carrying garden shears and hoes and things, sneaking about the place, and you expect me to believe no one touched the machines." He shook his head. "My mum was there! I know what she and her sidekicks are like."

"They didn't touch them," Miriam insisted. "We were all attacked by the dogs before we got there!"

"Well, we'll just go with that story, then," Collins said. "I have no desire to arrest anyone for vandalism to illegal machinery, anyway."

Mortimer looked at Gilbert. He was examining a flower with great interest, an anxious grey flush creeping up his neck. Amelia had sat up and was staring at him fixedly, half a sandwich still in one paw. "You brat," she said, loudly enough that everyone looked at her.

"What?" Gilbert said in a small voice, still not looking away from the flowers.

"You didn't just wait for Isobel to bring the others! *You* did it!"

"Oh dear," Beaufort said, and had a gulp of elderflower. "Really?"

"Someone had to do something! What if they *had* been coming for the woods? What if—"

Collins covered his ears. "No one has confessed. I have heard nothing that makes me need to take action."

"Me either," Adams said, with a final look at Alice. "Unfortunately."

Alice smiled, and said, "You were looking for a reason to arrest me? Again?"

"Of course not you! I just want to know about this mysterious husband!"

"He seemed most unsatisfactory," Alice said. "More cordial?"

"Which is exactly what you called *your* mysterious missing husband the first time I met you!"

"I understand there are many unsatisfactory husbands in the world."

"She's right," Miriam said. "That's why I never bothered."

DI Adams snorted and gave her arms an exasperated sort of wave, as if to wash her hands of all of them. "Fine. *Fine.*"

"I'm calling the whole thing a success," Thompson declared. "No one got eaten, all our tracks are covered, and the farms are saved. Go, us!"

"Indeed," Alice said. "Go, us!" She raised her glass, and everyone followed suit, even DI Adams.

"Go, us." They drank, then the DI added, "Can I just point out, though, that it all would have gone a lot easier if everyone had just listened to me?"

"And still she thinks the Toot Hansell Women's Institute might listen to her," Thompson said.

"I live in hope." DI Adams waved a sandwich past Dandy's nose, and he rolled over, snapping it from her hand.

"So weird," Collins said. "To me, that sandwich just vanished into thin air."

"Better than seeing it go down, I would imagine," Beaufort said.

"And definitely better than seeing him in person. In hulked-out form, or whatever he was."

Miriam made a face, and picked up a plate of cucumber sandwiches. "DI Adams, are you back to Leeds now?"

Collins burst out laughing, and DI Adams looked as if she wanted to throw something at him. "No," she said, her voice stiff. "I'm staying."

"You're staying?" Miriam squeaked, and Alice smiled.

"Oh, well done, DI Adams. I'm very pleased to hear that."

"Wonderful," Beaufort declared. "We shall see more of you!"

DI Adams screwed her face up as if she wasn't sure that was really a good thing. "It just makes sense. I spend half my time running out here anyway, because you lot can't keep out of trouble."

"Here?" Miriam asked, dropping half a cucumber sandwich on her lap, then yelping as Dandy vacuumed it up. Mortimer wondered if it was really any more alarming than seeing those long yellow teeth and hulking, dreadlocked shoulders.

"Not *here*. Bloody hell, no. Skipton. I'm not that far gone."

"I knew she'd come around," Collins said. "It's working with me that's the main draw, obviously."

"Obviously," Beaufort said gravely, and DI Adams gaped at him, then laughed and shook her head. Mortimer hadn't heard her laugh before. It was a warm sound, and it belonged to someone younger than she usually felt, younger than the steel-blue threads of tension that always wound through the canary-yellow scent of her.

"I guess this is the next step in my career, then. The dragon detective and her invisible dog."

"That sounds most wonderful," Beaufort said, and DI Adams leaned over to put a hand on his shoulder, her fingers long and strong against the rich gold of his scales. Dandy nudged her arm, jealous, and she leaned back in her chair, lifting her face to the sky, letting one hand rest on the dog's head.

"It may be tolerable," she announced, and Mortimer smelt the scent of her changing, less strawberries after a thunderstorm and more the crisp smart scent of shadows in the dawn. He looked at Alice, who smelt of old books and sharply folded thought, and Miriam, who was a wonderfully confused jumble of colour and light, rainbows shattering on heather, and Collins, who was less familiar, but had a definite taste of bad puns and liquorice to him. And he thought about the fact that his kind could still be treading careful old paths, scavenging for wood in the night and bartering worthless treasure with dwarfs when the wood ran out in the winter and they needed coal. Needed coal to stop the eggs dying and old dragons falling into a frozen hibernation from which they would never wake, the caverns cold and still, mausoleums to dragons who crept across the world on fearful feet.

Beaufort put a heavy paw on Mortimer's shoulder and regarded him with those old gold eyes, and Mortimer thought that the High Lord knew exactly what he was thinking. He started to flush lilac, wanting to explain that he wasn't congratulating himself or anything, but Beaufort leaned his head close and said, "Magic walks with dragons again, lad."

Mortimer looked at his paws and found he was entirely his own rich purple-blue, luminous with happiness, and thought that Beaufort was right. Because if friendship between kinds wasn't magic, he couldn't imagine what was. He took the scone that Miriam offered him, putting the whole thing in his mouth before the cream could melt and the jam fall off, and amended the thought. Friendship and scones. *That* was magic.

And it was beautiful.

THANK YOU

Lovely reader, thank you so much for coming along on another Beaufort Scales journey. I hope very much that you enjoyed *Game of Scones*, and I'd appreciate it hugely if you could take the time to pop a quick review up on the website of your choice.

Reviews are absolutely the best way to inform others of how best to deal with dodgy property developers, and (more importantly) how to prepare for dragons. Which are both important things to be aware of. Plus, reviews are writer fuel. We write much better when well-fuelled.

And if you'd like to send me a copy of your review, chat about dragons and baked goods, or anything else, drop me a message at kim@kmwatt.com. I'd love to hear from you!

Until next time,

Read on!

PS - head over the page to discover the complications of a Toot Hansell Christmas, and also to claim your free collection of dragon-approved recipes!

GET SOME DRAGONS IN YOUR FESTIVITIES

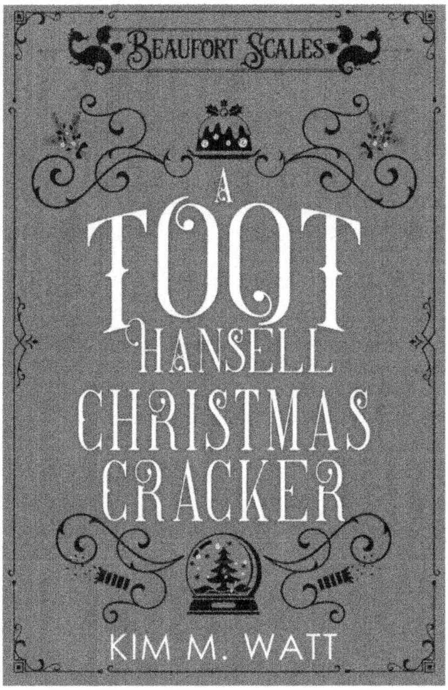

Rebellious Christmas wreaths. Mysterious welly-dwelling eggs. A plague of irate water fowl.

And ten ladies of a certain age who are by no means the least troublesome of Toot Hansell's residents, as far as Detective Inspector Adams is concerned.

But Christmas is almost here. Things can't go too wrong … can they?

Well. It is Toot Hansell …

Grab A Toot Hansell Christmas Cracker today to discover a collection of interconnected, festive tales and accompanying tasty treats!

Scan above or head to books2read.com/TootXmas to continue the adventure! (Just mind those lizards ...)

DON'T FORGET YOUR RECIPES

Your free recipe collection awaits!

Lovely person, I hope you're now fully appraised of the perils of local politics, and are ready to arm yourselves with the appropriate array of baked goods before tacking any of your own.

Of course, to make sure you are properly prepared, I've got a collection of summery Toot Hansell treats for you! I've even included the infamous elderflower cordial, although it shouldn't have *quite* the same quirks as Gert's ...

Plus, if this is your first visit to Toot Hansell and my newsletter, I'm also going to send you some story collections - including one about how that whole barbecue thing started ...

Your free recipe collection is waiting - grab yours now!

Happy baking!

Scan above or head to https://readerlinks.com/l/2369426/gospbr to start baking!

ABOUT THE AUTHOR

Hello lovely person. I'm Kim, and in addition to the Beaufort Scales stories I write other funny, magical books that offer a little escape from the serious stuff in the world and hopefully leave you a wee bit happier than you were when you started. Because happiness, like friendship, matters.

I write about baking-obsessed reapers setting up baby ghoul petting cafes, and ladies of a certain age joining the Apocalypse on their Vespas. I write about friendship, and loyalty, and lifting each other up, and the importance of tea and cake.

But mostly I write about how wonderful people (of all species) can really be.

If you'd like to find out the latest on new books in *The Beaufort Scales* series, as well as discover other books and series, giveaways, extra reading, and more, jump on over to www.kmwatt.com and check everything out there.

Read on!

amazon.com/Kim-M-Watt/e/B07JMHRBMC
bookbub.com/authors/kim-m-watt
facebook.com/KimMWatt
instagram.com/kimmwatt
x.com/kimmwatt

ACKNOWLEDGMENTS

I would like to extend another apology to the people of Skipton for taking terrible liberties with their road layout. That street was just not steep enough for what I needed. Also, I'm quite sure their councillors are much more efficient and less cake-obsessed.

The parts to do with dragons are, of course, entirely true …

And to you, lovely reader, who has taken a gamble on a book about tea-drinking, mystery-solving dragons, thank you. Whether it's your first time in Toot Hansell or your fourth, thank you. You are entirely awesome.

As always, to all my wonderful reading and writing friends, who have encouraged, cheerleadered (that's a word. I'm a writer), beta-read, critiqued, given feedback, shared bad jokes, and generally been amazing and wonderful and made me feel so very lucky to know you. You know who you are. You are amazing.

To Lynda Dietz at Easy Reader Editing, who is unfailingly funny, wonderful, supportive and just generally one of the best people I know. She really does the most extraordinary job of making sure I don't embarrass myself with confusing word order (especially the question of whether the garden or the person smells of cut grass) and the weird UK/US English hybrid that I speak. Any mistakes left in are mine. Except for cheerleadered. Like I said, that's a word.

I did not forget the Little Furry Muse. How could I? But I'm trying not to draw her attention to Thompson. He's being far too cooperative for her tastes.

ALSO BY KIM M. WATT

The Beaufort Scales Series (cozy mysteries with dragons)

"The addition of covert dragons to a cozy mystery is perfect ... and the dragons are as quirky and entertaining as the rest of the slightly eccentric residents of Toot Hansell."

– Goodreads reviewer

The Gobbelino London, PI series

"This series is a wonderful combination of humor and suspense that won't let you stop until you've finished the book. Fair warning, don't plan on doing anything else until you're done ..."

– Goodreads reviewer

The DI Adams Mysteries

"... will grip you within its story and not let go so be prepared going in with snacks and caffeine because you won't want to put it down."

– Goodreads reviewer

The Hollowbeck Paranormal Cozy Mysteries

(With Amelia Ash)

"It's a no-brainer to recommend this one to anyone who enjoys cozies. Or laughing. Or paranormal stuff. Or sarcastic wit. Or great writing in any form."

- Amazon reviewer

Short Story Collections

Oddly Enough: Tales of the Unordinary, Volume One

"The stories are quirky, charming, hilarious, and some are all of the above without a dud amongst the bunch ..."

– Goodreads reviewer

Need more stories?

Join the Ko-fi membership site for monthly, member-exclusive short stories, behind-the scenes content, early access to ebooks, and more!

Free stories!

The Cat Did It

Of course the cat did it. Sneaky, snarky, and up to no good – that's the cats in this feline collection, which you can grab free by signing up to the newsletter. Just remember – if the cat winks, always wink back ...

The Tales of Beaufort Scales

Modern dragons are a little different these days. There's the barbecue fixation, for starters ... You'll get these tales free once you've signed up for the newsletter!

Printed in Dunstable, United Kingdom

84137420R00194